D1587317

CURTAIN OF FEAR

CURTAIN
OF FEAR

by

DENNIS WHEATLEY

THE BOOK CLUB
121, CHARING CROSS ROAD, LONDON, W.C.2.

PRINTED IN GREAT BRITAIN
BY EBENEZER BAYLIS AND SON, LTD., THE
TRINITY PRESS, WORCESTER, AND LONDON

For my friend of many years
THE RT. REVEREND
CYRIL EASTAUGH, M.C.
Lord Bishop of Kensington.
Most affectionately.

AUTHOR'S NOTE

Stalin died shortly after I finished writing this book. The change in Soviet policy since his death provides the greatest riddle of modern times. Was he so all-powerful that it was his monstrous will alone which held down by terror not only the satellite countries behind the Iron Curtain, but also all his colleagues and two hundred million subjects? Or can it be that those colleagues welcomed the old man's death as a most timely excuse on which to hang a change of attitude?

At least we know that the rearmament programme forced upon the West by the menace of Stalin's Russia has now relieved us from the fear of being swiftly overwhelmed, and that the reigns of terror in Central Europe have resulted in a steady falling off of Communist Party membership in every country this side of the Iron Curtain. In other words that the *policies associated with Stalin* were no longing paying dividends.

Naturally we all hope that the change of heart displayed within the Kremlin is genuine and will prove lasting; but we have no guarantee whatever that it is not a ruse to induce us to reduce our armaments again, and to build up once more strong fifth columns of Communists in the countries of the West.

In any case, I am told by those who are in a position to know, that this story gives a by no means exaggerated picture of the state of things in Prague this time last year, and—as I am of the opinion that dyed-in-the-wool Communists do not give up their ultimate objective any more readily than leopards change their spots—I send it to press unaltered.

*   *   *   *   *

Birmingham has been chosen for the opening scene of this story solely owing to the suitability of its geographical situation. The author has no knowledge whatever of any of the Professors at the University there, and those portrayed in this book are, therefore, entirely imaginary characters.

D.W.

CONTENTS

CHAPTER I

"THE PATH OF TRUE LOVE . . ."

"WHAT about a little kiss from my teacher?" said Wendy with a smile.

"Come right up to the top of the class, darling," Nicky smiled back.

The door of the class-room had barely closed before her arms were round his neck. She was a senior student and he a junior professor at Birmingham University. About three minutes had elapsed since he had finished his morning lecture. During them they had both made an impatient pretence of packing up their notes and books until the other students had left the room. At last they were free to snatch a few moments' bliss together.

For a dozen heart-beats they stood tightly embraced, then drew apart to smile into one another's eyes. Wendy Stevenson was twenty-two, a well-built athletic-looking girl with dark curly hair, a straight nose, rather full cheeks and a generous mouth. Nicholas Novák was thirty, tallish, with a slight stoop, red-headed and so thin-faced as to be almost cadaverous, but his lively brown eyes gave his face charm and strong personality.

A glance at their clothes was enough to indicate their very different backgrounds.

As it was May and a sunny day, she had put on a gaily-coloured print frock. It was new and she would not have worn it for any other Professor's class that Friday morning; but her bag, shoes and the small attaché case which contained her sandwich lunch all spoke of ample money. Her father was a rich manufacturer and she lived with her parents in a big house with a pleasant garden out at Solihull.

He was wearing an old tweed jacket, baggy grey flannel trousers and a dark blue shirt. His tie was a rag, his shoes needed

1*

re-heeling, and the satchel into which his packet of sandwiches was stuffed with his books was gaping at the seams. This seediness about his things was not altogether due to the carelessness of appearance common among intellectuals, as when new they had been cheap and shoddy. His father had been a Czech commercial traveller who had married an English girl and taken British nationality shortly after the First World War. Both had been killed by a flying bomb in 1944 and, from the age of twenty-one, Nicholas had been left to fend for himself with very little money.

This was the second term that Wendy had sat as one of Nicholas' students in Political Economics. From the beginning she had admired his quick, vital manner and fine intellect; while he had soon, rather grudgingly, admitted to himself that for a spoilt little rich girl she showed unusual promise as a student; but their real 'discovery' of one another was much more recent. They had been drawn as partners in the mixed doubles for the first tournament of the year at the University Tennis Club. She had asked him out to her home to practise and, with the suddenness of blossom bursting on a warm day in spring, their acquaintance had become a passionate yearning for one another.

Wendy had philandered happily with half a dozen young men in her own wealthy set, but this was her first serious affair. She felt to the very bottom of her being that Nicky was the only man she could ever possibly marry. Never having had to bother about money, she did not do so now. Imperiously she had swept aside Nicky's uneasy admission that he could not afford to get married. For her it was enough that with his brilliant gifts he was certain to go to the top of the tree. In the meantime, her father would provide; or, should he refuse, that would be a challenge to her love which she would readily accept, as in her ignorance of living meanly the prospect of life with Nicky in a tiny flat appeared to offer all the delights of a gay adventure.

Nicholas, too, had never before had a serious affair. His struggle to achieve professorship without money or influence had begotten in him a bitter class hatred; he loathed and despised what were loosely termed the 'idle rich'. Yet he was fastidious

by nature and had acquired an illogical snobbishness about
women which had, up till now, made him reject any permanent
association with such girls as had been within his reach. On the
few occasions when his loneliness had caused him temporarily to
succumb he had afterwards despised himself; yet he despised
himself still more for secretly hankering after the beautifully-
turned-out daughters of the rich, whom he thought of as spoilt
and empty-headed. But Wendy had carried him off his feet.
She was neither idle nor foolish, but everything he had ever
longed for. That she should return his love still seemed to him a
miracle. He knew that to marry her on his income would be
madness, and his every instinct revolted against accepting help
from her father; but, all the same, a week before he had put all his
scruples behind him and they had become secretly engaged.

They thought it a foregone conclusion that her parents would
oppose the match, as Novák was very far from being the type of
man the Stevensons would have chosen as a son-in-law; but
neither of the love-bemused couple was unduly worried about
that. Wendy had a fine chin and a will that went with it; while
Nicholas at least had prospects and, although he remained
adamant about becoming what he termed a 'parasite', had been
persuaded to agree that it would be unreasonable to insist on
Wendy's refusing a handsome increase in her dress allowance.
In consequence they were confident that now Nicholas was prepared to forgo any attempt to make his young wife entirely de-
pendent on him in near poverty, consent could be won after a
display of sufficient persistence.

Yet one thing secretly troubled them; it was their diametrically opposed views on politics. As a professor and a student of
Political Economics, both of them took all questions of government and ideologies with extreme seriousness. Unhappily, he
was as Red as any Leftist could be, while by upbringing and conviction she was a True-Blue Tory.

During the early stages of their acquaintance they had found
it a fascinating game to argue their differences. Wendy, whose
earnestness was leavened with a sense of humour, had had a lot
of fun seeing him get hot under the collar when she shrewdly

quoted examples of the incompetence the Socialists had displayed while in office; and Nicholas had felt a pleasant sense of elation whenever he had forced her to admit one or other of the barbarous circumstances in which the governments of the rich had for many generations compelled the poor to scrape a living. But now that they were eager to marry, these differences of outlook had become like hideous insects gnawing at the core of their happiness.

Each time he came to her home she was fearful that he might give free reign to his boundless admiration for Mr. Aneurin Bevan—whose very name was anathema to her father; while on these visits he sometimes went white with the strain of holding his tongue when her family spoke with love and admiration of the man he always thought of as 'that deceitful, imperialist warmonger, Churchill'.

Passionately as they were drawn to one another, honestly as they admired each other's minds and characters, determined as they were to exercise every possible restraint where their political feelings were concerned, both of them were horribly conscious that this was the one rock upon which their love might founder. And a crisis that held all the ingredients for bringing about such a wreck was far more imminent than either of them imagined.

They had been talking, in half breathless snatches between kisses, for only a few minutes when Wendy said: "Darling, I've got an awful chore for you. I know you'll hate it, but will do it for my sake and be on your best behaviour."

He smiled at her. "Of course I will. What is it?"

"I've fixed up for us to stay the weekend after this with Aunt Agatha," she replied a little hurriedly.

His sudden frown did not surprise her. Aunt Agatha was her mother's sister, and the widow of Colonel the Honourable George Lis-Hartley. She had been left extremely well off and lived in almost pre-war luxury at Lis Court, a fine old Georgian manor in Shropshire. She entertained lavishly, ruled her estate despotically, and still rode to hounds enthusiastically at the age of fifty-eight. In fact she represented everything that Nicholas most heartily condemned.

"Now don't be difficult, my sweet," Wendy hurried on before he could reply. "As you are going to marry me you'll have to meet her some time, and the sooner you get it over the better. You really must get it out of your head that everyone who has a title or a lot of money is necessarily horrid."

"I never said they were."

"But you are inclined to think it, aren't you? Anyway, Aunt Agatha is a dear. She's fat and jolly and awfully kind."

"If you say so I'm sure she is, darling; but all the same I can't accept her invitation."

"Oh, Nicky! But you must. As I was telling you the other night, I'm her only niece, she's awfully fond of me and has made me her heir; so it would be not only stupid but most unkind to offend her. You really needn't be nervous about staying at Lis Court, or about the people you'll meet there. I know you haven't got a dinner jacket, but you could easily hire one, and . . ."

"Thanks!" He cut her short with an edge on his voice. "I don't need to wear their absurd livery to hold my own with a bunch of snobs." But he added quickly, "Sorry, darling! I didn't mean that. I haven't yet got used to thinking of such people as your friends; and I'd willingly dress myself up, even as punchinello, to please you. It isn't my ingrained dislike of all that your amiable aunt represents that makes me say no, either."

"What is it, then?"

He hesitated a second, angry with himself now at having put off telling her before, because he felt certain that his intention would displease her; then he blurted out:

"Next weekend I have to attend a conference of the new I.L.P. at Llandudno."

Her brown eyes opened wider. She was aware that he contributed articles to several Left-wing journals, but had not known that he took an active part in extremist politics; so she asked:

"Do you often attend such meetings, Nicky?"

"No," he shrugged. "Only those that I think may be of particular interest."

"Then surely, as it is to please me, you wouldn't mind terribly not going to this one?"

"I'm afraid I must. You see, it has been specially called to discuss a matter of major policy, and some of my friends who will be there are counting on my support. I'm sorry, darling. Really I am. I'll come to your aunt's any other week-end you like, and I'll be as good as gold about hiding my red light under a bushel."

Dropping her eyes she murmured, "All right, then. I suppose it can't be helped. I'll make some suitable excuse to Aunt Agatha."

After a moment's awkward pause, he plucked up the courage to say, "I'm afraid I've got another disappointment for you, sweetheart. I've had to scratch our game in the tennis doubles for to-morrow."

She looked up quickly. "Oh, Nicky, why?"

"My cousin telephoned me last night."

"Your cousin! I thought your only relatives lived in Czecho-slovakia."

"They do, except for Bilto. I've seen very little of him during the past few years, and I suppose that's why it never occurred to me to mention him to you. He came here as a refugee soon after Hitler marched into Prague. As he is a very able scientist he has done quite well for himself. During most of the war he was employed on atomic research in Canada and the States, and he now holds a senior appointment at Harwell. Anyhow, he rang me up to say that he wanted to see me urgently on an important family matter, so I promised to meet him in London tonight. In the circumstances, I couldn't possibly refuse."

"No, I quite see that," Wendy agreed. "But if you are seeing him to-night, what is to stop you catching a train back to-mor-row morning? Even quite a late one would get you here in time for our match."

Nicholas shifted uncomfortably from foot to foot, then he said uneasily, "Darling, I'm afraid you are going to be awfully annoyed with me, but I've committed myself for the whole weekend. You remember I told you about this new economic monthly that Igor Sinznick is planning to start. He has been urging me for the past three weeks to go up and have a really long talk with him about it, but I've kept putting it off because of us. I can't afford trips to London often, and since I've got to go up to see Bilto anyhow, this seemed the perfect opportunity. The Sinznicks can always give me a bed at their house in Cricklewood, so I wired Igor this morning, saying that I'd arrive late to-night, and would stay over with them till Sunday evening. I had no chance to discuss the matter with you, and when I sent off my wire to Igor I didn't think you'd really mind."

"But I do mind!" Wendy took a swift pace back from him and her mouth became a firm, angry line.

"Oh come, my sweet!" he protested. "You have to go to a party to which I am not invited on Saturday night, and as Sunday is your grandfather's birthday you are tied up for dinner that night as well. It is unreasonable to expect me to forgo this chance of spending the weekend with one of my oldest friends just to be with you for a few hours on a tennis court."

"It's not that!" she flared. "It is that you are going back on your word. When we became engaged we solemnly agreed that we would not allow politics to interfere with our private lives."

"Yes, that's what we agreed; and I stand by what I said."

"How can you say that, when you have just refused to come to Aunt Agatha's next weekend because you want to attend a conference of the Independent Labour Party, and this weekend you are scratching our match in order to stay up in London for the purpose of planning the issue of some filthy red rag with a Communist agitator?"

Two crimson spots appeared in Nicholas' lean cheeks, as he snapped, "Igor may be an agitator, if by that you mean a man who has the courage to speak openly in defence of the downtrodden masses, but he is not a member of the Communist Party, and I resent your stigmatizing our honest project to expose capitalist abuses in a new periodical by terming it a filthy rag."

"All right, then! Resent it if you like; but I refuse to be

treated like this. If we are to make a success of our marriage, from now on you must give your political activities second place to our life together."

"Wendy, my work is not for myself but for others; so I cannot give it up. But I swear to you that I'll do my best to honour our agreement."

"Very well. Meet me half way, then. Either come to Aunt Agatha's next weekend or get back here to-morrow in time for the match."

"Damn it, I can't," he cried in sudden exasperation. "I am already committed for this weekend and next."

She was very near to tears as she stammered, "I think you're horrid. I'd . . . I'd have half a mind to give you back your ring, if . . . if your head had not been too full of your beastly politics for you to think of giving me one."

"I'm sorry about that," he said contritely. "I meant to but I've had little chance. I'll get you one while I'm in London and give it to you on Monday."

"I may not feel like accepting it," she retorted angrily. "Stay up in London if you like, but while you are there you had better think things over. If by Monday you have not decided to meet me half way and come to Aunt Agatha's, I shall consider our engagement at an end."

"Wendy, please!" He held out his arms to her, but she evaded his embrace, turned on her heel, stalked swiftly to the door, wrenched it open and slammed it furiously behind her.

It was not until she was half way down the corridor that she realized that she had forgotten to snatch up the attaché case that held her sandwiches. Nothing would have induced her to go back for them, and she felt in no state to face her fellow students in the canteen. The prospect of a lunchless interval added further fuel to her anger, and during it she shed bitter tears in a quiet corner of the grounds. As she finally dried her eyes her resolution was taken. She had faced the fact that on this question time could be no healer. She must make her stand now, before she became further committed by publicly announcing her engagement. Desperately as she loved Nicky she must force herself to give him up unless, on his return from London, he was prepared to put her happiness before his other interests.

CHAPTER II

THE ATOMIC SCIENTIST

On his journey to London that evening Nicholas was a very worried man. One of the things he admired most about Wendy was her strength of character. She was not the sort of girl who could be cozened into meek submission by a display of tact and a little petting; and he had an uneasy feeling that she really meant what she had said. The thought that she might stand by her ultimatum appalled him, for he had never wanted anything so much in his life as he wanted her. Yet how could he possibly continue with what he had come to regard as his life's work if he ceased to collaborate actively with the little group of people who thought as he did, and believed that given the power to do so they could remedy all social ills?

That damnable problem had been lurking in the back of his mind ever since the wonderful evening when Wendy had first confessed her love for him. For the past fortnight his overwhelming joy in being with her and thinking of her had enabled him to put it out of his thoughts for the greater part of the time, but at unexpected moments it had kept popping up and he had known that sooner or later it must be faced.

Idealist as he was, Nicholas was by no means unconscious of the practical benefits which would accrue to him from marrying the rich Miss Stevenson. Apart from the delights and material comforts that a loving wife in any circumstances would bring him, now that he had agreed to let her accept the help that her

doting father would almost certainly offer he could look forward
to exchanging his dreary lodgings for a pleasant home. Enter-
taining on a modest scale would not be beyond them, and Wendy
already had her own little car. Once the Stevensons were recon-
ciled to the marriage they would probably insist on providing
the means for the young couple to take pleasant holidays—perhaps even trips abroad—and if there were children it was certain that old man Stevenson would make himself responsible
for seeing that they had the best education money could provide.

As Nicholas had thought of all these things he had suffered
certain qualms of conscience, recalling uneasily his own past
diatribes against 'worthless parasites who battened on the
rich'; but he had succeeded in persuading himself that provided
he did not use any of the 'tainted' money for personal ends he
need not reproach himself. That he could not avoid benefiting
from it indirectly was inescapable, but against that he set the
argument that it would be little short of brutal to compel a girl
who had had Wendy's upbringing to scrape and slave when
there was no necessity for her to do so. Moreover, he considered
himself far from worthless, and further placated his scruples by
the somewhat cynical reasoning that marrying a girl with money
must result in his having far more free time which could be
devoted to his political work.

About that, too, he had, up till now, managed to lull himself
into a false optimism. As a student Wendy had shown such
promise that he had felt certain that with her good brain she
could in due course be brought to see 'the Light', abandon the
shibboleths of her bourgeois antecedents and be moulded into
his right-hand in the great crusade for internationalism and
equality. Only in the past few days had he begun dimly to realize
that her patriotism, fervid loyalty to the monarchy, and belief
that the Socialists were incapable of governing the country in its
best interests, were far more the fruit of her own reasoned
convictions than habits of thought accepted instinctively from
the world of comparative affluence and privilege in which she had
always lived.

Another pleasing prospect that had taken shape in his imagination was that as a result of marrying Wendy he might hope for professional advancement. It so happened that her father and his immediate chief were friends of many years' standing, as they had been brother officers in the First World War. The latter, Professor Benjamin Salting-Sala, was regarded by Nicholas as a charlatan of the first water; and it was probably true that he owed his present position more to the connections he had made during half a lifetime spent at Oxford, and his flamboyant personality, than to his academic achievements. He was a fat, florid *bon viveur* with charming manners and a cynical wit that made him excellent company. Being a rabid anti-Socialist he lost no opportunity of using his occasional lectures as a vehicle for tilting with derisive mockery at the revolutionary tenets that Nicholas held most dear. Had they both lived in Paris in 1793 and Nicholas had been a crony of Robespierre's, he would have seen to it that Salting-Sala was given a specially high priority for a one-way trip to the guillotine; as things were, the corpulent, luxury-loving professor was far too occupied with his own concerns even to be conscious that the most intelligent but disreputable-looking of his juniors was not among his many admirers.

His blindness in this respect was now, in view of Nicholas' marriage prospects, particularly fortunate, for Salting-Sala was a power to be reckoned with in the University; and while he was too much of a snob to extend his patronage to a member of his staff whom he looked upon as his social inferior, all the odds were that, having no personal prejudice against Nicholas, he would readily do so to him, as John Stevenson's son-in-law.

The thought that he might be about to achieve through favouritism the promotion which he had earned by merit, but was denied by lack of influence, was another that made Nicholas' conscience squirm. Yet again he had quieted it with the sophistry that the higher his standing in the academic world the greater would be the regard paid to his articles championing the rights of the toiling masses.

In fact, during the past fortnight his mind had taken on an entirely new orientation. Almost unconsciously he had come to accept that Wendy would bring him not only married bliss but a new life of ease and comfort, and hitherto unhoped-for opportunities to become a more potent force in the political field.

But that morning he had been rudely awakened from this happy dream. She had made it unmistakably clear that their political views were utterly irreconcilable. He could still have her and the ease and comfort, but there was a price to be paid for those things. Not only had his cherished plan of making her his willing helpmate finally gone up in smoke; she was not even prepared to tolerate a continuance of his own activities on their present modest scale.

Despite his very human tendency to find plausible excuses for wandering from the straight and narrow path, Nicholas was at heart a man of great integrity. Desperately as he wanted Wendy for his wife, he knew that he could not have her on those terms.

As the train rumbled into Euston he made up his mind about that. On Monday he must tell her that he meant to adhere to the undertaking he had given his friends to attend the Conference of the resurrected I.L.P. the following weekend. That was, he knew, to risk that she might throw him over there and then, once and for all. That risk had to be taken; but there was at least a hope that she would give him another chance. If she did he would meet her wishes as far as he possibly could in the future, and by treating his political work as a thing apart, do his utmost to prevent it from interfering with their social life; but whatever happened he must continue his self-imposed task of writing and speaking on behalf of the helpless millions who were incapable of writing or speaking for themselves.

At half past six he arrived at the Russell Hotel, and having left his bag in the cloak-room, went through to the cocktail bar, where he had arranged to meet his cousin. Bilto Novák was there at a table in a corner drinking a whisky and soda. He was ten years older than Nicholas, a shade shorter, a little broader in the shoulders, and had a touch of grey above the ears in his red hair; otherwise their physical resemblance was striking. Their faces were the same shape, their eyes the same colour, and both had the lean cheeks and jutting chin inherited from a common grandfather; so anyone seeing them together would at once have assumed them to be brothers.

That they had seen little of one another in recent years was mainly due to Bilto's long stay in Canada and the United States, and since his return to England the opportunities for them to meet in London had been few and far between. But in the early nineteen-thirties Nicholas had spent several of his summer holidays with Bilto's parents in Prague. He had then been a schoolboy and Bilto a University student, but despite the difference in their ages a strong affection had grown up between them, and the mutual memory of it made them greet one another now with the happy handshake of old intimates.

Asked what he would drink Nicholas chose a gimlet, and Bilto ordered him a double with another whisky for himself. Then, with that directness which was one of Nicholas' characteristics, he asked his cousin the reason for this urgent request to meet him in London. Glancing at the nearby tables, two of which were occupied, Bilto lowered his voice and replied, "It is a private matter so I'd rather not talk about it here. After dinner we'll go up to my room and settle this business there. In the meantime tell me about yourself. How are you liking it at Birmingham?"

Nicholas shrugged. "I've no complaints. I know I'm doing a good job and I think I'm pretty popular with my students— with those who come from the lower income groups, anyway —and one can hardly expect the minority who have capitalist backgrounds to like some of the policies that I advocate in my lectures."

"Do they allow you a free hand to say what you like?"

"Oh yes. That's one of the good things about England; and the tradition that no one should be penalized for the free expression of his political views is particularly strong in the universities. Of course, I don't go the whole hog, as my bosses would be bound to kick at that; but I'm managing to give a useful grounding in the principles of true Socialism to a number of highly-absorbent young people."

"What do you imply by the term 'true Socialism'?" Bilto inquired.

"You ought to know," Nicholas replied quickly, "since you grounded me in it yourself when I was a kid and you were a student in Prague."

"It is generally referred to by another name," Bilto said with a grin.

Nicholas grinned back. "I know; but 'a rose by any other name would smell as sweet'; and it's getting the principles of the thing into the heads of the coming generation of intellectuals that counts."

"Your subject, Political Economy, provides the perfect vehicle for that. But how about your colleagues? Don't they see what you are up to?"

"As I've just implied, it is very much a live-and-let-live world, and quite a lot of the younger ones incline in varying degrees towards the Left. Unless someone monitored all my stuff and that of the others too, they would have difficulty in differentiating between our shades of opinion."

"Yes, I suppose that's true. Have you any prospects of advancement?"

"Not as things stand at the moment. The Senior Professor who has the most influence over my section is an old crook named Benjamin Salting-Sala. His principal assets are an acquaintance with half the people listed in Debrett and a Rabelaisian humour. He is the sort who goes about pinching the cheeks of the girl students, and gets away with it. God knows why, but they seem to like it, and look on him as a kind of funny uncle."

"I seem to have heard of him somewhere," Bilto remarked.

"That is quite probable. His influence is very far-reaching. His opinion is nearly always asked when the question arises of appointing a new Headmaster at one of the Public Schools; and it goes much further than that. It is said that he is even consulted from time to time by members of the Cabinet, on subjects entirely outside his own province."

Bilto nodded. "It is one of the queer things about the English that they often take major decisions on the advice of people who have no real qualifications to give it. That is why their foreign policy is so hopelessly unpredictable."

"Maybe you're right. Anyhow, you can well imagine that a man of Salting-Sala's type has little use for a junior like myself. His patronage is strictly reserved for those who can afford to ask him to dinner and fill him up with Château Claret."

"Still, you're a personable chap, Nicky; so I take it you manage to have quite an enjoyable social life on more modest lines."

Nicholas' mind was so saturated with thoughts of Wendy that his immediate impulse was to tell Bilto about her; but he temporarily repressed it and replied, "The various under-takings for furthering the movement we are both interested in are always short of funds, and I feel it is up to me to help as much as I can. That keeps me pretty short, but I know a few interesting people and go out with them for drinks or a snack now and again. I'm having more fun, though, now the tennis season has started again."

The cousins were both tennis enthusiasts, so while they had another drink they talked of the game, and the prospects of their favourite players in the approaching championship tournament at Wimbledon. Then, after a while, Bilto glanced at the clock and said:

"It's a quarter past seven. Come on; let's go in to dinner."

Before they were half way through the meal Nicholas could restrain himself no longer, and blurted out, "I'm by no means certain of things yet, but I'm hoping to get married in the fairly near future." Then he launched into a glowing description of Wendy.

After listening to him for a few minutes, Bilto shot him a swift apprehensive look, and said, "From all you say she sounds a typical bourgeois, and not at all a suitable wife for anyone who thinks as we do. Does this mean that you have succumbed to the flesh-pots and are going over to the enemy, Nicky?"

"Not on your life!" Nicholas declared. "But it is that which makes things still uncertain. Her father is the typical blood-

lusting Briton produced by the Public Schools. He won a D.S.O.
as a young Major in the First World War, and served in the
second as an Intelligence Officer. If a third broke out to-night
he would chuck up his business to-morrow to get back into any
sort of uniform—if they'd have him; so it is hardly to be wondered at that the whole family is for all Queen and Country, and
regard even futile old Attlee as first cousin to the Devil."

"I see; and having been a conscientious objector in the last
show-down puts you on a pretty bad wicket."

Nicholas flushed slightly and looked down at his plate. "They
don't know about that, and I see no reason why I should make
my case worse by telling them. I've let them assume that I spent
the war working on a farm because my health was not then up
to the standard required by the Services."

Again Bilto glanced a little apprehensively at him, and
asked, "Isn't that putting one foot on the slippery slope?"

"No. I don't regard it in that way. The past is past, and all
that really matters is that I should have a clear conscience about
the future."

"Anyhow, I take it that the girl's family are opposed to her
marrying you, and that is the fence you have got to get over?"

"No, that's not it. Wendy reckons she can manage her family
if we get that far; it is her own attitude that is the real trouble.
She has been reasonable enough in agreeing that we should both
stick to our own ideas on politics and not argue about them; but
she is trying to make it a condition of our marriage that I should
put our social engagements before my political obligations. And
that I am determined not to do."

"Good for you, Nicky!" Bilto nodded quickly. "It would be
a tragedy if you allowed this young woman to persuade you to
throw your hand in. If you keep faith with your convictions
you may go far; what is more, if things really go our way, in a
few years' time I may be in a position to do something pretty big
for you. I've read some of your articles and I think they are
absolutely first-class."

Nicholas beamed with pleasure. "Do you really?"

"I do. So for God's sake don't soften up with this girl of

yours. If you can get her under your thumb, though, and then marry her, that should be all to the good. In the future as we visualize it, everyone will be provided for in accordance with their past or present usefulness to the World State, and no form of currency will be necessary; but as long as things remain as they are, money is not only a necessity but a most potent weapon; so it is up to all of us to get control of as much of it as we can."

"You wouldn't think it wrong, then, to marry a woman solely for her money?"

"Certainly not, if your intention is to use the bulk of it for the furtherance of the cause; but if it so happens that you want to marry her anyway because you are in love with her, and she is willing to have you, then you're a mighty lucky fellow."

Bilto took a drink of the second large whisky that he had had with his dinner, sat back, and, after a moment's pause, went on. "As a matter of fact, although I haven't mentioned it before, I am hoping to get married myself. My intended is in no position to bring me any filthy lucre, but as my future prospects happen to be very different from yours, that is immaterial. Like you, though, I have been faced with certain difficulties, and I still dare not count my chickens."

Nicholas looked across at his cousin with quick interest. "That we should both be in much the same boat at the same time is most intriguing. Do tell me what sort of difficulty you are up against."

"I think I'm pretty well over it now," Bilto replied. "All the same it was a very tricky one. My girl—or woman, I suppose I should say, as she has already been married twice—is a Czech, and certain people who have their hooks in her have been making her play a very dangerous game. My problem has been to get them to release her so that we can both settle down to marry with quiet minds. The job was further complicated by the fact that although she is under their thumb, she looks on it as her duty to work for them, so would not willingly give it up. In fact, like your girl, if she were free to choose she might decide to throw me over rather than agree to lead the sort of life I want her to; so in case she felt impelled to sabotage my plans before the deal went through I haven't even dared to discuss them with her. The only way I could see to work it was to present her with a *fait accompli*. Once she knows that she has definitely been sacked and stands no chance of being re-employed, I am quite certain that she'll marry me; then it won't be long before she realizes how darned lucky she is to be out of it, instead of being liable at any time to find herself behind bars."

"And you reckon you've fixed it?"

"As good as. Very fortunately I was able to dovetail the whole thing with certain other plans of my own. I have good reason to believe that by this time she is already on the right side of the Iron Curtain and out of danger."

Into Nicholas' mind there floated a vague picture of an attractive widow in the middle thirties who possessed courage and intelligence, and had either been working for the Czech underground or been sent into Czechoslovakia from time to time as a secret agent on behalf of one of the United Nations' espionage bureaux. His memories of Prague were still clear, and for a moment he tried to imagine this woman of Bilto's moving furtively along the darkened streets at night on her dangerous secret business.

Anxious to get a clearer idea of her, he asked Bilto where he had met her; to which Bilto replied that he had first known her several years before, when she had been married to her first husband, and had fallen in love with her then; but he seemed loath to vouchsafe any further information. He was just starting on another double whisky which, counting the nearly-empty glass that had been on the table when Nicholas joined him, made five in less than two hours. Although he showed no signs of drunkenness, it suddenly struck Nicholas that he was drinking exceptionally heavy, but that might be because he was worrying about the safety of his woman, and was trying to keep his nerves steady during the ordeal of waiting until he learned that she was safely out of Czechoslovakia.

In any case, once having spoken of her, it seemed that she had taken permanent possession of his thoughts, for during the remainder of the meal he was obviously preoccupied and made little attempt to respond to Nicholas' conversational openings.

They did not have a lengthy meal, so it was only a little after eight when he paid the bill and took Nicholas up to his room. As soon as he had closed the door behind him he asked:

"Nicky; do you still remember enough Czech to speak it?"

"Yes," Nicholas nodded. "I learnt it just at the right time to retain a fair knowledge of it all my life."

"Good! Then we had better use that language. In this business of mine we can't be too careful."

One glance round the room had shown Nicholas that Bilto's things were only half unpacked. As he lowered himself into the single arm chair, he wondered what was coming next. Bilto moved some clothes off the bed, sat down opposite him and breaking into Czech, went on:

"First I would like to have an absolutely definite reassurance about your feelings. I hadn't expected to find you involved with a rich young woman who has reactionary sentiments. Are you quite certain that has made no difference to your outlook?"

"None whatever," Nicholas declared emphatically.

"So far, so good. Now give me the basis of your political beliefs?"

"I believe that the primary requirement of mankind is lasting peace, as the only condition possible for the development of a World State in which the peoples of all nations will be relieved of the levy now made on their earnings by the capitalist system, and enjoy equally the full benefits of their labour, the produce of the earth, and the inventiveness of man. I believe that the only serious menace to a lasting peace is the attitude of the capitalist governments towards the Union of Soviet Socialist Republics, and that every possible means should be exploited to bring about the downfall of those governments, so that they may be replaced by governments truly representative of the masses, who will co-operate in uniting the workers of the world in one brotherhood."

"Excellently put." Bilto's lean face broke into a smile. "I am now entirely satisfied about you. I take it, though, that since we last met you have not actually become a Communist Party member?"

"No. I have been approached about it, but thought it wiser to decline."

"And you were right—at all events for the present. The work you are doing will have every bit as much value if you remain what they now call a 'fellow traveller', and you will receive just as much credit for it in the long run. It suits my book better, too, as if you were a member of the Party the Special Branch might be keeping tabs on you."

"I am a member of the 'Friends of the Russian People' and several Peace organizations; but I have no reason at all to think that the police have ever taken an interest in me."

"Good. Naturally I don't belong to any of those things. It would be out of the question for anyone employed at Harwell to do so. I don't think there is any definite regulation forbidding it; but it's quite extraordinary how effective the English technique is of putting a stop to things they don't like by merely indicating that they 'are not done'—anyhow in a closed community like that. In these days, even the suggestion of an interest in the Russian point of view would set all sorts of alarm bells clanging down there. In fact I've never even risked anyone on the station finding me in possession of one of the type of periodicals for which you write. I have bought them on trips into Oxford, read as much as I wanted to of them in the lounges of the hotels in Abingdon on the way back, and left them there for the instruction of anyone who might chance to pick them up. However, that is by the way. We scientists who are working on nuclear projects are now subject to retain regulations, and I am going to break one of them. It is about that I want to talk to you."

Here it comes at last, thought Nicholas, settling himself a little more deeply in his chair.

Looking him straight in the eyes Bilto went on, "Since Bruno Pontecorvo hopped it during his Italian holiday, all of us have had to sign an undertaking not to attempt to leave the country without first having obtained permission to do so. I have to go abroad, and I am going without it."

After a moment's thought, Nicholas said, "If they catch you on the way out it will cost you your job; and you will probably be arrested on some charge connected with the breaking of your undertaking, into the bargain. Is taking such a risk really necessary? Wouldn't it be wiser to apply for permission, and so regularize the trip you have to take?"

"No. You are not making due allowance for the fact that, although on account of the highly-specialized war work I was doing they granted me British citizenship in 1942, I was born a Czech. And before the War broke out the Nazis did their utmost to deprive refugees like myself of the means of earning a living. It is quite on the cards that their Embassy passed information to the British about my Communist activities as a student, and later in Prague. If so, it was probably discounted when the question of my naturalization was gone into, on the grounds that it had all the hallmarks of a typical piece of malicious Nazi slander; but it would still be on my file. If I applied for permission, I have no doubt that the authorities would be very nice about it. The reply would probably be that owing to pressure of work I could not be spared. But it is a hundred to one that they would turn my application down."

"Why not anyhow try applying first, and take the law into your own hands only if you meet with a refusal?"

"No; that would be fatal. The security people are nervous as cats now about anyone connected with nuclear projects. From the moment my application went in they would order a special watch to be kept on me. My only chance is to slip out before M.I.5 is tipped off that I'm contemplating going abroad. And anyhow, I cannot possibly delay my departure. That is now out of the question."

"I see your point," Nicholas agreed. "And I take it this step is rendered both necessary and urgent on account of the woman you propose to marry. Go ahead, then, and tell me in what way you want me to help you?"

"Thanks," Bilto nodded. "I felt sure I could count on you;

and my request is quite a simple one which cannot possibly get you into any trouble. As you have pointed out yourself I may be caught on the way out and find myself under arrest. Anyhow my absence is bound to be discovered soon, and when it is they will start poking into my affairs; so I want you to take charge of my interests here."

As he spoke he rose to his feet, picked up a brief-case, put it on the dressing-table, opened it and took out a number of papers; then he went on, "I have here a Power of Attorney made out in your name. That will give you the necessary authority to deal with everything. There are shares here worth about two thousand pounds, and a Post-Office Savings Book with a credit of nearly two-fifty. Then there is the log-book of my car; it is a 1950 Morris, and ought to be worth five hundred. My things at Harwell won't fetch much, but add whatever they bring in to the pool. You will appreciate, of course, that I dared not dispose of all my assets myself in case doing so gave rise to suspicions about my intentions; but I want you to sell everything. If I am arrested, use the money to secure me the best legal defence you can get; if not, take five hundred for yourself and distribute the rest in any manner you consider will best serve the cause."

Nicholas sat bolt upright and stared at him in astonishment. "But . . . but . . ." he stammered, "that would be crazy. If I did as you suggest you'd be left without a brass farthing when you get back."

Bilto gave a very slightly drunken laugh. "You've become mighty slow-witted all of a sudden, Nicky. If they catch me leaving with the papers I'll have on me, it will mean ten years in prison. I wouldn't have any use for money there. I won't need any where I'm going, either. To-night I am being flown to Prague, and I am not coming back!"

CHAPTER III

THE TERRIBLE DILEMMA

FOR a moment Nicholas said nothing. He was desperately endeavouring to re-orientate his thoughts. To gain a little time he fished out a packet of cigarettes, and lowered his glance from Bilto's while he lit one. He had assumed that Bilto was under the necessity of going to Western Germany in order to ensure the freeing from her entanglement of the woman he proposed to marry, and that he hoped to get back without anyone at Harwell suspecting that he had used his leave to go abroad. It had not even occurred to him that an atomic scientist of his cousin's standing would dare to risk going behind the Iron Curtain; far less, that he had deliberately arranged to do so and meant to stay there.

Taking his silence for agreement, Bilto said, "I have been contemplating this step for some months. With the knowledge I have acquired at Harwell, I feel the time has come when I can be of much more use working on the other side than by just passing on odd bits of information."

"Bilto." Nicholas' voice was a trifle thick. "Have you really considered the full implications of what you are about to do? I mean, it is one thing to work for peace and quite another to make the Russians a present of our latest discoveries in the nuclear field."

A sudden frown creased Bilto's broad forehead. "I don't agree about that; and since you are a convinced Internationalist I am surprised that you should even question the ethics of the step I am about to take. It has always been a principle among scientists that all advances in knowledge should be shared, and it is only this accursed nationalism which has prevented a continuance of that ancient practice in recent times."

"Yes, you are right about that."

"Of course I am! If the British and Americans had not withheld the results of their nuclear experiments from the Russians, and ceased to collaborate with them in many other ways directly the war was won, there would have been no cold war—the cost of which is to-day keeping many millions of wretched people on both sides of the Curtain in a state of semi-starvation—and no likelihood of a third world-wide blood-bath. Instead, the nations would be living in friendship and prosperity, and atomic energy would have been developed solely for its potentialities in saving labour and making life easier for everyone."

"Again I agree with you. It was such ideas which impelled Alan Nunn May to disclose atomic secrets to the Russians through their Embassy in Canada; and I've always felt that he was fully justified in doing what he did at that time. But remember, on his return to England in 1946 he refused to continue supplying them with information because by then conditions had changed."

"You mean that by then the leaders of the capitalist nations had already alienated the Soviet Government, and begun to envisage the desirability of planning a war to destroy Communism."

Nicholas shrugged. "You know well enough which side I am on, but one must be fair; and it would be fairer to say that both sides had become suspicious of the future intentions of the other."

"Do you suggest that the Soviet Government had begun to plan for a war against the Western powers?"

"Certainly not. From the beginning it has given abundant evidence of its desire for peace, and still continues to do so. Russia has absolutely nothing to gain by war, and everything to lose. She has more territory than any other nation, and in it abundant resources of all the raw materials necessary to her well-being. It is self-evident that her dearest wish must be a continuance of peace, so that she may develop those resources for the benefit of her people instead of having to squander them in what for her could only prove a pointless and probably indecisive war. We all know that her ultimate object is to bring the people of all nations freedom and security as citizens of Workers' Republics modelled on the U.S.S.R., but she does not need to go to war to achieve that. It will take time, but can be done internally by people like ourselves, and, one hopes, without bloodshed."

"Of course it can. The spread of education is bound to bring it about. Gradually the thick-headed masses will become conscious of the fact that they are still being exploited for the benefit of an upper class, and that their own interests demand the total elimination of that class by the establishment of proletarian governments. But we are getting away from the point. Do you agree that Russia has done her utmost to bring about a better understanding with the nations of the West by initiating innumerable international conferences, and that their basic object has been to secure a lasting peace?"

"I do." Nicholas stubbed out his cigarette. "And you can go further than that. These conferences might have proved successful had not the governments of the capitalist countries consistently thrown spanners in the works, and frequently taken steps to prevent the attendance of delegates whose presence would have rendered them truly international."

Bilto smiled. "We seem to be having a rather one-sided argument. It is clear that we both feel that no blame attaches to Russia for the present deplorable situation, and that as an internationalist, poor old Fuchs was right in doing his best to redress the balance."

"No, I didn't say that. I said that I thought Nunn May was justified in what he did, because his only object was to enable the Soviet to share equally in our new scientific discoveries."

"That is not strictly true, Nicky. Although he refused to give away his contacts he did confess to his own activities, and at his trial he stated that he had embarked on those activities because he felt it was a contribution he could make to the safety of mankind. In other words, he hoped, by telling the Russians what he knew, to give them parity with the West in the development of atomic weapons, to prevent a war by putting the capitalists in a situation where they would know it to be suicidal to launch one."

"Perhaps; but there was no likelihood of war then; and as

2

soon as he recognized the signs that things were heading that way he stopped giving information to the Russians. Fuchs, on the other hand, came on the scene much later, and deliberately disclosed vital secrets that he knew would be used against this country in the event of a show-down. Surely you see the difference?"

With an impatient gesture Bilto exclaimed, "Nicky, you are splitting hairs! You have agreed that Russia does not want war, and obviously the best hope of preventing it still lies in providing her with the means to defend herself if she is attacked."

"I don't think that the majority of people in Britain or America want war either."

"The British don't, naturally, as they at least have sense enough to know that they would be in the front rank of the battle; and since Fuchs and Bruno Pontecorvo did their stuff even Churchill and his warmongering pals have been pulling their horns in. That's why they jibbed at the Yanks' attempt to make them take a strong line with China. They are scared now that any extension of the hot war might ultimately lead to the devastation of London and the Midlands, and they reckon that's too big a price to pay for the loan of a few billion extra dollars. But the situation in America is very different. Big business there is fed up with pouring money into Europe, and what would happen if they turned off the tap altogether?"

Having flung out the question Bilto paused for an answer, and Nicholas replied, "Without dollar support most of the European governments could no longer carry on. In effect, the American money buys the votes that keeps them in power, as without it they could not possibly maintain the living standards of their peoples. Within six months there would be chaos and starvation. In France and Italy, and probably several other countries too, the masses would turn to Communism as the only way out."

"Exactly; but America dare not let that happen. And now that even the middle classes there are kicking at the prospect of having to pay heavy taxes for the rest of their lives, as the price of halting the spread of Communism in Europe, what is the only alternative? It is to go in and smash Communism once and for all at its fountain head."

Bilto paused again, then went on, "They argue that the United States is still too far from Russia to suffer serious damage to her cities, but that it may not be if they give the Russians a few more years to perfect the new weapons. Therefore their best bet is to strike now."

"Do you really think they are prepared to sacrifice their allies? Because that is what it would come to. Western Europe is still only half armed, so could not possibly stand up to a Russian onslaught. Most of its cities would be bound to go up in flames, and unlike the last war, there wouldn't be much left worth picking up afterwards."

"The type of American I am thinking about doesn't give a hoot about Europe. His only concern is that its factories, ship-yards and material resources should not come under Com-munist domination by peaceful means, so that while still intact they could be used as war potential against the United States."

"Yes, one can't deny that a lot of them do think like that."

"Looked at from their point of view, you can't blame them either. Their reasoning is entirely logical. That is why the movement there to force a show-down is growing in strength every day. Only one thing can stop it—the knowledge that the Russians are in a position to give as good as they get, and that if America starts anything her own cities will promptly be laid in ruins. There you have my reasons for the step I am about to take; and if you had the power, as I have, to make this great contribution to preventing war, I am sure you would make the same decision."

"I suppose I would," Nicholas murmured unhappily. "I can't help feeling, though, that there is another side to it. God knows, no one could ever accuse me of being swayed by silly, sentimental patriotism. I've denounced it too often as one of the major evils leading to war. But, all the same, England has done a lot for you and me; particularly for you, as she took you in when you were a hunted, penniless refugee, gave you protection and enabled you to earn a good living at your own chosen work.

It seems pretty mean to me that in return for all that, you are now about to place in the hands of her enemies something that they may use to bring untold misery to her people."

"Nicky, be your age!" Bilto said impatiently. "Stick to the broader issues and stop befogging your mind with clap-trap. The kernel of the issue is that I believe I have it in my power to prevent another major war."

"I know. But if you give the Russians the benefit of your knowledge, there is always the possibility that it might tip the balance the other way and decide them to strike first. Even as things are, a lot of people think that they may be tempted to bank on their colossal man-power and launch a war of preservation while they still have a big superiority in the more orthodox weapons."

"God Almighty!" Bilto threw up his hands. "To think that I should ever live to hear you spouting capitalist propaganda! You can't possibly believe that there is the least truth behind such scaremongering."

"No. I can't honestly say that I do," Nicholas admitted a little shame-facedly. "Still. . . ."

"Still what?"

"Oh, nothing. It is only that I can't bring myself to approve whole-heartedly of what you are about to do. But, of course, you have the inalienable right of the individual to decide on your own actions, and if you insist on going through with this it is not for me to set myself up as your judge." Having made this admission, Nicholas added a moment later in the same rather pompous strain, "Naturally, too, as your only relative here, quite apart from the affection I bear you, I should regard it as a duty to agree to your request about looking after your interests."

"Thank God for that!" Bilto muttered. "Come on, then; let's get the job over."

Nicholas stood up and together they went through the papers that Bilto had produced. As he handed over the Power of Attorney, he said, "I should get a solicitor to handle the collection of my assets on your behalf, as there is no point in drawing down opprobrium on yourself by letting it be more widely known than necessary that you are acting for me."

"That is bound to come out," Nicholas shrugged. "But naturally I shall deny having been an accessory before the fact to your departure; and fortunately it is against their principles in this country to persecute the relatives of anyone they consider to have committed a crime against the State."

When he had pocketed the Power of Attorney and the other papers, he lit another cigarette and perched himself uneasily on the edge of the bed. Then, after taking a few nervous puffs, he stood up again and announced abruptly:

"Well, as there is no more to be said, I might as well be going."

"Oh, don't go yet." Bilto was smiling now. "Have a drink first to wish me luck." As he spoke he rummaged in his suitcase and produced a bottle of whisky, then went into the bathroom next door and returned with a tooth-glass. Filling it half full with the neat spirit he held it out to Nicholas.

"No, thanks." Nicholas shook his head. "I don't want a drink. All the same, on purely personal grounds, I hope that you don't find yourself in prison to-morrow morning. If you do get away safely I expect you will feel a tremendous sense of relief. Keeping secret rendezvous with Russian agents all these months, and never knowing that at any time you might be caught out, must have been an appalling strain."

Bilto took a gulp of the neat whisky, coughed, spluttered, then replied, "It was nothing like as bad as you might think. The Russians are past-masters at that sort of thing. They are much too clever to involve their informants in the least unnecessary risk, and they show great patience in allowing considerable intervals to elapse between meetings. That enormously lessens the chance of M.I.5 being on one's tail when a meeting does take place. In my case, too, until I actually took the decision to leave England, they employed only one contact, which is a good insurance against betrayal. You see, only that one person had it in his power to identify me as the man he had met; so if any of their other agents were caught and tried to get off lightly by

giving away what they knew I stood no risk of being incrimi-
nated."

After a moment Nicholas remarked, "I'm a bit foxed about
this woman you are interested in. I naturally formed the impression that she was in Prague and working against the Russians;
but from what you have said since dinner that doesn't seem to
make sense."

"She was, until they caught her husband. It was then they
got their hooks into her; but she has since become a convert,
and a very useful one. I only found that out when I met her
again."

"In that case I should have thought you would have been
willing for her to carry on with her work."

"No; it's too risky. I'd never have any peace of mind with
her dodging about Europe and liable to arrest every time she
left Prague. That is why I have stipulated that she should be
there to meet me when I arrive, and not be given any further
missions. In view of my usefulness to them, I don't think it
likely that they will go back on their bargain."

Nicholas gave a pale smile. "Then if all goes well to-night,
you will be with her, and making plans for getting married, to-
morrow morning."

"I certainly hope so."

Again Nicholas stood up. "Well, I wish you luck about
that; but really I think I had better be getting along."

Bilto swallowed the rest of the whisky. "No. What's the
hurry? Stay and keep me company while I pack. I won't detain
you long. A car will soon be coming to fetch me."

As he spoke he began to cram the rest of his things into the
open suit-case, and Nicholas asked:

"Do you know from which airport you are leaving?"

"I have no idea," Bilto shrugged. "It was up to them to make
all the arrangements for my journey. I was simply told to be here
at a certain hour and that a car would be sent to pick me up."

After a glance round he added, "I may as well have a quick
wash and brush up before I repack my sponge-bag."

Then he walked into the bathroom.

The moment Nicholas was left alone, he passed a shaking hand over his eyes and endeavoured to collect his racing thoughts.

He was in the unhappy position of a man convinced against his will. From early boyhood he had always liked and admired his cousin. It was from him, when in the most formative years, that he had imbibed with such enthusiasm the Marxist doctrines; but he had since fully convinced himself of the rightness of those beliefs in hundreds of discussions with scores of intelligent people. All the arguments that Bilto had put forward in justification of his proposed act were, he felt, entirely sound and he had time and again used them himself. Yet, just supposing. . . .

Just supposing there was something in the contentions of men like John Stevenson and old Benjamin Salting-Sala. They held that the Soviet rulers had long since abandoned the Communist doctrines that had inspired their youth; that when they now quoted Marx and Lenin, it was only hypocritical lip-service which enabled them to continue gulling their people; that Stalin had succeeded in forcing on Russia a rule more autocratic than that of any of the Czars, and that like the Czars his policy was governed by an old-fashioned nationalism with insatiable imperialistic ambitions. According to them Stalin maintained his vast armies and air forces only with a view to future conquest, and would already have launched them into Western Europe had he not been deterred by fear of the United States' lead in atomic weapons.

Such ideas Nicholas regarded as the wildest nonsense. From being in touch with various pro-Communist organizations he considered that he was far better informed on Kremlin policy than were these elderly scaremongers. As he saw it, Russia's efforts to secure a permanent understanding with the West had been unceasing, and that they had failed had been entirely due to sabotage by the old capitalist interests. There was, too, ample evidence in Stalin's speeches that he had never deviated materially from the Marxist line, but confined himself to enlightened interpretation of the original doctrine. And the fact that he continued to maintain vast armed forces had an obvious explanation. Menaced as he was by the capitalist conspiracy to destroy Communism root and branch, he would have been failing in his duty had he not kept his people in a constant state of preparedness to defend Russia—the heart, soul and world-wide hope of the movement—from attack.

Yet at the back of Nicholas' whirling brain there lurked one uneasy thought. The cost of the cold war to Russia must be as great as it was to the Western powers, but her industrial potential was less. How long could she stand the strain without breaking? What if the men in the Kremlin felt that Russia was nearing the point when she could no longer bear such a burden, and must either fight while it was still within her power to do so, or collapse from internal exhaustion? Supposing that awful choice was already looming on the horizon, might not the information Bilto was about to take then prove the deciding factor, through providing those who advocated war with a stronger case for claiming that Russia would emerge from it victorious?

A slight sweat broke out on Nicholas' forehead as he thought of that. War was war whichever side started it, and whatever their reason for doing so. Ever since he had been able to think clearly he had been an ardent pacifist, and the horror of the air-raids in the last conflict had made him positively fanatical on the subject. The next would be infinitely worse. It would mean the blotting out of whole cities, the slaughter of helpless people in their tens of thousands, and in most frightful circumstances. He recalled reading of the effects of the atom bomb dropped on Hiroshima. Its victims who had been blown to pieces had been fortunate; great numbers of survivors for miles around had died days and weeks later. Their hair and teeth had first fallen out and they had suffered the most frightful tortures from flash burns or internal injuries caused by gamma rays. A picture flashed into his mind of Wendy, stripped naked by the blast and screaming.

With terrible suddenness it was borne in upon him that it was he who now held this ghastly power in his hands. If he did nothing Bilto would give it to the Russians, but he could still step in and prevent that. It seemed to him that for a few moments

of time the future of the whole world lay in his keeping; that by
acting or refraining from doing so, he must inevitably shape
history for many generations to come. By his decision he might
decree misery and death for countless fellow human beings, or
spare them to live out their lives in peace and security. He wondered if such an appalling responsibility had ever been thrust on
any man before.

Then his mind subconsciously took in the fact that the sounds
of Bilto splashing in the basin next door had ceased. In a few
minutes they would be face to face again. Half numbed with
horror, he realized that he was not to be granted any time for
calm, reasoned thought. The decision had to be taken—and
taken swiftly.

Like a swimmer who fears he may drown before reaching the
shore, he strove desperately to keep his head, to thrust out the
nightmarish speculations that filled it, and make a final effort to
concentrate on the choice of striking out or passive floating.

To prevent Bilto giving aid to the Russians would be to go
against the principles that he had always cherished. That in itself
was difficult enough; but the broader aspects of the problem
dwarfed such a personal one into insignificance. The awful
thing was that Bilto might be right about feeling in the United
States. If he were and the war party there got the upper hand,
the only thing that might prevent them from attacking the
Russians was the knowledge that Bilto had taken the latest
nuclear secrets over to them. On the other hand, if a crisis was
approaching in the Kremlin, to let Bilto go ahead was to present
them with a newly-sharpened sword, and tempt them to save
themselves by using it. His palms sweating and and almost sick
with horror, Nicholas faced the fact that whether he stopped
Bilto or let him go, his decision might in either case equally well
result in precipitating the most terrible war that man had ever
known.

Bilto had dried his face and hands, and pulled the plug out of
the basin. Nicholas could hear the water gurgling down the
waste. In a frenzy he sought for some touch-stone which would
resolve his doubts. Were the Americans, or the Russians, the

more honourable, restrained and humane? That was no good. It was part of his creed that race made no difference to the fundamental goodness or badness of people. From which side would an onslaught be least likely to prove disastrous to himself and Wendy? No! To think on those lines would be the lowest degree of baseness. In which event would Britain stand the best chance of survival? There could be no doubt about the answer to that; but could he, as an internationalist, honourably accept it as the deciding factor? He had reproached Bilto for his proposed betrayal of the country that had sheltered and fed him; but only half-heartedly, because he believed the well-being of any portion of the human race should always be sacrificed when it conflicted with the general interests of mankind. No. He must not allow himself to lapse into sentimental patriotism, because he happened to have been born British. What of his friends? They formed an infinitely smaller group, so the same argument applied to them. But was there not another that overrode it; an obligation imposed by love of a few people that one knew intimately, and affection for many others, that transcended all demands made by the cold logic of intellect? Unless a man stood by his friends he was a mean and worthless being. He was on friendly terms with Hindus, Chinese and Negroes, as well as people of many European nationalities, all of whom were living in London and working for the cause. There were several of his fellow professors at Birmingham whom he liked and admired; quite a number of his old students still wrote to him in the friendliest way; and there was the present crowd, the majority of whom looked up to and trusted him. Again, as faces and figures raced through his mind, he visualized the blinding flash and deadly purple dust of the atom bomb that had been exploded over Hiroshima.

Suddenly his decision was taken. These people must be given the best chance to escape such an appalling fate. It was more likely to overtake them if Russia launched another war than if it was started by the United States. He must stop Bilto leaving England. But how?

Further argument was obviously futile. To call in the police

and have him arrested was unthinkable; for Bilto had trusted
him, and to do so would be the worst possible form of betrayal.
He could be leapt upon as he emerged from the bathroom and
taken by surprise, overcome; but what then? To tie him up,
then stand on guard over him indefinitely, was out of the question. To leave him there locked in his room would be only to
postpone the issue.

In his agitated quest for a solution to this new and urgent
problem, Nicholas had risen to his feet. His glance fell upon the
dressing-table and remained fixed there. Among the papers
Bilto had taken from his brief-case, several of which were still
lying on it, was his passport. At the sight of it the thought
flashed into Nicholas' mind that Bilto would not be able to leave
England without it. In two strides he reached the dressing-table,
snatched the passport up and thrust it in his pocket.

Had he delayed a minute longer he would have been caught
in the act, for barely thirty seconds later Bilto emerged from the
bathroom. He was carrying his sponge-bag and brushes, and
with no more than a casual glance at Nicholas, he put them into
his suit-case, then shut down the lid.

Nicholas' one anxiety now was to get away before Bilto
discovered that his passport had been stolen. His hands felt
clammy and his throat was as dry as if he had chain-smoked a
hundred cigarettes. He hardly recognized his own voice as it
rasped abruptly:

"Well, you're all packed up now, and I really must be
going."

Bilto did not appear to notice the sudden hoarseness of his
cousin's voice, or the fact that his glance had become nervous
and wavering. The last whisky had proved just one over the
odds, so his perceptions were now dulled, his eyes a little bleary,
and his movements beyond complete control.

"Good-bye, then," he said a shade thickly. "If what I am
about to do fails to prevent a show-down, I don't suppose anyone will get much warning that . . . that things are about to
happen. Still, there is always a chance that you may just have
time to see the red light. If . . . if you do, chuck everything,

skip to the continent and slip behind the Iron Curtain. We'll take good care of you if you manage to get through. But there . . . there is always the hope that America will stop sending dollar aid to Europe, and that these damn countries will go bust. Should that happen you'll be seeing me back again, and . . . and I'll get you made a Minister."

"Thanks," Nicholas managed to mutter. "Thanks very much." And he found himself adding instinctively as they shook hands, "I hope everything will go all right for you."

"Don't worry about me," Bilto grinned, with the casual confidence inspired by the whisky he had drunk. "Take care of yourself, Nicky. And don't let that girl of yours pull the wool over your eyes about the rights and wrongs of things. We can't afford to lose a good man like you."

"No, I won't let her do that," Nicholas promised with a sickly smile as he turned away. He actually had his hand on the door-knob when, to his consternation, Bilto called him back.

"Hi! Half a minute. I'd forgotten." As he spoke he swung about and walked quickly towards the dressing-table.

In an agony of apprehension, Nicholas remained by the door, his muscles tensed, his eyes riveted on his cousin's back. Every second he expected Bilto to notice that his passport had disappeared, but apparently he had forgotten that he had taken it from his brief-case. After fumbling in the case for a minute, he pulled out a thick wallet, opened it and thumbed five crisp five-pound notes off a hundred-pound wad. Turning, he strode back to Nicholas and held them out to him.

"Here. Take this! Little present! Buy yourself something when you get married."

Flushing with shame, Nicholas shook his head and stammered, "No, really. It's too much—and you may need it."

"Nonsense! It won't be much good to me this time to-morrow. On the rouble exchange one doesn't get much for pounds." Bilto thrust the notes into Nicholas' unwilling hand.

"Thanks!" he blurted. "It's awfully good of you! So long, old chap!" Then, with crimson face, he pulled open the door, stepped through it, and suppressing a gasp of relief, closed it behind him.

His mind still in a turmoil, he walked down the corridor. Bilto's last generous gesture had almost made him repent, but he told himself that it was absurd to allow the spontaneous act of a half-drunken man to weigh so much as a hair in the major issue. All the same, he was still by no means fully convinced that he had acted for the best.

As he went down in the lift, new qualms beset him. Had he really been right to allow his personal feelings for a small circle of people to govern his decision? Should he not have been prepared to sacrifice them as well as himself? After all, the Russians were the champions of everything that he believed in, and the Anglo-American capitalists were the enemy. Yet he had taken a step which would result in allowing the wrong side to retain an advantage that might tempt them to launch a war. And if war really was inevitable, whatever the cost, his creed dictated that he ought to aid Russia to win it. He suddenly felt that he must have been temporarily seized with a fit of madness. Still, he could go back to Bilto's room, confess what he had done, and restore the passport.

Although he had refused a drink from Bilto, on entering the Palm Court and seeing a number of people sitting there drinking he was seized with the thought that he wanted one desperately badly. Plumping himself down at a table near the orchestra, he told a passing waiter to bring him a double brandy, and soda. When it came he wondered why he had ordered brandy, as he ordinarily never drank it, but after a couple of gulps he felt a little steadier, and began to wrestle with the question of whether he should go up and return Bilto's passport, or stick to it.

After a few minutes, now that he was well away from Bilto, his ideas began to clarify. He decided that, as far as he was able to judge personally, Bilto had been wrong about the United States. Unquestionably there were quite a number of millionaire businessmen there who would welcome a war to destroy Communism; but the great majority of Americans must have had a bellyfull last time, so were most averse to having to leave their homes again. It seemed very unlikely, too, that America would start a war without first having made certain that she could count on the active support of the British Commonwealth, and as Britain's geographical situation made her so vulnerable to an atomic war, she would never willingly agree to America launching one. Therefore, the only real menace to peace lay in Russia being driven to make a gambler's throw as the last hope of saving herself from economic disruption.

As he reached this conclusion he heaved a heavy sigh and took another drink. The decision he had taken had been the right one after all. He now felt really positive about that. He need no longer feel any qualms of conscience about having prevented Bilto going abroad by stealing his passport.

A minute later a thought came to him that, in view of his final conclusion, threw him into sudden panic. Had he really succeeded in preventing Bilto from going abroad? Bilto had said that he was soon to be picked up by a car, but he had not known from what airfield he was leaving, and earlier he had said he was 'being flown to Prague'. Did that mean that he was not going by any orthodox route but from some small secret airfield that the Russians owned near the coast? If so, he would not need a passport. In a new fit of perturbation Nicholas realized that by stealing his cousin's passport he had not done enough. The ghastly responsibility for the future now once more rested with him. If he was to make certain that Bilto did not leave the country he must take some further step.

At that moment a page-boy passed through the lounge chanting shrilly, "Mister Nov-ák. Mister Nov-ák."

On hearing his name Nicholas looked round automatically, beckoned the boy over to him and said, "Yes, I'm Mr. Novák."

"Thank you, sir," replied the boy. "The car you are expecting has called to pick you up."

CHAPTER IV

THE BLACK LIMOUSINE

NICHOLAS was not expecting any car. It was on the tip of his tongue to tell the boy that there must be some mistake. He had actually opened his mouth to do so, but he closed it again. Suddenly his brain had ceased its panic groping among a maze of possible courses to pursue, and clicked. The page supposed him to be Bilto, and the car was the one that had been sent to collect his cousin.

As the boy turned to recross the Palm Court, Nicholas followed, his mind once more down to earth. If he could get rid of the car, that might upset all the arrangements for Bilto's journey. Swiftly he began to assess the possible results of such a stroke.

Since Bilto had no idea of the place at which he was to board the aircraft he could not have himself driven to it in a hired car; and he had made it clear that he maintained only the most tenuous contact with the Russians. It was possible that he had been given a telephone number for use in an emergency, and might ring up when he got really worried by their failure to collect him. If so the check to his leaving would be only a temporary one. But it seemed more probable he would assume that the Russians had postponed the hour of his departure for good reasons of their own, and do nothing. He might even think that they had refrained from picking him up because they had discovered that he was being watched; in which case the odds were on his abandoning all thought of his journey and endeavouring to save his bacon by a swift return to Harwell.

"Would you mind, sir?" It was the waiter who had come hurrying after Nicholas with his unpaid bill. Flushing with embarrassment, he fished in his pocket, found that he had not enough silver, so had to give the man a note. The waiter was short of change, and with a muttered apology went off to cash it, leaving Nicholas standing awkwardly in the middle of the great room.

Although he had decided that the chances were against Bilto trying to make contact with the Russians, there remained the possibility that they would get in touch with him. To get him safely out of the country was, for them, obviously a matter of immense importance. As soon as it became known at the Soviet Embassy that the car had come away without him a number of people would be near having heart attacks.

That thought did not come to Nicholas from any belief in the stories that Soviet officials who failed in their undertakings were promptly recalled and sent to Siberia, or, at best, reduced to the status of the lowest manual workers. He regarded such tales as dirty capitalist lies. But he did believe that every member of the Communist Party considered it a sacred duty to carry out any task with which he was entrusted, so he felt certain that everyone concerned with Bilto's journey would move heaven and earth to see that he accomplished it according to plan.

It followed that, unless the reason he gave for sending the car away was a really plausible one, the driver would refuse to accept it, or if he did, return quite shortly with some bigger shot bent on making a personal investigation; or again, someone would ring Bilto up, with the result that the car would once more be sent post-haste to collect him.

By now Nicholas felt himself morally pledged to prevent Bilto from leaving England, but—short of turning him over to the police, which he felt he could not possibly bring himself to do— it seemed that there was small hope of succeeding unless the Russians could be headed off from him. While striving to think of a story likely to have that effect he stared with unseeing eyes across the Palm Court, quite oblivious of the fact that his gaze appeared to be riveted on a pretty girl who, as she was sitting with her fiancé, found his attention far from welcome.

She was spared further embarrassment by the waiter returning with Nicholas' change. As he tipped the man, he gave him a swift glance and thought to himself, 'I wonder what you would do if you had an old friend upstairs, and knew him to be about to go over to the Russians with our latest atomic secrets?' From that it was only a step to picturing the scene if suddenly he shouted to the band to stop, seized the microphone of the first violinist and announced his own situation. 'Ladies and gentlemen, at this very moment there is a car outside the hotel with a Russian secret agent in it. I should like your advice how . . .'

With an inward shudder he recognized the symptoms of hysteria, and jerked his mind back to the necessity of immediately settling on a plan. Again, he would have given anything for a little time in which to think things out; but he dare not delay. At any moment Bilto might ring down for his bag to be fetched, and learn that the car had already come for him. For that matter, it was quite possible that he was now on his way down in the lift. The thought that Bilto might yet get to the car first and be driven off in it spurred Nicholas to action. Striding forward, he entered the hall.

The page was waiting for him there, and handed him over to a junior hall-porter. After giving the revolving outer door a thrust, the man followed him through it, indicated a car standing about a dozen yards to the left of the entrance, and made to accompany him down the broad steps.

With a murmured, "I am not leaving yet," Nicholas waved him back. He had no idea what course events were likely to take in the next few moments, but he now had his wits about him sufficiently to realize that it might later prove extremely awkward if a witness had stood by and listened to whatever was said.

As he walked quickly down the steps he was toying with the idea of saying that Bilto had changed his mind and gone back to Harwell; but he suddenly saw that if he made a statement of that kind it would imply that he had been let into this highly-dangerous secret. To establish his *bona fides*, and allay fears that he might betray it, he would then have to disclose that he was Bilto's cousin; and he felt most averse to 'giving hostages to fortune' by letting anyone know that he had been made accessory before the fact to Bilto's intended treachery.

The car was a large, rather old-fashioned, black limousine.

Still fearing that Bilto might emerge from the hotel behind him, Nicholas hurried across the pavement. He had covered more than half the distance, and was still groping for a plausible line to take without involving himself, when inspiration came to him.

He would say that Bilto had been seized with a slight heart attack, and while in no actual danger would certainly not be fit to travel for the next few days. In order to carry conviction, and at the same time provide an adequate cover for himself, he would pose as the hotel doctor. Having implied that Bilto was a complete stranger to him, he would add that when called in to such emergency cases, he often had to see to alterations in his patients' arrangements, then politely enquire if there was any message he could take back.

The bonnet of the limousine was pointing away from him, so he saw its driver only as a broad-shouldered man wearing a flat, chauffeur's cap. But he did not give the man a second glance. His attention at once became concentrated on the figure of a woman seated in the back. The car's interior was unlit; so he could see only that she appeared to be young, was dressed in black and had fair hair. On catching sight of him, she leaned forward and threw the door open. As she did so, the light from the nearest street lamp fell full upon her face.

Its thinness showed up her high cheek-bones, and its pallor was accentuated by the fact that she wore no lipstick; but she had a good chin, broad forehead and well-spaced eyes. They were green, and in the left one there was a slight cast. She was not wearing a hat, and her hair, which hung loosely to her shoulders, was of so pale a gold as to appear almost silver.

For a second he caught a rather startled expression in her eyes; then he blurted out, "I'm sorry to say I have bad news for you. It is not a matter for serious concern, but just one of those sudden things that are quite unforeseen. Had it occurred earlier I would have telephoned to save you the trouble of coming, as the car will not be . . ."

Her brows drew together in a frown, and suddenly she cut in: "What on earth are you talking about, Mr. Novák?"

At her words Nicholas' plan to pose as the hotel doctor went up in smoke. Breaking off in mid-sentence, he wondered for an instant how she could possibly know who he was, then jumped to the conclusion that Bilto must have told her about him and mentioned having invited him to dinner that evening. Silently but profoundly, he cursed Bilto for having involved him in this unsavoury and dangerous affair. But his wits were working quickly. He saw that the only thing he could do now was to fall back on the story that at the eleventh hour Bilto had decided against leaving England, and fearing trouble, had asked him to break the unwelcome news to his Russian friends.

"The fact is . . . ." he began a trifle hoarsely. Then, out of the corner of his eye, he caught sight of a man who had just halted under the near-by street lamp to read something in an evening paper. A cold shudder went down his spine at the sudden thought that the loiterer might be a detective who was keeping the Russians under observation. While seeking a way to put matters so that his words should convey nothing incriminating if overheard, he muttered:

"I'm sorry to upset your arrangements, but there's been a bit of a hitch."

She gave him a long, queer look; then, just as he was on the point of continuing, exclaimed, "So that is why you have no hat or coat! No matter; all that concerns me is that you are here! I had expected you to be ready to leave at once, and if some hitch has delayed you in getting your bags packed, that is unfortunate. But it cannot be allowed to alter our arrangements. Everything you need can be provided for you. Please get in."

Subconsciously he noticed that the slight foreign lilt in her voice was overlaid by an American accent. But once more his brain was whirling. She did not know who he was, after all. Like the page, although for a different reason, she believed him to be Bilto. Evidently she had never met Bilto but had been given a description of him, and it was his likeness to his cousin which had misled her. Dare he revert to his plan of posing as the doctor? No; since she believed him to be Bilto, she would not swallow that. She would think that Bilto had got cold feet at the last moment and was himself acting a part in order to provide a reason for wriggling out of his engagement. Believing she had seen through his imposture, she would challenge him, then do her utmost to persuade him to change his mind again. Protests and an argument would ensue. She might use threats. The loiterer would overhear it all, and if he was a detective. . . .

Evidently she, too, had noticed the man, as after a quick glance in his direction she again cut into Nicholas' racing thoughts. Leaning towards him, she said in a low, urgent voice:

"Whatever has happened this is no place to discuss it. Get in; we can talk on the way."

With the suddenness of lightning illuminating a dark landscape, her words clarified his mind. For him to let her drive him off was a certain means of depriving Bilto of the car. Better still, instead of her returning to the Soviet Embassy at once to cause consternation by reporting that Bilto had failed them, as long as she continued to believe that he was his cousin no endeavour would be made to get in touch with the real Bilto.

Scrambling into the car, he took the seat beside her. She tapped on the front window with the end of a fat little umbrella, the chauffeur started up the engine, and they drove off.

Nicholas' exhilaration at this sudden solution to the problem of how to upset Bilto's departure was short-lived. He had hardly sunk into the well-sprung cushions of the elderly limousine before he became uncomfortably aware that he was now faced with several others. When she asked him about the hitch he had mentioned, what story was he to tell? Sooner or later he would have to disclose his real identity; what explanation was he to give for having fooled her like this? At latest, when they reached the airfield the game would be up; how could he delay their arrival, and thus increase the probability of having sabotaged all chances of Bilto's being flown abroad that night?

To his relief while the car rolled down Southampton Row the girl did not ask him any questions; so he assumed that the only thing that really mattered to her was doing her job of picking him up. Whatever the cause of her silence, he was grateful for it, as it gave him a few minutes in which to think.

On reaching High Holborn the car turned west along it, and by the time it entered Oxford Street he had decided on a plan. It was governed by the thought that when the Russians found out how they had been tricked they were going to be very angry people; so it would be asking for trouble to let her take him either to a private airfield, or to some house at which her boss might be waiting to have a talk with Bilto before his departure. Whatever happened, he considered it unlikely that they would do him serious injury; but with such a prize as a leading atomic scientist in view, he felt certain that they would not hesitate forcibly to detain him, so as to prevent his further interference, until they had managed to get the real Bilto away.

The only sure way of evading such an unpleasant possibility was to leave the car before it reached its destination. As a first move to ensure his being able to do so, Nicholas turned to the young woman at his side, and asked:

"Are you taking me direct to the airfield?"

She shook her platinum-blonde head. "No. My part in this ends when I have delivered you at a certain address."

"Whereabouts?"

"That, it is not necessary for you to know. But as you had to leave your hotel without your baggage, it is fortunate that you have to go to this place before catching your plane. They will be able to provide you there with a suit-case and things for your journey."

Nicholas considered this for a moment. The phrase 'catching your plane' implied there was no aircraft waiting specially to fly Bilto out from some secret airfield, but that a place had been taken for him on one of the regular night services to the continent. That cheered Nicholas a lot. If his delaying tactics worked, by the time circumstances made it necessary for him to confess to his imposture it would be too late to collect Bilto with any hope of getting him on his plane. Feigning annoyance and anxiety, he said:

"There is more to it than having had to leave my things behind. As I told you, something quite unforeseen has happened, and if I could have got your Chief on the telephone I should have asked him to put all arrangements for my journey off until to-morrow. In any case I cannot possibly leave London without seeing a friend of mine."

"My orders about you do not permit of any deviation."

"I can't help that. I learned by chance that my going may bring this friend into danger; but that can be avoided provided I tell him what to say should he be questioned. I have been trying to get hold of him for the past four hours without success, but he was expected home by half-past eight, and it must be well after that now."

"You can write him a letter before leaving. I will undertake to see that it reaches him within an hour or so."

"It is not the sort of thing one can explain in a letter. I must see him personally."

"I am sorry, but to get you away safely is a matter of great importance. We cannot afford any delay which might cause you to miss your plane."

"What time does it leave; and from where?"

She shrugged. "I wouldn't know. Anyway it's not my business."

Nicholas took a firmer tone. "Mine is to do my utmost to see that my friend does not get into trouble on my account. If you refuse to take me to his house, when we stop at the next traffic lights I shall get out."

After a brief silence, she asked. "Where does your friend live?"

"In Cricklewood."

"That is quite a way, isn't it?"

"It's not very far in a car. We are already going more or less in the right direction. If we turn north at Marble Arch it's only about ten minutes' run up the Edgware Road."

"By the time you have seen your friend and we get back to Hyde Park we shall have lost half an hour."

"Well, the people who have fixed my trip must have allowed some margin; and there is always a certain amount of hanging about at an airport. If need be, the person you are taking me to see must forgo any idea of a cosy chat in his house and come to the airport with me; then he can say what he has to say on the way there."

"Do you absolutely insist on this?"

"I do. Otherwise I'm getting out when we have to pull up at Marble Arch; and we'll be there in about two minutes."

"All right, then. What is the address?"

"Number fifteen, Lister Road, Cricklewood."

Leaning forward, she slid open the glass panel and spoke to the chauffeur. Then, as she sat back, she remarked, "Somehow, that address is familiar. I feel sure that I recently wrote to someone there. Ah! I remember now. It is that of Igor Sinznick."

He turned to look at her in astonishment. "How very extraordinary that you should happen to know the person living at the one address I gave you, in such a vast place as London."

"It isn't really." Her voice held a warmer note. "Not when you remember that all three of us are members of a very small political minority. In the case of Mr. Sinznick and myself the circle is still further narrowed, because we are both writers."

"May I know your name?" he asked.

"It is Hořovská. I doubt if you have ever come across it, though. I'm not a novelist. I sell a short story or an article now and again, but most of what I earn comes from translating Czech into English and vice versa."

Her name and slight accent told him that she was a Czech herself, which suggested that the Russians were making use of their Czech underlings to handle this affair; but the idea did not strike him as at all surprising seeing that Bilto was a Czech and they had planned to fly him to Prague. Glancing at her again, he enquired:

"Do you know Igor well?"

"No. I have met him only a few times at literary parties and more recently at the flat of a mutual friend. I wrote to him because my friend told me that he was about to start a new monthly, and I hoped to interest him in my articles."

It was on the tip of Nicholas' tongue to say that one of his objects in coming to London was to discuss the new monthly with Igor. Just in time he remembered that he was supposed to be Bilto; so instead, he asked to which periodicals Miss Hořovská contributed; but he listened only perfunctorily to her answers. The car had now turned up the Edgware Road, and with secret satisfaction he was contemplating the further development of his plan.

He felt that once he had persuaded his companion to drive him to the Sinznicks' he had got over the worst hurdle; for instead of having to leave the car prematurely as the only alternative to getting himself into a packet of trouble, he now stood a good chance of detaining it for quite a long time. His intention was to leave Miss Hořovská sitting in it outside number fifteen Lister Road, until her patience was exhausted and she came in to fetch him. Still posing as Bilto, he would then say that he had suddenly been struck with qualms of conscience at the thought of betraying the country that had given him asylum from the Nazis. That would provoke an argument in which she would use every line she could think of before resigning herself to leaving him, and facing the anger her report would arouse in her boss. Nicholas reckoned that by the time she reported, he would in any case have thrown Bilto's programme out by an hour, and, with one proviso, for very much longer. The proviso was that he could get the Sinznicks to abet the continuance of his imposture, as the Russians would then continue to believe that Bilto had left the Hotel Russell and, having gone sour on them, was spending the night at Cricklewood; and he felt sure that the Sinznicks would do anything within reason that he asked.

As the car entered Kilburn High Street his sense of humour was suddenly tickled by the thought that, although he would have to borrow things for the night from Igor, he had got himself a free ride all the way from Russell Square to Cricklewood, which would have cost him at least six shillings in a taxi. But next moment a new thought struck him, which made it look much more likely that he would be an extra six shillings down before the night was out.

The appalling responsibility which had been thrust upon him that evening would not be lifted simply by having kept Bilto out of the Russians' hands for a few hours. His knowledge and abilities would be just as valuable to them to-morrow or next week, and within a day or two, at most, they would know how they had been fooled, have got in touch with him again and be making fresh plans for getting him away to Prague. Somehow he must be persuaded to give up his idea of leaving Britain. Nicholas saw that as soon as Miss Hořovská had left him to report, he must return to the Hotel Russell and have it out with Bilto. If arguments failed threats must be used; but by hook or by crook, as a first step, he must be got back to Harwell.

Nicholas had gone only so far with his intensely-worrying preoccupations, when on reaching Brondesbury Park Station the chauffeur slowed down and asked to be directed. A few minutes later they entered Lister Road and pulled up in front of number fifteen. It was a rather dingy, but solidly-built, semi-detached house in a row typical of the houses that, during the reign of Edward VII, had spread like a rash over the old-world gardens and small estates which had previously been the principal feature of London's inner suburbs. The conflicting sounds of two radios tuned in to different stations shattered the twilight peace; but otherwise a respectable quiet reigned in the short street. Murmuring "I'll be as quick as I can"—which was a flat lie—to Miss Hořovská, Nicholas got out, walked up the short gravel path and rang the bell.

The door was opened to him by Igor, a short, fat, cheerful Jew wearing thick-lensed glasses. Shaking Nicholas warmly by the hand, he pulled him inside and called to his wife. "Judith! I think you have won your bet; he has had his hair cut."

Nicholas was too deeply absorbed in his own affairs to take much notice of this somewhat strange greeting; and shutting the front door quickly behind him, he followed his host into the sitting-room. The two were about the same age, and their histories had a certain similarity, as their fathers had come to England in the same year and both had married London-born girls.

Igor's father had been one of the original Russian-Jew associates of Trotsky, and later had been made a member of Arcos, the Bolshevik trade mission which, early in the 1920's, had taken offices in the Strand and reopened Anglo-Russian relations after the breach caused by the revolution. An ardent Marxist in his early years, the excesses of the revolution had shocked his sensitive nature, and he had abandoned the 'Comrades' in favour of making permanent his association with a pretty Whitechapel Jewess. Yet, like so many of his kind, he could not see that the rapings, burnings, and butcherings by the mobs were the inevitable outcome of his gospel, and he had continued in the belief that had not power corrupted men like his old leader, Communism would have turned Russia into a Utopia. Igor had inherited his father's ideas and, like Nicholas, believed that whenever possible Russia should be aided in her efforts to spread Communism through the world. They had met during the war as inmates of the same labour camp for conscientious objectors.

The sitting-room was in its usual state of chaos. It was also used as a work-room by Igor, for dressmaking by Judith, and as an extra spare bedroom when, with their boundless generosity, they had taken in more lame ducks than they could otherwise accommodate. As Nicholas entered it he saw with relief that there was no man or woman with a pathetic, half-apologetic face, preparing to make up a shakedown on the divan, there to-night. But before he could get out a word of what was on his mind, Igor had swept a pile of books from a chair, pushed him down into it, peered into his face, then exclaimed with a happy laugh:

"I am sure Judith was right. The reason for your having neglected to answer so many of the questions in my letters for this past month is that you have fallen in love. You have begun to take trouble with your hair, and never before have I seen you sporting an expensive silk handkerchief."

It was true that for Wendy's sake Nicholas had recently begun to take a little more thought for his appearance, and the handkerchief in his breast pocket was a present from her. As he glanced down a little self-consciously at its quietly-patterned silk, he realized how for the first time in weeks her image had been blotted from his mind for one whole waking hour. It now returned with redoubled vividness; and as he acknowledged Igor's innuendo by a half smile and a nod, he again cursed Bilto, this time for having been the cause of his leaving Birmingham and so quarrelling with his beloved fiancée.

At that moment Judith came in from the kitchen, carrying a tray with coffee and a cake upon it. She was the thin type of Jewess, with a high-bridged nose and large intelligent eyes. Like her husband, she wrote articles and made speeches; in addition she spent several hours every week handing peace propaganda, and other Communist-inspired literature, to women and girls as they left their factories. This accounted for the untidiness of the Sinznicks' home, the unpunctual and indifferent meals, and the usually grubby condition of their three children, who, although healthy, were shockingly neglected. But her husband would not have had things otherwise; and being much the more fanatical of the two, it was she who carried them over the bad patches when he grew despondent and was tempted to soft-pedal his Marxism, in order to sell some of his articles to the Pink press because it paid better than the Red.

Setting down the tray, Judith gave Nicholas a quiet smile, and said: "I am so glad for you, Nicky. For a man of your age to be without a woman is not right; and for a long time now I had been hoping that you would find a nice girl to take care of you. Do tell us all about her?"

"I will," he replied quickly, "but later on. There's something much more pressing I've got to talk to you about. It is typical of Igor that he should have noticed my new tie, but not that I arrived here without a hat, coat, or suit-case. The fact is I am in a bit of a difficulty and I want your help."

Igor's eyes grew round behind his thick-lensed glasses, and he breathed apprehensively. "Is it that the police are after you?"

His reaction was due to the fact that although he and his wife were both British born, neither of them was of British blood and more than half their friends were aliens; so they had never come to accept the average British citizen's view of the police, as the unbiased and unbribable guardians of law and order. Instead, the continental belief that all policemen were spies and bullies was still held by them, and as they spent a good part of their lives frothily denouncing the British Government, they were never quite free from an uneasy feeling that sooner or later the police would pounce upon them.

"No," said Nicholas. "It's not the police; and I don't quite know how to explain, really. Will you forgive me if I don't attempt to for the moment? You see, this mess concerns a cousin of mine named Bilto more than it does myself, so I am not altogether free to talk about it."

"That is your cousin the scientist, isn't it?" remarked Judith. "The one you told us about two or three years ago, when he returned from the United States to take up an appointment at Harwell?"

Nicholas had hoped that they had forgotten about Bilto and his connection with atom bombs, as for the sake of everyone concerned he felt that the less near the truth their speculations led them the better; but he nodded and continued.

"That's right. Well, certain people are very anxious to talk to him; but he doesn't want to talk to them. He is a bit older than I am, but we are very much alike and might easily be mistaken for one another by anyone who had only a description of one of us to go on. To-night he asked me to impersonate him for a few hours while he . . ." Nicholas hesitated then continued rather lamely, ". . . er, while he got away quietly to the country. I agreed, and let myself be driven off in a car that had been sent to fetch him."

He paused for a moment, and Igor said quickly, "Go on; what happened then?"

"I had no idea where she was taking me, and I was afraid that I might find myself in trouble when . . ."

"Who d'you mean by 'she'?"

"The girl who was sent in the car to fetch Bilto. She is waiting for me outside. As a matter of fact . . ." Nicholas was about to add, 'it seems that she is an acquaintance of yours. Her name is

Hořovská'; but his sentence was cut short by the shrilling of the front-door bell.

He had not been in the house more than three minutes, and he had counted on at least ten before Miss Hořovská lost patience to the point of coming to rout him out; but at this hour it seemed unlikely to be anyone else, so there was no time left for him to elaborate his story. Seizing Igor's arm with one hand and Judith's with the other, he gave the astonished couple a slight shake and said hurriedly:

"That will be her! I made her bring me here, but she's expecting me to go on with her. I'm not going. I shall tell her I've changed my mind. But she must continue to believe that I am Bilto. Is that clear? I'm going to send her away, but she must go thinking that it's Bilto she's left behind. That's terribly important. For God's sake don't let me down."

"Of course we won't," Judith assured him, and Igor gave him a friendly pat on the shoulder before going out into the narrow hall.

A minute later Igor reappeared. Throwing open the sitting-room door, he said in a slightly flustered voice, "Judith! This is an unexpected pleasure. You remember Comrade Hořovská?"

The tall ash-blonde remained standing in the doorway. Nicholas could see her better now. Her lack of lipstick made her thin face so pale that it might have been that of an invalid, but her green eyes were full of life and extraordinarily compelling.

Judith gave her a quick look of surprise, then smiled. "Why, yes. We have met several times at Mr. Kolin's. Please come in and join us. We were just about to have some coffee."

The young woman shook her head. "Thank you, Mrs. Sinznick, but I'm afraid I can't stay now."

Igor stepped past her and spread his arms wide, as though to usher her into the room. "Oh, come; this is the first time you have been to our house. We shall be quite offended if you will not take some refreshment."

"Another time, perhaps. My business is with Mr. Novák."

"Then why not discuss it here? If you wish, Judith and I will leave the two of you together."

Ignoring him, she turned impatiently to Nicholas. "You were with Mr. Sinznick quite long enough to give him the warning you spoke of. Every moment is now precious. Please come with me at once."

Nicholas gave a quite passable impression of embarrassment by shifting from one foot to the other and lowering his glance at the floor, before he said in a low voice, "I'm sorry; but I don't think I can."

"Why not?" Her brows drew together in a frown.

"Well, the fact of the matter is . . ." he hesitated artistically. "I've changed my mind."

The Sinznicks glanced in silence from her to him and back, then uneasily at one another, as she snapped, "It is no good telling that to me. You must tell it to the person who sent me to fetch you."

He shook his head. "You can quite well do that for me. I'm sorry to have taken up your time for nothing, but there it is." Then, feeling that even at the risk of the Sinznicks' guessing the truth about Bilto he ought to do his best to detain her as long as possible, he attempted to lure her into an argument by adding, "I have decided that it would be morally wrong to take the step I contemplated."

"I don't care what you have decided." Her voice was harsh. "You are coming with me."

"I'm not," he countered firmly. "I am staying here."

"You are wrong about that." For the first time she smiled, showing good teeth, but her green eyes remained as hard as pebbles. Taking a pace forward into the room, she half turned and waved a hand towards the doorway. "I had an idea you might try to double-cross us; that's why I brought Rufus in with me."

Only then did Nicholas become aware that the chauffeur had been standing behind her in the semi-darkness of the hall. It was the first time he had seen the man face to face. He was a powerfully-built negro, well over six feet two in height. His

white teeth flashed in a grin as he held up his right hand for
Nicholas to see. Folded back over the knuckles there gleamed
the five-inch blade of a cut-throat razor.

The girl with the ash-blonde hair said in a matter-of-fact tone,
"You are quite a good-looking man, Mr. Novák. It would be a
pity if I had to tell Rufus to spoil your face for life. I think you
had better come quietly."

CHAPTER V

THE PERSISTENT NEGRO

NICHOLAS was not a coward, but the idea of fighting a big negro
armed with a naked razor made his flesh creep. His vivid imagination instantly conjured up pictures of fingers being half severed
from his hands as he strove to protect his face, then of his cheeks,
lips and nose gashed to the bone and pouring with blood. Yet
the alternative had suddenly assumed a very frightening aspect.

From the moment he had stepped into the limousine he
had realized that if he did not get out of it before it reached its
journey's end he might find himself temporarily a prisoner. The
idea of having to spend the weekend in a coal-cellar while they
got the real Bilto away had been bad enough, but now he was
seized with a foreboding that if he got into the car again he
would be letting himself in for something very much worse.

This threat to slash his face to ribbons was a terrifyingly-clear
indication of the lengths to which they were prepared to go,
rather than be disappointed in their hopes of getting Bilto behind the Iron Curtain. It could therefore also be taken as fair
warning of the danger to which he would be exposed once they
became aware that he was not Bilto. If they were prepared to
disfigure and abduct a scientist from whom they expected so
much, rather than allow him to go back on his word, what

might not their rage lead them into doing to someone who had deliberately jeopardized their chances of getting him abroad at all?

In a matter of seconds Nicholas decided that here—in the Sinznicks' house, with them to aid him and neighbours who could be brought swiftly on the scene by cries for help—he would stand a much better chance of getting away uninjured than if he allowed himself to be taken to some place where circumstances might render escape impossible.

The door of the room opened inwards and at the moment stood wide. Nicholas was near its edge, the negro was still in the hall, and the pale-faced girl just inside the room. Both Igor and Judith were further back, behind a small table on which the latter had set down the coffee tray.

In one swift movement Nicholas seized the door-knob with his left hand, thrust out his right fist, and flung himself forward. His fist caught the Hořovská girl in the chest. With a gasp she went over backwards. The door crashed to, shutting Rufus outside.

The key was on the hall side of the lock. Nicholas had had no chance to transfer it. With his shoulder pressed firmly against the door panel, he kept a tight grip on the knob with one hand, while with the fingers of the other he sought frantically below it for a bolt. There was none. He knew then that once the negro threw his weight against the door it would be impossible to keep it shut for more than a few moments. Desperately he called to his friends.

"Quick, Igor! Help me to hold this door. Judith! Open the window as wide as it will go, so that I can get out that way!"

He was still shouting when the door shuddered under the first impact of Rufus' heavy body. At the second, Nicholas' feet slithered and the door was forced open a few inches. By straining every muscle he managed to get it shut again. Igor had answered his appeal by grasping a four-foot square, open bookcase that stood near the door. He was clumsily slewing it round so that it would block the entrance.

With a loud thump Rufus' shoulder hit the door again. The

shock temporarily threw Nicholas off his balance. The door gaped open, but he flung himself at it and was in time to prevent Rufus getting more than a foot in.

Igor was still struggling with the bookcase. Over his shoulder Nicholas caught a glimpse of Judith. She had not moved. "Judith!" he gasped. "For God's sake get the window open!"

Still she did not move. She did not even seem to hear him. Her features expressed distress, but her big eyes held a look of resignation, and they were riveted upon her uninvited visitor.

The girl had staggered to her feet. Two bright spots of colour flamed in her thin, pale cheeks; her green eyes were blazing. For a moment she stood there panting, then she sprang forward and seized Igor by the shoulder. Pulling him back, she cried:

"This is none of your business! Keep out of it, or I will see to it that you have cause to regret your interference."

The door strained and creaked. Suddenly Rufus withdrew his foot and it slammed to. Nicholas guessed that the negro was about to make another charge. Swinging round, he put his back against the door and planted his feet firmly against the plinth of the heavy little bookcase that Igor had dragged from the wall. He could now see the whole room. Judith had still not moved, but stood with drooping shoulders on the far side of the table. The Hořovská girl was glaring at Igor, and he was staring at her uncertainly with his full-lipped mouth hanging a little open.

Sweating and panting from the strain of holding back the door, Nicholas no longer had breath enough to shout, but he gasped:

"Igor! Igor! What's come over you? Don't you see what they mean to do to me? Dial 999! Ring up the police!"

"No! No!" Igor exclaimed, a look of consternation coming over his fat face. "Not the police!" Then he waved both his arms in a helpless gesture, as though he was experiencing a nightmare and realized the futility of attempting anything except to shake himself awake.

When Nicholas had slammed the door in the negro's face he had counted on his friends taking his place at it and blocking it

3

for the few minutes which were all he needed to reach the street by way of the window. Their failure to give him the help he had expected now rendered his situation desperate. Between him and the window stood the girl. He could not possibly hope to reach it without her either tripping or clinging on to him, and the second he took his weight from the door Rufus would come charging through it. The negro, whirling that terrifying razor, would be upon him before he could even free himself from her, let alone get the window open and scramble out of it. At the thought of the razor he instinctively flattened his back against the door still more firmly, and strained every limb to the utmost, expecting at any moment to have to resist the shock of the two hundred pound human battering ram on its other side.

For the past half minute there had been no sound outside in the hall. Nicholas took the brief silence for the lull before storm, and tensed his muscles. Suddenly they went slack, his mouth fell open, and his eyes started out of his head. The other door of the sitting-room had been jerked open. The negro had come round through the kitchen, and now stood there grinning at him. Taking the razor from the pocket of his chauffeur's coat, he folded it back over his hand.

Igor took a faltering step forward and cried, "No, no! Please! He is my friend."

The girl swung upon him sharply. "I warned you to keep out of this. It is a Party matter." Then she turned to Nicholas and asked, "Are you now prepared to leave without making any further trouble?"

He nodded, and stepped away from the door. "It doesn't seem that I have much option."

Rufus put away his razor, walked up to Nicholas, patted him on the shoulder and said, "Sorry I had to scare you, Comrade. I wouldn't have used that razor on you; honest I wouldn't. Worst I'd do is jus' to give you a lit'l tap on the head. But you be good now, an' nothin' unpleasant won't happen to you at all."

He spoke in quite an educated voice, and Nicholas accepted his assurance with considerable relief. All the same he could not help wondering uneasily how far it would hold good once the cat was out of the bag about his not being Bilto.

His one hope now of escaping that issue lay in the chance that the Sinznicks' neighbours might have been aroused by the shindy. If they had and were on the point of coming to enquire if all was well, or were even looking out of their windows, he could make a bolt for it when going down the garden path, as it seemed unlikely that the negro would dare to set upon him in front of witnesses. But he was quick to recognize that the prospects of his being given such a chance were far from good. The rumpus could not have lasted for more than three minutes from start to finish. The only really loud noise had been from the series of thumps as Rufus had thrown himself against the door. Nicholas alone had raised his voice above normal, and then only in half a dozen brief sentences. Fervently but uselessly he wished now that instead of dissipating his strength in keeping the door shut he had used it to yell for help with all the power of his lungs. Momentarily he had forgotten the menace of the razor, and he was still berating himself for having bungled the best opportunity of regaining his freedom that he was likely to get when the platinum-blonde administered the *coup de grâce* to his lingering hope that he might be saved through outside intervention.

Looking across at Igor, she said, "It is possible that the people next door may have heard the noise and be wondering what is going on here. Go outside and see if there are any signs of them. If so, apologize. Say that you were getting a heavy trunk downstairs, and that you are sorry if the bumps it made disturbed them. Then see that the street is clear. When all is quiet, come back and let me know."

"Comrade Hořovská . . ." he began in a voice that was near to tears; but she cut him short.

"Do as I tell you! If you refuse I shall report you for showing bourgeois-individualist sympathies."

The term bourgeois typified for Nicholas the smug middle-class that he had taught himself to hate, and even in his present straits her application of it riled him. Rounding on her angrily, he cried:

"If you are referring to Igor's sympathy for me, I resent being called a bourgeois. I consider it an insult."

"Is that so!" she replied quietly, as the shamefaced Igor slunk out between them. "Yet only a few minutes ago you were talking about having changed your mind owing to moral scruples. No lapse could better show the cloven hoof of the religio-bourgeois."

He saw the trap he had dug for himself and hastily protested. "I said nothing of scruples. I was referring to the fact that I had made a reassessment of my obligations."

She shrugged. "What is the difference? It was clear to me within a few minutes of picking you up that you were a waverer, and that I might have difficulty in getting you to our destination. But in front of the traffic lights at Oxford Circus is not a good place to have a show-down. I should have had to get Rufus to drive us to some dark cul-de-sac, had you not asked me to bring you here."

Judith gave her a bitter look and suddenly put in, "You showed little consideration for us, Comrade Hořovská, in choosing our home as the place in which to . . . to arrest one of our friends."

"You should be honoured that the use of your home chanced to coincide with the Party's interests," came the retort. "It was further than I would have come from choice; but at least I knew that if I allowed Professor Novák to come in here I should have no difficulty in getting him out again; so to take him where he wished to go was the obvious thing to do. Now that we have had the opportunity of making his situation plain to him, I do not think he will give us any further trouble."

At that moment Igor returned and, avoiding Nicholas' glance, said dully, "There is no-one looking from our neighbours' windows and no-one is about."

"Good!" The girl nodded, then gave a sharp warning to Nicholas. "No nonsense, mind; or Rufus will give you a headache that you won't forget in a hurry."

As she turned to lead the way from the room Judith called after her in a voice which betrayed a touch of anxiety, "I take it, Comrade Hořovská, that this having happened here won't be held against us in any way? I mean, no difficulty will be made about letting us have the money to start the periodical?"

The girl cast a slightly contemptuous glance over her shoulder and replied, "No. I have no reason to complain that you or your husband have hindered me, Mrs. Sinznick, so you need not worry about the money."

Nicholas laid a hand on Igor's arm, gave a wry smile and said, "So you and Judith are members of the Party. I wasn't aware of that."

"No." Igor shook his massive head. "We have never been members. But one must go along with them, otherwise what hope is there of making any progress?" Through his thick-lensed glasses he peered into Nicholas' face and added, "Please do not think too badly of us. I am most distressed by all this; more distressed than I can say. I do hope things will work out all right for you . . . Bilto."

This belated use of his cousin's name filled Nicholas with sudden consternation. He guessed at once that Igor had called him it as the only means he had of showing that, in spite of the weakness he had displayed, he still wished to help in any way he could. By doing so he had taken the risk that he might later be accused of having deliberately misled his paymasters: but unfortunately he had ignored the fact that Nicholas' situation was now very different from what it had been when he had asked to be supported in his imposture. Then, he had expected to be able to send the people who had brought him there away still believing he was Bilto. Now, they were on the point of forcibly removing him with them, and he had just decided that the only means of preventing them from doing so was to disclose his real identity. In fact, he had at that very moment been about to throw his hand in, and call upon the Sinznicks to confirm that he was Professor *Nicholas* Novák.

For a few seconds he still considered declaring himself; but it now seemed unlikely that he would be believed. How could Igor possibly explain away just having called him Bilto? No doubt he intended, if questioned later, to deny ever having done so, but he could not possibly get away with such a denial in the next few moments. Neither, in view of his evident dependence on the goodwill of Comrade Hořovská, would he dare admit to having attempted to help Nicholas deceive her. To make an immediate issue of the matter would place him in a frightful predicament, and probably lead only to his continuing to maintain that Nicholas was Bilto.

By now Nicholas needed no telling that he had got himself into the very devil of a mess; but, anxious as he was to get out of it, he decided that his unsupported account of the trick he had played was unlikely to prevent his being carried off as a prisoner; so it would be better to spare his friends further embarrassment and save his breath for a more favourable occasion. In an attempt to comfort Igor he said:

"Thanks for the good wishes. I quite see that you and Judith couldn't have acted in any other way. I'll be all right. Don't worry about me." Then he followed his blonde captor out into the hall.

As they reached the front door Rufus took his arm and spoke to him in the firm but friendly manner that he might have used towards a naughty boy. "Now, Mister Bilto, you're not goin' to give us any trouble, are you? Comrade Hořovská, she's often driven this old bus, so for the rest of the way she'll be doin' chauffeur while you sit in the back with me. I jus' wanta warn you, though, that if we pass a copper don't you start nothin'; 'cause in situations like that there isn't no time for argument. I'd havta hit you real hard at the very first sign you meant to holla, and I don't wanta have to do that."

Nicholas had just begun to toy with the idea of sitting quiet until the car was brought to a halt by traffic lights, then giving Miss Hořovská a swift back-hander to keep her from grabbing hold of him, wrenching open the door and making a bolt for it. Now it was clear that no situation was likely to arise in which the conventions of chivalry would be outraged by his hitting a woman. It was equally clear that the chances were extremely slender of any profit being derived from administering a quick slap to Rufus. Contemplating these obvious truths somewhat ruefully, Nicholas got into the limousine, the negro followed him, the girl took the wheel and they drove off.

Resigned now to being taken to some Russian or Czech official, Nicholas could only hope that he would prove a superior type of man, who would not become violently vindictive when he learned how his people had been tricked. In the meantime he endeavoured to console himself with the thought that the longer he kept up his imposture, the less likelihood there was of their getting Bilto away to the continent that night.

As they turned back into Kilburn High Road his thoughts reverted to the Sinznicks, and it was with considerable dismay that he ran over in his mind again all that had happened at their house. In retrospect it had a most unpleasant resemblance to the stories he had so often heard in his youth about the sort of thing that went on in the countries controlled by the Nazis.

At first he was inclined to suppose that the thought had come to him only because it so chanced that the Sinznicks were Jews; for no midnight visitors could be less like the smart, uniformed thugs of the Gestapo than the ash-blonde girl and the ebony-skinned negro. Yet the fact remained that their behaviour had been on the traditional lines of Hitler's secret police. There had been the same unwarranted intrusion into the privacy of a home, cynical disregard for the feelings of its occupants, and reduction of them to frightened onlookers by means of threats, the resort to violence and, finally, the removal of a friend of the family against his will to an unspecified destination.

On consideration, Nicholas decided that the methods employed by the cloak-and-dagger people of every nation were probably much the same, and it was the fact of his having been kidnapped in the heart of London which made the whole thing so fantastic. Then another moment's thought told him that this could never have happened had not the Sinznicks meekly played the part that had obviously been expected of them, and his musings turned from the broad unsavoury picture as a whole to the mental attitude that Igor had displayed.

Although it had transpired that the new periodical was to be financed by the Communist Party, and Judith had shown anxiety about that, Nicholas knew Igor too well to believe that he had been influenced by either money or self-interest. The crux of the matter lay in his statement that he saw no hope of progress for the things they believed in except through keeping in with the Party. What he had really meant was that he had come to the conclusion that his own interpretation of the Marxist doctrines, which were the very breath of his life, could not be brought to more than a very limited public without the aid of Russian money. Therefore, although he was not a member of the Party, to secure that aid he had become subservient to it, and had accepted its discipline to a degree that had caused him to place its interests before his natural desire to protect a personal friend.

With something of a shock it recurred to Nicholas that less than an hour before, when he had been seeking some acid test to apply to his own dilemma, he had rejected all but the one fundamental concept—that a man should place the safety and well-being of the people that he knew and loved before the furtherance of any abstract ideology, however convinced he was that its acceptance would ultimately benefit all mankind. It was, in fact, in the belief that he might give Igor, Judith and a few score people like them, as well as Wendy and himself, a better chance of escaping a horrible death in an atomic war, that he had stolen Bilto's passport and then impersonated him.

Igor's conduct showed that on this question of ethics their views were diametrically opposed, and Nicholas had a great respect for Igor; so he began to wonder if after all he had allowed sentiment to warp his judgment. Yet the thought had hardly come to him before he dismissed it, becoming once more fully convinced that he had acted rightly, and that a better world could not be built by debasing individuals to a level at which they were ready to sacrifice their personal loyalties when ordered to do so.

At the bottom of Kilburn High Road, instead of continuing on down Maida Vale, the car turned south-west in the direction of Paddington. It was a part of London that Nicholas scarcely knew, and although he endeavoured to memorize the way they

THE PERSISTENT NEGRO 73

were taking he soon found it hopeless, owing to the irregular nature of the succession of mean streets through which they passed. Presently they entered a broader thoroughfare that he thought might be Ladbroke Grove, then after two more turns they pulled up outside a two-storied house standing in its own small garden.

As he got out, with Rufus again holding him by the arm, he saw that it was typical of the larger houses in that decayed neighbourhood. It had been built to accommodate a prosperous middle-class Victorian family, but all signs of prosperity had long since vanished from it. Beyond a low wall of stucco balusters the light from the nearest street lamp showed a strip of garden that neglect had turned into a dust patch. Only a few weeds struggled for existence round a small fountain that leaned awry in an empty basin. The short flight of steps leading up to the front door were cracked and broken. The paint had flaked in great patches from the walls of the house, giving it a leprous appearance. Its windows were shuttered and no lights showed in any of them.

The girl leaned out from the driver's seat and said to the negro, "You take him inside while I put away the car. If anybody wants me I shall be here for about ten minutes; but that's all, as I've got a date to keep up West."

Her casual announcement sounded so much like that of an ordinary business girl just about to go off duty that Nicholas was quite taken aback. He wondered vaguely what her date would be like. She certainly did not strike him as a woman's woman, and although she was not his type he could imagine her extreme pallor coupled with the ash-blonde hair proving attractive to quite a lot of rich, rather jaded, middle-aged men. Had he known more about women he would have realized that her well-worn black coat and skirt were hardly up to the sort of supper and dance at one of the big hotels that he was visualizing as her destination; but momentarily the idea that she had a more glamorous life, quite apart from that necessitated by this under-cover work, greatly intrigued him.

As she turned the car to back it in through a pair of double

3*

gates which were already open, the negro drew Nicholas across the neglected garden and round the side of the house. His thoughts now focused on what the next few moments might hold for him. It seemed probable that the person to whom he was being taken, or anyhow someone on his staff, would know Bilto personally; so the balloon would go up at once. If that proved the case, there would be nothing for him to do but endeavour to modify their anger and use either reason or threats, whichever seemed most appropriate, to induce them to release him right away.

Should he not be unmasked at once, that would give him the option to carry on his imposture a little, but not very much, longer; as he felt that anyway he must throw his hand in before they took him to the plane, otherwise he might be given into the charge of some unreasoning but highly duty-conscious Comrade, like the Hořovská, which could lead to a frightful scene, or even a struggle, at the airport. He had no intention of risking anything of the kind; so had already decided that in the very near future, if nobody did it for him, he must now play for safety by bringing his imposture to an end.

The back of the house appeared almost as lifeless as the front, but a few chinks of light showed along the tops of the ground-floor windows where the thick curtains that had been drawn across them did not quite meet the upper part of the window frames. Rufus halted in front of a garden door half hidden by a broken-down trellis. Slipping a hand behind the rotting wood-work, he pressed a concealed button and a buzzer sounded faintly somewhere inside. After a moment the door was opened by a tall young man, with pale blue eyes and a receding chin, who said with a heavy foreign accent:

"So! At last it is you. We have been much worrying. You are late by half an hour, or more."

His words put heart into Nicholas, for they were an assurance that he had not got himself into a mess to no purpose. It was over three-quarters of an hour since they had left the Russell, and evidently Bilto had made no move to find out why he had not been picked up; so the odds against his doing so now were considerable. By this time he might even have panicked and decided to return to Harwell.

The young man led them down a short passage and into a brightly-lit room. Unlike the outside of the house it was spotlessly clean, but its decoration was uninspiring. Nicholas guessed that it had once been the drawing-room of the house, as it had a big bay window facing the garden, and arch-shaped recesses with shelves which might once have held ornaments on each side of the fireplace. Now it was in use as an office, and had the bleakness associated with bureaucracies whose expenditure is limited to essentials. The walls had been distempered off-white, the floor was covered with linoleum, the recesses and mantelpiece held rows of files, and the furniture, which consisted only of a desk, a large bare table and a set of stiff-backed chairs, was of the type which can be obtained very cheaply second-hand.

A man had just risen from the desk. He had a thin intellectual face with rather sleepy-looking eyes, short grey hair cut *en brosse* in the German fashion, and he was toying with an old-fashioned pince-nez which hung round his neck on an inch-wide black ribbon. Coming forward, he held out a blue-veined hand, smiled, showing a gold filling at one side of his mouth, and said in crisp English:

"Professor Novák, this is a great pleasure. My name is Vaněk, and although I do not play any public part at our Embassy, I am the principal representative of the Czechoslovak People's Government in this country. Your decision to return to your own land, and give the Communist Party the benefit of your great knowledge in their struggle to bring freedom to the workers of all nations, has filled us all with joy. I feel honoured in having been given even so small a part to play in your return as, shall we say, your travel agent."

Not liking to ignore the outstretched hand, Nicholas shook it; then, as soon as he had the chance, he said, "Thanks very much, but before we go any further there are certain things I want to explain. This affair has not gone at all as you arranged."

Vaněk gave a quick nod. "I gathered that something must have delayed you, but nothing matters now that you are here.

I have only to give you the papers for your journey, and we still have just time for a glass of wine together. It is a pity you were held up, as I intended to offer you supper, but I must now deny myself that pleasure."

Another wave of elation swept through Nicholas. Obviously he had succeeded in so reducing their time margin that they could not possibly get Bilto away to the continent that night, whatever happened now. In addition an idea had suddenly come to him of a way in which, when they learned that their plan had been sabotaged, he might divert their fury from himself to the absent Bilto. He was still hurriedly working out the best way to put over this line of self-preservation when Rufus cut in defensively:

"Ai'd jus' like to say, Comrade Vaněk, that it weren't no fault of Comrade Hořovská's or mine that we're back late. Mister Novák, he insisted that we take him to see some friends of his who live right up out Cricklewood way."

Seizing on the negro's protest as a good lead for a bold attempt to carry off the situation, Nicholas nodded. "That's true; and since Rufus has raised the matter I'd be awfully grateful if, when I've explained things, he could run me back there. You see, it is with those friends that I have arranged to spend the night."

"To spend the night!" Vaněk's grey eyebrows shot up. "I do not understand. . . ."

"No, but I'm trying to explain. I had always intended to go on there after dining with my cousin; and I felt I must look in on my way here to make certain they did not give me up and lock me out. It was only . . ."

The Czech had been impatiently fiddling with his pince-nez. Dropping them, he exclaimed, "Forgive me, but I am quite lost! Unless I have been completely misled by my subordinates, to-night was the night fixed for your journey at your own wish."

"Not my wish," Nicholas took the plunge. "At the wish of my cousin Bilto."

"Then you, you . . ?" Vaněk's face had suddenly gone as white as a sheet.

"I am Professor *Nicholas* Novák, of Birmingham University." Nicholas paused a second, then launched out on the distorted version of the night's events by which he now hoped to transfer the wrath to come from his own head to Bilto's. "My cousin rang me up last night and asked me to dine with him this evening. We hold the same political views, so when we met at the Hotel Russell he confided to me what had brought him to London. Then he said that after thinking matters over all this afternoon, he had decided that he couldn't go through with it."

"You cannot mean this!" The blood had now streamed back into Vaněk's face, and he looked as if at any moment he might have a fit.

Nicholas nodded. "I do. Naturally he realized that you would be very upset, and he felt very badly about having to let you down. But he has definitely made up his mind to remain in England. For him to have to come here to tell you so himself would have meant only a most distressing scene, so he asked me to send your car away when it arrived to fetch him. I went out intending to do that; but we are very alike to look at, and Miss Hořovská mistook me for him, just as you did. There was a lounger who I thought might be a detective standing near the car, and I didn't like to risk explaining to Miss Hořovská in his hearing; so I suddenly decided that the best thing to do was to let her bring me here and explain matters to you myself."

For a moment the Czech stood there goggle-eyed and dumbfounded, then Rufus' rich voice came like a bomb-shell from behind Nicholas.

"Comrade Vaněk, don' you go believin' that story. It ain' true. No, sir, not a word of it."

"How d'you know that?" his chief rapped out, instantly recovering himself.

"Ai don' say Mister Novák hasn't changed his mind 'bout goin'. He told us so himself. He said that very thing. He told Comrade Hořovská that he'd decided it 'ud be morally wrong, but . . ."

"What the devil are you talking about?" Vaněk cried in puzzled fury. "Are you telling me that you've seen Professor Novák? The real one—the scientist—I mean?"

"No, Comrade. I mean yes, I mean . . ."

"He doesn't know what he means," Nicholas cut in quickly.

"Be silent! Kindly refrain from interfering while I get to the bottom of this," Vaněk snapped, and having administered this sharp rebuke, swung on Rufus. "Now, Comrade Abombo, tell me at once what you are driving at."

The negro grinned and pointed a thick finger at Nicholas. "That's him. That's Mister Novák, numbers one an' two. There ain't no other. He said all that 'bout changing his mind up way out at Cricklewood. He asked us to take him there, but he didn't wanta come along here to see you, like he says. Oh, no! Ai hadta do a lit'le forcible persuadin', by showin' him ma razor, to induce him to do that."

"He's got an entirely false impression of what happened," Nicholas protested in a desperate attempt to maintain his own version of the story. "Naturally I could not speak freely about this business in front of my friends, and that led to a misunderstanding."

"Ai don't misunderstand nothin'," declared Rufus doggedly. "There's only one Mister Novák, an' you'se him."

Vaněk gave his coloured underling a doubtful glance. As he did so, the tall, thin young man who had opened the back door, and had so far remained a silent spectator of the scene, put in, "There *are* two Professor Nováks. The other writes articles. I have read, not always with approval. But most times yes. He is at heart one of us, and puts his thoughts clearly."

"Thanks," said Nicholas, giving him a quick smile. "That's the one I am. My cousin the atom scientist's name is Bilto; mine is Nicholas."

An awful deep chuckle came from Rufus. "You go tell that to the Marines. If your name's Nicholas, why did that li'tle fat Jew friend of yours out up Cricklewood way call you Bilto?"

"We will soon have the truth of this," Vaněk declared with a hard stare at Nicholas. "Turn out your pockets. Put their contents on my desk."

Seeing Nicholas hesitate, Rufus and the thin young man closed in on him. Realizing that he had no option, he began to unload the miscellaneous collection of things he was carrying. The moment he produced Bilto's passport, Vaněk grabbed it, gave a quick look inside and exclaimed:

"Enough! This is all the proof we need. You are Professor Bilto Novák; but for some reason that we shall discover later you have ratted on us, and are endeavouring to escape being sent to Prague by pretending to be your cousin."

Nicholas shook his head. "No, that is Bilto's passport, but I am not Bilto. He was afraid that when you heard that he had changed his mind about going you might send people to attempt to coerce him. He asked me to take care of his passport as a precaution; because he felt that to be without one was the best guarantee against being hustled into an aircraft."

"He is . . . I mean you are very ignorant if you suppose that it is impossible for me to send anyone abroad without his own passport," Vaněk remarked with a sneer. "Given a little time our experts can easily make good such a deficiency."

Jamming the pince-nez more firmly on his nose, he began to run quickly through the other papers. Then, after a moment, he said, "What is this? It appears to be a Power of Attorney made out by Bilto Novák in favour of Nicholas Novák."

"Yes; that's what it is," Nicholas agreed. "And you could hardly ask for better proof that I have been telling you the truth. How could I come to have that in my possession if I were not Nicholas?"

Vaněk examined the document more carefully, shook his head, and said, "I suggest that you had this made out when it was still your intention to go to Prague. When you changed your mind there was no longer any point in giving it to your cousin. That is why it is still on you, and I regard it as a further proof that you are Bilto."

"All right, then!" Nicholas cried in desperation. "Let's say I am Bilto, and that I have changed my mind about leaving England. If I refuse to go you can't make me, so the sooner . . ."

"Can't I?" Vaněk cut him short. "You are quite wrong about that."

Nicholas caught his breath, then stammered, "But . . . but,

even if you could, there would be no point in doing so. An un-willing scientist is no use to anyone. Surely you don't mean that you . . . that if I were Bilto, and didn't want to go, you would send me just the same?"

"Certainly." Vaněk smiled unpleasantly, showing the gold filling of his tooth. "An arrangement was entered into by two parties. As the representative of one of them I have been given certain orders. A last-moment change of mind on the part of the other party does not relieve me of my responsibility. Besides, this change of mind may be only temporary. In any case, pro-viding it is in my power to do so, I must carry out my orders. Unless you can satisfy me beyond all doubt that you are not Professor Bilto Novák I shall have you put on the plane for Prague."

"You'll be making a fool of yourself if you do!" Nicholas retorted with rising agitation. "I tell you I'm not Bilto. I swear I'm not. There were other papers in my pockets that you haven't looked at yet, and they will prove it."

The thin young man had been turning over some of the items that Nicholas had produced, and he remarked, "He is I think right, Comrade Vaněk. For conclusions we must not make jumping. Here three letters are, all to Professor Nicholas sub-scribed. Also one ticket for season entry to a Birmingham con-cert series. How could the scientist Professor Novák of Harwell these papers have come by?"

"Exactly!" Nicholas snatched gratefully at the welcome support. "I can understand your having been foxed by my having the Power of Attorney; but the fact is that Bilto was not altogether easy in his mind about what might happen when he got back to Harwell. He thought there was just a chance he had failed to cover up certain indications that when he left he in-tended it should be for good. That's why, having had this Power of Attorney drawn up, he insisted on my taking it—so that if the security people had got on to him and he found himself in serious trouble, I could take charge of his affairs."

Now, uncertain and agitated, Vaněk fiddled with his pince-nez. After a moment's thought he said a shade less aggressively,

"You have still failed to explain why, if you are Nicholas, while you had yourself driven to this place in Cricklewood you continued to pretend that you were Bilto, and why you refused to come on here until you were forced to do so."

Nicholas passed a hand wearily through his red hair. His brain was now so tangled up with the lies he had told that he could no longer think of the best answer to make. At that moment he understood why it was that people under third degree lost the thread of the arguments on which their defence depended, and collapsed. He had an awful feeling that he was going mad; and while he was still groping for a reply that would not hopelessly compromise him, the rich voice of Rufus came again:

"Comrade Vaněk, why are you gettin' you'self all het up 'bout this when it's plain sailin'? This is Bilto, make no mistake about that; otherwise why would his Jew friend have called him Bilto? That's not all, either. How come that Comrade Hořovská mistook him for Bilto if he weren't?"

Vaněk turned to him with sudden relief. "Comrade Abombo, you have hit upon the one certain way of settling this question. I should have thought of it before. Find Comrade Hořovská and bring her here at once."

Rufus shrugged. "Maybe she's gone. She did say somethin' 'bout goin' dancin' with a boy-friend. But I'll go look see if she's still here."

For the few minutes that Rufus was away, not one of the three that remained said anything. At length the strained silence was broken by his return with the platinum-blonde.

Putting on his pince-nez, Vaněk tilted back his head and addressed her rather pompously. "Comrade Hořovská. It is you who until quite recently have been our sole contact with Professor Novák. During the past two years you must have met and talked with him at least half-a-dozen times. Is this the man that you have always known as the atomic scientist Bilto Novák?"

The young woman looked faintly surprised at the question, then she nodded. "Of course it is."

"Are you absolutely certain?"

Her green eyes were fixed unwaveringly on Nicholas' as she replied, "As I have had to let him make love to me, how could I possibly be mistaken?"

Nicholas returned her stare, and wondered if he really was going mad.

CHAPTER VI

IT *CAN* HAPPEN HERE

"Thank you, Comrade Hořovská." Vaněk gave a sigh of relief. "What you tell us puts his identity beyond further dispute."

Suddenly Nicholas found his tongue. "It's a lie! A flat lie! I've never so much as laid a finger on her."

She continued to look straight at him. "You need not be ashamed of admitting it because you knew I had no option. Everyone here realizes that there are occasions when a woman Comrade is proud to submit to things which are personally distasteful to her if they are rendered necessary by her work."

"Are you suggesting that I made you sleep with me against your will?"

"That first night at Marlow you made it quite clear that if I wouldn't, you meant to break off our association; and you knew perfectly well that the importance of maintaining it left me no choice."

Her voice was coldly indifferent, but her expression gave him the idea that she was laughing at him. Then he realized that was owing to the small cast in her left eye which, in the strong light, he could now see again.

"Damn it, I've never been to Marlow," he burst out. "I've never even set eyes on you until to-night."

"It is unnecessary to pursue the matter further," Vaněk declared with a smile of approval at the pale-faced girl. "Before

I sent for you, Comrade Hořovská, he was endeavouring to persuade us that he was Professor Nicholas Novák, Bilto's cousin. That is why he so stoutly denied his relations with you."

"I see," she returned his smile. "I knew already that he'd got cold feet and was trying to wriggle out of going to Prague. I expect Comrade Abombo has told you that we had to bring him here from Cricklewood against his will. He is more of a fool than I thought him, though, to try such a silly stunt as this. No family resemblance could be close enough for a girl to have any hesitation about identifying a man she has slept with."

That was the very point which was making Nicholas wonder if he was not living through some evil dream. Bilto and he were certainly very alike, but there was ten years' difference in their ages. The girl's eyes showed no sign of weakness and, even had she been nearly blind, it seemed utterly incredible that she could mistake a man she had never seen before for one with whom she had been having an affair over many months.

"It is settled, then!" Vaněk gave Nicholas a belligerent look. "You are Professor Bilto Novák, and I shall send you to Prague."

"I am not!" Nicholas protested angrily. "And even if I were, what would be the use? I left the hotel with only the things I stand up in. All Bilto's notes—or mine, if you insist that I am Bilto—are still there in his luggage. What good would an atomic scientist be to anyone on the other side of the Iron Curtain if he had left all his data behind?"

Vaněk waggled his pince-nez with a knowing look. "Ah, but you carry most of your knowledge in your head. If you still prove recalcitrant when you get there, our friends will find ways to extract it. But come! We have already wasted a further ten minutes disposing of your wicked lies. Time is now short, and to guard against trouble at the airport, we must give you special treatment. Comrade Abombo, go and tell Comrade Lubitsch that we have a reluctant passenger. Ask him to get his things together and come here as quickly as possible."

"What d'you mean to do?" cried Nicholas in sudden apprehension.

"To give you a small injection." Vaněk's gold tooth flashed

in a brief smile. "Nothing that will upset you seriously. You will be quite well again to-morrow; but for the next few hours it will make you feel as though you were drunk, and slow up the action of your brain."

Nicholas' face went a shade whiter. Swiftly he took stock of the situation. The negro had left the room. Vaněk was well on into middle age and of frail build. The tall young man did not look as if he had much stamina. It seemed hardly likely that the girl would be capable of going very much to help them in a rough-house. It was three to one, but now or never. He clenched his fists.

"Stay where you are!" Vaněk had noticed Nicholas' gesture and guessed his intention. In one quick movement he stepped back to the side of his desk and thrust a hand behind him into a half-open drawer. When the hand appeared again it was clutching a pistol. Pointing the weapon at Nicholas, he said:

"You will achieve nothing by resorting to violence. I am a good enough shot to stop you with a flesh wound, so we should still be able to send you to Prague. Keep your hands by your sides—unless you prefer to go as a stretcher case."

Short of risking a bullet, there seemed no reply to that, so Nicholas did not attempt one. No words could have expressed the mixture of anger, exasperation, fear, doubt and indignation that seethed within him; so he remained silent while Vaněk turned to the girl:

"Comrade Hořovská, as he left without any luggage we must provide him with a suit-case and enough things to make a show. Go upstairs and collect what is necessary from the ward-robe room. While you are there pack a case for yourself as well."

Nicholas happened to be looking at her. He sensed rather than saw the blood drain from her face. It could hardly have gone paler, but the line of her eyebrows became more clearly defined, and by comparison with her cheeks, her lips became quite pink.

"A . . . a suit-case for myself," she stammered. "But why, Comrade Vaněk . . . why?"

"Because I wish you to go with him," Vaněk replied quietly.

"No! Please!" she gasped. "I have a date. Someone I promised to meet at half past ten up in the West End."

"You are not down in my book for any assignment. Has something arisen unexpectedly in connection with one of your cases?"

In three quick strides she came round the end of the table to within two feet of her chief, and said in a low, urgent voice, "Comrade Vaněk, this is a private matter, but it means a very great deal to me. I have always . . ."

Tilting back his head, he looked at her through his pince-nez and said severely, "I am amazed, Comrade Hořovská, to hear you use such bourgeois expressions. For those of us who have dedicated ourselves to the creation of a Workers' World State, there are no longer 'private matters'. It is most distressing to me to learn that you are still subject to the type of weakness you suggest, and I must strongly recommend you to discipline yourself."

"I'm sorry, Comrade Vaněk." She began openly to cringe. "Of course I realize how anti-social such emotions are, and I assure you that I would never allow anything of that kind to affect my Party-consciousness. But . . . but is it really necessary for me to go to Prague?"

"Even were it not, I should send you there now," he declared with the harshness of a fanatic. "It would be a fitting exercise for you in subordinating all thoughts to the priority of politico-endeavour. But it *is* necessary. Experience has taught us that when cases such as we now have on our hands travel accompanied by a woman there is less likelihood of awkward questions being asked. I had intended that Konečný should go with him as his courier. Now someone who can at the same time act a nurse-mistress-secretary role will be more suitable, and in view of your intimacy with him. . . ."

At that instant Nicholas leapt forward and grabbed at the pistol in Vaněk's hand.

For the past two minutes the girl's unexpected reluctance to accept an order had diverted the attention of both Vaněk and the thin young man from their prisoner. Nicholas had watched the pistol gradually slew away from him and downward till it was pointing towards the floor. Seizing his chance, he attempted to snatch it, but the force of his spring made him overshoot the mark. Instead of his fingers closing on the weapon they met round Vaněk's wrist.

The Czech jumped backwards in an endeavour to jerk free his hand, but only succeeded in pulling Nicholas after him. For a moment they stood a foot apart with their arms thrust out sideways, both fearful that the gun would go off and wound them.

"Quick, Konečný! Seize him! Seize him!" Vaněk cried in Czech, and the thin young man threw himself at Nicholas from behind. But Vaněk was no match for his younger antagonist. Before Konečný could come to his help Nicholas hit him hard in the stomach and at the same moment gave his wrist a violent wrench. He groaned, doubled up, and the pistol fell with a dull thud on the floor.

Nicholas had no time to turn; he could only throw his body to one side as Konečný came at him. The young Czech had aimed to grasp both Nicholas' arms and hold them fast behind his back, but the movement frustrated his intention. He succeeded only in catching hold of Nicholas' left elbow, and the wrench he gave it swung Nicholas round towards him.

As Vaněk staggered away, retching and gasping, the two younger men closed. The Czech was slightly the taller, but Nicholas was more sturdily built. For some twenty seconds they remained almost motionless, striving for mastery; then Nicholas broke the other's hold. Stepping back a pace, he clenched his fists and lashed out with all his strength. His left thudded into the Czech's ribs and his right took him squarely on his receding chin. Clutching frantically at the air, he went over backwards.

Panting from his exertions, Nicholas looked swiftly round. Vaněk was now leaning heavily on his desk, still trying to get his breath back. The girl had picked up the gun, but she was not pointing it at him. As his glance met hers he saw her eyes flicker towards the passage. It looked as if his swift double victory had taken her so much by surprise that it had robbed her of the initiative to hold him up, and she was now counting on the sounds of the struggle bringing prompt help. Praying that by the time she recovered her wits it would be too late for her to use the pistol, Nicholas made a dash for the door.

Konečný lay sprawled in the way. The blow to the chin had dazed him but not knocked him out. He was rolling his head from side to side and making futile movements with his arms. It was the worst possible luck for Nicholas that as he sprang forward Konečný should have rolled right over. Instead of his right foot landing firmly on the floor it came down on the calf of Konečný's leg. It twisted under him and he fell in a heap on top of his victim. Konečný, still only half-conscious, and believing that he had again been set upon, let out a shout, struggled up on to his knees and struck out wildly. The sudden hunching of his back threw Nicholas against the table, he struck his head a sharp blow on its edge, reeled with the pain and tumbled over sideways.

Vaněk had now recovered sufficiently to re-enter the fray. Dodging out from behind his desk, he ran at Nicholas and kicked him savagely in the ribs. Already off balance as Nicholas was, the kick sent him right over. His cheek and shoulder hit the floor on the far side of Konečný, and his feet flew up into the air. As he wriggled over Konečný's still squirming body Vaněk came at him again, but this time he saw the kick coming and managed to grab the Czech's ankle. Heaving himself over, he brought the older man down on top of him, and as he fell used his free hand to strike at his face. The blow was little more than an upward jab, but it landed on Vaněk's mouth, cutting his lip badly.

The attack by Vaněk had lasted long enough for Konečný to get back some of his wits. Regaining conscious control of his limbs, he ceased to flail them blindly, dragged himself free of the other two and grabbed Nicholas by the hair. Nicholas twisted free, again hit him under the chin, then kneed Vaněk in the stomach. Gasping for breath, his eyes watering from pain, bruised, shaken and half winded, he struggled up between them into a half-kneeling position. Konečný had fallen back with his mouth hanging loosely open and Vaněk now lay face downwards on the floor making horrible animal noises. Instinctively Nicholas realized that he need fear no more trouble from either of them. Swaying as though slightly drunk, he pulled himself to his feet and lurched towards the door.

But the delay caused by his having tripped over Konečný proved fatal to his chance of escape. Vaněk's first shouts had alarmed the house, and even the few moments occupied by the recent melée on the floor had been sufficient for several people to reach the scene of the trouble.

As Nicholas made his second attempt to reach the doorway, a hard-faced middle-aged woman appeared blocking his way. Close on her heels came Rufus and a big blond man with china-blue eyes. They were followed by another, very fat woman, wearing a check apron, and an elderly man with a drooping moustache, whose hands were black with printer's ink.

In a matter of seconds Nicholas was surrounded. Several people struck him at once, and he was temporarily too exhausted to do more than ward off the most savage blows. Fortunately for him, the good-natured Rufus saw that he was incapable of serious resistance, so thrust the others aside and pushed him into a chair; then, more in sorrow than in anger, proceeded to read him a lecture:

"Mister Bilto. Didn't ai warn you not to start nothin'? What for d'you wanta go actin' so an' gettin' you'self hurt? They tell me that way down in your heart you's one of us, an' it's all wrong for us proletarian-ideologists to go gettin' at cross purposes. 'Tain't sense for you to pretend you's not you'self and don' wanta go to Prague no more. That's where duty calls you; an' doin' our duty is what qualifies us to be equal members of one great big happy family. Yes, sir, we must all do that if we's to see the fine new Communist world that Comrade Stalin[1] is workin' so hard to create for all the poor simple folks who can't create nothin' for themselves. Now Comrade Stalin, I reckon he'd be mighty hurt if he knew how you been behavin' this evenin'."

"Oh, go to hell!" groaned Nicholas, sinking his aching head between his hands. But he could not shut out the babble of

[1] See 'Author's Note' opposite contents page.

voices that now filled the room. Most of them were using Czech, but he caught snatches of English and German. The hard-faced woman was dabbing with a handkerchief at Vaněk's cut mouth. The fat one, whose apron suggested that she had come from the kitchen, was fussing over Konečný. The big fair man and the old fellow with the drooping moustache were asking the Hořovská girl for details of the trouble. Then, after a minute or two, Vaněk was helped back into the chair behind his desk, and he called for silence.

As the din subsided, he gave Nicholas a malevolent look and said, "If you were not so eagerly awaited in Prague, I would have you disciplined for this; but in order to get you to the airport on time I must deny myself that pleasure. We have wasted enough time already and must now work fast." Turning to his subordinates, he added:

"Comrade Konečný, your bag is already packed. Put some things in another for Professor Novák and take them both to the car. You, Comrade Hořovská, will pack a bag as I told you, and join him there. Comrade Abombo, take a firm hold of the Professor, so that Comrade Lubitsch can proceed with the injection. The rest of you can return to your duties."

As they began to file from the room, Rufus stepped round behind the chair in which Nicholas was sitting, grabbed the lapels of his jacket, and in one swift movement pulled it back over his shoulders. The trick had the effect of pinioning his arms at the level of the elbows and exposing his shirt from a little above the waist upwards. Setting his teeth, he jerked himself forward and made an attempt to rise; but by pressing down hard on his jacket the powerful negro was able easily to prevent him from struggling up out of the chair.

Meanwhile, the fair man who had been addressed as Comrade Lubitsch opened a small attaché case that he had been clutching as he ran into the room, and laid out on the table the things needed for an injection. Vaněk came from behind his desk and, as Nicholas was still squirming from side to side, took a firm grip of his right ear. Giving it a sharp twist, he said:

"Be still now! You will only make matters worse for yourself if you jerk about and cause the needle to snap off in your arm."

Tears of pain had already started to Nicholas' eyes at the tug on his ear; and seeing the sense of the admonition, he reluctantly decided that, for the moment, discretion was the better part of valour.

Lubitsch produced a pair of scissors, made a four-inch slit with them in his victim's shirt, jerked up the short sleeve of his vest, dabbed the skin with surgical spirit and pressed home the hypodermic. As the needle came out Rufus relaxed his grip on the jacket and slid it back round the prisoner's shoulders. The speed and efficiency with which they did the job suggested to Nicholas that it was by no means the first time that the two of them had collaborated in giving an injection to a patient who might have made difficulties about partially undressing; and now that he had a few moments to think in, he wondered grimly how many unwilling people had been similarly treated at this apparently derelict house hidden away in a once respectable part of central London.

For some minutes he felt no effect from the drug at all, and by the time Vaněk went to the door to shout in Czech an impatient enquiry if the others were ready, he was contemplating making another attempt to get away as they led him out through the garden to the car. However seedy the district might be, there could be no doubt that the majority of its inhabitants would be honest citizens, and that like any other it must be patrolled by the police. Even if he was unable to break free and run for it, if he began to shout for all he was worth just as they reached the gate it seemed a certainty that help would arrive before he could be forcibly carried off.

In response to Vaněk's shouts someone could be heard clattering down a flight of uncarpeted stairs, and next moment Konečný appeared in the doorway. Leading him over to the desk, Vaněk unlocked a drawer in it, took out a bundle of five-pound notes, counted several off, and as he gave them to him said:

"Here is money for an extra seat on the plane. If there is no t one free you must give yours up to Comrade Hořovská; but I would prefer you to go with them as far as Paris in case she needs your help. There you will be met by someone from our Embassy, and as arranged you can hand over. But she must continue on to Prague with him, in case the Paris-Prague plane has to make an unexpected landing and it is necessary to explain his state."

During the next few minutes Nicholas began to feel a little drowsy; so that when the Hořovská girl came hurrying along the passage carrying a suit-case, and Vaněk went to the door to give her a batch of papers, he felt that he could not be bothered to strain his ears sufficiently to make sense of the Czech phrases they were using.

As the sharp tapping of her high-heeled shoes receded towards the garden door, Vaněk turned and made a sign to Rufus. The negro put a hand beneath Nicholas' arm and helped him to his feet. Lubitsch then stepped up to him and gave him a hard slap in the face.

In spite of all that had gone before, Nicholas' immediate impulse was to return the blow. Instinctively he sought to raise his fists, but he found that it needed a great effort even to drag them from his sides, and that his knees were now distinctly shaky. While he swayed there ineffectively glowering and thickly muttering curses, the big blond man gave a contemptuous laugh, said in German to Vaněk, "He will do, Comrade," and, stepping back, lit a cigarette.

Vaněk nodded and said to Rufus, "You can take him to the car now, Comrade Abombo. Report to me on your return." Then he stood aside for the negro to lead Nicholas from the room.

While going down the passage, Nicholas made a resolute effort to rally his resources for the attempt to escape that he had been contemplating; but it was fated to die stillborn. As soon as he got out into the fresh air, instead of it reviving him each breath he took seemed to make him fainter and more giddy. His footsteps faltered, he was almost overcome by a feeling of acute nausea, and even had he forced a shout, the weak sort of cry which was all he could have managed would not have been heard by a passer-by, for Rufus did not take him within sight of the street, but through some stunted bushes at the back of the house straight to a side entrance of the garage. As he stumbled into it he felt that nothing he did could now prevent these people from carrying him off to the other side of the Iron Curtain.

CHAPTER VII

UNHAPPY LANDING

FROM that point Nicholas' limbs continued to function only lethargically and a little eccentrically, while his mind became distinctly hazy. He knew fairly well what was happening round him at any given moment, but his sense of time deserted him, and between fighting down bouts of nausea a variety of scenes seemed to telescope into one another.

Konečný and the girl put him in the back of the car between them. Again he found himself staring at Rufus' broad shoulders and flat chauffeur's cap. Somewhere they pulled up and all got out while he was sick as a dog at the side of the road. When they arrived at the airport Konečný left them, and Rufus carried their bags to the reception counter. While his blonde companion produced the tickets Nicholas leaned against the desk, dull-eyed and breathing heavily.

He felt very drunk, and the place seemed to be going up and down like a ship on a slowly heaving sea. At the back of his mind he knew that it was terribly important that he should say something, but he could not think what. With difficulty he focused the pretty face of the receptionist. She was eyeing him with disapproval, and as she handed the tickets back she said:

"I take it that as you are travelling together, Madam, you will be responsible for this gentleman. We have the right to refuse to accept passengers who might prove troublesome in the aircraft."

"He won't be any trouble." The Hořovská girl gave a rueful smile. "I'm used to him. Once he's on board he'll settle down to sleep."

The girl gave her a sympathetic glance, weighed their bags, then said that as their flight had been signalled they could go straight through. Rufus handed the bags over to a porter, wished them a good journey, touched his peaked cap like a well-trained servant and turned away.

At the emigration desk Nicholas made another desperate attempt to control his wandering mind. The sight of the passports gave him a vague clue, and in his head the words 'I am not Bilto, I am Nicholas' formed themselves; but when he strove to get them out, his tongue felt like a lump of leather in his mouth and he could only mumble incoherently.

After staring at him for a moment, the officer looked at the pale-faced girl who was supporting him, and asked, "What's the matter with your friend?"

"He's been ill," she replied calmly. "Nervous breakdown following severe shock; and to-night when my back was turned he got at the whisky bottle."

"It is against regulations to allow persons 'under the influence' to board an aircraft," the man remarked rather dubiously.

"He is not drunk in the ordinary sense, and he has to go abroad to complete his cure. I am his nurse, and will be responsible for him."

"Very well, then." The official shrugged and stamped their passports.

In the customs room Konečný caught them up, but did not immediately approach them. Instead, he waited until Nicholas, on turning away from the bench, staggered slightly. Then, playing the part of a stranger, he raised his hat politely and offered his help to get him to the plane.

On the way to it, Nicholas was sick again, and so racked with physical suffering that he was rendered temporarily incapable of even registering what was taking place round him. Only his legs continued to function sufficiently for him to be helped on board without actually collapsing, and once he had been lowered into his seat he drifted off into a coma.

His next impressions were even vaguer than those of his transit through the airport. Physically his condition had improved, as his stomach had settled down, but his brain was still leaden from the drug and he no longer felt any impulse to fight it. As though in a dream he saw arc-lights alternating with patches of darkness, felt himself walking with the stilted gait of a somnambulist, and knew that he was being transferred from one aircraft to another in the middle of the night. He could hear people talking in French, and was aware that a short fat man had taken Konečný's place. The movement made his head ache intolerable, and it was an incredible relief when he was able to relax again in the second aircraft. It seemed much smaller than the first, and the half-dozen people in it all kept staring at him while chattering together excitedly in Czech. Soon after it had taken off the Hořovská girl opened her bag, and taking some tablets from it, forced two of them into his mouth. He closed his aching eyes, and slept.

He was woken by her shaking him. Morning had come and bright sunlight was streaming through the ports. He wondered how on earth he came to be in an aeroplane; then as he turned his head and found himself looking into her green eyes, everything flooded back to him.

His mouth tasted frightful, but his brain was now perfectly clear again. In fact it seemed to have a special clarity, as though he were subject to one of those happy hangovers induced by drinking only wine, which cause the toper to call gaily on his friends to renew the carousel on the morning after. Having flexed his limbs he decided that all he needed was a drink to cleanse his mouth, and he would then be as fit as a fiddle. Momentarily, relief at finding that Vaněk had not lied about the temporary effects of the drug occupied his mind to the exclusion of all else, and he found himself smiling into the green eyes that were watching him so intently, with the intention of asking if he could have a pot of tea.

Before he could open his mouth, she put a finger to her lips, made an anxious grimace enjoining silence, then passed him a slip of paper. On it was written:

"We shall soon be coming into Prague. Both of us are in great danger. You must pretend that you have not yet recovered from the drug. Say nothing whatever, and do exactly as I tell you. Destroy this at once."

Slowly he tore the note into fragments and pushed them into the ash holder. Pleasure at his sense of physical well-being was swiftly crowded into the background by a host of questions crying out to be answered, and the resurrection of acute anxiety about the future. So much had happened in so short a time before he passed out that he had never really had a chance to sort the awful muddle and get things in their right perspective.

He had himself to blame for starting the chain of events; but they need not have brought him here, several thousand feet up in the air somewhere over western Czechoslovakia, had it not been for the girl. It was she who had browbeaten the Sinznicks, and had him carried off against his will to the secret headquarters somewhere in the decayed part of north-west Kensington. It was she who, when his identity had been in doubt, had falsely established it as Bilto's by positively declaring that she was his mistress. For some purpose of her own she had deliberately got him into this mess, and in order to do so had deceived her own people. Now, apparently, she was in a mess herself and hoped to get out of it by persuading him voluntarily to continue the deception. But why? Why? Why?

The carefree light-headedness, sometimes resulting from a glass too much of champagne, came over him again. Fishing in the inside pocket of his jacket he found that his private papers and Biro pencil had been put back there; so he took out a letter, tore a piece off the envelope and wrote on it:

"Dear Comrade in Imaginary Sin. My present inclination is to take the first opportunity of throwing you to any wolves who may be chasing you. But I have a kind heart and am susceptible to bribery. Get me a pot of tea and I will reconsider the matter."

When she had read what he had written she gave him a look in which anger was mingled with alarm and impatience. Then she wrote on another piece of paper:

"This is no time for fooling. Our situation is much too serious. Beg you to do as I ask."

To that he replied on another strip of envelope. "Only pot of tea will induce me to listen to reasons why I should play your game."

After reading it, if looks could have killed her glance would have slain him. She sucked the point of her pencil for a moment, then produced a third effort.

"We are on Czech diplomatic plane. To order drink would indicate your partial recovery. Imperative you continue to appear in semi-stupor. Only possible chance for me to get you on plane returning Paris."

That had the effect of putting an abrupt end to Nicholas' levity. Visions of long interrogations, possible imprisonment, and the prospect of worries and difficulties of all kinds when called on by the Czech authorities to explain how he came to be in his present situation, again surged to the forefront of his mind. If only she could save him from that by having him promptly flown out of Prague, what matter the axe she was grinding on her own account. He nodded, scribbled on his last piece of envelope: "All right, I'll play", then settled back in his seat once more.

Lack of movement on the part of the other occupants of the plane suggested that they were still dozing, but as it began to descend they roused up and started getting their things together. Nicholas then closed his eyes and pretended to be asleep; so he did not see from the air, as they came in to land, the fine city he had last visited when a boy.

A gentle series of bumps told him that the aircraft had landed, and again he felt himself shaken by the arm. His memories of his feelings while being shepherded through the airport the previous night were still so vivid that he had no difficulty in counterfeiting a slightly milder version of the appearance he must have presented. Wide-eyed and mumbling a little, he allowed the cause of all his troubles, and the short, fat man who had joined her in Paris, to help him from the plane.

The latter's name, Nicholas learned, was Kmoch. He had soft spaniel-like brown eyes and was wearing a light overcoat that was much too long for him. Evidently he was a Comrade of authority, as he carried a small badge that he had only to flash under the noses of the immigration and customs officials for himself and his companions to be passed straight through; but as soon as these brief formalities were completed and they reached the main hall of the airport, a violent argument arose between Nicholas' male and female escorts. As he leaned against a pillar there, he appeared incapable of taking in what was said; but actually he found his Czech quite good enough to follow their wrangle, and listened with intense interest to it.

The man had ordered a car, which was outside waiting to take them to the city, and he was anxious that they should set off without delay. The girl maintained that it would be an ill service to the Party if they allowed it to leak out that it had been necessary to drug the famous atom-scientist in order to get him to Prague. He agreed, but said he saw no way of making him appear normal when he obviously was not. She declared that given an hour in the airport restaurant with the Professor, and plenty of black coffee, she would have him round to normal, or very near it.

He at first demurred, from fear that he would get into trouble if he did not obey his instructions to take the Professor straight to the hotel at which rooms had been reserved for him. She said that he would get into much greater trouble if he ruined a first-rate occasion for disseminating valuable propaganda, as it was certain that a big official reception would have been ordered for such a distinguished arrival. He said that a luncheon had been arranged for later in the day, and he felt sure that nothing of that kind would have been planned to take place until then. She argued that even if that were so, he would risk a severe reprimand if, for the sake of an hour, he took the Professor into the city for all-and-sundry to see in his present state.

After some hesitation he admitted that she was right; then

4

said that he would telephone explaining the cause of the delay and afterwards join them in the restaurant, as he could do with some coffee himself. At that she flared up into a passion and asked if he had not the sense to realize the importance of getting the Professor mentally as well as physically presentable; adding that as she was his mistress, she had a good chance of doing both if left alone with him, but could certainly not hope to overcome his resentment at having been drugged should her efforts be handicapped by the presence of a third person.

The possibility that the Professor might recover his wits, only to create a violent scene in the lounge of one of the biggest hotels in Prague, was obviously against the interests of the Party; so again Kmoch had to admit the soundness of her arguments. In the end it was therefore agreed that she should be left to do her utmost with the Professor, while he went to telephone by the private line at the airport police post, have some coffee there, and come to collect her and her charge from the restaurant in an hour's time.

The moment that Kmoch turned his back, the girl winked at Nicholas; then she took him by the arm and led him towards the restaurant. As they entered it, under cover of the noise made by the revolving door, she whispered in English:

"Everything depends now on whether a friend of mine is still working here; and if so, what he can do for us. You can act normally, but ask no questions, and leave all the talking to me."

Immediately Nicholas was inside the long, low room, he saw that it was not a restaurant in the true sense but run on the lines of a cafeteria. None of the tables were laid, but on a metal counter, behind which stood several girls, there were piles of cutlery, cups and saucers, trays with slots in them, and steaming food containers. Very few of the tables were occupied, as it was still early and the peak of the morning traffic was not due for at least another two hours. The only concession to making the room something more than a cheap eating place was a semi-circular bar at one end. Behind it a dark-haired man of about thirty-five, in a white jacket, was polishing glasses.

Nicholas' companion led him straight over to the bar, unobtrusively made the sign of the cross on it with her thumb-nail, perched herself on a stool, and said in Czech, "Good morning, Jirka, I was hoping you'd still be doing the early shift. How's business?"

The barman grinned at her, nodded to Nicholas, and replied in a loud voice, "Fine, fine. There isn't a bar to touch this in London, Paris or New York, for variety of good liquor." Then he added under his breath, "Lousy; and the only thing I've got fit to drink is some matured Slivowitz that I keep under the counter. Want a couple, or is it too early?"

"No," she smiled, producing some Czech money from her bag. "Set them up, Jirka; I need a bracer."

As he produced the bottle and glasses, she lit a cigarette, and keeping her hand over her mouth with the cigarette between her fingers, continued to talk softly through them. "I'm in a spot, Jirka. Unless I can get out of here pretty quick, I'll be a dead duck."

"That's bad," he murmured without looking at her. "Either way you'd be a big loss to the Legion."

"I'm sorry to quit. Please tell everyone that. I've had a long run for my money, but now it's a case of get out or go under. How's the funnel working?"

He poured two generous portions of Slivowitz, and pushed the glasses over. "Pretty good; but those jobs need careful organizing. How close are the Com's to catching up on you?"

"I've just got rid of that little swine Kmoch for an hour. If we're still here when he gets back we'll have to go with him. He's not fly yet, but I reckon the balloon will go up about mid-day. The odds are against my getting a chance to go to earth between leaving here and then; so I'll be up against it unless you can pull a fast one for me."

Jirka made a wry face. "Any of us would take big risks to get you out of trouble, Fedora; you know that. But it would be asking for coffins all round if we tried to smuggle you aboard a kite without proper preparation."

Lifting her glass, she said aloud, "Here's damnation to the American imperialist aggressors," drank a little of the plum brandy, set it down and added under her breath, "I was afraid that's how it would be. But I could think of no other chance that might save us from having the Com's take us both to little pieces."

Jirka glanced at Nicholas. "Him as well, eh? To get two of you out would make the job even more difficult."

She nodded. "I know; but I got him into this, so it's up to me to get him out—if I can. If you can't help us now, have tabs kept on us, and try to get us a break if they take us from headquarters to a prison."

"I'll do that," he promised, noisily mopping up his bar with a damp cloth. "But the odds against getting you out once you've been pulled in are pretty poor. Can't you possibly keep yourselves off the ice until this afternoon, then come back? I reckon by then I can fix something."

"We've no passes, Jirka; so we can't get out of the airport. But talking of ice, what about the cold store?"

He grinned, showing a double row of teeth so even that Nicholas thought they were probably dentures. "You're thinking of the time we had Oldřich in there. Yes, that's certainly an idea. There's so much sabotage goes on these days that they'll hardly give a thought to just one more breakdown in the electric system. You'll have to take a chance on getting pneumonia, but as soon as the current's cut the temperature will start to go up."

Her eyes brightened. "Could you fix it for us, Jirka? If we could lie low there for a few hours, we'd be over the worst fence. Then, even if you can't work the funnel for us, we could get clear of the airport in the darkness and go to earth somewhere in the city."

They could only just catch his words, as he began to chip bits off a block of ice with a pick and hammer. "Yes. No one goes in but the store-keeper. He and the electrician are both Legion men. But I've got to get you there. The girls are all reliable except for the blonde at the far end. She's a Com, and was put in here recently to keep tabs on us. She mustn't see that you don't leave by way of the hall. The rest of us will swear you did when Kmoch starts asking questions. I'll have to get her out of the way. Send her a message she's wanted on the 'phone, or something. You had better get yourselves a meal. All to the good to have something hot inside you. I'll get the electrician to cut the current off, see the store-keeper, then fix the blonde. As soon as you see her leave get up and walk through the door marked 'Toilet'. Beyond it there's an anteroom. I'll be there to take you along to the store."

Whispering their thanks, they drank up their Slivowitz, left the bar and went over to the long food counter. Both of them chose stew, as the most sustaining item on the very limited menu, added rolls and cups of coffee to their trays, then carried them over to a table near the door marked 'Toilet', so that as few people as possible should notice their leaving when the time came for them to slip through it.

Nicholas had been quite worried enough when he had thought that the worst he would have to face was a spell in prison, until the Czechs had definitely satisfied themselves that he was not Bilto and could be persuaded to repatriate him; but the recent conversation had both puzzled and rather scared him; so as they sat down opposite one another, he said, hoping for reassurance:

"You and Jirka weren't speaking literally just now, were you? I mean when you talked about dead ducks, coffins and taking people to little pieces?"

"No," she said. "Not really. It's just a game we play in these parts. We Czechs have a queer sense of humour. It amuses us to scare people who come from the other side of the Iron Curtain."

Seeing his look of relief, she went on, "By coffins we mean the decorations our Government dishes out to encourage independence of thought and action."

He had often read how, at the great Party Conferences in Moscow, the Communist leaders stressed the healthiness of criticism from the lower ranks, and believed it; but from the slight twitching of the corners of her pale mouth, he could see that she was laughing at him; and he said a little sullenly:

"It's obvious that you are against them, and mixed up in some anti-Government movement; so naturally you would like me to go back believing all the nonsense one hears about the Iron Curtain countries behind held down by terror. But unless they are after you for murder, it is fantastic to suggest that you really fear a death sentence."

"I don't fear that," she replied quietly. "Although that's what I'll get if we're caught. I'm not afraid to die. It's the thought of being taken to bits first that's so unpleasant."

"Oh, come. I know the Communist Party maintain a strict discipline, but there is no resemblance whatever between them and the Nazis. You're pulling my leg again."

She sighed. "All right. Have it your own way. The truth is that the Nazis were benevolent uncles compared with these people. But you'll find that out for yourself soon enough if they get us. They'll probably start the party by hanging you up by your testicles."

"Me!" he gasped. "But why? What have I done?"

"Plenty! You are the big fish in this pond; I'm only your girl friend."

"Look here!" he raised his voice suddenly. "I've had enough of this. It's time you gave me an explanation. First you lie like a trooper, to make out that I am my cousin when you know darn' well I'm not. Then . . ."

With an agonized grimace, he stopped in mid-sentence. She had given him a vicious kick on the shin under cover of the table. Leaning forward, she smiled sweetly, while almost hissing between her teeth:

"Are you crazy? D'you want all Prague to know the jam we're in? For God's sake keep your voice down, or that blonde stool-pigeon will start to take an interest in us. Then she'll smell a rat and refuse to go when Jirka sends to say she's wanted outside."

He scowled at her, but said in a lower tone, "Sorry, I'm not used to this sort of thing. All the same, if you want me to go through with it, I insist that you tell me the truth about yourself."

"Now is not the time for that. Either it won't be necessary, or we will have all day to talk about the love-life of the glowworm and anything else you like, while we are in the cold-room."

"Between intervals of physical jerks to keep ourselves from freezing, I suppose," he remarked bitterly.

"That's it. Now for goodness' sake try to behave normally. It will probably be another ten minutes or more before Jirka has fixed the electrician and the store-keeper. Pretend to be enjoying your breakfast, and make a show of talking to me as if you liked me—even if you don't."

He had already had several mouthfuls of the stew and, while disposing of two more, tried hard to think of something to say; but the extraordinary circumstances which had brought them together there seemed to rule out any ordinary conversational opening. At length, after glancing out of a window near which they were sitting, he said rather lamely:

"It's a lovely day, isn't it?"

Appreciating his difficulty, she smiled and tried to help him out. "Yes. Tell me what you would do during it, if you could spend it any way you liked?"

His answer came without hesitation. "I would have one of those aircraft out there fly me to Birmingham, so that I could take part in a tennis tournament there this afternoon. What would you do?"

"I would get you to drop me off in London; then I'd do my utmost to catch up on a date I missed last night."

"Listen," he lowered his voice again. "Trying to fit this jig-saw together is making me go crackers. You simply must tell me what it's all about?"

She shook her head. "I daren't, here. It would take some time, and if we keep on whispering that blonde girl may become suspicious of us. I will tell you everything as soon as we are alone. In the meantime, it's essential to give the impression that we haven't a care in the world. The easiest way to do that is to go on with our game. Which aircraft shall we choose to travel in?"

Glancing out of the window again, he studied the half-dozen planes that were scattered about the nearer part of the airfield, then replied, "I don't know much about aircraft, but I rather favour the long thin one over there on the left. Which is your pick?"

Half turning in her chair, she followed his glance. Suddenly her mouth opened, and she suppressed a gasp.

"What's the matter?" he asked with swift concern.

"Kmoch!" she murmured. "Didn't you see him. He's only about a hundred yards off, and walking this way. It's not twenty minutes since he left us. Something's gone wrong."

Nicholas gave a quick look at the bar, then at the food counter. Jirka was still absent and the blonde girl at her place. As he turned back to his companion he saw she had lit a cigarette. While holding it in her mouth, just as she had done at the bar, she began to talk softly through her fingers:

"For some reason we'll soon know he's gone back on our arrangement, and is coming to pick us up. Otherwise, he would have spent the whole hour with his cronies at the police post. Any hope of our being able to hide in the cold-room has gone up in smoke now. We'll have to go with him; but unless he has rumbled us already we can still play for time. This means that for the present you'll have to keep up the fiction that you are Bilto."

"I won't!" he muttered resentfully. "If I did I'd only get myself in deeper; and I'm damned if I see why I should. Anyway, I couldn't maintain the part once they began to question me."

"Yes, you could," her low voice was insistent. "Pretend to be a bit dopey still, and very angry. For the moment, the only really nasty one with which you will be faced is to give a plausible explanation why, after having agreed to come here voluntarily, it should have been necessary for us to drug you before we could get you into the plane."

"There is no answer to that except the truth—and that's what I'm going to tell them."

"Oh, no, you're not; and there is an answer. You can say that the thought of changing your mind about coming had not even entered your head. It was simply that you wanted to postpone your departure for twenty-four hours, but Vaněk would not agree to that. Blame the whole thing on him. Accuse him of acting arbitrarily and demand that he should be punished."

He grinned suddenly, but his whisper held a sneer. "You'd like to see him get it in the neck, wouldn't you? For that matter, so would I. But it's about the only desire we have in common."

"Still, you'll play the game out on the lines I suggest?"

"No, it would be pointless. If I've got to meet a lot of other scientists at this reception lunch Kmoch spoke of, within five minutes they will tumble to it that I am not Bilto."

"You fool! You wretched moron!" Again her words came faint but clear from between half-closed lips. "Haven't you the sense to realize that it is the next three hours I want you to play for? Give me the morning, and with luck you won't have to attend the lunch. Our one last chance to escape lies in your keeping up for a little longer the deception you started yourself."

"You knew that I wasn't Bilto from the beginning, then?"

"Of course I did! But what's that matter now? Kmoch will be here any minute. What d'you mean to do?"

"Tell the truth and shame the devil," he replied tersely. "We are on opposite sides of the fence. I don't know what you're plotting; but you are a reactionary, and I refuse to involve myself with you further. I believe in Peoples' Governments, so I intend to rely on the good-will and decency of this one."

Opening her bag, she took from it a small capsule, pushed it over the table to him and said: "I've been a fool to bother with you; but as it's through me you're here I'd still like to save you from the worst. Hide that if you can until you have lost your illusions about the sort of treatment you are likely to receive from the People's Government; then pop it in your mouth. It is cyanide, and will give you a quick get-out."

CHAPTER VIII

BEHIND THE IRON CURTAIN

At that moment the restaurant door opened and little Kmoch in his too-long overcoat came in. Picking up the capsule, Nicholas slipped it into his breast pocket; then, instinct bidding him cover the action, he pulled out his handkerchief and blew his nose. He was still blowing it when the short, fat man halted beside them, bent over their table so that his voice should not carry to anyone else, and said:

"I telephoned Comrade Frček and he was much distressed to hear of the Professor's state. He says we were quite right not to take him to the hotel, and that I am to bring him and you, Comrade Hořovská, at once to Headquarters."

"The Professor is much better already," she said quickly. "You can see that for yourself. I'm sure he won't give us any trouble now, but he needs rest after his journey, and Comrade Frček is much too important a man to be bothered about such matters unnecessarily. I suggest that we go straight to the hotel, and you can telephone him again from there to relieve him of his anxiety."

"No." Kmoch shook his head. "It is an order." Then he turned to Nicholas and said, "Now that you are recovered, please allow me to welcome you back to Czechoslovakia. We are very proud that Prague should have produced such a distinguished scientist."

"Thanks," Nicholas replied non-committally. He was still a little staggered at the thought that he was now carrying the means of instant death in his pocket; and having been given it to use on himself in an emergency had once more thrown him into a state of frightful indecision. But Kmoch was obviously anxious not to keep his chief waiting; so without further remark, he hurried them out into the hall. Having flashed his pass in front of two state policemen on the main door he led his charges over to a car driven by a third, told them that their bags were already in the boot, and bundled them in.

Much of the country round Prague is well-wooded and beautiful, but after a few miles the road from the airport lost its attraction owing to ribbon development. Subconsciously Nicholas noticed occasional rows of jerry-built, ill-kept looking bungalows, with here and there, near factories, big blocks of workers' flats; but he was much too absorbed in his own problem to take the interest he would normally have done in the new suburbs of the Czechoslovakian capital.

For years past he had read avidly all the Left-wing material that had come his way on conditions in the Soviet satellite countries. That, and innumerable discussions with people who thought as he did, had given him a fixed belief that they were governed for the benefit of the great mass of their people. The fact that in them land, property and accumulated fortunes had been confiscated for the benefit of the State he entirely approved. Those measures necessarily created a discontented minority who would stop at nothing to sabotage the smooth running of these worker-republics, and obviously such activties had to be severely repressed. Such suppression he accepted as the unavoidable birth-pangs of a new and better order, but he was convinced that the stories of nation-wide terror and arbitrary imprisonment were capitalist lies.

On this basis he realised that only active enemies of the State had anything to fear from it. Obviously the blonde young woman now sitting beside him was such an enemy. That had been made clear beyond doubt by her conversation with Jirka, the barman. But he, Nicholas, was not. On the contrary he was in entire sympathy with the regime. Therefore, it seemed, he had only to tell the truth—apart from the fact that he had deliberately impersonated Bilto to begin with in an endeavour to prevent his going to Prague—to be certain of a sympathetic hearing, and humane treatment afterwards. Whereas should he continue the deception and be found out, his association with the girl would be taken as proof that he was a member of the subversive 'Legion' to which she belonged, and he would no longer have any reasonable cause for complaint if they treated him too as a potential saboteur.

On the other hand it would be necessary to lie about how he had first got drawn into the affair, and—would he be believed? If not, should they decide that he had been her willing confederate all along, he would in that case, too, be treated as a saboteur, and—what would happen then?

He was still of the opinion that she had deliberately over-dramatized her situation, and that neither of them stood in any danger of torture or death; but all the same it was difficult entirely to discount the fears she had expressed to Jirka and his immediate acceptance of them. Even the lurking thought that the Czech state police might have found it necessary, in their war against sabotage, to follow the example of the Nazis—under whom their country had suffered for so long—was distinctly unnerving. She had looked as if she really meant it, too, when she had said that she did not fear death but dreaded the treatment she expected to receive before it.

It occurred to him then that although, if he could tell a few convincing lies, he might get himself in the clear, that would not necessarily clear her. What lay behind her having had him brought to Prague still remained a mystery; but evidently it tied up in some way with her subversive activities, and she had left him in no doubt that her only hope of escaping exposure was his continuing to play her game. Presumably, therefore, if he did not, ruling out her exaggerated fears, she would shortly find herself in prison.

He thought that she probably deserved it; and his immediate reaction was that, anyway, he owed her nothing. But on second thoughts he recalled her attitude to himself—that having got him into this mess it was up to her to get him out of it. That showed a generosity of spirit which it was not easy to ignore; and he felt it only fair to assume that the course she had urged upon him was the one she believed offered the best hope for them both.

Her attempt to evade the interview at Headquarters had been promptly blocked by Kmoch; but if they could get past Comrade

Frček, who was evidently Kmoch's chief, and were allowed to go on to the hotel, there seemed a good prospect that, with the help of her underground associates, they could manage to disappear. If so, and Jirka's 'funnel' worked, they might both be outside the Iron Curtain before morning.

Putting aside, on the one hand, his inclination to tell the truth, and on the other, his natural reluctance to be the cause of anyone's being sent to prison, Nicholas again strove to weigh up the chances. After they had covered another mile he decided that in the final analysis they must be judged on what was likely to be believed by Comrade Frček, and what was not. The odds were obviously heavy against his acceptance of a statement that the man brought before him was *not* Bilto, because it could never even have crossed his mind that it would not be the person he was expecting; from which it followed that, apart from the remote possibility that he had known Bilto in his student days, he would have no reason to suspect an impostor. Therefore, in the first case detention was certain, but in the second unlikely.

There still remained the disturbing thought that while the chances of deceiving the police chief were good, the hope of continuing the deception if faced with a gathering of Prague's leading scientists at luncheon was virtually non-existent; so Nicholas had to face the fact that should the young woman who was the cause of all his troubles fail to get them away from the hotel in the hour or two he could gain for her, his last case would be very much worse than his first. But finally he decided to risk that, and gamble on her succeeding both in obtaining for him a quick get-out and saving herself.

The car was approaching the capital from the north-west, and from a long way off Nicholas had been able to see the outline of the vast Hradčany Castle. When they came within clear sight of its steeply-sloping roofs and myriad-pointed gables, he expected that they would turn off to it, for he knew that it was now used as the central administrative offices of the People's Government; but instead they continued on round the shoulder of the hill across which it sprawled. From the high ground he could now see a good part of Prague, and the bend of the river

Vltava that separates the richest residential district from the greater part of the city. Beyond the beautiful Charles Bridge lay the Old Town with portions of its original walls and many fine medieval buildings. He could pick out the Powder Tower, the Týn Church and the Town Hall; then, further off, the massed buildings covering the slopes on which lay the New Town with its big hotels and principal shopping streets. Another few minutes and the car was running down between the big old private houses and blocks of one-time luxury flats. It crossed the river to the east bank, ran on through several streets, crossed the broad Příkopy, and two hundred yards further on pulled up in front of a tall modern concrete office block.

Kmoch got out, told the driver to take it round to the garage and continue to stand by, then shepherded his charges into a lofty pillared hall. A number of very smartly turned out State Police were standing about there, and a few civilians most of whom had the appearance of tough plain-clothes men. One of a row of pretty uniformed lift girls smiled ingratiatingly at Kmoch and took them up to the top floor. There an even prettier secretary received them and ushered them into a comfortably-furnished waiting room; but they were not kept waiting long. After speaking over an intercom, she took them along a short passage, and showed them into her boss's office.

It was a fine oblong room, one of its longer sides being entirely formed of glass, which gave it a magnificent view over the rooftops of the ancient city. The floor was uncarpeted but of a slightly yielding synthetic rubber substance that made it pleasant to walk upon. The walls were panelled in light woods, the fittings chromium plate, and the furniture tubular. At one end of the room Comrade Frček sat behind a glass-topped desk that had on it only a writing pad, an intercom and a battery of different-coloured telephones.

He was a biggish man, but bulky rather than tall, and at first glance it struck Nicholas that there was something old-fashioned about him. The impression was probably due to the fact that he was wearing a stiff white collar with a black jacket and pin-stripe trousers, yet he looked more like a well-paid artisan in his Sunday best than the traditional senior civil servant. His features, too, were the reverse of intellectual. Jet black hair and bushy eyebrows sprouted from his massive head, which was set upon a short thick neck; his nose was pudgy and his mouth gross. Only his round, black, piercing eyes gave any indication of the liveliness of his mind, and they stood out with special vividness because the skin of his moon-like face had the unnatural matt pallor sometimes seen in men who are incapable of growing a beard.

Getting up from his desk, he came round it, and ignoring the others shook Nicholas warmly by the hand, booming meanwhile in a deep bass voice that belied any lack of virility suggested by his beardlessness.

"My congratulations, Professor, on your safe arrival. Your decision to leave the decadent democracies of the West and return to the land of your birth has been warmly applauded by all your fellow-countrymen who have so far been permitted to know of it. As a representative of the People's Government, I speak for the dumb millions whom it is our privilege to serve, in welcoming you back amongst us. I can only add how distressed I was to learn that there had been some sort of . . . er, trouble about your departure from London."

Nicholas' bent in life did not lie towards amateur theatricals, but he knew that half the secret of success in the histrionic art lay in throwing oneself heart and soul into a part; so, having decided to play Bilto, he returned the vigorous handshake and replied in the pompous manner that he felt best suited to the circumstances:

"Comrade Frček, I accept your welcome to Prague in the spirit in which it is given. I should never have left it, had not my position as a known Marxist-front-worker meant death if I had stayed on after the city fell into the hands of the Nazi-imperialist-swine. But I have a most serious complaint to lodge against your London headquarters staff. Are you aware that they laid violent hands upon me there, and that at the orders of Comrade Vaněk I was forcibly given an injection?"

Frček's moon-like face showed sympathetic concern. "Comrade Kmoch reported to me half an hour ago that you had been sent as . . . er, what we term 'a parcel'; and I am completely at a loss to understand it. That you no longer appear to be suffering from the effect is some comfort. But come and sit down, and we will go into the matter."

With a glance at the others, he added, "Comrade Hořovská, Comrade Kmoch; please also be seated." Then, when they had settled themselves, he went on: "Now, Comrade Professor, perhaps you will give me an account of what occurred?"

Nicholas ran a hand through his rumpled red hair, and said with a frown, "Everything had been fixed up satisfactorily about the date of my departure, and all my own arrangements for leaving went without a hitch, until the last moment. Then an unforeseen crisis arose. I learned by chance that my going might implicate an old friend of mine—a Marxist comrade of long standing whose work is of great value to the Party in London. Both friendship and the interests of our cause decided me that I must postpone my journey for twenty-four hours in order to inform him of the steps that he should take for his protection. In consequence I allowed myself to be taken to Comrade Vaněk's headquarters as arranged, but only with the intention of telling them there what had happened, and that I could not travel that night. Comrade Vaněk then acted in a most arbitrary fashion. He said that in no circumstances could my journey be postponed. When I refused to leave he orderd his people to seize me. I was overpowered and given an injection which made me extremely ill. Comrade Hořovská was present the whole time and will bear out all I have said."

She nodded her sleek blonde head. "Yes, Comrade Frček, that is exactly what happened."

Frček continued to look sympathetic. "Of course, Professor," he said after a moment, "you will appreciate that in the Party an order is an order. Comrade Vaněk had his instructions to send you to Prague on a given date, and he would naturally have been most reluctant to disobey them unless he could afterwards give a fully satisfactory reason for having done so."

"He could hardly have had a better one," Nicholas retorted

truculently, "as my decision to put off my journey was in the interests of the Party."

"Quite, quite. But I wonder if you made that really clear to him?"

"Unless he is a complete fool, he could not possibly have misunderstood what I said."

Frček's black eyes bored into Nicholas' brown ones, as he asked quietly, "Do you not think it possible that Comrade Vaněk may have got the idea when you said you wished to put off your journey that you really had in mind a longer postponement than twenty-four hours?"

This sudden switch to dangerous ground caused Nicholas' throat to contract, but he returned the stare unwinkingly. "Certainly not. I gave him no reason whatever to suppose so."

The big man tapped his desk thoughtfully with thick, pudgy fingers. "You see, Professor, you are of great value to us. If Comrade Vaněk formed the impression that you had become troubled by doubts at the last moment—in fact that you had changed your mind and did not mean to come here after all— he would have been fully justified in acting as he did. I suppose you hadn't changed your mind?"

"I regard that as an insult!" Nicholas cried indignantly, jerking himself upright in his chair. "My whole life vouches for my devotion to the workers' cause! There must be scores of Comrades still living in Prague who will remember me as a leader of the Marxist student group."

The words were hardly out when he wondered anxiously if he had gone too far. If Frček sent for some of the old Comrades he claimed to have led, the game would be up. But his bold stroke had had the desired effect, at least for the moment.

Frček was smiling as he said, "I intended no insult, Professor, and I accept your version of this unfortunate affair. Comrade Vaněk was obviously over-zealous in carrying out his orders. In an experienced and responsible official that is almost as bad a fault as slackness; so I shall at once send a severe reprimand to London. Regarding those old Comrades that you mention, a number of them are greatly looking forward to a reunion with you at the lunch we have arranged in your honour. But if I may say so, you look remarkably young to be their contemporary."

At that Nicholas felt a cold chill run down his spine. It had temporarily slipped his memory that he was ten years younger than Bilto, but a second's thought told him that nothing could be behind the remark. Forcing a laugh, he said:

"A youthful appearance runs in the family. My grandfather hadn't a grey hair on his head when he died at the age of seventy."

Again he could have bitten out his tongue. It was of his English grandfather he had been thinking. One of Bilto's grandfathers had died before Bilto was born, and the other when under sixty. He had given himself away completely if Frček knew anything about the Prague branch of the Novák family. For a moment he held his breath, while realizing to the full the awful strain and terror of slipping up which must afflict a guilty criminal under cross-examination. His sigh of relief was almost audible as the big man gave a casual nod, then stood up and addressed Kmoch:

"Everything is now in order. You will take the Professor to Engelsův Dům and see that he has everything he requires to refresh himself before the reception."

"Certainly, Comrade Minister. Kmoch hesitated a second, then asked, "What about Comrade Hořovská? She told me at the airport that she is the Professor's Comrade-companion."

Frček smiled. "In that case arrange for her to be accommodated there with him. I remember now that some undertaking was given for one of our women agents to be placed at his disposal when he arrived in Prague, and naturally we wish to do all we can to make him comfortable here."

For a moment his glance rested on the quietly-dressed girl, taking in her big green eyes, the fine-spun silvery hair that fell to her shoulders, and brazenly stripping the clothes from her slim figure; then he turned to Nicholas with a vulgar leer:

"Congratulations, Professor. Your taste in women does you credit; but when you tire of her let me know, and I will arrange for you to be given an opportunity to pick another. We have in Prague a good selection of Comrade-companions for the recreation of the privileged few, and the importance of your work will entitle you to be counted among us."

His reference to 'the privileged few' left no doubt in Nicholas' mind that a joke was intended, and while he regarded such humour as in the worse of taste, he thought it advisable to play up to it; so he laughed and said, 'Thanks for the offer, Comrade. It is nice to know that you retain the good old customs of the Austrian nobility."

The big man gave him a queer look and remarked rather sharply, "They were decadent parasites battening on the life-blood of the people; we work tirelessly for the welfare of the people and give expression to their will; so I fail to see the point of your analogy."

Nicholas was greatly puzzled, and now quite out of his depth, as it seemed to him that this must be another joke, but he could not be certain; so he said hastily, "I . . . er, I'm afraid my Czech is not very good. It's so long since I spoke it that you must have misunderstood me."

"Perhaps I did." The black eyes in the big white face, which looked like currants in an uncooked bun, became guardedly affable. "In any case, I will not detain you longer now, Comrade Professor. It is no part of my functions to attend the type of luncheon at which you are to be the guest of honour to-day, but I shall hear all about it. I am sure we can rely on you when making your remarks to raise no controversial questions, and to impress everyone present with the relief you must feel at having thrown off the shackles of slavery under the British oligarchical-plutocracy."

Although Nicholas had often referred in his artickes to the wage-slavery of dock-labourers, cotton-operatives, ship-stokers, and others who were still 'exploited' under private enterprise he had never really thought of them as slaves, much less himself. But he felt that due allowance must be made for hyperbole and Comrade Frček's probable lack of knowledge of actual conditions in Britain; so he said that he would do his best, and with heartfelt relief at having got safely through this dangerous interview, accepted his dismissal.

Little fat Kmoch shepherded Nicholas and his blonde 'Comrade-companion' down to the ground floor, summoned his car and told its driver to take them to the Engelsův Dům. The way to it lay through the so-called 'New Town', which in the old days was the fashionable heart of Prague, and Nicholas could not help being struck by its deterioration.

He was neither surprised nor sorry to see that all the jewellers, milliners, modistes, antiquaries, and other de luxe shops which pandered to the foibles of the rich, had disappeared, and that their places had been taken by others showing only cheap clothes or utility goods. But his expectations were sadly disappointed when it was borne in on him that many of the shop windows were half empty and that none of them seemed to have had a coat of paint for a generation. He noticed, too, that while every tram they passed was packed to overflowing, there were very few private cars about, and that the people in the streets, although reasonably well clad, had a generally despondent and down-at-heel appearance.

As the car turned into the broad Wenzeslas Square, Kmoch said quietly, "I should tell you that as neither of you have yet been given official papers it would not be a good thing for you to go out into the town. Not that you will have much time to do so before the reception, but I mention this to save you the unpleasantness of being turned back by the door porters should it have occurred to you to take a short walk. They have orders that no one unable to produce an identity card should be allowed to leave the hotel."

Nicholas quickly suppressed the impulse to give a worried glance at his Comrade-companion. He wondered anxiously if she would be able to find a way for them to evade this formidable obstacle to getting out. He needed no telling that he had burnt his boats with Frček; so if she could not he was in it up to the neck.

CHAPTER IX

LUXURY SUITE FOR TWO

Two minutes later his mind was temporarily taken off this new anxiety by being diverted to memories of his youth. The car pulled up before the Engelsův Dům, and it turned out to be the old Hotel Ambassador now renamed in honour of Karl Marx's collaborator. As he followed the others into it he smiled a little grimly to himself. Long ago Bilto had pointed it out to him as a sink of iniquity, at which millionaire industrialists squandered the wealth wrung from sweated labour in such pastimes as bathing French chorus girls in champagne and drinking it out of their slippers. As a youngster he had often afterwards stared at it in passing with a mixture of curiosity, awe and secret envy; but he had never expected to enter it, let alone with the prospect of being given a room with a young woman who, if more suitably dressed, or undressed, would have qualified for a place in the Folies Bergère.

Yet, within five minutes of Kmoch having spoken to a subservient under-manager, that was precisely the situation in which Nicholas found himself. Kmoch had accompanied them up to the second floor, then rid them of his unwelcome presence; their bags had been brought up, and the porter had left them facing one another in a large double bedroom adjoining which there was a spacious bathroom.

With a sudden return of the levity he had felt early that morning he smiled at her and said, "Now all we need is the champagne."

She pointed to the telephone beside the bed. "If you feel like a bottle, you have only to ring down and they'll send one up."

"No," he shook his head. "It was just a silly thought about the sort of thing that used to go on up in these rooms in the old days. We have no time to waste on drinking. I've got you the break you asked for. Now I want the truth about you, and to hear your plans for getting . . ."

In one swift step she closed with him, flung her right arm round his neck and pressed the palm of her left hand over his mouth. Her voice came in a frightened whisper:

"For God's sake be careful! Don't you realize that all these rooms are wired. As we're new arrivals someone in the basement will have been put on to listen in to every word we say."

Tearing his face away, he muttered angrily, "Oh, cut it out! You're suffering from persecution mania, and have got spies on the brain."

With an imploring look she seized his arm, pulled him to the bedside, picked up the telephone from its cradle and turning it over showed him its underside. In it there was a round hole covered with a mesh of fine wires. Setting it down again she drew him away to the far end of the room, then put her lips to his ear.

"That's the mike. I daren't interfere with it or they'll smell a rat. Having got us this last chance, don't act like a fool and throw it away. You did your stuff splendidly in front of Frček. Now both of us have to play a part. I'm supposed to be your mistress; so you must call me 'darling' or Fedora. Make love to me, or pretend we're having a row and beat me if you like. But whatever we say out loud must be on lines that will sound normal to our unseen audience."

Everything that had happened to Nicholas since his arrival in Prague had seemed so like a cheap melodrama that he could still hardly bring himself to believe that he was really living in it; yet that little wire mesh arrangement under the telephone cradle had certainly looked like a microphone.

"All right," he whispered. "But I've got a girl of my own at home, and I'm not going to be unfaithful."

"I didn't ask you to," she countered. "And they wouldn't expect us to play those sort of games at this hour of the morning."

He hesitated. "I . . . I've never taken a young woman away for the weekend, so I'm at a bit of a loss all round. Give me a lead by saying the sort of thing you said to Bilto when he took you to Marlow."

She gave a low laugh. "He didn't; and I've never been to Marlow."

"What on earth led you to say you had, then?"

"People like Vaněk expect their women agents to sleep with the informers they are nursing, as part of the drill. It was the first place that came into my head, and saying I was your mistress was the most certain way of convincing him that you were Bilto."

"Blast you! What in hell's name impelled you to make him believe that?"

He had raised his voice slightly. With an angry "Shush" she murmured quickly, "We have been whispering long enough. They will regard our silence as unnatural." Then she stepped away from him and added loudly, "Shall I unpack for you, darling?"

He took the cue. "Thanks. I wish you would. I had to leave in such a hurry that I hardly remember what I put in my bag. I hope I didn't forget my shaving things."

She undid the suit-case that Konečný had packed for him, and took out some of the contents. "No, here they are. And thank goodness you brought a cake of soap."

"Why?" he asked in mild surprise.

"Because it is rationed here, and the allowance is sufficient only to enable people to wash themselves once a day and bath once a week." Under her breath she went on. "To wish to do so more frequently is to proclaim oneself a decadent bourgeois."

With a rather crooked smile he said loudly, "And that is how it should be, Fedora. Fats are important in our economy. To waste them in unnecessary washing is sabotage."

She gave him a smile of commendation. "Of course; and it is a pity that we did not bring more while we were about it. We could then have saved our ration and at the same time helped a little in depleting the stocks of the capitalist-warmongering English."

Stepping over to her side he took a quick look at the things she was unpacking. They were a miscellaneous lot, but adequate enough to have prevented the British Customs from wondering why he was travelling without any personal belongings. Most of them were of poor quality, but he had never been used to expensive clothes or gear, so that did not worry him; and in any case he hoped that it would not be necessary for him to make use of any of them except the toilet articles. Picking up an imitation silk dressing-gown, he threw it across the end of the bed, and remarked:

"This is a nice room they've given us, isn't it?"

"Yes," she replied. "But I don't think I shall be altogether happy here. To live in such luxury is apt to make one forget the lot of the less fortunate, and all our thoughts should be given to them."

"How right you are, Fedora!" he exclaimed with genuine feeling; but he saw from her expression that she was only playing her part and speaking hypocritically, as she went on, "It is not right that just because you have a fine brain you should be pampered and have servants to wait on you. I would much prefer to share the lot of the workers and live in a tenement."

For the first time he began to wonder if a world in which everyone lived in tenements would be a very happy one. After all, no one but a fool lived in a tenement if he could afford something better; yet it was against his creed that any privileged class should be left to enjoy benefits denied to the masses. With obvious sincerity he put his own point of view to her:

"There is nothing anti-social in wishing to live in comfort. It is not our object to bring everyone down to the lowest common level, but to raise the standard of life of all to that enjoyed by the old middle classes."

"What wonderful thoughts you have, Bilto! I wish I had a brain like yours," she said in a honeyed voice ; then added in a sarcastic whisper, "You are so clever it should be easy for you to think of a way of providing everyone in the world with a thousand a year."

He knew that she had hit upon the snag which had rendered impracticable the successful application of the doctrines of Karl Marx by every workers' government that had so far adopted them, even in a modified form. When the riches of the rich were taken from them the people individually became no wealthier, and the national income began to shrink because there was a limit beyond which the workers could not be taxed without making them worse off than they were before. He was honest enough to admit to himself that actually that was what had happened in Russia, and that poverty there was now almost universal; but he still pinned his faith in the Communist statements that it was due to, and would continue only during, the period of transition.

Again and again he had told himself that complete nationalization in every country, and the pooling of assets on a world-wide plan, was the only possible basis for assuring a fair share for all. Yet this was not the first time that he had caught himself wondering a little dubiously what that share would be. His creed demanded that black, brown and yellow men should share equally with whites. Could the world's resources ever provide each family with goods and services equivalent to an income of even five-hundred a year? Given governing bodies of unimpeachable integrity and brilliant planning at the top, with the whole world population educated up to a Utopian standard of unselfishness, devotion to duty and pride in achievement, it might be possible. But that was to ask perfection of mankind, which was another thing that Karl Marx had failed to provide a receipt for achieving.

"Dreaming great dreams, my love?" the honeyed voice enquired; then came the whisper: "Or can it be that people like you find it easier to destroy than to build up, and that you haven't really got any of the answers?"

He had been silent for almost a minute and looked up to see her making a rude face at him, as she went on aloud, "Our journey must have tired my great man. Why don't you lie down and rest for a while? Perhaps you would like me to massage your head?"

"Not now, Fedora darling; but bless you for the thought," he replied with equal sweetness. Then he picked up the toilet things. "I think I'll go and shave."

The bedroom had evidently been done up since the war, and its furniture was of the vulgar skin-thin-walnut-on-deal-with-fussy-embellishments type, that has flooded cheap furniture stores all over Europe for a generation. But the bathroom had been left untouched and was a true relic of the Habsburg régime. Nicholas had never seen such a large one before. Its chequered floor, consisting of slabs of black and white marble, was large enough to have held a ping-pong table and four players. In one corner there was a huge bath encased in solid mahogany, with a step up to it, and a yard-wide oval basin with a marble surround was fixed below a mirror that ran nearly up to the ceiling. The only incongruous note was two small towels on airers designed to hold old-fashioned bath-sheets.

He had got only as far as lathering his face when Fedora came in. He saw that she had slipped on a different dress and tidied her hair. Walking over to the bath, she turned the taps full on.

"Why are you doing that?" he asked.

"First because there will be a mike in here, too, and the sound of rushing water is one way to defeat it. Secondly because I thought that as we have been given a private bathroom owing to the fact that you are one of the 'privileged few' here, you might like to have a bath."

Nicholas gave her a suspicious glance. "You're not suggesting that Frček really meant that, are you? I thought his remarks in the worse of taste and most embarrassing for you; but obviously he was only joking when he implied that a sort of private harem is kept for Party leaders."

Her mouth hardened. "You wouldn't find it much of a joke if you were a pretty girl, or the attractive young wife of a man who is not a member of the Party. They don't keep a harem, as such; but one of them has only to fancy a face or figure that he happens to notice in the street and order its owner to be pulled in. Then it's 'into bed you get, my girl, and like it; or your family will be sent to a labour camp'."

"Nonsense!" he retorted angrily. "I don't believe a word of it. You are the worst type of reactionary, and simply doing all you can to put a smear on the Czech People's Government."

"All right. I am a reactionary. And you, it seems, are a Com. I knew you must be pretty far Left from your friendship with that Sinznick couple, but I thought . . ."

"You're wrong!" he interrupted. "I'm not a Communist."

"No!" her voice was vibrant with scorn. "Since you insist on splitting straws, you're something worse. You are one of those clever-dick Professors who couldn't earn an honest living running a cigarette shop, but think they know how to run the world. You're a typical example of the criminally irresponsible professional teacher, who spends his life cramming young people's heads with impracticable ideas that make them discontented. The really evil men only climb on the band-wagon when the damage is done. It is crazy idealists like you who are the fundamental cause of countless happy homes being plundered, and the best elements in whole nations being treated like criminals or done to death."

He made a gesture of exasperation. "Oh, cut it out. If you feel like that go and try to blow up the Kremlin, or something. And why in God's name did you get me here? That's what I want to know."

"I should have thought you would have guessed by now." She gave an unpleasant laugh. "But why I am remaining with you is quite another question. There doesn't seem any logical answer to that, so I must be a bit crazy myself. After all, why should I bother about a mind-poisoner like you, when it would be easier for me to get away on my own?"

It was on the tip of his tongue to retort, 'Then for God's sake go to it.' But it flashed upon him that if she took him at his word he would find himself in a really ghastly mess. If he went back to Frček and told him the truth, he would be regarded as a liar and a criminal who had got cold feet. If he waited where he was until the time came for him to attend the reception he would be found out and hauled off to prison, and should he attempt to go to earth on his own his arrest within a few hours was certain, as he had no papers he could show and no Czech money.

Suppressing the anger he felt at her insults, he said, "Listen,

Fedora. It's clear that politically we are poles apart but at the moment that has no bearing on our situation. Against my own better judgment and at your most earnest request, I burnt my boats with Frček this morning. As I understood it, your whole object in persuading me to do that was to have us brought here, because you believed that you could fix a get-away for us both within the next hour or so, and then with a little luck have us smuggled out of Prague on a plane leaving later to-day. What you do or where you go once we are safe, I don't give a damn. But till then, I think it's up to you to do the best for me that you can."

She nodded. "Yes. You're quite right. I always meant to, and how we got into that stupid argument I don't quite know. I came in to tell you what I am about to do. I dared not start anything while Kmoch was still likely to be hanging about, but now we've been up here for ten minutes or more he should be safely out of the way; so I am going downstairs. You heard what he said about identity cards. The Government lodges its most important foreign visitors here, and it is to keep a check on all their comings and goings that the entrances are watched; but that applies to us too, so I can't go out as I had hoped to do and make contact with my friends. But there are several members of the Legion on the staff here, and I feel certain they will devise some way of smuggling us out past the watch-dogs. It may take me some time to arrange it, though, so don't get any silly idea that I've left you in the lurch. Have a nice bath while you've got the chance; but don't use both those skimpy towels as I mean to have one too, if there's still time when I get back."

When she had left him he finished shaving, undressed and got into the bath. It was the first real chance he had had to sort out his ideas, and the pleasant warmth relaxed the tension to which he had been subject. Although Fedora seemed to think that by now he should have guessed why she had lied to Vaněk about his being Bilto, he could still find no answer to that riddle. That she had been Bilto's contact was beyond doubt, but as the Marlow weekend had been an invention it seemed he had been wrong in assuming her to be Bilto's mistress.

He had ruled out at once the idea that she might be the woman Bilto hoped to marry, as she did not at all fit the description, but as the widow presumably lived in Prague and Bilto lived in England, he had thought it probable that his cousin had been consoling himself for that separation by having parties on the side with Fedora. Apparently that was not the case. But what about the widow? Where was she?

Frček had known about the promise made to Bilto, but had not apparently regarded that as any part of his business. No doubt such arrangements were handled by another department of the police administration. If so, it seemed probable that she was to be produced and formally handed over at the reception, by whoever was to act as official host. Frček having said that he was not attending the lunch added to the plausibility of such a theory.

Nicholas devoutly hoped not to be there either, as it seemed certain that if he had to appear that would lead to his landing up in prison; but he already had Jirka, the barman's, unsolicited testimonial to the esteem in which Fedora was held by the Underground, and ample evidence of the strength of character she could display when she wanted anything; so he was reasonably confident that she would succeed in getting them smuggled out of the hotel.

He could not quite make up his mind if he liked or disliked her. Now that he had seen her smile and heard her laugh he thought her much more attractive than he had formerly. That pale face of hers, and her green eyes, lit up in a most extraordinary way when she was amused by anything, and the little cast in the left one held a curious fascination for him. He thought it a pity that she did not dress more smartly, as if she had given more care to her appearance and made up her face she could have passed for a beauty; but he supposed her shortcomings in that respect were due either to lack of money, or, in view of her work, a deliberate wish to remain as inconspicuous as possible. Her obvious courage and resource were qualities calculated to appeal to any man, but her violently reactionary sentiments and her constant attempts to traduce the Workers' State, in which he so fanatically believed, made her personality unsympathetic to him.

He was still thinking about her when it entered his mind that her political beliefs were, in essence, the same as those of his beloved Wendy. It therefore seemed strange that he should find the mentality of the one girl grate upon him, while he ignored it in the other and adored her. Wendy's lovely image took possession of his thoughts, and he toyed with the idea of how marvellous it would be if, free of the danger in which they stood, she was sharing this luxury suite with him instead of Fedora. During the past three hours his brain had had such a surfeit of puzzling, guessing, wondering and straining to arrive at sound conclusions, that he allowed it to continue this most pleasant form of daydreaming until the water began to chill, resuming his anxious speculations only as he began to dress.

When Fedora got back he was still in his shirt-sleeves. He heard her quick footsteps crossing the bedroom, then she poked her head round the door and gave a smiling nod, to let him know that things were going all right. Seeing that he was nearly dressed, she came in, closed the door behind her and, putting her fingers to her lips, tiptoed over to his side. The water from his bath was still running out, and they watched it in silence for a couple of minutes. When the last of it had drained away she turned on the taps again, and said:

"I've fixed it. But it's going to be pretty tricky, because you will have to attend the reception."

"Good God!" he exclaimed aghast. "I can't do that! Those old Comrades of Bilto's student days that Frček said would be there are certain to realize that I'm not him."

"I don't agree," she countered quickly. "To look at, you are quite extraordinarily like Bilto. You have a much closer resemblance to one another than most brothers; and it must be twenty years since Bilto was a student in Prague. That is a long time to remember anyone's features. In this case, too, your being younger than he is will prove an advantage, for their memory of him will naturally be as a young man."

"Perhaps you're right," he murmured uncertainly. "But

what about the scientists? It's certain they will have their top boys to meet me, and I'm not an atom man. If they start talking technicalities to me I'll be out of my depth in no time. They'll smell a rat, and under cross-examination I'd be completely sunk."

"Then don't talk technicalities. Be frightfully hush-hush, and say you never discuss your work outside a laboratory."

He shook his head. "No; it's no good. There's one thing you've forgotten—that's the woman. Even if I could get past the old pals and the back-room boys, I couldn't possibly hope to deceive her."

"What woman?" Fedora gave him a puzzled look.

"Bilto's woman, of course. The one he was expecting to meet in Prague."

"Frček said something to that effect; but it didn't seem to fit in. As he handles so many cases, I thought he would have only skimmed through Bilto's dossier and had got things muddled up."

"He had. He took you for Bilto's woman. In the circumstances that was quite understandable; but if he'd gone properly into things he couldn't have, because she is a middle-aged widow and is living in Prague."

"How do you know that?"

"Because Bilto told me so. He has been in love with her for a long time and wants to marry her."

Fedora sat down on the side of the bath. For a moment she was silent, then she asked, "Are you quite certain of this? Somehow, it doesn't sound like Bilto."

"I don't know why you should think that," Nicholas replied thoughtfully. "He's quite a normal sort of chap. He had a pretty hectic youth, but I think his work has been his main preoccupation for a long time past, and now he is forty there is nothing at all extraordinary in his deciding that he would like to have a wife and proper home. About the details of the matter I'm a bit hazy, as he really said very little, but about the main facts I have no doubt at all."

"Did he definitely say that she was living in Prague?"

"No, I couldn't swear to that; but it was the impression I

got. Something he said about having known her when she was first married gave me the idea that she was a girl-friend of his in the old days, Anyhow, it was a part of the deal he made on agreeing to leave England that she should be here to meet him on his arrival, and that the authorities would relieve her of the work she was doing so that they could marry and settle down."

"Are those the only grounds you have for supposing that she will be at the reception?"

"Yes. As she wasn't at the airport it seems pretty certain that they are holding her in reserve, so that the cameras can click on this touching reunion between Bilto and the love of his youth."

"Do you think they will produce a wedding-cake in advance, or present the happy couple with a set of fish knives as a token of their esteem?"

He was adjusting his collar and tie in front of the mirror, but the sarcastic note in Fedora's voice made him turn and glance down at her. With a bitter little laugh, she went on, "If so, you'd better think again. There won't be any wedding-cake or fish knives, or love of Bilto's youth either. You may put right out of your silly head any idea that you will be brought face to face with her."

"What makes you so certain of that?"

"The well-proved fact that one of the first principles of Communism is never to keep a promise. You may be right about their having dangled in front of Bilto the prospect of marrying this woman, as an inducement to get him here; but that doesn't mean a thing. She may quite well have been dead for years, or a semi-lunatic in one of their labour camps. If she is not, they will have her under arrest by now, with the intention of keeping her on ice indefinitely as a hostage to Bilto's good behaviour."

Nicholas made a grimace of distaste. "I do wish you would stop this childish mud-slinging. It doesn't impress me in the least."

"O.K., Professor." She gave a heavy sigh and stood up. "All the same, I'd bet you my last dime that you won't be called on to meet Bilto's woman when we go downstairs."

"If I do we'll be blown sky-high; but if you're right there's just a chance we may get through. I wish to goodness, though, that you had managed to fix things without my having to face such a big risk of exposure."

"So do I," she agreed. "But there was no other way. Still, it may comfort you a bit to hear that you won't have to go through the whole thing, and that we may get away before most of the guests have arrived. That minimizes the danger of someone who used to know Bilto really well having any chance to talk to you long enough to realize that you're a fake."

As she was speaking she stooped down, took hold of the hem of her dress with both hands, and with one smooth movement stripped it off over her head.

"Hi!" he said. "Give me a chance to get out of here."

She shook her head impatiently. "Stay where you are, and listen to me. I've got to tell you what I've arranged; but the reception starts at midday; time's getting on and I don't want to have to go without my bath. I told the manager that you are a diabetic, and that it is part of my job to ensure that you eat nothing which might upset your metabolism. Then I asked to see the luncheon menu. That enabled me to say I'd like to see the Chef and arrange with him that one or two special dishes should be prepared for you. The Chef is a Legion man, so as soon as we were alone I was able to get down to brass tacks."

While she talked she continued to undress herself. Nicholas had been telling the truth when he said he had never taken a girl away for the weekend; neither had he ever seen one undress in a bedroom. His few fleeting affairs had been confined to necking parties in front parlours with the lights out, tremulous embraces on the way home from dances, and one afternoon he always looked back on with pleasure that he had spent with a girl in a haystack. By the time Fedora had got down to her elastic belt and begun to peel off her stockings, he felt himself going hot all over, and exclaimed:

"Look here! I think I'll go into the bedroom, and you can whisper the rest to me later."

She gave him a look of contempt. "Don't worry. I've neither

the time nor the inclination to seduce you. And I had no intention of stripping in front of you, anyhow."

"Well," he muttered uneasily, "you're not far off it."

"Oh, shut you, you wretched prude!" she snapped at him. "You must have seen hundreds of girls on beaches with much less on than I have; and time is precious. We've got to go to this reception because there is no plausible excuse for the Chef to send a bowl of salad, or something of that kind, up to us; and even if he did they couldn't get us out if the bomb exploded up here."

"The bomb!" he exclaimed in horror.

"Yes, but you needn't get the wind up. We never kill the Coms without a very special reason, because their reprisals are too drastic. This will be a combined smoke and tear-gas bomb. The Chef showed me the place where you will be expected to stand for the reception. We are to get down a little early and take our places while the preparations for lunch in the next room are still going on. A waiter will come in carrying a bowl of something, and as he passes behind you the bomb will go off. Whether you are temporarily blinded or not, you must stagger about and then collapse as if you had had a heart attack. By then there may be a score or more people in the room, but the smoke and the gas will cause confusion. Before anyone is sufficiently recovered to take an unwelcome interest in what is going on you are to be picked up and carried out to an ambulance that will have been waiting round the corner. Our friends here will tell the Coms afterwards that it just 'happened' to be passing along the street; so they hailed it, but they don't know where it came from or where it went. As your ever-loving Comrade-companion I shall naturally go with you in it. The ambulance, of course, will be manned by Legionnaires, and with luck they will whisk us away to a place where the Coms will never find us."

Nicholas nodded. "The plan sounds daring enough to have a good chance of success, but everything will depend on the timing. I only hope your friend the Chef is a good organizer."

"You needn't worry about that." She gave him a grim little smile. "If he wasn't he wouldn't have stayed the pace as long as he has. In this game anyone who leaves loose ends untied soon finds them round his own neck. Now you had better leave me; unless you want to be properly shocked."

He gave a sudden grin. "Since you called me a prude, it would serve you right if I came back when you've got the rest of your things off."

"No! Please don't." She at once became serious. "But I like you better for having one back at me and showing you are at least a little human."

When he reached the bedroom he sat down on the edge of the bed and anxiously thought over the ordeal that lay before them. He felt that if he had to be in the reception room only for some five to ten minutes, he ought to be able to cope with any of Bilto's old acquaintances or scientists who were among the first arrivals, but he was still much perturbed about Bilto's woman. Habit of mind still made him very loath to accept Fedora's statement that the Communist leaders were entirely unprincipled, and if she was wrong it seemed highly probable that his official host would bring the lady with him. In that case the balloon would go up before the party had even started.

For a good ten minutes he cudgelled his wits for some way of dealing with such a situation, but in vain, and he was still fruitlessly going round and round the problem like a squirrel in a cage when Fedora, again half-dressed and carrying her frock over her arm, came hurrying in. Sitting down at the dressing-table, she beckoned him over to her and said in a whisper:

"I've got to do something about my hair, and we've so little time left that you must help me. I keep it long because I'm rather vain about it, but it makes me damnably conspicuous. There's always the chance that something may go wrong outside and we'll have to take to our heels. If that happens I don't want my silvery locks to be spottable from half a mile away, so I'm going to do them up in half-a-dozen plaits and stuff them under a beret. You do the back and I'll do the sides."

It was a novel employment for Nicholas, and in other circumstances he would have been amused at playing barber to a pretty woman. As it was he worked away as quickly as he could plaiting up her fine silky hair, and tying the ends with some pieces of blue ribbon that she had snipped off from a clean nightdress. When they had finished the plaits, she coiled them into a coronet on the top of her head and secured them rather precariously with half-a-dozen safety-pins. Then, turning her head from side to side, she smiled at her reflection in the mirror and whispered:

"There! How do you like me now?"

Nicholas never had a chance to answer. At that instant without knock or warning, the bedroom door was thrust open and Kmoch walked in. For a moment he stood surveying them with his sad brown spaniel eyes, then he said:

"I have ordered the lunch to be put back for half-an-hour. You are to return with me to Headquarters. Comrade Frček wishes to put to you a few more questions."

CHAPTER X

IN THE NET

NICHOLAS' first reaction was not fear, but indignation. Fedora had known that it would be a race against time to get her hair rearranged before they were summoned to the reception, so she had not bothered to unpack her dressing-gown before sitting down to the job, and she was still in her undies. To Nicholas their actual relationship in no way invalidated the fact that events had placed upon him some of the responsibilities of a husband, and his strong sense of decency had been outraged. Turning on Kmoch, he demanded angrily:

"How dare you come barging in like this? It is disgraceful that you should show so little respect for people's privacy."

Kmoch gave him a faintly surprised look. "Only people who have something to hide desire privacy, so it is against the prin-

ciples of the State to permit it. The police have access at all
times, everywhere; and unless the lunch is to be further postponed we must hurry. That is why I came up to fetch you myself. Please, Comrade Hořovská, get your clothes on quickly."

Silently, Fedora slipped on her frock and adjusted her beret to
cover the coronet of plaits. Then they went downstairs and
followed Kmoch out to his car.

On the short drive Nicholas hardly knew whether to be
pleased or sorry about this unexpected intervention, which had
temporarily saved him from the ordeal of having to face the
beginning of the reception. He was hoping now that some new
factor might have arisen which would enable him to manœuvre
Frček into a discussion that could be sufficiently prolonged to
result in the function being put off altogether; but the fact that
Frček wished to put further questions to him so urgently was
extremely disquieting.

At the police headquarters they were taken up in the lift to
the top floor, and shown into Frček's long wide-windowed
room. Without getting up from his desk, he waved them to
chairs and, drawing his black caterpillar eyebrows down into
a frown, said to Nicholas:

"An hour ago a cable came in from London. When it had
been deciphered and handed to me, I was much disturbed by its
contents. Comrade Vaněk reports that in an endeavour to prevent him sending you here you pretended to be your cousin.
Explain, please?"

"That's right." Nicholas rose to the occasion with an apparent
confidence that he was far from feeling. "I told you of the importance I attached to putting off my departure for twenty-four
hours, and how he refused to listen to me. When he threatened
to use force I felt fully entitled to get out of being sent, if I could,
by a trick; so I tried to make him believe that I wasn't the man
he thought I was."

Frček nodded his broad head. "I see. But surely that was a
stupid thing to do when Comrade Hořovská was at hand to
prove conclusively that you were."

"I suppose it was; but she wasn't in the room at the time and it was the only line worth trying that I could think of on the spur of the moment."

"Comrade Vaněk further reports that you then attacked him, and did your utmost to escape by means of violence."

"Well, what about it? Wouldn't you have done the same if you decided that to remain in England for a day longer was in the best interests of the Party?"

For a moment Frček appeared to ponder this, then he said heavily, "Once you had stated your case, Comrade Vaněk was the best judge of that. His report fully justifies his having used force, and sent you here as 'a parcel'."

"There I disagree," Nicholas replied firmly. "But no doubt he considered that to do so was his duty, and since you seem to feel that way too, I withdraw the complaint I made against him. The whole thing was most unfortunate, but it is all over now and here I am in Prague; so it doesn't seem to me that there is much point in our arguing the matter further."

"I am not so sure." The black eyes bored into Nicholas'. "There is another passage in Comrade Vaněk's cable which I regard as most disquieting. He says that when, in face of Comrade Hořovská's positive identification, you admitted that you were Professor Bilto Novák, you then declared that you had changed your mind about coming to Prague, and that if he sent you against your will you would not co-operate with us."

"That is not true. What I said was that as I had left all my notes behind at the Hotel Russell I should not be much use here without them."

"To say that was to split straws. The loss of your notes could have proved only a temporary set-back. Your principal value lies in your abilities as a nuclear-scientist of the first rank and the information concerning capitalist-imperialist experiments in that field that you carry in your head."

Nicholas shrugged. "That may be true; but it was all part of the same business. I was putting up any line that occurred to me, that might have induced Comrade Vaněk to let me remain for another day in London."

"You definitely maintain that the postponement for which

you wished was only temporary, and that your intention to place your knowledge at the disposal of the Socialist Soviet Republics has never wavered?"

"I do."

"Then you are ready and willing to set my mind at rest by giving me a sample of that knowledge?"

"Certainly." Nicholas covered his uneasiness with a smile, while praying that he would be able to fake up enough scientific jargon temporarily to fool this gimlet-eyed, but probably not very educated, police chief. A question followed instantly:

"Tell me the gross weight of the Dr. Penney bomb that was exploded by the British off Montebello Island?"

To attempt evasion would have been fatal; in fact the only hope of averting suspicion lay in a quick, direct answer. Nicholas had nothing to go on other than the statement made in the press at the time, that the bomb was a comparatively small one; so he gambled on that and replied: "A little over nine hundred-weight."

Frček's round pasty face showed no emotion, but suddenly he shot out, "It was heavier—very much heavier. We had a report from a man who had excellent opportunities for observation."

There was no other course open to Nicholas now but a determined bluff. With a contemptuous gesture he exclaimed, "How could anyone judge weight merely by observation! The construction of fission bombs is entirely different to that of the H.E. variety. The old types were packed solid with explosives, whereas the interior of the new ones is mainly hollow to allow for the plunger mechanism."

"Our source would make allowances for that."

"Perhaps. But would he have done for the new alloy the British are using in the manufacture of these bombs to improve their weight-distance ratio? That has been kept a very close secret."

"His grading is very high. I cannot believe that he would be so far out in the estimate he gave us."

Again Nicholas shrugged. "If you prefer to accept the guess of a secret agent to the statement of a scientist who assisted in designing the bomb, you must do so. But what object could I possibly have in attempting to deceive you?"

"I don't know." Frček continued to stare at him. "If you are, in time we shall find out. We always do. But at the moment I am not satisfied." For over half a minute he said nothing, then he went on:

"I may be wrong—quite wrong; but I cannot afford to take any chances. I will speak frankly to you. The situation here is not altogether as we should like to see it. As a Czech yourself, you will know what a stubborn race we Czechs are. It has proved very difficult to convince a great part of our better-educated citizens that they should give up thinking for themselves and allow the Government to think for them. In quite a different way the rural populations of Moravia, Slovakia and Ruthenia have proved equally non co-operative. It can, of course, be only a matter of time before all sections of the population recognize the benefits of living under a People's Government, but that time has not yet come. The country is riddled with anti-social movements, and one of my major tasks is to prevent them from receiving any encouragement."

Again he paused for a moment, before continuing: "It would be contrary to established policy to inform the capitalist-imperialists governments of your arrival here by a public announcement, so from the beginning we had to deny ourselves any prospect of a broadcast by you to the Czechoslovakian nation; but we had hoped to make use of the considerable kudos that your return brings to the Party, through a small but influential circle. The gathering which is now assembling at the Engelsův Dům consists not only of old Comrades and physicists, but also the senior faculty of the University and numerous other leaders of thought in our communal life. The majority of them are undoubtedly heart and soul behind the People's Government, but others—well, I regard their loyalty as at least questionable. The sort of greeting speech we expected you to make—one in which you would have affirmed your relief and joy at having escaped from the slavery imposed upon you by the capitalist-warmonger English—might have done considerable good with these waverers; but even a hint that you had not come here willingly, given in private conversation to one of them, would far outweigh any good your speech would do. In no time the grapevine would have spread it all over Prague, and it would provide fresh ammunition for the people's enemies."

"Your doubts of me are entirely unjustified," Nicholas protested. "But since you have them, why don't you call off this lunch?"

"That is what I intend to do. I was explaining only why it is that I cannot afford to take any chances. I felt I owed you that because I still hope that we shall find you to be entirely loyal to us, and I should not like you to think later that I am taking this step without good reasons."

Leaning forward, Frček pressed down the little lever on his intercom and said in to it. "Telephone the Engelsův Dům. Tell them that the guests are to be given drinks and light refreshments, but there will be no lunch. Professor Novák was taken ill on his journey here and is not yet sufficiently recovered to attend. It is hoped that he will soon be fully recovered, and that a lunch to welcome him will be given in a few days' time."

Nicholas had been so dreading the possibility of something going wrong at the reception that he had deliberately made his bid to get out of it, and he was now greatly relieved. He reasoned that if Fedora's desperadoes were capable of undertaking such an elaborate escape plan as the bomb plot, they would easily be able to arrange a less spectacular and less dangerous method of getting her and himself out of the hotel that night. But he was counting his chickens before they were hatched. Frček turned to him and said:

"In these new circumstances, Professor, I shall be glad if you and Comrade Hořovská will be my guests at lunch to-day here. In the meantime I will issue instructions for a few of the men whom you were to meet at the Engelsův Dům to report here at three o'clock. They will be our leading men in your own field of research. After lunch you shall have a short discussion with them, and that will remove from our minds any doubt at all about your willingness to give us your complete collaboration."

5*

Nicholas only just prevented himself from giving a gasp of dismay. It was as though he had been hit hard in the pit of the stomach. The saliva ran hot in his mouth, and he felt the palms of his hands becoming moist. He knew that within five minutes of such a meeting he must be revealed as a fake; and as he was to be detained there until the Czech scientists arrived to question him, there seemed no possible means of escaping it. Desperately he sought a way, but all he could think of was to blurt out:

"I'm afraid that's no good. As I've told you, I left my notes behind."

"You will not need any notes," replied Frček smoothly. "All I have in mind is that you should meet the men with whom you will be working in future, and exchange with them ideas on a few general principles."

"It's no good, I tell you," Nicholas' voice was slightly hoarse. "It would not be at all satisfactory. I must have time to prepare a proper paper, then read it to them and answer their questions afterwards."

Frček's black eyebrows drew together. "Am I to understand that you refuse to hold any preliminary discussion with our scientists?"

"Yes. For the time being, anyway. All nuclear projects are of great complexity. It is certain that they have been working on totally different lines from myself. Without being taken stage by stage they would not understand. . . ."

"It is you, Professor, who do not understand."

"In what way?"

"You evidently do not understand the alternative that your refusal to meet these Comrades will force me to adopt. I shall have to detain you here—or rather in another place, which you may not find very comfortable."

Less than twenty-four hours earlier Nicholas would hotly have denounced as a dirty capitalist lie any suggestion that a high official of the Czech People's Government would use menaces in an attempt to extract information from a scientist unwilling to give it; but the morning's events had played such havoc with his preconceived idea that he now hardly knew what to believe; so Frček's threat did not take him entirely by surprise, and he stammered, "You . . . you mean you will send me to prison?"

"Yes. You have now made it quite clear to me that Comrade Vaněk was right in his fears that you had changed your mind. I still hope we may find that change to be only a very temporary one. Should you maintain your refusal to meet our scientists, you will go to prison and remain there until you have proved your willingness to give them all the information and assistance of which you are capable."

"You can't make a scientist give of his best unless he is treated decently and his heart's in his work," declared Nicholas truculently, in a forlorn hope that by a display of defiance he might yet gain a respite. "To send me to prison is the one certain way of making me dig my toes in and refuse to talk."

"About that I don't agree. We have considerable experience in dealing with stubborn people." Frček took a sheaf of papers from a drawer in his desk, and began to go through them as he went on quietly, "I will give you a few minutes to make up your mind. You can either accept my invitation to lunch and to discuss atomic matters with our experts afterwards, or I will send you downstairs to await conveyance to quarters very different from those you have been allotted at the Engelsův Dům."

Nicholas stood up and walked over to the side of the long room that formed one huge window. It was a lovely May morning, and the spires and domes of Prague glittered in the sunshine; but he stared out at them with unseeing eyes. He knew that he was really up against it, and it did not take him long to decide that only one course now lay open to him. He must do as he had wanted to do from the beginning—tell the truth about himself.

For a moment he wondered how his doing so would affect Fedora, but it did not seem that whatever he said now could make much difference as far as she was concerned. If he allowed himself to be exposed by the Czech scientists she would be involved in his exposure, and presumably in no worse case than if he anticipated matters by a voluntary confession now.

The memory of the way in which he had allowed her to involve him filled him with rage at his own stupidity. If only he had followed his own instincts in the first place he might have got a sympathetic hearing, whereas now it was a foregone conclusion that Frček would have put him in prison—anyhow for a time. But that was the whole crux of the matter.

If he went to prison as Nicholas there would be no point in keeping him there for very long. At the very worst it seemed unlikely that they would give him more than two or three months for having entered the country under false pretences. On the other hand, if he let them put him in, still believing him to be Bilto, they might keep him there indefinitely. He would certainly never be able to buy his freedom on Frček's terms, and the longer he left it before he declared himself to be Nicholas, the greater would be his difficulty in persuading anyone to believe him.

The more he thought about it the more obvious it became to him that sooner or later he would have to come clean, as the only possible way of getting out of this ghastly tangle; and that the sooner he took the plunge the better his chances would be of escaping a prolonged spell of detention. Having no further doubts on the matter, he turned about, walked over to Frček's desk and said in a firm voice:

"Comrade Frček, I have an admission to make to you. I also wish to apologize for having caused you a certain amount of unnecessary trouble. However, I should first like to assure you that although I am not actually a member of the Communist Party, I have spent most of my life working in close sympathy with its aims. It was here in Prague as a youngster that I first embraced the cause of the workers, and it has been my inspiration ever since. I am a regular contributor to the principal British Left Wing periodicals; I am a member of the Friends of the Russian People and of all the major associations working for the preservation of peace. I know that I have acted wrongly and foolishly; but the fact is that I am not really guilty of anything worse than playing a stupid practical joke, and I feel that on account of my past labours in spreading the doctrines of Karl

Marx I am entitled to ask you to take a lenient view of the matter."

As he paused for breath Frček asked with a puzzled frown, "What the devil are you talking about?"

Nicholas stared down into the round, moon-like face. "I was on the point of making a solemn declaration, that while I was doing my utmost to prevent Comrade Vaněk from sending me here I told him the truth. I am not Bilto but his cousin, Nicholas Novák."

Frček's voice came in a snarl. "You didn't fool Vaněk and you can't fool me! Is it likely that we should be taken in by such a barefaced lie?"

"It is the truth," Nicholas protested.

"It is a lie!" Frček banged on the desk with his clenched fist. "It is a lie, and an absurdly childish one. You have been identified by the woman who Vaněk informs me has slept with you on and off for months, and is still your mistress; so about your identity there can be no shadow of doubt."

Nicholas turned and shot a quick glance at Fedora. During the whole interview he had not dared to look at her for fear that Frček might jump to some conclusion from their expressions as their eyes met. She was now sitting with her legs crossed, staring down at the floor. Her face showed no emotion and she appeared to be perfectly relaxed, but one little thing revealed the strain she was under. Her hands were clasped in her lap, and clasped so tightly that the knuckles showed white."

"You will gain nothing by looking at her," Frček snapped. "Her identification of you was positive. Should she go back on it now I should take that only as evidence that she is in love with you. I should not believe her."

"I think we can leave her out of this," Nicholas retorted. He had no obligation whatever to champion Fedora—far from it—but ordinary decency impelled him to do his best for her, and he had thought of a line which he hoped might save her with himself from prosecution on any charge worse than having committed a misdemeanour. Quickly he went on:

"These are the facts. Bilto did need another night in London to advise a valuable Comrade on the story he had better tell if he found himself implicated. But my cousin foresaw that Comrade Vaněk might not agree to his postponing his journey, so he asked me to do the explaining for him. When I joined Comrade Hořovská in the car she knew perfectly well that I was not Bilto, but I made her have us driven off and explained to her. Then I was suddenly seized with a silly notion. I have so often been mistaken for Bilto that I thought it would be rather fun to see how far I could carry the deception."

"This whole story is a tissue of lies," Frček interrupted grimly.

"It is not," Nicholas insisted. "As a boy, I loved Prague, so I thought it would be intensely interesting to visit it again and see for myself the great improvement in the workers' status that has taken place here. Counting on my resemblance to Bilto to get me past Comrade Vaněk, I persuaded Comrade Hořovská to let me try out an impersonation of my cousin. We intended no harm, because we believed that Bilto would be following me to Prague to-day, and that when he arrived we would both have a good laugh with people here about my having fooled everyone. Then when I came face to face with Comrade Vaněk, I realized that what I was doing was both liable to be misunderstood and dishonourable. I tried to back out by confessing that I was Nicholas. Comrade Hořovská was not in the room at that time. When she was called in she had no idea that I had abandoned our little plot to get me a free trip to Prague, so of course she swore that I was Bilto. After that no one would listen to me. I tried to get away, but I was overpowered and sent here as 'a parcel'. It had not been intended that Comrade Hořovská should travel with Bilto; but Comrade Vaněk sent her to look after me. When we woke up side by side in the aircraft early this morning, we talked over the awkward situation in which my silly prank had landed us. Then I'm afraid we both became irresponsible again. We could not help seeing the funny side of it. I mean, that even against my will my impersonation had actually got me to Czechoslovakia. So we decided to see just how long I could manage to keep it up after landing. From start to finish the whole of this business has been nothing more than a series of misunderstandings arising out of my original impulse to play a joke on Comrade Vaněk and get sent to Prague without paying for a ticket."

As an explanation made up on the spur of the moment it was not a bad one; but it did not get past Frček. Without hesitation he picked on its weak spot, and sneered:

"I do not believe one word of this. Where the work of the Party is concerned its members have no sense of humour. To do so would be anti-social; so it is forbidden. Your assertion that Comrade Hořovská consented to collaborate with you in a joke, which had as its object making a fool of the Comrade from whom she received her instructions, is enough to qualify you for an asylum. I am quite used to people lying to me. I do not mind it. But to expect me to believe that sort of lie is to insult me."

Nicholas saw then that in trying to extricate Fedora he had strained the plausibility of his explanation too far; but no story could hold water that did not somehow or other account for her identification of him as Bilto; so he felt that even had he been thinking only of his own interests, he could not have cooked up anything more likely of acceptance. All he could do now was to stick to his guns, and he cried angrily:

"If you don't believe it I can't make you. But that's how it was; and neither you nor anyone else in the world will ever be able to alter the fact that I am Nicholas Novák."

"Your mulish persistence with these stupid lies makes no impression on me whatever," Frček bellowed back. "All you have succeeded in doing is to convince me that since you decided of your own free will to come to Prague something has happened to change your outlook. Therefore, having got you here in order to exploit your brain, it will now be necessary for us to exert severe pressure on you."

"If I were Bilto, to do so would be to dishonour the People's Government that you represent," Nicholas stormed. "But I am not; so however long you may keep me in prison you will never succeed in extracting from me one single item of useful information."

Frček sighed. "Really, you tire me. All this is too absurd. Why not admit that you are Bilto, have lunch with me, and meet the Comrades with whom you will sooner or later find yourself compelled to collaborate? That would save you much unpleasantness and me some trouble."

"Damn it, can't you see that to do that would simply be a waste of time? I'm Nicholas, I tell you, and . . . and . . ." A sudden inspiration had come to him, and he ended triumphantly, ". . . what is more, I can prove it!"

"How do you propose to do that?" asked Frček sceptically.

"Quite simply. Apparently you are Lord and Master here. All you have to do is to send for my relatives. Some of them may have died since I last heard of them, but Bilto and I must have several mutual uncles and aunts and cousins still living here in Prague. At the time of my last visit I was only fourteen, but all the same they couldn't possibly mistake me for Bilto. If you really want the truth, send for them and you will get it."

For the first time Frček looked a little shaken, and his voice held just a trace of doubt. "You are again trying to make a fool of me. What you suggest could result only in a farce."

"It will prove that no amount of wishful thinking can turn a sow's ear into a silk purse," retorted Nicholas. "Or myself into my brilliant cousin the atomic-scientist. I challenge you to confront me with all the members of the Novák family that you can get together."

Frček shrugged his broad shoulders. "All right. It shall be as you wish. I will have these people hunted out and brought here this afternoon." Turning to Kmoch, he added, "Take them both downstairs and have them put in the cells until I send for them again."

Nicholas was already standing. Kmoch came to his feet like a jack-in-the-box, and Fedora stood up more slowly. Frček had apparently again become absorbed in his papers and did not give them another glance as they left the room.

Outside on the landing one of the pretty lift-girls turned her automatic smile on them as they stepped past her, swiftly closed the gates, and at a word from Kmoch pressed the lowest button on the indicator. Taking advantage of the whirring noise as the lift shot down, Fedora said softly to Nicholas in English:

"I'm afraid we're finished now you've thrown your hand in. There was always a chance that you might have bluffed your way through the meeting with the scientists; but once your relatives have identified you Frček will charge us with having conspired to enter the country in order to spy for the British."

CHAPTER XI

THE PEOPLE'S REPRESENTATIVE

KMOCH was facing the lift gates, so had his back turned; but he caught Fedora's murmur before Nicholas could reply, and, swinging round, ordered her to be silent.

Ignoring him, she whispered a single last sentence. "All the same, whatever happens now, I want you to know that I thought it very generous of you to try to get me out as well as yourself."

"Be silent, I tell you!" Kmoch said in a sharper tone.

Nicholas gave him an angry look and asked in Czech, "Why shouldn't we talk if we want to? We are not criminals. We haven't even been charged with anything yet; and this is supposed to be a free country."

Kmoch waved the protest aside. "You may speak in Czech, but to talk in a foreign language is forbidden."

The lift had arrived at the basement, and Kmoch took them across a corridor to a small office. Particulars of them were entered in a ledger, then Fedora was led away by a gross-faced, huge-limbed wardress. Nicholas called after her in English, "Keep your chin up", and was marched off by an equally brutal-looking warder, who locked him in a cell.

There was nothing particularly cell-like about it, and except for the grille in the door it might have been a small private ward in a hospital, as it smelt strongly of disinfectant. The narrow iron bed looked reasonably comfortable; it had a chair, a table, a bed-side lamp and a water bottle. Sitting down on the bed, Nicholas went over in his mind the happenings of the past half hour.

He wondered uneasily if Fedora had been right, and he ought to have stuck to his guns a bit longer. Evidently she reasoned that if he had succeeded in bluffing his way past the scientists they would then have been sent back to the Engelsův Dům and so secured another chance to escape; whereas by his confession, although it had not been believed, he had finally burned their boats.

After some cogitation, he decided that her hopes had been based on false premises, as she could hardly be expected to appreciate the sort of discussion his meeting with the Czech scientists would entail. He was certain that he could never have got through it; so to accept the challenge would have been only to postpone the evil hour, and having reconvinced himself of that he dismissed the matter.

Her belief that they would be charged with espionage sounded alarming, but he was not inclined to take that very seriously. All along she had displayed a fanatical hatred of the People's Government, and a conviction that it employed the most barbarous methods to keep itself in power. His experiences in the past few hours had badly shaken his own belief that this Socialist Soviet satellite country was all that his Marxist friends in England had painted it, but he argued that people like Frček could not be truly representative of the Czech Communist leaders. After all, Frček was a policeman, and all over the world bad police chiefs sometimes abused the licence they were given to carry out their job of maintaining law and order. Therefore, it did not follow in the least that the People's Government denied individuals a reasonable freedom, and failed to protect them from being imprisoned without trial or otherwise unjustly treated.

That he might, as Nicholas, be sentenced to a few months' imprisonment for having entered the country illegally, he now glumly accepted; but he decided that Frček could only have been bluffing when he had threatened him, as Bilto, with imprisonment for an indefinite period. At the time the threat had rattled him; but now he could regard it calmly he felt sure that the Government would never allow that sort of thing.

Fedora's fears, he told himself, could be put down to undue pessimism. If it came out that she was a member of this anti-social resistance group known as the Legion, things would certainly go badly for her; but there seemed no reason why it should. At the moment, if he stuck to his story about her false identification of him being part of a silly joke that they had agreed to play, she could be accused only of having failed in her duty towards the Party, and that was a very minor offence compared with a charge of spying for the British. As far as he was concerned the idea seemed absurd, as Frček had only to order a check-up in London to be informed that the record of his pro-Communist activities placed him above all suspicion of being a spy in the service of the warmongering Tory Government.

Somewhat comforted by these reflections, he lay down at full length on the bed and after a conscious effort succeeded in turning his mind to more pleasant things. Wendy was his natural target for such thoughts, and fond day-dreams about her merged imperceptibly into sleep.

As his eight hours or so of unconsciousness during the night had been mainly drug-induced, and since waking he had passed through a long morning every moment of which had been exceptionally exacting, the sleep into which he fell was a very deep one; so he did not hear the guard enter his cell, and roused out of it only when the man shook him roughly by the shoulder.

Still only half awake, and not realizing where he was, he stumbled out into the corridor; then as they turned into a cross-passage, he caught sight of Fedora and the wardress who looked like a female all-in wrestler. His brain at once began to tick over again, and, assuming that he was now being taken up to be confronted with his relatives, he wondered which of them he would shortly be seeing after a lapse of so many years, in

these unhappy circumstances. On reaching the office he saw
from a clock in it that it was nearly five, and with a smile at
Fedora he said:

"It seems that I've been asleep for over four-and-a-half
hours."

She returned his smile a little wanly. "I didn't do as well as
that, but I managed to doze for quite a while."

At that moment the gates of one of the lifts opposite rattled
open and they were ordered into it by their hefty guardians.
Two minutes later they stood once more in front of the moon-
faced, caterpillar-browed Frček, with fat, spaniel-eyed little
Kmoch beside them, and their respective keepers standing
rigidly to attention two paces behind their backs.

This time Frček did not invite them to sit down. Having
ordered the male and female gorillas to stand back on either side
of the door, he stared hard at Nicholas for a moment, then
said:

"I have had three members of the Novák family unearthed
and brought here. When they enter this room I shall ask them
if they know who you are, and I will not permit that their answers
should be influenced in any way. You will, therefore, remain
absolutely silent until they have given their opinions. I take it
that is understood, as this test is being carried out at your request,
and will otherwise be rendered useless?"

"That sounds fair enough to me," Nicholas replied; upon
which Frček nodded to Kmoch and said, "Bring them in."

Kmoch went out and returned a moment later leading a short
procession of five people. It consisted of a stooping white-
haired woman, an old man, another woman of about Nicholas'
age and two state policemen. The policemen took up positions
standing as stiff as ramrods beside the warder and wardress, the
others sidled with obvious reluctance after Kmoch until he
halted them a few feet from Frček's desk.

With knitted brows Nicholas surveyed the three civilians
who had been produced as his relations; he could not recognize
any of them.

Frček addressed the trio. "Look well, please, at the male

prisoner. Have any of you ever seen him before? If so, tell me who he is?"

The old man only shook his head; but the old woman broke into a swift, frightened gabble. "No, no, Comrade Minister! We do not know him. Why should we? If you have the idea that we mix ourselves up in the resistance movements you are quite mistaken. We are quiet people who do just what we are told, and every day we feel more thankful for the simple, happy life that Comrade President Gottwald and the People's Government have made possible for us."

Suddenly the younger woman took charge of the situation. She was plain, thick-set, with reddish hair that was turning grey, and a sullen mouth; but she had a determined chin. Laying a restraining hand on the older woman's arm, she said:

"Be quiet, Mother. The Comrade Minister can have no reason to be angry with us if we tell the truth. This man is Nicholas. Surely you and Dad remember him. He is your English nephew, Nicholas."

Frček gave a loud grunt. The elderly couple looked at their daughter, nodded uneasily, then stood staring at the floor. It was obvious to Nicholas that whether or not they had recognized him at first sight, they were reluctant to admit it: but by now he had placed them all.

The old people were his Uncle František and his Aunt Anka; the younger woman was his cousin Ludmila, whom he had last seen as a fat-faced girl of fourteen with a couple of thick plaits. To see them as they were now shocked him profoundly. He knew that his uncle and aunt could only be in their later fifties, yet their lined, unhappy faces and stooping shoulders gave the impression that neither of them could be less than seventy. The clothes of all three were threadbare, and in any city they would have been taken for people of the working-class. Yet in the old days the Nováks had been, if not wealthy, at least moderately well-off. The family had owned a glass-manufacturing business, and its profits had been sufficient to maintain them all in solid middle-class comfort. As one of the junior members of the firm Nicholas' father had been sent to travel its products in England, but for several generations its senior members had lived in quite large houses with three or four servants and had enjoyed the respect of all who knew them.

Another thought which distressed Nicholas acutely was that by addressing Frček as 'Comrade Minister' they confirmed the impression given earlier by Kmoch, that he was a member of the Government, and so a fully responsible representative of it. But feeling that Ludmila's spontaneous recognition of him had now released him from his undertaking to remain silent, he thrust these thoughts aside, stepped forward and said:

"I am sure, Aunt Anka and Uncle František, you remember me, but I am most distressed to see you all in such poor shape."

"Oh, we are well enough, nephew, well enough," his uncle replied quickly. "Your aunt and I are still quite capable of doing our shift at the factory; and we enjoy it."

"But Aunt Anka never used to work there in the old days." Nicholas' voice held both surprise and disapproval.

"Ah! But we were still criminally blind to what each one of us owed to others, then," Uncle František hastened to reassure him. "You remember your cousin Bilto, and how greatly we all disapproved of his Marxist politics. We were wrong, very wrong; and he was right. We know better now, and we are doing our best to show our repentance for the evil, reactionary-bourgeois lives we lived, almost in idleness while taking the lion's share of the profits that really belonged to our workers."

Nicholas knew that as a joint managing director of the factory his uncle had worked far longer hours than any of his employees. What sort of menial job the poor old man had been given to do there now could only be guessed at. With his heart suddenly gone leaden he forbore to enquire, but asked:

"What about the rest of the family? How are they?"

The old couple uncomfortably averted their eyes, and it was Ludmila who answered, "There was the occupation, then the war. Our family was greatly reduced by the Nazi bandits. Some fell as honourable victim-martyrs in the purges, others were conscripted for the wicked war against our Russian brothers and we have never heard what happened to them." A bitter note entered her voice as she added, "Your cousin Máša is still in Prague. She has had the good fortune to please one of the Comrade Food Controllers; but she was always the lucky one, and she is too grand to know us now."

At a loss for a suitable reply, Nicholas turned to his aunt and enquired: "Are you still living at the house in Pelléova?"

Her glanced flickered in Frček's direction, and her wrinkled old face broke into a cringing smile. "Yes; oh, yes. Everyone has been most kind to us. Of course the house was always far too big for just us three, so several families live there now. But they have let us keep the basement and . . ."

Frček's booming voice cut her short. "That will do! I have heard quite enough to satisfy me." He turned to Kmoch. "Get rid of these people. No! Wait a minute. They may talk about this meeting with a Novák from England, and I don't want any rumours to start getting about. We had better detain them for a few days. Let the warder take them down to the cells. I wish the wardress and the two troopers to remain here."

Aunt Anka let out a sudden wail, and, clasping her feeble hands, made a move to throw herself on her knees in front of Frček's desk. It was her daughter who prevented her, by seizing her arm and exclaiming:

"Mother! Be sensible! You heard what the Comrade Minister said. If you behave he will allow us to go home in a few days' time; but if you make a scene he may send us all to one of those labour camps."

Nicholas felt the blood hammering in his temples. He was horrified at the state to which his relatives had been reduced, and even more so at the implications of the sort of treatment to which respectable families of their kind were now subjected. He wanted desperately to intervene, but realized that it would be futile. Clenching his teeth and hands, he stood rigid with helpless indignation as the moronic-looking warder hustled his aunt, uncle and cousin from the room.

As the door closed behind them Frček said to him, "Well; you have proved your case. I little thought that my insistence on your meeting our scientists would produce such an unexpected result; but I see now that faced with it you had no alternative to throwing in your hand. I think you had better tell me about this imposture of yours from the beginning."

"There is nothing to tell," Nicholas shrugged. "I mean, nothing that I haven't already told you. Bilto asked me to explain to Comrade Vaněk why he wanted another night in London; then on the way to him I thought it would be fun to see if I could get myself a free trip to Prague, and persuaded Comrade Hořovská to help me carry through my silly prank. That's all there is to it."

"You say this idea occurred to you only when you were on your way to see Comrade Vaněk."

"Yes."

"And that Professor Bilto Novák definitely intended to come to Prague the following night?"

"Yes."

"Then how do you account for the fact that you travelled on his passport?"

When Nicholas had hastily made up his story, that was a point he had entirely overlooked. Instantly he saw that it blew the whole thing wide open. No possible explanation could reconcile those two parts of his statement that Frček had picked upon so swiftly. Seeing his sudden discomfiture, the bull-like police chief leaned forward across his desk, and thundered:

"I will tell you how your cousin's passport came into your possession. You stole it."

No shot in the dark could have been better aimed. In vain Nicholas stammered a denial. The fact that the accusation was true temporarily deprived him of the wit even to grope for an alternative to account for his having come by it. Pressing his advantage, Frček shot out a thick pointing finger and repeated:

"You stole it! Yes, and I will tell you why! It is not easy for people from the West to enter Czechoslovakia now. On learning of the arrangements for your cousin to come here you realized that it was a unique opportunity to get in unchallenged. You lied to him, had him arrested, killed him—for all I know—

so that you could take his place. Once in, you hoped to disappear, ferret out our secrets, then slip back across the frontier and sell them to our enemies."

Nicholas paled. For a second he was struck dumb by this sudden revelation that Fedora's worst fears had been really justified. Then he cried, "You're crazy. I've already told you that I am a life-long follower of Karl Marx. If you don't believe me, ring up London. Get Comrade Vaněk to find out about me. There are a score of people prominent in the Peace Associations who will vouch for it that nothing would ever induce me to serve the British Government as a spy."

"Peace Associations!" Frček's voice rang with contempt. "Surely you do not think that we pay any serious regard to the sort of people who sit on the platforms of those puppet shows. They are valuable only as a means of sabotaging the rearmament drives of the pluto-democratic West. We pull the strings, but the people who sponsor them publicly are no more than a collection of cranks, visionaries and fools."

As though struck in the face with a tumblerful of ice-cold water, Nicholas winced. He could hardly credit that he had really heard that cynical exposure of what lay behind the crusade that he had participated in so enthusiastically and for so long. Before he could recover sufficiently to speak again, Frček went on:

"Irresponsible idealists who have never submitted to the discipline of the Party often go through a period in which they regard themselves as radicals of the extreme Left; but such people are an easy prey to other political ideologies, and quite frequently they become converts to Fascist-imperialism overnight. That may be your case. But I neither know nor care. I am concerned only with the fact that you entered this country as a spy."

"I deny it! You have not one atom of proof on which to base such an accusation. Even your theory about Bilto does not make sense. Is it likely that I would have betrayed my own cousin? Who would credit for one moment that, unless he had trusted me implicitly, he would ever have confided to me the

deadly secret that he meant to come here and place his knowledge at the disposal of the Soviets?"

"I never said that he confided in you."

"Then who else could have told me about his intended
journey?"

Frček's black eyes flashed. His arm shot out, and he pointed
at Fedora.

"Her! This woman who is in love with you, of course! She
was Professor Bilto's contact. She knew all the arrangements.
She disclosed them to you; then the two of you hatched this plot
in which you were to impersonate him."

"You're wrong! Utterly wrong! I'd never even seen her until
the car came to the Russell Hotel to pick Bilto up."

"You lie! And do not dare to repeat to me that childish
story about her pretending that you were Bilto as a joke entered
into on the spur of the moment. Your having his passport in
your possession disproves it. That is conclusive evidence that
the whole business was arranged beforehand."

Standing up, Frček walked round his desk and halted in front
of Fedora. For a moment he stared at her in silence, then he
said: "You were Professor Bilto's contact. You must have
known him intimately, yet you identified this other man as him
to Comrade Vaněk. Why did you do that? Was it love for him,
or was it for money; or is it that for a long time you have been
in secret a traitor to the Party? Answer me?"

In a low, expressionless voice she replied, "I have nothing to
say."

Stretching out his left hand, he seized her beret and the coiled
hair beneath it. Then, raising his open right hand, he slapped
her with all his force across the side of the face.

The blow would have knocked her flat had he not been holding her up by the hair. Staggering sideways under it, she let out
a choking gasp.

"You swine!" yelled Nicholas, and, reckless of the consequences, he sprang upon the Minister. Grabbing him by the
shoulder, he swung him round, then aimed a blow with his
clenched fist at the cruel, pasty, moon-like face.

Frček ducked the blow and took a quick step back. Nicholas got no chance to strike at him again. Kmoch had been standing at his side, and only a pace away from him. Whipping a small automatic from the pocket of his long overcoat, the fat little detective rushed in and jammed its barrel against Nicholas' ribs.

"Move again and I fire," he cried. "Put your hands on your head and keep them there."

The two uniformed thugs had dashed forward at the first sign of trouble, but their assistance was not necessary. White with anger and still panting slightly, Nicholas did as he had been ordered.

For a moment no one moved or spoke. Slowly Frček's black eyes travelled over Fedora, surveying her from head to foot, then he looked at Nicholas and said:

"Your childish attempt to play champion to Comrade Hořovská tells me one thing. Whether or not she is in love with you, it is obvious that you are in love with her; otherwise you would never have risked the sort of punishment to be expected for aiming a blow at me. I mean to get to the bottom of this business. I want to know all the things you were instructed to try to find out while acting as a spy here, and full details of your contacts with the British Secret Service. Men can be stubborn about such matters, but they usually soften up when obliged to witness certain things done to a woman that they love. I think I shall learn quite quickly all I wish to know about you through her."

He raised his hand, beckoning the two thugs and the wardress. Then, pointing to Fedora, he said:

"Strip her."

CHAPTER XII

A TASTE OF SOVIET JUSTICE

KMOCH still had the barrel of his pistol jammed hard against Nicholas' ribs. In spite of that Nicholas lowered his arms and cried in ringing protest, "This is monstrous! Your order is a violation of all human decency."

Frček's underlings were just about to seize Fedora, but he waved them back, and said, "Whether my order is carried out or not lies with you. I am ready to cancel it if you are prepared to tell me what I wish to know."

"How can I?" Nicholas' voice was high-pitched with anger and exasperation. "There's nothing to tell! No one gave me any instructions! I don't know a thing about the British Secret Service!"

"Then we must see if Comrade Hořovská's tears will refresh your memory."

"Nothing could make me remember things I never knew. And you're quite wrong in believing that I am in love with her."

"Then why should you show such recklessness in her defence?"

"Good God, does that need an answer! Any man would do his utmost to prevent a woman being treated as you are treating her."

"Prevent it, then, by a full confession."

"I have nothing to confess."

"Your stubbornness certainly suggests that you do not care for her very much; but we shall learn the truth about that after we have taken off her clothes."

"Your attempt to extract information from me by threats of what you will do to her reduces you to the level of the Nazis."

"If you intend that as an insult to my way of conducting this affair, it is without point," Frček replied quietly. "The Nazis were self-seeking protectors of a bourgeois-industrialist society; and therefore of criminal mentality. But their methods of dealing with spies and saboteurs were most efficient, and therefore admirable."

Nicholas glared at him. "To proclaim such a belief shows you to be utterly unprincipled."

"My principles are the teachings of Marx-Lenin as interpreted by Comrade Stalin, and no one has ever accused me of deviation. But we waste time. Are you or are you not prepared to answer my questions?"

"How can I? You might just as well ask me if there are men on Mars!"

Frček signed to his underlings to go ahead. The police troopers each took Fedora by a wrist. The hefty wardress stooped down, grasped a handful of skirt on either side, and pulled it up to her waist.

"One moment!" Nicholas threw up a hand. "Please listen to me."

Again Frček checked his underlings, then enquired, "Well?"

"Am I right in believing you to be a Minister in the Czecho-slovak People's Government?"

"You are."

"Then in the name of the People I appeal to you not to sully your honourable position by such unworthy conduct."

"As Minister of Police it is my duty to protect the workers from traitors like her, and capitalist-spy-swine like you."

Nicholas let the terms of opprobrium pass and said, "All right; but the essence of this affair is that you believe us to be guilty of having committed some crime against the State."

"Your admission that you entered this country on another man's passport, and that the woman abetted you, makes that obvious."

"To you, perhaps. But it has not been properly proved. I insist that we should both be formally tried in one of the People's Courts, and . . ."

"You will be in due course; but not until I have got the truth out of you."

"To extract statements from the accused under threats is the negation of the basic principles of jurisprudence. Whatever you may think we have done, we have the right to demand that we should not be subjected to further examination before we have received legal aid, that specific charges against us should be formulated, and that our case should be heard before a court which is properly qualified to administer justice."

Frček shrugged. "Within a few minutes of your first being brought before me I realized that you were one of those half-witted socialists who believe that it is possible to run a country by State planning and at the same time preserve individual freedoms. In the Socialist Soviet States nobody has any personal 'rights'. As for justice, that is my affair. If I conclude that any-one has been falsely accused I order their release; if not I in-form the court of the sentence that I wish to be inflicted on them."

Horrified beyond measure by these brutal revelations, Nicho-las found himself temporarily bereft of words. Frček muttered disdainfully, "I have given time enough to answering your childish quibbles." Then, turning to the group about Fedora, he called, "Get on with it, now!"

The two men thrust her wrists up as high as they would go while the woman peeled her frock upwards until it covered her face. They had got no further before Nicholas attempted to intervene again. Starting forward, he cried:

"I won't stand by and see this!"

"Stay where you are!" snapped Kmoch. "Stay where you are, or I'll put a bullet into you!"

Frček swung round on his subordinate. "No! Be careful with that gun! I don't want him shot—yet." Then he shouted at the nearest police thug. "Here, you! Take care of the man; two people are quite enough to get the clothes off a woman."

The blue-jowled policeman threw himself in the advancing Nicholas' path and hit him hard beneath the jaw. The impact sent him staggering back and left him momentarily dazed. Kmoch pocketed the pistol and seized one of his arms; the policeman grabbed the other. Before he had time to recover, they had put a double half-Nelson on him. Kmoch then left matters to the brawny uniformed man, who took a firm grip of both Nicholas' arms and held them behind his back as tightly as if they had been pinioned.

Fedora offered no resistance. She had the sense and self-control to realize how futile it would be. Without any aid from the man the gorilla-like wardress could easily have overpowered her. As it was she neither helped nor hindered, but the wardress was well experienced in such tasks and had her naked except for her shoes and stockings within two minutes.

When they had pulled her suspender belt off they let go of her and stepped aside. She stood there motionless looking down at the floor.

Frček walked over to her, took her chin in his hand, tilted up her face and looked down into it. One cheek was sadly disfigured, having turned a bright scarlet from the slap he had given her; but he now favoured her with a smile of approval, and said:

"You and I must have a little private session later on. If you behave yourself I might make things much easier for you. But we mustn't let such ideas interfere with our present business, must we? Since your boy-friend doesn't care enough about you to talk, perhaps you would like to start the ball rolling by telling me what you know about him? If you give me some good hard facts I may decide to go no further for the moment, and twist his tail instead of yours until he gives me the rest of the story."

Again, in a low expressionless voice, she said, "I have nothing to say."

He shrugged and said to the underlings who had stripped her, "Turn her round and put her up against the wall."

Swinging her about, they gripped her wrists again, marched her over to the panelling and held her flat against it with her arms spread wide above her head, so that with her body they formed a 'Y'.

She was tall and slender, with good shoulders and boyish hips. Nicholas gazed at the triangle of her back, thinking how beautifully proportioned it was. The muscles in it rippled slightly when the man and woman who held her jerked her arms slightly, and having been stretched taut they became still.

Frček had stooped down behind his desk and opened one of the bottom drawers in it. As he straightened up Nicholas saw that from it he had taken a whip. It had a thick handle ending in a round knob, so if reversed it could have been used as a formidable cosh; its lash was of thin plaited leather and about two feet along.

"You can't do that," Nicholas shouted. "You can't do that."

A sadistic smile spread slowly over Frček's round pasty face. "I can, and I am going to," he said softly. "Even if you decide to talk, as you have kept me waiting I mean to keep you waiting until I have made a pretty pattern on your mistress's skin. To watch me will give you only a mild idea of the much more painful treatment that I may order her to be given later, should you not talk fast and to the point when I am ready to listen to you."

Raising the whip, he gave it a preliminary crack. Fedora, her nerves strung to the highest pitch, jerked spasmodically as though she had already been struck. Nicholas swore.

Like most social revolutionaries he was an agnostic, so it did not occur to him to pray for divine intervention. Nevertheless he shut his eyes. By doing so he hoped to blot out the harrowing scene, but the attempt was futile. In his mind he could still see the big room, with its long stretch of window, through which the afternoon sunlight was coming at an angle. He knew the position of each person in it, and saw them as though they were wax-work dummies posed in a grim tableau. Above all, the central figure remained clear. Fedora's body spread-eagled against the dark panel was vividly etched upon his closed eyelids.

Although he had not heard the whip come down he heard her give a sudden gasp. Automatically his eyes flickered open. Frček had not struck her. He was standing there grinning. All he had done was to administer an unexpected shock by using the end of the whip to tickle the base of her spine.

But next moment he stepped back, raised the whip and brought it down smartly just below the spot he had tickled. She gave a sharp cry and jerked herself erect. One of her stockings slithered down into a ruff round her ankle. Frček raised his whip again and gave her a quick cut on the calf of the exposed leg. She had set her teeth and did not cry out this time but automatically drew up the hurt leg. At her movement the stocking on the other floated down, and with a swift flick Frček gave its calf similar treatment. Then, crossing to her other side, he gave her another vicious cut. She twitched violently and let out a low moan.

"You brute!" Nicholas shouted, and began to struggle with the man who held him; but his arms were gripped behind his back as though in a vice.

Frček only smiled at him and said, "I've hardly started yet." Turning again to Fedora, he began to strike at her back and shoulders. Once, twice, thrice, the lash descended. Still with clenched teeth she choked back all sound other than a low, quivering moan. But at the fourth stroke, she burst into tears and sobbed out:

"Oh, God! Oh, God! Help me, I beg. Help me! Help me!"

Nicholas had closed his eyes and opened them again. Beads of sweat had broken out on his forehead. The sound of Fedora's sobbing drove him into a frenzy of fury, but he knew that he was powerless to help her. Each time he made the least move, the police thug gave an upward jerk to one of his arms that caused him acute pain and threatened to wrench it from its socket. He could only mutter useless curses.

Standing back, Frček admired his handiwork. He had not lashed Fedora hard enough to draw blood, but red weals now stood out where the whip had cracked down on smooth flesh. With an amused glance at Nicholas he said:

"Now, I think, we must give her a pretty girdle round that slender waist." Once more he drew back the whip, this time sideways on, and the vicious stroke curled round her body so that the end of the lash cut into her stomach.

At that, she let out a scream and began to struggle, but the man and woman who held her by the wrists had little difficulty in keeping her in position. Frček lifted the whip again, but Nicholas could bear no more.

6

"Stop!" he yelled. "Stop! I'll tell you everything you want to know."

Frček lowered the whip, laid it on his desk, and said, "All right, I'm glad you have come to your senses." Turning to his underlings, he added: "That will be enough for now. Let her sit down."

They led Fedora to a chair, and she collapsed into it, still sobbing. But after a moment she leaned forward, picked up her dress from the floor, pulled it in a bundle across her middle and hunched her smarting body over it. As her sobs eased Frček sat down behind his desk, and said to Nicholas:

"Now, let's have the truth! If you attempt to tell me any further cock-and-bull stories, I'll have her straddled over the back of that chair so that I can use my whip on her in a way that will be really painful."

Nicholas knew that it was no longer the least use to beat about the bush, or even to give the true account of how the whole thing had started by his deciding to impersonate Bilto on a sudden impulse. He would not be believed. Unless this brutal scene was to continue, and mount to a revolting barbarity the thought of which made him feel sick, he must now lie, and lie to the limit. He had got to tell Frček the sort of thing he expected to hear, and pin his hopes on some fresh turn of events enabling him later to escape the consequences.

Drawing a deep breath, he said, "The facts are these. You are right about my being a British secret agent, although I became one only a few weeks ago. It was after my cousin Bilto told me of his intention to come here. I went and reported that to the police. They took me to see a man at the War Office. I had several interviews with him, and eventually he persuaded me to impersonate my cousin. As you guessed, the idea was that I should let myself be brought to Czechoslovakia in his place and disappear as soon as possible after landing. My task was to find out all I could about the resistance movement here, and how it could best be assisted."

Frček nodded. "So far, so good. At what point did your woman accomplice enter the scene?"

"Only a few days ago. Naturally, from the moment I had given Bilto away they put him under constant observation. That's how they got on to her. They pulled her in, told her they knew everything, and that they would get her a ten-year prison sentence unless she would agree to play. It was just the one job of getting me put on the plane for Prague, or ten years; and, of course, she had no idea then that your people would send her with me. She decided that to keep her freedom was worth the risk of Vaněk's finding her out, and who can blame her?"

"I do. She wilfully betrayed the interests of the Party. There is no worse crime than that."

Nicholas heaved a mental sigh. He had done his best for Fedora all along. He was putting himself in it up to the neck to save her from acute physical suffering now; but he had seen no possible way in which, if he was to be believed, he could do more than attempt to palliate her offence. With a little gesture of helplessness, he went on:

"A meeting was arranged between us, and we fixed everything up. She let me know the date planned for Bilto's departure, and on that day I came up to London again. Bilto and I both used the Russell Hotel on our occasional visits to Town, so he didn't think it particularly strange when he ran into me there. The police knew that he had left Harwell, of course, and were at the Hotel waiting to arrest him. We agreed to dine together and afterwards went up to his room. A few minutes later the plain-clothes men came in and took him into custody. I simply collected his passport, went downstairs, and waited there until Comrade Hořovská picked me up in the car. There you are. Now you know everything."

For a full minute Frček's round, pasty face remained expressionless; then he said, "I think we are now getting a little nearer to the truth. But there are several points that you have so far failed to explain. Unless a man is a professional agent, and earns his living by betraying people, it is usual to feel shame in the presence of the person about to be betrayed. Why, if the police were in any case going to arrest Professor Bilto so that you could obtain his passport, did you go out of your way to dine with him? There was no necessity for you to see him at all, or even for him to know that it was you who had betrayed him. In Comrade Vaněk's report, too, he stated that a Power of Attorney made out by Professor Bilto in your favour was found upon you. If you put yourself in his way at the hotel, giving him the impression that you were there only by chance, how does it come about that he had had the document prepared and was still carrying it on him when he did not expect to see you again before his departure? Another point: If you had planned to impersonate him for the purpose of coming to Czechoslovakia, why, when everything was going well, did you risk missing the plane in order to visit a house in North London? Why, too, above all, did you later resort to violence in an attempt to escape from Comrade Vaněk, and make it necessary for him to send you here as 'a parcel'?"

Nicholas' brain was reeling. The whole awful business had become such a frightful tangle that his mind no longer registered the innumerable lies he had told about it, or to whom he had told them.

"I . . . I tried to get away from Vaněk because . . . well, because I got cold feet about coming at the last moment," he stammered.

"Then why did this Hořovská woman get you sent here against your will, by her positive identification of you as Professor Bilto?"

That was one which Nicholas himself could not answer truthfully, for he still had not the faintest idea. As he floundered for a reply, Frček went on. "She had done all that could be expected of her, so could not have been blamed by your Secret Service friends if fear led you to back out. She must have known, too, that the British would publish the fact of Professor Bilto's arrest in their papers, so that Comrade Vaněk would soon learn of it. If she had held her tongue no-one could have proved afterwards that it had not been her intention to double-cross you and give you away to Comrade Vaněk at the first opportunity, but by insisting to him that you were Professor Bilto she damned herself quite unnecessarily. Another thing occurs to me. If you had planned to impersonate the Professor in advance, why did you not either take his luggage or set out with some of your own?"

Leaning forward, the bulky, black-haired Minister tapped the glass top of his desk with a pudgy forefinger. "Broadly speaking the admissions you have made are satisfactory, but I am picking holes in your story because there is one part of it that does not ring true. It is of what took place on the night of your departure. Why had the Professor got the Power of Attorney on him? Why did the Hořovská continue to insist that you were him when she need not have done so? Why had you no luggage? Why did you go out of your way to dine with your cousin? Why did you make a visit to your friends in North London? I require answers to all . . ."

Suddenly breaking off, he got quickly to his feet. For Nicholas, the prospect of a respite of even a few moments came as a most blessed relief. Hearing swift footsteps behind him, he looked round to find out the cause of this most welcome interruption.

Unannounced by any knock, a small man with a close-clipped moustache and dark hair, neatly parted on one side, had entered the room. His features were slightly Mongolian, and when he spoke his pronunciation of Czech proclaimed him to be a Russian. From his undistinguished appearance anyone would have put him down as a very minor official; but after a single glance at Nicholas, he snapped at Frček:

"Get rid of your uniformed people."

At once Frček made a sign to the two police thugs and the wardress, telling them to wait outside. Kmoch remained, and once more producing the pistol murmured to Nicholas, "If you start anything, I shall not hesitate to put a bullet through your foot."

As soon as the door had closed behind the underlings, the mild-looking little Russian said to Frček in a cold, contemptuous voice:

"So you and your friends in London have bungled this most important matter."

"Yes. London has slipped up badly, I'm afraid," Frček

admitted hastily. "Here, though, we are now getting to the bottom of the affair. But how did you know already that our Novák has turned out to be a fake?"

The reply was acid. "Realizing that failure to get a full report to Moscow at the earliest possible moment might land us both in a Labour Camp, I took the quickest means of finding out."

Frček gave the Russian a reproachful look. "I assure you, Comrade Gorkov, that I have lost no time; and I am surprised to learn there were any quicker means than those I have adopted."

"You could have done as I did, and put an 'immediate' enquiry through to London. As it was, when you informed me soon after midday of your reason for cancelling the Novák lunch, you were so over-confident that this was the atom-scientist that you did not treat the matter with any urgency at all. You were quite content to wait about all this afternoon until your police could rake up some members of the Novák family to say whether or not he was the right man."

In a low, rather nervous voice, Frček made a respectful protest. "Permit me to point out, Comrade Gorkov, that unless you have known the facts for some time, your method of finding them out has proved no quicker than mine."

"And what have you found out?" sneered the Russian. "Simply that the man is a fake and the woman a traitor. Who cares about them? Or what they are, or what they've done? In this affair—and it is one in which the Kremlin has stressed that our vital interests are at stake—the only thing that matters is, what has happened to the real Professor Novák?"

"Ah! That I can tell you," cried Frček. "Although I greatly regret to report such a misfortune. He was betrayed by his cousin here, and arrested in his presence by the British police."

"You incompetent fool!" The Russian's eyes glinted angrily. "You can have nothing but this man's word for that and it is not the truth. With their usual speed in high-priority cases, my Embassy in London has found out the facts and cabled a full reply to my enquiry. It was deciphered ten minutes ago. Professor Bilto Novák is still at the Hotel Russell, and there is no reason to suppose that he is being kept under observation. One of our agents contacted him, and fresh arrangements are now being made for him to fly here *via* Paris to-morrow night. He had no idea at all why your people had failed to collect him, and was waiting to receive some explanation. Had no one got in touch with him over the weekend, he intended to return to Harwell first thing on Monday morning; but if he had had to do that it might have been a considerable time before he could have left again without arousing suspicion. Had such a serious delay resulted from your failure to find out if the real Professor Novák had left London, you would be making a trip to the Urals from which you would never come back. Unless you wish me to send in an adverse report on you to Moscow, in future you will give less time to self-indulgence and more to thinking about your work."

Nicholas was savouring the first unalloyed pleasure he had experienced for many hours. It was clear that although Frček might be Minister of Police in the Czechoslovak People's Government, Comrade Gorkov was his master; and it was a most enjoyable sight to see the bulky pasty-faced brute cringe under the lash of the little Russian's tongue. But Nicholas was soon given something far less pleasant to think about. In a servile effort to escape further censure, Frček said:

"Comrade Gorkov, you are much cleverer than myself; so please do not be too hard on me. I assure you I have been far from idle, and between us we shall have the best of both worlds. While you have ensured the arrival after all of the real atomic scientist, I shall be able to offer a fine propaganda trial of the false one. He has already begun his confession, and from the witness-box he will testify to the world how he was sent here by the warmongering English as a spy."

While forced to witness Fedora being stripped and whipped, Nicholas' emotions had been harrowed as never before. His final intervention had sprung from a desperate urge to prevent her being tortured further, and he had had no time to give proper consideration to its possible consequences. Now, the repugnant and humiliating price he might be forced to pay was brought home to him with brutal suddenness; and next moment an even blacker chapter of the nightmare serial, in which he had become a helpless actor, was opened to him.

The Russian gave Frček a bleak smile of approval. "Such trials are always of considerable value, so at the Kremlin they will be glad to learn that you have secured the basis for one. But here you have no experts in training the accused in what they are to say. Have the woman looked to, so that she is fit to travel, then send them both on the evening train to Moscow."

CHAPTER XIII

A MIND IN TORMENT

"I WILL give orders to that effect at once, Comrade Gorkov."

Frček's reply came promptly enough, but he looked a little crestfallen. After a slight hesitation, he added, "However, I hope you will not take it amiss if I remark that as this is a Czech affair it might be more suitable to hold the trial in Prague."

"Propaganda trials need careful preparation," answered the Russian testily. "Your crude methods of beatings and threats are good enough to extract first confessions, but they are never any guarantee that a prisoner will not retract afterwards; and to produce a physical wreck in open court invalidates the whole object of such operations."

"Of course, Comrade; of course!" Frček immediately became submissive and fawning. "I am well aware that the M.V.D. are more skilled in these matters than my people. The results achieved by their psychologists with the aid of the new drugs, and physical treatments that leave no trace, were wonderfully successful in the trial of Slánský and his thirteen fellow traitors last year. It is only that as a young Soviet Republic, we are in much greater need of further demonstrations of that kind than they are in the U.S.S.R.; so I was hoping . . ."

With an impatient gesture, Gorkov interrupted, "Had you allowed me to continue, I was about to say that to ensure the success of such trials it is necessary first to destroy the prisoner's mind, then build him up as a new, docile personality. That can be done only in Moscow, and it may take two or three months; but the sooner you send them off the sooner they will be mentally conditioned, and in a fit state to be returned here for trial."

"Ah!" Frček beamed. "Forgive me if I jumped to a wrong conclusion; but it was in my eagerness to take advantage of any event which may help to enlighten the people of Prague."

Gorkov said sourly, "That I understand. From the beginning the whole country has shown a most stubborn resistance. Our task is like beating upon a rubber sponge. It is not enough to crush it; no means should be neglected which will help to lessen the qualities of recoil that are inherent in its nature."

After a glance at his watch, he added, "We are due at that meeting at the Hradčany at six o'clock, and it is nearly ten minutes to now. You had better get rid of these people quickly, or you will be late for it." Turning on his heel, he walked out of the room.

Frček wasted no time in obeying the orders he had been given. At his shout the three underlings returned. As they resumed their places by the prisoners, he said to Kmoch:

"Have them both taken to the basement. Get the doctor to put some stuff on her weals, then let her lie down until it is time to take them to the train. It's clear now that, as I supposed, he was telling us a tissue of lies about what happened between him and his cousin at the hotel; so teach him a little lesson by putting him in an X-cell. That will give him a taste of Moscow in advance. Telephone the station for a coach with a barred compartment to be added to the train, then make their dossiers up to date. You will accompany them yourself, taking any escort you think fit. As soon as you have delivered them send me a telegram; then report back here."

Fedora had been crouching, still half stupefied by pain, in her chair. The mark on her left cheek and jaw, where she had

6*

been slapped, stood out more vividly than ever, but her whole face now looked hot and feverish. At the urging of the wardress she stood up, and, turning her back, began to dress. As anything tight would have aggravated her whip-sores, she made no attempt to put on her belt or brassiere; but with the wardress' help she wriggled into her slip and frock, then tucked the other things and her long-strapped satchel bag under her arm.

As she moved a little unsteadily towards the door Nicholas stepped forward and said, "Do lean on my shoulder."

She laid her hand only lightly on his forearm, and gave him a faint smile. "Thanks; but I'm not all that bad. No bones broken, anyway."

Frček was already collecting the papers that he would require for his meeting, but he looked up to snarl with sudden venom, "If the Russians don't break them, I'll break them for both of you after your trial. This pretty plot of yours very nearly resulted in my having to make an explanation to the Kremlin, and I'll not forget that in a hurry."

Both of them half turned and caught a glimpse of the implacable hatred in the pasty moon-like face, then they were hurried from the room. But it was neither of broken bones nor devilish ingenuities practised by unscrupulous psychologists in Moscow that Nicholas was thinking as they were taken down in the lift; he was wondering what an X-cell was like. Five minutes later he knew.

It was virtually an upright box three feet square and five feet high. He could neither sit, lie nor stand upright in it, and it had eight glaring electric lights covered with unbreakable glass— one in each corner of the ceiling and one in each corner of the floor.

For a few minutes he stood with bent neck, his rumpled red hair pressed against the ceiling; then he managed to get himself into a slightly less uncomfortable position by sliding his feet forward to the door and leaning his back against the wall. In that way he could just keep his head clear, but he soon found the relentless glare of the lights almost unbearable. Even when he shut his eyes it came through their lids as a steady pink glow.

Only by keeping his hands over them could he get relief; and with his palms pressed to his face, he tried to think.

That morning he had been in the position of a man convinced against his will, and so 'of the same opinion still'. Fedora's talk with Jirka the barman, their confinement to the hotel, the microphone in the bedroom, the things that Fedora had said there, her bold arrangements with the Chef for their escape, and their interview with Frček, had all proclaimed a state of things which it seemed impossible to explain away. Yet the convictions of a life-time had died hard in him.

He had argued to himself that, although forced upon him by circumstances as a temporary ally, Fedora was in fact the enemy of all he stood for. He had discounted her attitude as inspired by bitter, unreasoning hatred of the régime, and decided that nine-tenths of the things she said about it were baseless accusations concocted by a wild imagination and neurotic urge to dramatize every situation in which they found themselves. For the rest, he had reasoned that the police in any country were justified in taking strong measures to check the type of movement in which Fedora obviously played an active part; and that Frček's attitude could not be taken as evidence that the People's Government was a mockery controlled by evil men who were exploiting the masses, and ruling by tyranny, injustice and torture.

But his experiences in the past hour had stripped from him every vestige of belief he had had in the splendid fellowship of Communism. Its vaunted 'Welfare State', in which all men were free, equal and cared for by a paternal government truly representative of the workers, had proved a ghastly myth. Frček's threats of the morning had not been a justified bluff to extract information from prisoners suspected of criminal activities; they had turned out to be a terrible reality. Moreover, it had emerged that he was not just a police chief, but a Minister; and to suppose that the government was ignorant of the horrors that went on at his headquarters was unthinkable. Still worse, it was not the People's Government of Czechoslovakia alone that had fallen into evil hands. Comrade Gorkov had made it clear beyond all doubt that Frček and his colleagues were only puppets controlled by Moscow; and the cold little Russian's terrible intentions towards the prisoners made even Frček's physical brutalities pale.

Nicholas groaned aloud as he thought how often he had argued that the Soviet trials of saboteurs were not ingeniously stage-managed affairs, and that the confessions made at them were in fact the outcome of prisoners having, after long free discussions, at last been brought to 'see the Light', so that they willingly testified their past errors to the world. Now, he knew the awful truth.

He recalled a book that he had read by Paul Galico called *Trial by Terror*. He had thought the scenes in the Paris newspaper office a brilliant piece of work, but had been both indignant and amused by those describing the treatment of the central character when, through his own fault, he had found himself in a Soviet prison. The idea of putting a tin pail over a man's head, and beating on it with a broom-stick until the drumming drove him to the verge of madness, had seemed a wickedly skilful piece of imagination. Now, with fear gripping at his heart, he wondered if that was one of the 'physical treatments that leave no trace' that would be inflicted on him in Moscow. Gorkov had spoken of destroying the prisoner's mind, then building him up as a new, docile personality. That was exactly the theme of Paul Galico's book. It couldn't be true. It was too terrible; and yet . . .

His arms were aching from holding his hands up over his face. For a few moments he removed them, but the glare was so blinding that he could not stand it for long. Taking out his big silk handkerchief, he folded it into a bandage and tied it over his eyes. That helped a little, but the light still penetrated through the fabric; so to give each arm a rest in turn he pressed the bandage over his eyes first with one hand for a while, then with the other.

It was stiflingly hot in the coffin-like cell, and his mind began to wander. The more he thought of his situation, the more fantastic and improbable it seemed. How could it possibly have come about that he—Nicholas Novák, a quiet-living, unadventurous professor of Political Economics at Birmingham University, an ardent supporter of the Peace Council, and a champion of Socialism in its most advanced form—should find himself imprisoned under a People's Government on a charge of being a British secret agent?

The term switched his mind to another book, and one he had read quite recently. It was about a thoroughly unscrupulous character who, between nights of love-making with a beautiful Countess, went about the continent murdering innocent policemen and others, because it chanced that their duties caused them to stand in the way of British objectives during the last war. He was instructed and abetted by a ferocious and evil old millionaire whose object in life seemed to be to force the domination of British imperialism upon as many countries as possible. The two of them drank champagne out of tankards while they glorified the sort of reactionary sentiments that had been current in Disraeli's day. They were absurd and unreal, and wickedly calculated to inspire anti-social ideas in the young. There had been a scene in which the central character, who rejoiced in the unlikely name of Gregory Sallust, had been present, although a civilian, at Dunkirk. He had refused to be taken off with the army because his old crony had charged him with some private murder assignment, and he had ranted to himself that he could not go home because it was his job to 'seek out and destroy the enemy'. That was just the sort of claptrap to inflame youngsters with the narrow nationalism and hide-bound patriotism that begot future wars.

As a picture of a British secret agent, Nicholas thought it might easily bear some resemblance to the truth; and here was he, charged with being that sort of revolting buffoon. Incredulity piled on incredulity; he was at that very moment in just the kind of situation in which that licensed thug had landed himself again and again in his unrelenting war against the Nazis. But he always argued, bluffed, laughed or killed his way out, and Nicholas saw no possible prospect of doing any of these things.

The book had been given to him by Wendy, otherwise he would never have read it. He remembered the name of the man

who had written it now; it had been by a blood-lusting blimp
named Dennis Wheatley. Wendy had said that he was the
family's favourite author. Of course it was just the sort of dangerous tripe that would appeal to a man like John Stevenson.
He and his friend Benjamin Salting-Sala flatly refused to accept
the term 'Commonwealth of Nations' as a substitute for 'The
Empire'. They opposed equality of status and self-government
for native races, because they believed that British governors,
residents and judges administered the territories in which they
functioned without any thought of lining their own pockets,
whereas the native politicians who would have replaced them
were mostly self-seeking crooks. Having stolen the poor Per-
sians' oil for half a century, they would have continued to take it
by force if they had had their way. They still believed in sending
battleships to 'see things done'. They even refused to kow-tow
to their friends the Americans, and wanted the Mediterranean to
remain forever a lake under the White Ensign. If they could,
they would have painted every land on the map bright red. No
wonder they liked the drum-banging Wheatley with his aged
flag-waving V.C. millionaire, and the trigger-happy, stick-at-
nothing Gregory Sallust.

And Wendy, his adorable Wendy, was as bad as the rest. One
evening he had asked her what her most cherished beliefs were,
and she replied quite simply:

"I believe in God, the Queen and England."

He had been so taken aback that he had not known what to
say. It seemed incredible to him that any intelligent person could
hold such outworn tenets in this modern age, much less un-
ashamedly proclaim them. God did not exist, the Monarchy
was an anachronism, and England a greater bar even than the
United States to World Federation. He had not expected her to
say anything about Social Justice, Equality, or the Welfare State,
but she had not even included Freedom, Liberty, Democracy.
Perhaps, he thought, she had the hopelessly erroneous idea that
all those were embodied in her three hoary old images. He could
only hope so, and had quickly turned the conversation to tennis.

Now, in acute discomfort, sweating from the heat, and panting heavily to absorb enough oxygen, his bemused mind continued to revolve round Wendy. He wondered what she was doing at that moment. Guessing the time to be about half past six, it seemed pretty certain that she would be drinking a cocktail, either at home or with friends. Knowing all her arrangements, he sought to get nearer the probability by working out what day of the week it was. The result seemed unbelievable. Not until he had checked through what had been happening to him three times could he fully convince himself that it was still only Saturday.

It seemed days ago since he had landed at the airport that morning, and weeks since he had left England. Yet barely thirty hours had elapsed since he had had that miserable quarrel with Wendy after his morning class in Birmingham. The small hands of the world's clocks had not even travelled twice round their dials since he had arrived at the Russell to keep his appointment with Bilto. Less than twenty-two hours ago he had not had so much as an inkling of this frightful nightmare into which he had been drawn. He had not yet been made the confidant of Bilto's awful secret; he had never seen Fedora, or known that such people as Vaněk, Kmoch, Frček and Gorkov existed.

That his circumstances, his beliefs, and his future prospects could all have been so unthinkably altered in so short a time seemed yet one more incredulity on top of all the others; but that was just as incontestable as the fact that without trial he had been condemned to occupy a cell which meant torture of a kind that no medieval tyrant had thought of.

With swimming senses his mind groped round Bilto. From what Gorkov had said it was clear that Bilto had not panicked; but, as he had at first supposed might prove the case, had assumed that the Russians had refrained from picking him up for good reasons of their own. He had simply lain doggo. And now they had got in touch with him again. Short of another intervention by fate, he and the atomic secrets that he carried were to be flown into Prague to-morrow, Sunday, night.

Nicholas passed a damp hand over his sweating forehead. From that moment in the Palm Court of the Russell, when he had dismissed his last scruples about attempting to prevent Bilto from leaving England, he had had few doubts about the rightness of his action. During the morning his conviction in that rightness had subconsciously strengthened. Now, he felt that not to have made the attempt would have been positively criminal.

He needed no telling that the world and nearly all its peoples were in a most hideous mess, and that the majority of them were further from enjoying a stable government, under which they could hope to live out their lives in peace and security, than they had been for many decades past. He had cherished the belief that a new era of enlightenment was dawning in those countries where the workers had thrown off the shackles imposed upon them for centuries by the triple tyrannies of birth, money and superstition. Now he knew that was not true.

People like John Stevenson might angrily declare that in twenty years 'a lot of dirty snivelling little bureaucrats', incapable of appreciating the grandeur of their inheritance, had robbed the British people of nine-tenths of the liberties that it had taken their forefathers six centuries of courageous endeavour, and sometimes martyrdom, to win. The fact remained that such glimmerings of individual freedom and protection from oppression as still lit the darkened world did not glow in any newly-fashioned neon lights behind the Iron Curtain, but from the little home fires maintained through many generations by the ancient civilizations of the West.

Through a mist of pain, exhaustion and semi-suffocation, Nicholas came dimly to realize that however justified the fight against privilege, capitalism and a narrow nationalism might be, until some better way of life developed from them it must be the first duty of all who knew the truth to protect those hearth fires of the West from being trampled into extinction.

To reach that final conclusion took him a long time. He had not wound up his watch that morning, and when he glanced at it he found that it had stopped at twenty past four; so he could get no idea how long he had been in the cell, but it seemed an eternity. The sweat was running down him in rivulets, his cramped position made his muscles ache intolerably, and from lack of air his head felt as though it was about to burst. Gradually his mind lost all coherence, and ranged without direction over a score of subjects having little or no connection with one another; but every now and again it drifted back to Wendy, Frček, Bilto or Fedora.

At length the heat and exhaustion overcame him. Automatically his limbs relaxed and he slid down on to the floor in a senseless heap. His last conscious thought was that if he could live the past twenty-four hours over again, fond as he was of Bilto he would have gone straight to the nearest police station and had him arrested.

When he came to, rough hands were hauling him from the cell. Two warders half dragged, half carried him along the corridor and into a wash place. There he slid to his knees and leaned against the wall, gasping in the welcome cooler air. Without warning one of the men threw half a bucket of cold water over his head. Gasping, he staggered to his feet, once more fully conscious.

They let him dry his face on a towel, then hurried him along to the basement office. Fedora was just outside it with the wardress. The side of her face which had been slapped was still red, but she was standing erect instead of with her shoulders hunched, and looked in an altogether better state than when he had last seen her.

Raising a smile, he said, "Congratulations on the way you have pulled yourself together. I'd never have believed anyone could look so good after what you've been through."

She made a little grimace. "Oh, it's just part of the service. The best of attention and the most expensive drugs without a penny to pay. The idea is that the quicker they repair the damage the sooner they can start in on you again without the risk of your passing out and bringing a premature end to their fun. But you don't look too good."

"I'll be all right as soon as I get a bit more air," he assured her. "But they kept me all night in a cell like a coffin and as hot as an oven."

Fedora smiled. "I expect it felt that long, but actually we've been down here only just over two hours."

At that moment Kmoch came out of the office and signed to them to enter the waiting lift. In the hall he collected two State policemen. One was a blue-eyed ruddy-faced young man, the other was older and had a black moustache. The little party went out to the street. A six-seater car was waiting for them. Kmoch made Fedora and Nicholas sit in the back, he and the black-moustached man took the seats opposite them, and the youngster got in next to the driver. As they settled themselves Kmoch produced his automatic from the pocket of his long overcoat, and said to Nicholas:

"Please observe that I can fire at you without any risk of injuring my men in front. If you make any attempt to escape I shall blow your knee-cap off. That will not prevent your appearing for your trial, but it will be a long time before you forget the pain that such a wound causes."

Fedora had lowered herself carefully into her place, but as the car started off she jerked up her head with a grimace of pain, then sat forward holding on to the strap so that her sore back should not come in contact with the cushions.

Nicholas had already decided that to try to escape would be hopeless, and as he looked about him he saw from a clock in a church tower that it was just after eight. It occurred to him that it was already past his usual supper time. Apart from the bowl of stew at the airport he had had nothing to eat all day, so he now felt distinctly hungry and began to hope that they would be given some sort of meal on the train.

The city looked very peaceful in the soft evening light, and except for the still overloaded trams, there was very little traffic in the streets though which they passed; so the police chauffeur drove swiftly. His klaxon wailed and the car sped through a big square to the south of the Přikopy. Beyond the square they shot down a narrow turning. A hundred yards along it the klaxon wailed again. A heavy lorry had emerged just ahead of them from a side-street.

Suddenly there came a shriek of brakes, shouts and a violent crash. The car stopped dead. Nicholas and Fedora were thrown forward on top of the two men opposite. She screamed as the unexpected movement lacerated the weals on her back, then fell upon Kmoch. Nicholas' right hand landed on the policeman's shoulder, and with it he thrust himself away.

Next second a single shot rang out. A man who was standing on the pavement had fired through a window of the car. It starred as the bullet made a neat round hole in its centre. The policeman with the black moustache gulped and clawed at his neck. It was spurting blood. His eyes bulged, then he slid over sideways.

Kmoch was yelling curses as he tried to thrust Fedora from on top of him. He had managed to get out his gun and was pointing it under her arm in the direction of Nicholas's legs. Nicholas made a grab at the pistol. As he seized it the weapon spurted flame and three shots crashed out from it. His wrist was seared but the bullets missed him, and smacked into the leather-covered cushioning behind his back. Forcing the pistol down, so that it pointed at the floor of the car, he strove to tear it from Kmoch's grasp. Suddenly Kmoch gave an awful scream and let go. Fedora had got her hands up and plunged her thumbs down into his brown spaniel-like eyes.

While they were still struggling two more single shots rang out; then came a burst of fire from a sten gun. Police whistles were blowing and people shouting. One glance through the glass partition of the car showed Nicholas that nothing was to be feared from the men in front. As the car hit the lorry the driver's head had shot forward and cracked the wind-screen. He lay slumped over the wheel of the car. The young policeman with the ruddy complexion had attempted to get out, but had been shot as his foot touched the road. He had fallen backwards and lay writhing half in and half out of the driver's box. The civilian who had fired from the pavement through the window of the car was now under cover in a shop doorway. He was yelling at the prisoners to jump out and run for it.

Nicholas needed no urging. Wrenching open the door of the car, he stumbled over the policeman who had been shot in the neck, and landed in the road. Turning, he grasped Fedora by the arm and pulled her after him.

For a moment he paused there, uncertain which way to take. Behind him the groans of the ruddy-faced youngster mingled with Kmoch's screams. To his right the big lorry blocked the view. Its driver was crouching beside its bonnet, a pistol in his hand. At that second he raised it and fired at someone Nicholas could not see. To his right, towards the square, the street had been blocked by another lorry; but there was no one in its driver's cab, and near it a still figure sprawled in the gutter. Three policemen emerged, running from behind it. All of them were holding their pistols at the ready. They shouted in chorus at Nicholas and Fedora:

"Stay where you are! Put up your hands!"

The sten-gun opened again with a staccato clatter. It was being fired from the first-floor window of a corner house over-looking the crossroads at which the crash had occurred. The foremost of the running policemen stopped dead in his tracks, threw up his hands, gave at the knees and crumpled up within a few feet of the dead lorry-driver. As the other two dashed for cover the man in the doorway ran out into the road and shouted:

"Follow me!"

Nicholas still had Fedora by the arm with his left hand; in his right he grasped Kmoch's gun. Hardly ten seconds had elapsed since they had scrambled from the car. Turning as one, they ran after their rescuer. He dived round the corner of the alley from which the lorry used for the ambush had come. As they followed several bullets whizzed past their heads and thudded into the lorry's canvas hood, but once round the corner they were tem-porarily safe.

Behind them the firing continued. It had roused the whole quarter. Some people were running to get clear of the danger area, others had flung up windows and were leaning from them, shouting questions at one another to find out what had started the battle.

The fresh air during the drive from the headquarters had com-pletely restored Nicholas, but he was worried about Fedora.

The man ahead was running fast, and knowing what she must be suffering from her recent whipping, he feared she might not be able to stay the pace. Glancing at her, he cried:

"Can you manage to keep it up?"

"Don't worry!" she panted. "I'll run till I drop! Better to die of heart-strain than be recaptured."

They had covered about sixty yards. Their rescuer was leading by some fifteen feet. He was within that distance of another crossroads. Suddenly two policemen, attracted by the sounds of firing, came charging round the corner towards them. Almost simultaneously shots crashed out from two directions. The man ahead pulled up with a jerk, his gun clattered to the pavement, and he grabbed at his right arm. One of the policemen seemed to rise on tiptoe, then he executed a graceful pirouette and fell flat on his face in the road. The other fired again, but still clutching his arm, the wounded man jumped sideways; then, with extraordinary agility, took a flying leap through the open doorway of a small restaurant that occupied the corner of the street.

The remaining policeman and Nicholas were left face to face with only about six paces between them. Never before in his life had Nicholas handled an automatic, much less fired one; but already he had instinctively pointed it at the policeman's body. He pressed the trigger and it went off. The policeman's mouth opened, he swayed drunkenly, then fell to his knees; but he did not collapse. He had been in the act of lifting his gun to fire a third time. As he was hit his arm had fallen to his side; but now he raised it again, although slowly as though the weapon he held was very heavy.

Nicholas stared into the kneeling man's eyes. The very idea that he might have killed a fellow human being shocked him to the depths of his conscience. In spite of all that had happened —the ambush, the shooting, their rescue and the danger they were still in—it never even occurred to him to fire again. In another moment he would most probably have been choking out his own life, had not Fedora intervened. Dashing forward she kicked the policeman in the face. His hand swung sideways and the gun exploded; the bullet shattered the plate-glass win-

dow of the restaurant. He gave a choking cry and rolled over
dead.

It was now Fedora who seized Nicholas' arm and dragged him
forward. "Hurry!" she cried. "Hurry! or we won't get away
before the squad-cars come on the scene!"

Stuffing the gun into his jacket pocket, he ran on with her
round the corner. They crossed the street diagonally and dived
down another turning. Before they were half way along it they
heard the wailing klaxons of the squad-cars behind them. Jerking
on Nicholas' arm to slow his pace, Fedora gasped:

"We must walk now! If they spot us running they'll be on us
like a ton of bricks."

They covered another thirty yards, then a klaxon wailed
ahead of them. Next moment a squad-car pulled up at the far
end of the street along which they were advancing. Four policemen tumbled out of it. The street was quite a long one, so they
were some distance off; but they spread out across the road,
turning back the few pedestrians who were coming towards
them, and barring it to traffic. It was useless for the fugitives to
retrace their steps, as the whole area in which the ambush had
taken place was now swarming with police.

Desperately, Fedora looked round. A little way further on
there was a neon-light sign, as yet unlit. It outlined a windmill,
and the Czech words above it were the equivalent of 'Le Moulin
Rouge'. Fedora nodded towards it.

"We'll go in there! Our best chance of escaping recognition
lies in mingling with a crowd."

Obediently he walked forward with her; but he was still
thinking of the awful staring eyes of the policeman who had
tried to shoot him, and he muttered:

"You saved my life just now! I almost wish you hadn't. I
killed that man. He was only doing his duty. It is a frightful
thing to have done."

She shook his arm impatiently. "Don't be a fool! This isn't
England, where the police are honest decent men. There are
no Czechs in our police-force now who haven't volunteered
of their own free will to take orders from the Russians. Every

one of them is a Com. They are the dregs of our race, ex-convicts and criminals of all kinds. There is no law for them, except obedience to their bosses; and they are all stinking with money that they have blackmailed out of shopkeepers and house-holders for small breaches of the regulations. You wouldn't spend a sleepless night if you had trodden on a slug in a garden, would you?"

As she finished speaking they were within a few yards of the entrance of the Moulin Rouge. An elderly, lethargic-looking doorman dressed in a shabby uniform said, "Welcome, Comrades; it's a good show to-night," in a tone which implied that he couldn't have cared less; and they went inside.

There was no entrance fee to pay and no pretension to smartness about the place; no welcoming cloak-room attendants and no semi-nude young ladies carrying trays with cigarettes, chocolates and sprays of flowers for sale. They walked down a broad, empty corridor and entered a large, lofty room.

It was the type of *nachtlokal* which is to be found in every central European city, and in the old days combined the functions of music-hall, restaurant, dance place and rendezvous for prostitutes. The raised stage at one end of it was large enough to hold a score of girls or a team of acrobats, a small space in the middle of the floor was left free for couples to dance in between the acts, and rows of small tables were set round it; behind them in a horseshoe were ranged a double tier of private boxes.

However, it was obvious that the place had degenerated sadly since Austrian nobles and rich Czech industrialists had been its principal patrons. Even the poor lighting failed to disguise the fact that it had not been painted for a decade and that the gilding on the scroll-work of the boxes had become tarnished. None of the customers was in evening dress, no food was being served and the stage show in progress was most decorous, as it consisted of a dozen peasants in traditional costume doing a village dance. The only things that linked it with its past were that drinking was permitted and that some of the tables were occupied by very seedy-looking women whose profession was obvious.

A bald-headed waiter with mean little eyes shuffled forward, and at a word from Fedora showed them into a lower-tier box. Without waiting for any order, or to perform any service, he closed the door behind them, and Fedora whispered:

"Occupying a box means we've got to pay for champagne, whether we drink it or not. I expect it's pretty filthy, but you might open it and see."

There was a bottle on the table, in an ice-bucket that contained no ice, and two thick tumblers. As Nicholas picked the bottle up he said uneasily, "I haven't got any Czech money."

"Don't worry about that, I have." She put up a hand and began to feel about under her beret among the tight plaits of hair. "That ghoul of a wardress went through my bag, of course, but she didn't get anything for her pains except small change. After our midday interview with sweetie-pie Frček I took the opportunity to hide the few Czech notes I brought with me from London."

Nicholas eased the cork out of the bottle and half filled the two tumblers. As the hour was still early, and the place had not been open long, the wine had not had time to lose entirely the chill of the cellar. It was Hungarian Sparkling Samorodny, and anyone accustomed to drinking the finer *cuvées* of the famous French houses would have taken a poor view of it. But Nicholas did not know one brand of champagne from another, and his two hours in the X-cell had given him an appalling thirst; so he drank it down gratefully.

He had only just set down his glass when he saw a woman come in. She was wearing a white straw hat decorated with imitation cornflowers. After a furtive glance round she sidled up to the box in which they were sitting. It was raised only a foot or so above the level of the main floor, so she could lean an elbow on its edge. As she turned towards them he looked down into her face. It was not old in years; she was probably no more than thirty, but it was loose-mouthed, pouch-eyed, and riddled with debauchery. There could be little doubt how she scraped a living.

In a swift whisper, she said, "I saw you come in. The police are questioning people outside and asking if they've seen a couple like you two. Old Jan, the doorman, is all right. He'll keep mum; but you had better pass the waiter something to shut his mouth. I came in to give you the tip-off, because I heard one of the top Coms tell some of his boys to run through this place—and they'll be in here in a minute."

CHAPTER XIV

NIGHT-LIFE UNDER THE SOVIETS

It was a very nasty moment. Nicholas was conscious of a horrid empty feeling in the pit of his stomach. Less than fifteen minutes ago they had been Kmoch's prisoners and on their way to Moscow. In the past few hours he had lost all his illusions about people receiving justice in any of the Communist-controlled countries. He had had all the evidence he needed that overnight he had been plunged back into a way of life in which barbarities were practised that had never been equalled in the Dark Ages. Even Ivan the Terrible had never included among his tortures a body of men charged with destroying men's minds and robbing them of their personalities.

As yet he had hardly had time to appreciate his rescue from that appalling fate; now he was threatened with it again. Desperately he looked round for some side-entrance to the hall by which they might escape, or a place where they could hide during the police raid that the prostitute had warned them was about to take place.

The blood had drained from Fedora's thin cheeks, but she did not lose her head. Crumpling up one of the notes she had just taken from her hair, she pressed it into the woman's hand, and said:

"Thanks, sister. We will be in greater danger if we leave our box, so will you see the waiter for us and try to square him with this? And . . . and, could you possibly lend me your hat!"

The gaily-dressed peasants on the stage were stamping and whirling through their dance; the attention of the audience was concentrated on them. The lights were dim and neither of the adjacent boxes had yet been taken. After a quick look round, to make certain that she was not observed, the woman took off the white straw with the cornflowers and slipped it over the edge of the box. Not only her mouth but her tired eyes smiled, as she murmured:

"It's my new one, for the summer; but you're welcome. If they don't spot you, when you've done with it leave it in the back of the box. I'll fix the waiter, then I shall make myself scarce; but I'll come back for it before the place closes. Good luck, dearie."

As she sidled away Fedora whispered, "Thanks, sister; and bless you." Then she turned to Nicholas.

"They will have the back entrance covered by now, so any attempt to get out will be hopeless. But they can't know for certain that we are in here. If the doorman and the waiter don't split, the Coms may content themselves with a quick look round, and not bother to have everyone paraded on the dance floor. Anyhow, we've just got to stick it out and keep our fingers crossed. If only this damn' thing still works we may escape recognition."

As she spoke she pressed a small button underneath the edge of the table. To Nicholas' amazement he felt the floor slowly sink beneath them. The table, the small couch behind it on which they were sitting, and an oval of floor nearly as large as the area occupied by the box were all supported on a single hydraulic pillar, making it like an open goods-lift.

On the continent, unlike in p⸺tanical Britain, there have never been any regulations limiting the width of curtains in private boxes, or other devices which could be used to screen their occupants from view; so that couples in them can, if they wish, ignore the show to indulge in more intimate amusements.

Had Nicholas been older when he was in Prague before, and owned the money to visit such places, he would no doubt have come across this ingenious and amusing idea of supper tables which could be made to sink below the level of the floor; as it was, he could only exclaim at this apparent miracle and wonder when it would stop.

The lift brought them to rest about six feet down, so that they were now in an almost dark pit with their heads about five feet below the level of the edge of the box.

Pulling off her beret, Fedora thrust it at Nicholas, and said, "Here, put this on to hide your red hair." Then she adjusted the flashy white straw so that it hid her silvery-blonde coronet of plaits. It was at that moment that the band abruptly ceased playing and the lights went up.

They could now see one another clearly in the glow coming from above, and she smiled at him a little wickedly. "I'm afraid you've got to play the he-man now and do your stuff. Try to imagine that we're back in the bad old days, and that you're an Austrian Count supping with the prettiest girl in the chorus."

Nicholas grinned. The tumbler of champagne he had drunk was beginning to have its effect, the danger they were in gave him a sense of recklessness, and he had not forgotten that only a few hours ago she had called him a prude. Without the slightest hesitation he put his arms round her, pulled her into a tight embrace and kissed her full on the mouth.

She shuddered, let him kiss her for a moment, then gave a low groan. In some surprise he took his mouth from hers and asked, "What's the matter. Didn't you really mean me to kiss you?"

"Of course I did, silly," she answered. "But it's my back, and my poor bottom. Hauling me into your arms like that hurt frightfully."

"I'm so sorry," he whispered. "I'll never forget what that swine did to you; but it had slipped my memory for the moment." Holding her more carefully, he kissed her again, then they snuggled down together and she began to return his kisses.

As they sat there embraced, anyone looking over the edge of

the box could have seen only the white straw, the beret, and parts of their arms and shoulders. They formed a tableau of silent rapture, which was just the sort of thing that a snooper peering down into the shaft would have expected to see.

For a good ten minutes they remained locked in one another's arms, then the lights went out and the band started to play again. They had not even known the moment at which a plain-clothes man, holding a pistol ready in his hand, had glanced down at the white straw, decided that its wearer could not be the woman he and his fellow searchers were after, and with a fleeting wish that he was off duty so that he could be making love to his own girl, dismissed them from his mind.

When darkness enveloped them again they cautiously drew apart, but Nicholas had one of Fedora's hands in his and he continued to hold it. She gave his fingers a slight squeeze, and said:

"You know, if I wasn't in love with someone else, I believe I could like you quite a lot."

He smiled at her. "That goes for me too."

"In that case we had better make the best of one another." She let her head fall back on to his shoulder. "I'm feeling pretty part-worn, and it's rather a comfort to have you hold me instead of sitting bolt upright, or leaning my wretched back against the sofa."

He put his arms round her again and laid his cheek against hers. "Yes; it gives me a more relaxed feeling too. Besides, if anyone pops his head over the edge of the box we'll be better placed for going back into action."

"I think the danger is past for the moment. We'll have to stay here for an hour or two, though, until it is dark."

"What do you think our prospects are of getting away?"

"Not too bad, if only we are not challenged in the street. My friends in the Legion should be able to hide us and smuggle us out of the country."

"I take it that it was Legion men who rescued us. But what beats me is how they knew we'd be at a certain place at a certain time, and so were able to make arrangements for the ambush."

"They must have been tipped off by someone at Frček's

headquarters. The police and warders are all swine, but some of the secretaries and lift-girls are good types. Theirs is a lousy assignment, as they have to sleep with whoever takes a fancy to them; but through them there's not much that the Legion doesn't get to know. One of them must have got a message out that we were being sent to Moscow on the evening train. The rest would have been simple."

"I suppose so—given the guts," Nicholas remarked, thinking of the dead lorry driver and the other man who had been wounded, and perhaps afterwards captured. "They must owe you quite a bit, to have fought a pitched battle with the police like that, in order to rescue you."

"I've helped to get a few people away now and then," she admitted modestly, "but all those who belong to the Legion must always be prepared to risk their lives, even if they have never met the brother or sister on whose account they are ordered to risk them. Otherwise they would never be accepted into the Legion to start with."

"Why is it called that?"

"Because it is the successor to the famous Czechoslovak Legion that fought under General Gaida in the First World War."

Somehow Nicholas did not like to confess to Fedora that he was a Pacifist, and, having a prejudice against even reading about wars, knew next to nothing about those which had taken place before his own time; so he said truthfully, "I remember my father telling me something about that, but I'm afraid I've forgotten the details."

Starting up, she exclaimed in a shocked voice, "Forgotten! Since you have Czech blood in your veins I'm amazed that you're not ashamed to admit it."

"It's a long time since I lost my father," Nicholas hastened to excuse himself, "and I was brought up as an Englishman. But I'd like to hear about it. Please tell me."

Apparently mollified, Fedora resettled her head on his shoulder. "Well, anyway, you must know that in August 1914 all our troops formed part of the Austro-Hungarian Army.

Many of them hated the Austrians and the old Emperor so much that as soon as the war started they went over to the Russians. Several divisions went over complete with their bag, baggage and officers; then as the war went on many thousands more allowed themselves to be captured. It was from them that the Legion was formed, to fight with the Russians for the liberation of Czechoslovakia."

"I remember now," Nicholas put in. "They got caught up in the Russian revolution, didn't they?"

"That's right. By the spring of 1918 there was a body of our troops 55,000 strong, in the middle of European Russia. Austria still held Czechoslovakia, and the Bolsheviks were trying to make peace with the Central Powers. The Bolshies tried to get our men to join the revolution and shoot their officers; but they wouldn't. They wanted to go on fighting for the Allies; but the trouble was that without proper supplies and munitions they couldn't form a front on their own, and there seemed no way to get them out of Russia. Then some bright boy at Versailles suggested that if they would march to Vladivostok, they could be taken off there and shipped right round to Europe to fight on the Western Front. Their officers agreed, so the Legion set out on its first great march. By then all Russia was in a state of anarchy, and not a day passed without them being attacked for one reason or another; but they crossed the Urals and fought their way through 5,000 miles of the worst country in the world, to the Pacific."

Nicholas had poured out the rest of the champagne, and Fedora paused a moment to drink some, then she went on, "By the time they got to Vladivostok the whole situation had changed. The Allies were getting on top in the West, and reckoned that they could finish the Germans without any help from the Legion; but they had come to regard the Bolshies as a lot of mad dogs who must be destroyed. So instead of bringing the Legion back by sea to Europe they asked that it should remain in Russia to fight the Reds. As an inducement they offered to recognize Czechoslovakia as an independent state when they had finally defeated the Central Powers. That was the thing nearest the heart of every one of our men, so they turned round and started on the second half of their 10,000 mile march. Fighting all the way, without support, reinforcements or supplies, they recrossed the vast Siberian wastes and the Urals, until at last, with hardly a rag of their uniforms left, their proud columns re-entered their homeland. The Allies kept their word; the Legion had earned Czechoslovakia her independence."

Fedora broke off again, then her low voice came with a ring of pride. "It was one of the greatest military feats that the world has ever known. Its aim was to bring freedom to our people, and it could only have been accomplished by a combination of courage and discipline. That is why we call ourselves 'The Legion', and we endeavour to prove worthy of our predecessors."

For all his ingrained Pacifist outlook, Nicholas could not help being impressed, and said, "Those original Legionnaires must have been darn' good soldiers; but I think the crowd to which you belong even braver, because they have to work alone and in secret. Are there many of you?"

"Yes; several thousand. There is hardly a village in the country now that is not organized to rise at a given signal. The only depressing thing is that until the West is strong enough to back us with active support, and shows its willingness to do so, we dare not give it."

"Was that poor woman who lent you the hat a Legionnaire?" Nicholas asked.

Fedora raised her eyebrows in surprise. "Not as far as I know. What leads you to think she might be?"

"Well, for one thing, the way she took a chance on being nabbed in order to help us; and for another, your calling her 'sister'."

"Oh, you don't have to be a Legionnaire to take a hand against the Coms. In these days it has become second nature to nearly everyone outside the Party and their hangers-on to throw gravel in the works at every opportunity. As for my calling her 'sister', why not? If I had offered to buy the hat from her she would have felt most terribly hurt, so the best way I could show my appreciation was to let her know that I regarded her as just another woman like myself, whom I would have been glad to help as she was helping me. After all, Jesus Christ put up the idea that we were all made of flesh and blood long before Karl Marx, you know."

Nicholas winced. Wendy had said very much the same thing to him only a few evenings before; but he was in no mood either to defend or to repudiate his old idol. Instead, at the thought of Wendy he said:

"The girl I'm in love with lives in Birmingham. Is your boy-friend a Czech, here in Prague, or someone in England?"

"He is in London at the moment, as far as I know."

"I'm hoping to get married. How about you?"

She rolled her head slightly in a negative motion. "I'd like to, but I don't know. It's all rather complicated, but I might be able to pull it off, if we are lucky enough to escape the Coms to-night and can get back to England."

That rang a big bell with Nicholas. Within a few minutes of having escaped from Kmoch, and while running down the street with bullets whizzing about him, he had found himself thinking, 'If only I can get away and across the frontier, I'll be able to stop Bilto. He has got to be rendered harmless somehow, even if it means having him arrested. If I get out of this gun-fight alive I must do my damnedest to get home at the earliest possible moment. If I can get back there's still a chance that I may be able to have him locked up before the Russians can send him over here.' The thought of Bilto now rang another bell, and he said:

"You know, you've never told me why you swore to my being Bilto, in front of Vaněk, when you knew darn' well I wasn't."

Fedora smiled. "For that matter, you've never told me why, in the first place, when you thought I didn't know Bilto and had mistaken you for him, you didn't attempt to disillusion me; but pretended that you were Bilto, and let me drive you off in the car instead of him."

"I did that on the spur of the moment. I'd meant to send the car away. But when it appeared that you took me for him, it seemed simpler to get rid of the car by letting you carry me off in it, than to enter into an involved explanation—particularly as I was afraid that chap by the lamp-post was a 'tec and was listening for anything we might say."

"But why did you want to get rid of the car?"

"In the hope that by messing up Bilto's arrangements I might prevent him from leaving England. He had told me less than half an hour before what he meant to do, and suddenly I decided that, somehow, I must try to stop him."

"Well, that more or less goes for me too. I'd been his sole contact for over eighteen months, but all the time I was working secretly for the other side. On every occasion that he gave me a sheet of those incredibly complicated notes and figures, I copied them out but altered them here and there before passing them on. I knew that he was boiling up to throw his hand in at Harwell and skip to this side of the Iron Curtain, but I thought I'd be able to prevent that. There was always a chance that he'd see daylight about the Coms and cool off; and, naturally, I didn't want to have a show-down with him until I absolutely had to. If it did come to having a show-down I reckoned I could scare him out of going by threatening to turn him over to Scotland Yard; but to do that was to risk his letting the Coms know that I was double-crossing them; and, without doing any crystal gazing, I had a pretty firm conviction that if that happened I could be written off as a very dead duck."

Fedora took another drink of champagne, and went on, "My plan fell down because I was by-passed. That's one of the worst things we are up against. What the top Coms will do next is always unpredictable. I don't think they suspected me, but somebody at the Russian Embassy must have decided that Bilto was ripe for a direct approach to desert to their side. Naturally it was made without my knowledge. Bilto was already toying with the idea and evidently agreed to it. Vaněk was instructed to make the arrangements. I hadn't seen Bilto for a month, and knew nothing about it at all until I was sent for, told what had been fixed up, and ordered to go and collect him."

7

"What did you intend to do if Bilto had come out of the hotel instead of myself?" Nicholas asked.

"I had decided to tell Rufus Abombo that I wanted to pick up something at my flat on the way down to Kensington; then on some pretext I'd have got Bilto to come up to it with me. I'd have come clean with Bilto then and done my utmost to persuade him to change his mind. I had known him a long time and he was fond of me. At least, I thought he was, until you told me about this old girl-friend of his that the Coms had promised to produce for him when he arrived in Prague. Anyhow, I had a gun in the flat; so if he refused to listen to me I could have held him up, made him go into the bathroom on the threat of telephoning the police if he refused, then locked him in there."

"How about Rufus, though? He was such a persistent type. You would have had a packet of trouble getting rid of him."

"Yes. That coloured boy is no fool, except for his lunatic belief that he and his half-educated, Com-financed friends could run his native Kenya better than the British. I hadn't had time to think out what to do about him, but I expect I would have managed somehow."

The disconcerting thought came to Nicholas that, until a few hours ago, he had held the same 'lunatic-belief' about Kenya and other native territories that were being 'exploited' by Europeans. Pushing it out of his mind, he said:

"I'm still not quite clear how your mind worked with regard to me."

"I shouldn't have thought that was difficult to fathom. Your likeness to Bilto is very striking, and as he had told me that he had a younger cousin I guessed at once who you were. The next thing I knew was that you were pretending to be him. I could make only the wildest guesses why; but one of them was that Bilto had suddenly got qualms of conscience and wanted a little more time to make up his mind. If that were so, he would have been afraid that if he didn't come out to the car, whoever had been sent to fetch him would come in and, perhaps, threaten him; and if he did come out to get rid of it that might mean a most unwelcome argument in the street. Therefore, he had persuaded you to go out in his place, and on some excuse or other stall whoever had been sent for him until it was too late for anyone to come and bully him into leaving that night."

"If that had been the case, he would have known that you knew I wasn't him."

"But he wasn't expecting me. I've already told you that I hadn't seen him for a month, and that the Soviet Embassy contacted him direct about going to Prague. He might have banked on their sending a Russian who had never seen him, or one who had only done so once, and so could have been fooled in the semi-darkness for half an hour by your resemblance to him. Anyhow, that was the rough theory that I formed the minute or two you were standing on the kerb; and I felt that if I was right nothing could have suited me better, so I urged you to hop in."

"I see. You thought that at Bilto's request I was getting him a bit of extra time, and that if he missed the plane you would be able to go back later and have a show-down with him; so in a way, unknown to each other, we were playing one another's game?"

"That's it," Fedora sighed. "How I wish we had realized it then. But that state of affairs didn't last long. When you asked to be driven to the Sinznicks' I knew that my theory must be more or less right, and that you were only playing for time. I guessed then that you meant to hang me up there as long as possible, then make some excuse for not leaving at all. How I thanked God that your friends happened to be people that I knew and could deal with. Half those Left-wingers and fellow-travellers are taking money off the Russians; so it was a certainty that I would be able to put the black on that wretched little man and his anarchist wife. Otherwise I might have had the very devil of a job to get you back into the car."

"But why did you want to? If you had let me remain talking to them for half an hour before coming in, it would have been too late to do anything about Bilto; so he would have missed his plane, and that was all that either of us was trying to ensure."

"Not by that time. Your impersonation had given me a golden opportunity. If I had detained Bilto at my flat, as I first intended, Rufus would have reported me to Vaněk, and he would have sent his cosh-boys along to get us. I'd have been taking a frightful gamble on being able to persuade Bilto, in half an hour, to do a disappearing trick with me; because if I'd still been there when they turned up I'd have been better off dead. And half an hour is mighty little to convert a pro-Communist into a Christian. That was possibility number one. Number two was that if I had let you remain at the Sinznicks' I would have had to report to Vaněk myself. Had I told him that you were an impostor, how could I have explained my picking you up in the first place, when he knew that I could not possibly have mistaken you for Bilto? If I had said that it was Bilto whom I had left at the Sinznicks' because he had changed his mind, Vaněk would have jumped in the car and gone out there to try to persuade you to unchange it, even if you had missed the plane for that night. You would have told him that you were Nicholas and I should have been caught out just the same. Number three was that if I hadn't gone back to report to Vaněk he would have gone to the Russell. So you see, whatever course I took I was going to be blown open. But by forcing you to go through with your imposture I reckoned that I could both have my cake and eat it. Apparently I would have done my job, but actually I would have gained a clear twelve hours at least in which to tackle Bilto and win him round."

"So you sold me down the river in order to get a free field with Bilto?"

"That's it, my dear. I didn't give a damn what happened to you if only it got me long enough to make him go back to Harwell. The nasty twist that I couldn't foresee was that Vaněk would send me here with you."

"Yes," Nicholas agreed, "and that resulted in a sort of stalemate as far as Bilto was concerned. But why couldn't you have done a bunk from the airport? You could have told Konečný that you were going to the 'Ladies' and not have come back."

"He would have said that there wasn't time, and I must wait

until I was on the plane. As it was, we caught it only by the skin of our teeth."

"You could have refused to board it."

"You were in no state to appreciate the set-up, but Rufus remained hanging about until the plane actually left, so that he could report to Vaněk that we had got you safely on board without any trouble. If I had defied orders at the last moment Konečný would have run back to tell him; then Rufus would have stuck to me like a leech. He had a car and I hadn't. As the only alternative to risking his slashing my face to ribbons with his razor, I'd have had to go back with him in it. Within an hour I'd have been in one of the private cells at the house I took you to; and when Vaněk learned that I had fooled him about your being Bilto I'd have been nice and handy for them to take me apart. As an alternative to finally being hacked into a dozen pieces suitable for putting into small weighted sacks, then feeding to the fishes in the Thames, I preferred to continue my role as your ever-loving Comrade-companion, and come on here."

"That clears up a lot of things that have been puzzling me," Nicholas said thoughtfully. "But tell me one thing more. It's clear that you know the ropes here, and you arrived still unsuspected. I'm sure that during the course of the morning you could have got away on your own. Why didn't you?"

"I really don't know. I suppose I felt that having got you into this I ought to do my best to get you out."

"No; that won't wash. You've just said that when you were planning to have me sent here on my own, you didn't give a damn what happened to me. And getting to know me better can hardly have made you regard me as a long-lost brother. This morning I nailed the Red flag to the mast and showed up as the type of chap you are fighting tooth and nail. When you found out that I was a pro-Communist I wonder you didn't throw me to the wolves and rejoice at having done so."

Fedora gave a low laugh. "You're not a Com; and the only flag you could hoist is a washed-out pink. You're just a woolly-minded Liberal with an infinite capacity for believing any lie he's told. You wouldn't hurt a fly yourself; and if people like you ever formed a government you'd be eaten up by the real Marxists in ten minutes. The only thing I hold against you is that as a teacher you are entirely lacking in responsibility. You are handing out mental Mills bombs and Sten guns to young people, some of whom may be evil enough one day to use them."

"Well, obviously that idea could not endear me to you," said Nicholas stiffly. "Why have you taken big risks yourself to stick with me and try to get me out?"

"If you must know," she replied lazily, "I suppose it is because I'm a woman. I got a silly maternal sort of feeling for you when you were sitting doped beside me in the aircraft. Then, later, it was so transparent that your head was filled with fool ideas only because you hadn't realized the truth. I didn't feel that I could possibly let you go like a lamb to the slaughter because I had made use of you. Another thing—you are quite different from most of the men I'm used to meeting, and by then I had decided that I rather liked you. I liked you all the more, too, for not making a pass at me when we were up in the hotel bedroom."

Nicholas felt insulted, awkward and flattered in turn, and muttered, "I'm afraid I can't take much credit for that. As I told you, I'm in love and engaged to be married."

"Oh, don't be stuffy!" she retorted with a little shrug. "Single, engaged, or married, there are few men of your age who wouldn't have tried their luck. That is the nature of men; and being in danger only makes them the keener to snatch at that sort of thing whenever they get the chance. But don't run away with the idea that I wanted you to. I'm in love with someone myself."

For a few moments they were silent, then she asked, "Now I no longer have to pretend that you are Bilto, what would you like me to call you?"

"My friends call me Nicky," he replied, "so I'd be glad if you would too; and I'll call you Fedora. But that's not a Czech name, is it? How did you come to be given it?"

"I was named after my maternal grandmother, who was a

Russian Baroness. She escaped from the Bolsheviks during the revolution and took refuge here."

"Then it is hardly surprising that you are such a dyed-in-the-wool reactionary. You must have imbibed it with your mother's milk."

"Don't talk like an inverted snob," she said sharply. "And don't get worried that you may have sold your spotless prole-tarian soul to the Devil by kissing me, either. I'm only one fourth noble; the rest of me is quite common Czech."

"I wasn't trying to be priggish," he protested. "I meant only that it is natural that you should always have been an anti-Communist."

"But I wasn't." Her tone had become friendly again. "At least, when I was a girl I had the same sort of advanced Socialist views that you seem to hold. It was seeing what they led to that made me change them. Even then I didn't become an active anti-Communist until 1950. My husband refused to allow me to be mixed up with his secret work, so I knew very little about the part he had played in the Legion until the Coms caught him and pulled me in. I was fool enough to think that by making a deal with them I could save him. They imagine that I believe that he is still living reasonably comfortably in prison as a hostage for my good behaviour; but I know for a fact that they did him in a few months after he was caught. By then, I'd already got in touch with the Legion myself, and I've been double-crossing the Coms ever since."

"It must have been pretty ghastly for you," Nicholas said sympathetically. "But if those old memories aren't too painful, I'd be awfully interested to hear more about your life and work."

Lifting her head from his shoulder, she shook it slowly. "No, not now. We have been down here long enough. Someone may think it queer, and tumble to the fact that we have been hiding, if we don't at least make a pretence of seeing something of the show."

As she spoke, she pressed the button beneath the table edge, and the hydraulic lift brought them slowly up to floor level.

The stage was now occupied by another set of dancers; but they too were clad in peasant costumes, and were doing a very similar dance to that of their predecessors; which caused Nicholas to remark:

"There doesn't seem to be much variety about this show."

Fedora smiled. "If you expected anything like the Folies Bergère you are going to be disappointed. The fact that the principal amusement of our rulers is making pretty women dance to their tune in private does not mean that they encourage, or even permit, anything at all suggestive in public. Leg-shows are ideologically connected with the bourgeois-capitalist exploitation of women, so barred as being both anti-social and frivolous. Even the films all have to be based on one theme— the unselfish worker who triumphs over some form of temptation and denies himself pleasure in order to produce more of something for the Soviets."

"How dreary. And does this place never put on anything but peasant dances?"

"Oh yes; physical drill displays, amateur ballet, and sketches by young would-be playwrights in praise of the Com régime. It is one of the many places that have been turned over to the Sokols for propaganda purposes and winning recruits for their organization."

Nicholas well remembered the Sokols. When he visited Prague as a boy it was the great national youth movement. Young people of both sexes and all classes had belonged to it, and their rallies had been a feature of the life of the nation. There were over 300,000 of them, and they prided themselves on their special code of honour and their physical fitness. At times as many as 12,000 Sokols gave marvellously synchronized displays of physical drill and community singing. Glancing at Fedora, he said:

"I should have thought the Sokols would have formed the best basis for the Legion, as they were such a patriotic institution and had their branches in every village as well as in all the towns."

"Is it likely?" Her low voice held a bitter note. "Do you

think the Coms are such fools as not to have realized the value of the movement? One of the very first things they did was to get hold of it and unobtrusively pervert it to their own uses. For years past thousands of helpless youngsters have been indoctrinated through it with the Com ideology, and many of them now are among our worst enemies."

After they had watched a succession of dance groups for about three-quarters of an hour, Fedora said, "It must be dark by now, so I am going to telephone. Don't worry if I'm away for quite a time."

"Why?" he queried. "Is the telephone service very bad?"

She shook her head. "No, it's not that; but I may have to telephone several people before I can fix up a hide-out for us. It is nearly three months since I've been in Prague, and a lot can happen in that time. Quite apart from Legionnaires being caught, there are the deportations. The Coms know that the old middle classes will always remain their enemies, so every month they make a swoop on several thousand unsuspecting people and send them either to the uranium mines or to Russia. One never knows from one day to the next when friends will disappear never to be heard of again."

"How terrible!" Nicholas breathed, as she stood up and left the box.

She was not, after all, away for very long; and when she returned, the bald-headed, mean-eyed old waiter followed her in. Producing her few notes, she waved a hand towards the empty bottle and asked:

"How much?"

He gave her a long, steady look. "More than you have there, Comrade. I want five thousand Koruny."

"Don't be absurd," she said with a slightly forced laugh. "That Hungarian muck isn't worth more than three hundred Koruny a bottle, and you've had a tip already. The girl who owns the hat I'm wearing took it out to you. I'm quite willing to give you another, but you must be reasonable."

With a slow unpleasant smile, he retorted, "Five thousand Koruny is reasonable, Comrade. You are the couple the Coms

7*

were after. You admitted it by sending that bit on account to keep my mouth shut. I kept it shut, but I want five thousand Koruny before you go; otherwise I'm going to open it."

"I . . . I haven't got it," she faltered. "Really I haven't. This is all I've got."

"Then you had better find some more. And don't think you can start anything, or get away without paying. There are twenty Coms sitting at tables out in front, and round about in the boxes. I've only got to give a shout, and pretend that I've just recognized you as the wanted couple. They'll nab you, or put bullets into you, long before you could reach the street."

"Listen!" she pleaded desperately. "We are in trouble; bad trouble. Please don't hold us up like this. Take all I have and let us go. My friend hasn't got any money at all on him; so with the best will in the world we can't find you any more."

"Oh, yes, you can," he replied, a gleam of cunning showing in his little eyes. "You must have friends somewhere in the city. This place won't be closing till midnight, so we've a couple of hours to go yet. One of you can go out and raise a loan. But the other stays here till the one who goes brings the money back."

Fedora's hand was resting on the edge of the table and Nicholas saw it tremble slightly, so he guessed that she was speaking the truth when she said:

"We only got into Prague to-day, and we know hardly anyone here. There is no one I could go to who is likely to have that amount of money available to lend me at this time of night."

The man's hard little eyes showed no trace of pity, and he gave a shrug. "Well, you can't say I haven't given you a fair chance. The Coms always pay a good reward to anyone who turns in people on the run. I'll claim that instead. We'll wait here till this act finishes. It won't be more than a few minutes. Then when the lights go up I'll beckon over a couple of tough Coms to take you in charge."

CHAPTER XV

THE FAITH THAT FAILED

NICHOLAS was almost choking with ill-concealed fury. To have escaped the awful prospect which had faced them only two hours ago, to have survived a street battle uninjured, to have thrown their pursuers off the track, and now to be menaced again with all the horrors that the word 'Moscow' had conjured up for him since that afternoon, seemed an unbelievably brutal twist of fate. That this new threat to their liberty, sanity and lives should have arisen solely owing to the avarice of the miserable little old man who had it in his power to betray them made it infinitely worse.

More shattering still was the thought of all that hung on the retention of their freedom. Fedora's refusal to accept the waiter's offer to go out and get the money made Nicholas suppose that her telephoning had been unsuccessful; for had she located friends who could hide them for the night, it seemed that she could have gone to them now and that, somehow, they would have managed to raise the ransom demanded. But, if she had failed, there remained Jirka at the airport.

The barman had implied that morning that, given a few hours to work in, he could get them both out through the 'funnel'. Since their escape from Kmoch, Nicholas had been counting on that. To get back to England within the next twenty-four hours was their one hope of preventing Bilto's leaving for Prague. Now that Nicholas had seen for himself the evil and ruthless régime of the Soviets, the thought of Bilto's placing his awful secrets at their disposal made him sick with horror. Their escape and the chance to stop him had seemed a deliberate dispensation of Providence. Compared with the appalling calamity which might ultimately overtake humanity as a result of Bilto's treachery if he could not be stopped, then their own lives counted for nothing. Yet it was impossible to explain to this wretched black-mailer how much hung upon their freedom from arrest. Either he would have disbelieved it, or thought that if there was any truth in it at all he might get a still bigger reward for turning them over to the police.

These thoughts rushed through Nicholas' brain in a matter of seconds, to be followed by another. Anyhow Fedora must accept the offer to go out and collect the ransom. If she could not get it that could not be helped. She, at least, would be free. Even if she had no friends to whom she could go at once, she could make her way to the airport before morning, and fix up with Jirka to get her out through the 'funnel'. Even if he could not get her out until the evening she would be in Frankfurt, or in some other city on the other side of the Iron Curtain, in time to telephone London and have Bilto arrested before he caught the night 'plane for Paris. And that was the one thing above all else that mattered.

Urgently, he said to her in English, "For God's sake stop arguing! Get out while the going is good. If you can't get the money that will be just too bad. But you're not to come back or worry about me. Somehow you've got to get through the Curtain to-morrow. You know why?"

In spite of the two hours' relief from strain she had had since their escape from discovery in the box, now that she was faced with another crisis pain and fatigue seemed to have temporarily dulled her mind. Shaking her head she replied in the same anguage:

"I can't! It's no use! I daren't leave here."

There was no time to ask her why. The gaily-clad peasants on the stage had entered on a wild Czardas that obviously heralded the end of their turn. At any moment they would cease their whirling. With the applause the lights would go up, and the horrid bald-headed little vulture blocking the way to the door of the box would be calling to some of the uniformed men in the audience to arrest them.

"All right," said Nicholas in Czech. "Then I'll go."

He did not wait for Fedora to make any comment, but added to the old waiter, "I think I know a man who will lend me five thousand Koruny." Then he pushed past him.

Nicholas had had only a matter of seconds in which to make up his mind. He had no hope whatever of raising the money, but with luck he might reach the airport and get Jirka to arrange for him to be smuggled out through the 'funnel'. On the other hand it meant abandoning Fedora, and that, after all they had been through together, he could not bring himself to do.

He had no sooner passed the waiter than he pivoted on his toes and stretched out his hands. As he fell with all his weight on the old man's back his clutching fingers closed round the skinny throat, choking back the beginning of a cry. His victim gave at the knees, and Nicholas, still grasping his throat in a vice, crushed him down on to the floor.

Instantly Fedora's look of helpless despair vanished. Leaning across the table she swiftly pressed the button below its edge, and the lift began to descend. It was not a moment too soon. A burst of clapping sounded from the auditorium; as the platform of the box came gently to rest six feet down the lights went up.

"Quick!" whispered Nicholas. "Get something to gag him with."

Fedora was stooping over the two writhing men. "No," she whispered back. "Keep your fingers pressed hard on his windpipe. He'll be dead in under two minutes."

Suppressing a shudder at her ruthlessness, Nicholas muttered angrily, "Is it likely that I'd kill him?"

"You must!" she breathed. "Our safety—and much more than that—may depend on it."

"I'll not become a murderer!"

"This won't be murder, but self-defence. Dead men tell no tales."

"What can he say about us that the police don't know already?"

"Nothing! But if you let him live I'm sure he will become an additional danger to us."

"I can't help that! It's bad enough my having shot that policeman. I'll not kill another man in cold blood."

"Nicky, be sensible! He's a dirty blackmailing swine. He asked for it."

"I won't, I tell you! Give me something to gag him, or I'll have to take one of my hands away to grope about. Then he may manage to cry out."

"You squeamish fool," Fedora whispered; but she grabbed up two rough paper napkins from the table and knelt down beside him.

With a heave Nicholas turned the waiter over on his back. His face had gone purple and his mean little eyes were bulging from their sockets. Seizing his nose between her finger and thumb, Fedora gave it a violent upward jerk, then crammed the paper into his gaping mouth. To complete the job she undid his rag of a black tie, pushed the middle of it between his yellowed teeth and tied the ends tightly behind his head, so that he could not possibly work the wad of paper out.

He was still too near strangulation to offer further resistance; so between them they got his coat off without trouble, and, tearing strips from its lining, first knotted them together, then used them to tie his wrists and ankles. Within three minutes of being set upon, he was trussed like a turkey and stowed out of sight under the table.

Their hearts were hammering heavily from the violence of their exertions, and Fedora said breathlessly: "We had better remain down here till the lights go out for the next turn."

He nodded; and as they reseated themselves on the sofa she added, "It's a pity to have spoiled the ship for a ha'porth of tar; but all the same, I take my hat off to you for the way you handled the little toad."

His laugh was a trifle nervous, and he was still trembling as he replied, "I'm sorry to have had to disappoint you about reducing the population here still further, but I have an old-fashioned respect for human life."

"As you have been behind the Iron Curtain only about fourteen hours, I suppose that is understandable," she remarked with a touch of sarcasm. "To get the full flavour of it you need to be here, and on the run, for twenty-four. If you survive that long you'll no longer need any persuading that if you don't kill an enemy when you have the chance the odds are you will be a dead duck yourself before the big hand has gone round the clock again."

"Perhaps you're right," he muttered. "But this fellow wasn't an enemy in the true sense—only a dirty little blackmailer."

"He is an enemy now," she argued, "because we had to make him one."

"Anyhow, we've rendered him harmless; and he is paying pretty heavily for the dirty game he tried to play on us."

Fedora gave a hard little laugh. "On the contrary, he got off darned lightly. If you hadn't moved when you did I should have smashed his head in with the champagne bottle. He escaped death by about ten seconds."

Nicholas' jaw dropped as he turned to stare at her. He had been feeling distinctly pleased with himself at the way in which his vigorous action had saved the situation; it was disconcerting to learn that she had been on the point of saving it herself. He could only mutter rather ungraciously:

"The little swine would have let out a yell the instant he saw you grab the bottle, and that would have raised the whole place against us."

"Probably; even then, with luck, we might have reached the street and got away. But if you had kept your wits about you we shouldn't have had to run any risk at all. I was waiting for you to pull out Kmoch's gun and stick it in his ribs; then he would never have dared to yell when he saw I meant to crown him. I can't tell you how worried I was getting to see you standing there doing nothing."

"I'm sorry, Fedora," Nicholas sighed. "The trouble is that I'm not used to this sort of thing. I had completely forgotten that I had the gun in my pocket."

Her hand found his and pressed it. "It is I who should apologize. In the excitement it slipped my memory that you are an 'innocent abroad'. Making allowances for that, you did wonderfully."

His good humour restored, he asked, "Was it because you were expecting me to cope with the situation that you refused to go out and get the money to buy him off, or because you had

failed to get in touch with any friends from whom you could
have raised it?"

"Oh, I got in touch with friends all right; and they could
have raised it for me. The snag was that I didn't dare to go and
ask them. As bald-head said, there is a big reward for turning
in people who are on the run, and that applies as well to anyone
who helps them. If I had gone out it is a hundred-to-one that
he would have had me followed, collected the cash when I
brought it back, then shopped us, and my friends who had given
us the money, to the police, so as to be able to collect from them
on both counts. In this game, the one unforgivable sin is know-
ingly to risk involving a friend; so I had to count on you, or, at
the worst, having to bolt for it with the whole crowd after
us."

"I see how you were placed now," he nodded. "Anyhow, it's
a great relief to know that you have located friends who will
help us. What do you think the chances are that they will be
able to get us out to the airport and smuggled into it while
darkness lasts?"

Fedora did not answer. The band had started a new number.
A moment later the lights went out. Without wasting a second
she pressed the button beneath the table edge. As the platform
slowly ascended she slipped to her knees on its floor and beckoned
Nicholas down beside her. When the lift stopped they rolled
the trussed body of the old waiter forward so that it lay below
the front of the box and could not be seen unless anyone deliberately peered over its edge. Before getting up she thrust
her hand into the hip pocket of his trousers and pulled out his
wallet. As she had expected, it held his night's takings and was
bulging with notes of all denominations. With a low chuckle
she held it up for Nicholas to see.

"Put it back," he whispered severely. "Whatever else we
have to do there can be no justification for theft."

"Be your age!" she retorted. "To carry on, the Legion needs
the sinews of war. Besides, I've a use for some of it myself."

Getting to their feet, they slipped quietly out of the box.
Under a light in the corridor she paused for a minute to extract

enough notes from the wallet to make up two thin wads each amounting to one thousand Koruny, before thrusting it into her bag. When they reached the entrance the doorman was standing just inside it. After a quick look round to see that they were not observed, she said to him:

"You know the girl who's hat I am wearing, don't you?"

"Yes, *Slečna*," he replied at once, giving her the old, respectful form of address. "She's a regular here."

"Good." Fedora smiled, pressing one of the wads of notes into his hand. "She told me you were to be trusted. But we've had trouble with that old, bald waiter. Tell her that I dare not leave her hat behind, as it might be used as evidence that she helped us. It would be safest too if she didn't come here for a while. When she comes for her hat, please give her that money and ask her to buy another with it."

The doorman nodded. "Very good, *Slečna*. I'll see to that."

"Thanks; and this is for yourself." Fedora held out the other thousand Koruny.

"No, no!" He shook his head. "You're on the run. You need it more than I do."

"Take it, brother, please." She tapped her bag. "We have plenty; and it may enable you to help someone else."

He smiled, and took the money. "All right, then. Good luck, *Slečna*. And may every one of those dirty Coms rot in hell for-ever."

With a quick "Good night" to him they hurried out into the now dark street, and Fedora said, "I'm afraid we've got a long walk ahead of us."

"In that case we had better keep a look-out for a taxi," Nicholas suggested.

"That's right; and we'll tell the man to drive us to the Berkeley."

"I'm afraid I don't get the joke," he said a little huffily.

She squeezed his arm. "I'm sorry. I shouldn't have pulled your leg, but you do rather ask for it by continuing to assume that Prague is not very different from London. The taxis are few and far between here; and if you do see one for God's sake don't hail it. All the drivers are kept on a string by the police. They have to put in a report about every job they do, giving a description of their passengers, where picked up, and where put down. It is all part of the universal check-up which enables the Coms to find out about people's private lives; and, of course for anyone on the run to take a taxi to their intended hide-out is as good as ringing up the police to ask them round in the morning."

There was no moon and the streets were not very brightly lit; but they could see a good way ahead, as there was practically no traffic and very few people about. The latter fact added to the danger of their being challenged; for, as Fedora told Nicholas, the police spent most of their time at night calling on pedestrians to produce their identity cards. For them, with no cards, such a challenge would have spelt disaster; so they took every possible precaution to avoid one.

To have hurried would have been to invite trouble, too; so they walked arm in arm at an easy pace, as though they were a young couple homeward bound after some innocent family celebration. But not for a moment did they relax their vigilance, and every time they saw the silhouette of a policeman in the distance they took the next side turning, rather than risk passing near him.

This precaution added greatly to the distance they had to cover, but zig-zagging from street to street they gradually made headway in the right direction. When passing the National Museum at the top end of the broad Wenzeslas Square they had a very nasty moment, as a policeman stepped out from the shadow of the great equestrian statue in front of the building; but Fedora had the presence of mind to pull up at once, wish him good evening, and ask if he could oblige them with the time.

Glancing at a gold wrist-watch, he told her that it was twenty-five to eleven; then asked where they were going.

"Home to bed, of course, Comrade," Fedora laughed. "And I bet you wish you had the luck to be doing the same thing."

Ignoring Nicholas, he grinned at her. "I wouldn't mind, if it was with you, baby. But I go off at midnight, and I've got a girl on ice for then."

"Give her a smack on the bottom for me," said Fedora, and with a good-humoured laugh, in which Nicholas joined, the policeman let them go on their way.

To the north-west of the Wenzeslas Square the streets became narrower, and Fedora led Nicholas through a maze of twisting ways until, at the far end of a gap between tall buildings, they glimpsed the river. They had now entered a commercial district in which there were no houses and few shops. It was mainly occupied by wharves and warehouses, all of which were dark, silent and deserted. The streets were ill-lit, and Fedora became uncertain of the exact situation of the building for which she was looking. Twice they crossed a canal which led down to the river, and for some minutes explored noisome alleys and sinister *culs-de-sac* without success. Then, from a pitch-black doorway, a man's voice came low but clear. He said:

"John Huss is dead."

Fedora halted in her tracks, and replied, "But his spirit lives on in his people and will endure forever."

Nicholas realized that a password had been exchanged, and knew that it referred to the great Czech pre-Lutheran martyr whose preaching had paved the way for the Reformation. A short, broad-shouldered figure then emerged from the blackness, took Fedora's hand, bowed over it and said in a cultured voice:

"Paní Hořovská, I am delighted to see you again. It is bad news that you are on the run, but you and your friend will be safe here with me."

"Thank you, Pan Smutný," smiled Fedora. Then she introduced Nicholas to him as Pan Novák.

Leading them through the doorway, Mr. Smutný bolted it after him, produced a torch and said, "Now follow me very closely, please, because in the building I have installed a number of trip wires; so that should anyone pay me an unauthorized visit they would set off a burglar alarm up in my flat, and give me warning of their approach."

As they advanced, Nicholas could see that they were in a large and lofty warehouse. Their guide led them upward from floor to floor, but not by a direct route. On each they followed him through narrow lanes formed of stacks of crates or sacks until another broad shallow staircase brought them to a higher floor. At length they reached the top floor, and it seemed that they could go no further; but in a corner, cunningly concealed by a rampart of boxes, hung a light wooden ladder suspended from the edge of a trap-door in the ceiling. When they had climbed it they found themselves in a long narrow hall-way with a carpeted floor and coloured prints hanging on its painted walls. Puffing a little, Mr. Smutný pulled up the ladder, closed the trap-door, and exclaimed:

"There! Now you need have no more fears. You are at home."

It was, indeed, with most heartfelt relief that Fedora and Nicholas followed him into his comfortable sitting-room; which, although small, with its handsomely bound books, pictures and *objets d'art*, might well have been situated in a luxury block. Smiling at their surprise, he told them that this flat of his was actually a six-roomed penthouse which he had had built on the warehouse roof in anticipation of the German invasion, and that he had lived there ever since, unsuspected by either the Nazis or the Communists who had succeeded them. No one but a few trusted workmen were ever allowed to handle the goods on the upper floor of the warehouse, and apart from them only a few members of the Legion knew that the penthouse existed. Its only inconvenience was that it was always semi-dark in day-time, as it was essential to keep it entirely blacked out at night, and the only satisfactory way of doing so had been to paint over the windows and the skylights.

Now that Nicholas could see Mr. Smutný properly he found that he was a man of about forty-five with black hair turning grey, intelligent brown eyes, and a fine broad forehead. As soon as they had seated themselves in the armchairs that he pushed forward for them, he went over to a cabinet and produced a bottle of Slivowitz and glasses; but Fedora said:

"Pan Smutný, it is food we really need, if you can possibly produce a meal for us. We have had nothing to eat since early this morning."

"You poor child," he exclaimed. "Of course you shall have a meal, and a good one; for I flatter myself that I am no bad cook. But a nip of this while I am preparing something will give you an even better appetite; and I would like to hear just how great the danger was that you have been in. I take it there is absolutely no chance of your being traced here?"

She shook her head. "No. You may be sure that I would never wilfully endanger a friend, and I am quite certain that we were not followed." Then, as they drank the Slivowitz, she gave him an outline of their exhausting day; but she made no mention of Bilto and gave no reason for being in Prague, leaving him to assume that the police had got on to them as suspected spies soon after their arrival that morning.

Discreetly, he refrained from asking her any questions; and, when she spoke of the whipping she had been given, although his face clouded he showed no surprise. On the contrary, after she had concluded her account, he said quietly:

"You were lucky to have been in their hands for so short a time and to have got off so lightly. The last poor girl that I know of who was rescued from them had to be taken straight to one of our secret nursing-homes. They had jumped on her stomach with their hobnailed boots, and she will suffer for the rest of her life from the internal injuries they inflicted. For you, Paní Hořovská, I recommend a saline bath to take the inflammation out of your cuts, while I am getting you some supper."

Nicholas raised his eyebrows in surprise. "I know salt heals cuts but surely its application to them is terribly painful?"

"Not when it is applied in the form of a saline bath made up in the correct manner," Mr. Smutný replied quickly. "It is just a question of balance. When the skin is broken the fluid rushes to the surface, causing pain. If salt is rubbed into the wound it causes the absorption of the fluid, which also causes pain. But the application of salt dissolved in the proportion of a cupful to a gallon of lukewarm water stabilizes the situation, and while soothing the pain helps to heal the wound."

Fedora hesitated. "I didn't feel too bad after they had treated me, and while we were sitting still in the Moulin Rouge, but our long walk has made my back hot and aching; so a saline bath sounds very tempting. The trouble is that it will be so painful getting my things off and on again."

"You must not dress after your bath. I can lend you a silk dressing-gown."

"Thank you, Pan Smutný, but we are very anxious to get out of Prague to-night, and I was hoping that you might be able to arrange it for us."

"You would be wiser to stay here, as the sort of whipping you have had is liable to give you a high temperature. In fact, from your flushed face I suspect that you have a temperature now."

"I'm afraid I have. But we must leave all the same if it can possibly be managed. It is of vital importance that we should get back across the frontier by midday to-morrow."

"In that case I will do my utmost to help you. What are your plans for getting out of the country?"

"I am afraid we can hardly call them plans at the moment," Fedora confessed. "They are no more than ideas on which I am pinning our hopes. Do you know a barman at the airport named Jirka?"

Mr. Smutný nodded. "Yes, slightly. Anyhow, I know quite a bit about him, and that he is one of our key men in operating the 'funnel'."

"Do you know where he lives?"

"No; but I can find out, and get in touch with him if you wish me to."

Fedora sighed with relief. "That's just what I do wish. I came to you because you are so high up in the Legion that I felt sure you would know about the 'funnel', but I couldn't be certain that you would be able to get hold of anyone at short notice who is connected with working it. As far as I know, the 'funnel' offers us the only chance of getting out of the country within the next twelve hours, and Jirka told me this morning that, given a few hours' notice, he might be able to fix it for us. We had no means of reaching the airport after we left the Moulin Rouge, and anyhow, as Jirka does the first shift in the morning, we couldn't have contacted him till then. Will you please get a message to him asking him to do his best; then, if possible, get us out of Prague while it is still dark to a barn, or some place where we can doss down for the remainder of the night, within easy walking distance of the airport."

Mr. Smutný reached for the telephone and after a short wait got his number. Then he talked for some minutes in cryptic phrases that sounded to his listeners as if he was conducting some complicated commercial transaction. When he put the receiver down, he said:

"So far, so good. I was speaking to a friend of mine, Pan Lutonský. He owns a small hotel now called the Soviet Worker-Hero Air-Mechanic, near the airport. He will go to see Jirka, who lives nearby, and then telephone me about your prospects." Mr. Smutný smiled at Fedora and added, "Now I will go and cook you some supper. In the meantime, if you are to face further exertions to-night, I feel more strongly than ever that you should relax for a while in a saline bath and have some soothing ointment put on your cuts."

Nicholas said tentatively, "Someone will have to put the ointment on; so if you'd like me to I'll help you get out of some of your things, and generally act as lady's-maid."

"That's right." Mr. Smutný gave a quick nod. "To boggle at conventions is stupid when so much hangs on people like ourselves keeping fit to continue the fight. Come with me, both of you."

He fetched salt from the kitchen, then led them to the bath-room, made up the bath, and produced a pot of ointment from a cupboard. As he left them Fedora gave a wicked little smile, and said to Nicholas:

"From your gallant offer, it seems that you have grown up quite a lot since this morning, Nicky."

He grinned. "That's true in more ways than one. But, anyhow, this part of my enforced vacation course may come in useful when I'm married."

They made no more jokes during the next few minutes. Fedora's frock came off easily enough, but her chemise was blood-stained where it had rubbed against the angry weals; so while she set her teeth Nicholas very gently eased it off her. To save her the pain of stooping he took off her shoes, and her stockings, which had stuck to the red slashes across her calves; then, leaving her to get into the bath, he turned away to the basin and began to prepare to have a thorough wash himself.

He spun the process out as long as possible, then killed another five minutes in experimenting with a lotion of Mr. Smutný's as a means of flattening his unruly red hair. By the time he had done he thought it probable that Fedora's bath was beginning to cool off, so he asked her if she was ready to get out. She told him to wait a minute; there was some splashing, and when she called to him again he turned to find that she was sitting on the edge of the bath with a towel round her middle. With another he gently patted her back dry, then anointed her wounds with the ointment and helped to get her clothes on again.

The warmth of the water had relaxed the stiffening tissues of her flesh, so she found that dressing was not such an ordeal as undressing had been, and when she thanked Nicholas for maiding her she said that her bath had not only made her feel much more comfortable, but had also refreshed her mentally.

Back in the sitting-room they found Mr. Smutný waiting for them. He at once took them into a small dining-room, where he had already laid two places at the table, then disappeared into his kitchen. A few moments later he opened a hatch in the wall and pushed through it a big ham omelette flanked by masses of chipped potatoes. As Nicholas took the dish the sight and smell of its tempting contents made him realize how desperately hungry he really was; so he lost no time in obeying his host's injunction to help Fedora and himself. Mr. Smutný then came round and sat down at the table so that he could talk with them while they ate.

At first he asked them many questions of a general nature

about the state of things in Western Europe, America and Southern Asia, as all news entering Czechoslovakia was very heavily censored before being put out in an almost unrecognizably distorted form; and it was by no means easy, even for members of the underground, to keep abreast with the truth about events on the other side of the Iron Curtain.

By the time they had finished the omelette his most pressing questions had been answered; and having brought them cheese, biscuits, and half a currant cake to round off with, he asked Nicholas:

"In what way do you earn your living, Pan Novák?"

"He is a Professor of Political Economics," Fedora answered for him with a slightly malicious smile.

"Then he occupies a highly responsible position," commented Mr. Smutný.

"I can hardly claim to do that," Nicholas replied modestly. "I am only a member of the junior faculty at my University."

"It was not your grade but your profession that I had in mind. All teachers, from the young woman who takes a class at a kindergarten to the most gifted academicians, by the very nature of their work are given power for good or ill, and in a far greater degree than that enjoyed by any other caste. Most unfortunately the financial rewards of teachers are generally far below what men and women of their standard of intelligence would receive in other walks of life, and that makes great numbers of them discontented. For that, a terrible price is being paid by the world to-day. Comparatively few of the most prominent Communist leaders have been professional teachers, but it is beyond question that teachers in the mass have been responsible for the strangle-hold that Communism has now secured on some seven hundred and fifty million helpless people."

"Do you really believe that?" Nicholas asked.

"Indeed I do. Forty years ago, even in most of the backward countries, people enjoyed certain rights and liberties. Why did they give them up? They could practise their own religions without fear; follow any occupation they preferred; read, write, print and publicly discuss whatever they chose; travel without restriction; emigrate with their families to other countries which they thought would offer them better prospects; and if accused of any crime expect a fair deal by their fellows. Why did they surrender all these freedoms that their forefathers had won for them?"

"It was because they believed that the sacrifice of individual liberty would bring an end to age-old abuses, and secure better living conditions for all mankind," Nicholas replied quickly.

"That is not true," said Mr. Smutný. "It was because they were taught to believe that there was a short cut to universal prosperity. By the end of the last century the majority of those in whose hands lay the moulding of the minds of the next generation had ceased to believe in God, and the wisdom of his Ten Commandments. Many of them had already imbibed the doctrines of Karl Marx and were setting up a graven image of 'The People's State' for their pupils to worship. A far greater number were merely embittered by their own lot and blindly groping for a means to overturn the old order. They rejected the healthy discipline which for so many centuries had held society together, and instead fostered resistance to authority. They taught that Monarchy was synonymous with tyranny, and that the Commandment to honour one's parents was a sly trick invented by Moses to enable the old to suppress and batten on the young. They taught that to confiscate the wealth of the rich for the benefit of the community was not stealing, and that to covet the possessions of those who were better off was not wrong."

"Even granted that there is something in what you say," protested Nicholas. "I cannot agree that the teaching profession can be held responsible for the Communist revolution in Russia, or for Communism having since become the form of government in numerous other countries. That was the work of politicians."

"In the event, yes. But even the most fanatical politicians are powerless to enforce any form of government without the initial support of a considerable proportion of their fellow countrymen. It was the teachers of the preceding generation who had provoked universal discontent. It was they who had led thousands of young people to believe that, merely from the fact of being human beings, they were entitled to be fed, clothed, housed and generally cared for by the State, irrespective of how much they contributed to its wealth; and that if the government had not sufficient funds to keep everybody in comfort, then the State must steal the property of individuals and deprive those who worked hard of their just rewards, in order to support those who were lazy. It was the teachers who had conditioned the minds of the masses to accept the blandishments and arguments of the Communist politicians, and sell their birthrights for a mess of pottage."

"You must admit, though, that under the old systems the poor had little chance of bettering their lot."

"Nonsense, my friend. In every age men of humble beginnings have found it possible to rise to the very top by hard work and intelligent endeavour. Pope Pius X was the son of a swineherd. Colbert, the greatest minister of France's greatest age, that of Louis XIV, began as an ill-paid clerk in the Treasury. Cardinal Wolsey started life as a butcher's boy in Ipswich."

"Oh, there were exceptions, of course; but it was next to impossible to get to the top in the professions reserved for the privileged."

"You are quite wrong there. Admiral Nelson was the fifth son of a village parson with little money and no influence; and General Robertson, the British Chief of the Imperial General Staff for the greater part of the First World War, rose from the ranks. In the fields of law, medicine, and science, one could quote innumerable examples. As for commerce and industry, think of the founders of the great fortunes in the United States. Every township there has its own story of its poor boy who became a millionaire. In a more modest way the same thing applied all over Europe, when men still enjoyed the right to work at what they liked for as long as they liked and keep the rewards of their labours. Most of them too, far from hoarding their gains, gave lavishly to bettering the lot of the less fortunate.

In England, for example, take your Lord Nuffield. He has given away over ten million pounds, and he started only with a little bicycle shop. Under Communism such men are killed or put into concentration camps; the inspiration they give to others and the good they do is lost; and the masses, deprived of God, ambition, hope or future, are reduced to a dead level of poverty-stricken uniformity."

"All the same, the Marxist ideal still has a great hold on the imagination of many honest and intelligent people," Nicholas remarked.

Mr. Smutný frowned. "It may have in the West. If so, it is for you teachers to counteract it before your pupils become the tools of unscrupulous politicians. The bait they hold out is the transformation of all countries into Welfare States, but that can be achieved only by dissipating the wealth of their nations. Wherever that happened a collapse would inevitably follow; and it is in taking such a risk, to achieve their own ends, that the Socialists play the Communists' game for them. A national collapse drives people to desperation, and it is then that in their despair they are only too apt to surrender their liberties to the soap-box orators who promise to save them. If their minds have been conditioned by Left-wing thinkers beforehand, they accept a Communist dictatorship without a struggle."

"The Socialists are certainly not playing the Communists' game in England."

"Less so perhaps than in many other countries; but they are playing it all the same. England cannot be altogether an exception to the rule that all over the world many Socialist leaders are crypto-Communists. That is, Party members who are under orders not to divulge the fact that they are Communists, because they can do much more valuable work for the Party by keeping it secret. It is such men who ferment unjustifiable strikes and go-slow movements, and, where they are Trade Union Officials, press for exorbitant wage increases; so that by these means industry is disrupted and the ability to keep up exports reduced. It is others of the same kidney in the parliamentary sphere who persuade or bully their innocent colleagues into adopting policies which will gain Socialist votes but can only be carried out to the detriment of Britain's financial stability. That is the danger of Socialism. Everywhere the Communists are using it as a lever to impoverish the countries of the West, in the hope of eventually creating chaotic conditions which will enable them to take those countries over, by a skilfully managed series of *coups d'état* that will have all the appearance of being 'by the will of the people'."

"And what do you think of their chances, Mr. Smutný?" Nicholas enquired.

"Nothing like as good as they were a few years ago," the little man replied. "For one thing, nearly every country your side of the Iron Curtain which tried a Socialist Government has now thrown it out; so, in spite of the terrible drain of the rearmament drive that the Soviets force on them, they have become more stable. For another, I think those crypto-Communists disguised as Socialists, of whom I spoke just now, are themselves beginning to see the red light. They can hardly have failed to observe the Kremlin's method. It is to use such men for the furtherance of Communist aims in their own countries, then when Communist governments take over they are appointed to run them. But for how long? Only for the few years needed by the Kremlin thoroughly to purge the armed services of that country, suppress its church and liquidate all survivors of its old ruling caste, so that there is no longer any great risk of a counter-revolution. Then those men who sold their country to the Soviets are accused of deviation, and liquidated themselves, to be replaced with the Kremlin's own nominees. All the world has seen that happen not once but many times in the Soviet satellite countries. The trial of the fourteen Czech Communist leaders here, headed by the infamous Rudolf Slánský, was typical. Therefore, I think that while the crypto-Communists of the West are perfectly happy to go on accepting money from Moscow to create every sort of trouble, most of them would now think twice before taking the plunge, if they had the chance to carry their task to its logical conclusion."

"Since you are opposed to Socialism, Mr. Smutný, what form

of government do you suggest? Surely not a continuance of the old reactionary systems?"

"Why not? Although I take exception to the word reactionary. All over the world, and not excepting Russia, there had been a steady improvement in the people's lot for many decades preceding the outbreak of the First World War. You may argue that it was slow, but surely that is better than upheavals in which millions of people lose their lives and the survivors are reduced to permanent slavery."

"You cannot be serious! You would not have kept the Czarist rule in Russia?"

"Her people would have been infinitely better off than they have become under Comrade Stalin. No one suggests that all the old Monarchies were perfect—far from it. But Monarchy, at its best, is the most sensible form of government so far devised by man, because it gives continuity and stability. To appreciate its virtues you have only to consider the Queen of England, and her predecessors. For many generations they have ruled through governments chosen by their people, without power to oppress but retaining the power to bring the leaders of opposing political factions together in times of crisis—as was done by King George V when the £ threatened to collapse and he initiated the formation of a National Government. They seek nothing for themselves, devote their lives to the well-being of their subjects, are above all Party strife, and fulfil the burdensome functions of Heads of State far better than any elderly harassed President could do. By comparison, consider how wasteful and inefficient is the constitution of the United States, where for one year in every four the whole country is disrupted by electioneering gone mad."

Nicholas smiled. "I suppose that's true. But what of the future? Do you think the Kremlin will succeed, one way or another, in dominating the world?"

Mr. Smutný returned his smile. "I can, thank God, say 'no' to that. Communism is already a dying faith. The only danger of its revival now lies in the West. If any country on your side of the Iron Curtain went Communist that would give the move-

ment a fresh lease of life. But whatever happens now, the years
—not the days but the years—of Communism are numbered.
It has been tried and found wanting. It is maintained only by
terror. Except for a few fanatics who are still too young to
appreciate the whole picture, even the members of the Party do
not believe in it any more. They carry on because they are the
privileged cast and receive jam with their bread and butter, but
they go in constant fear of one another. Christianity, Islam,
Judaism are still living faiths, but Communism has had its brief
day, and is recognized by all who have lived for any length of
time under it as the negation of all that man has ever striven for.
In fact it is already a back number."

"You amaze me. Do you think, then, that it is likely to
collapse?"

"Oh, no. Too many people have vested interests in keeping
it going. The only hope of its total dissolution in our time lies
in the Western Powers getting really tough."

"Do you mean by their launching a war aimed at destroying
it root and branch?" asked Nicholas apprehensively.

"No. To challenge Moscow outright would be too great a
risk. One side or other might then resort to atomic warfare, and
that would mean the destruction of most of the great cities in
Europe and America as well as in the U.S.S.R. Any attempt to
bring about the personal downfall of the men in the Kremlin
would result in their fighting like rats in a corner. But their
claws can be cut."

"How?"

"When the Western Powers have completed their rearmament programme they could demand the withdrawal of Russian
control over Eastern Germany. The Kremlin would give way
on that, rather than fight. I am convinced, too, that they would
give up Czechoslovakia, and all the other satellite countries in
turn, rather than face a show-down."

"What leads you to suppose that?"

"The fact that they did not fight to retain Yugoslavia, although
they were relatively very much stronger when it broke away
than they are now. Marshal Tito was the one fellow-traveller

who in due course openly declared himself, but had the sense to get out from under before his country was properly in the bag. He must have known much more about the minds of the men in the Kremlin than any of the Western Powers, and at that time they were in no state to give him effective military support, even if they had been willingto do so. But he took the gamble and he won."

"Yet their military might compared to his is overwhelming. Why do you think they refrained from marching in?"

"Because they cannot trust their troops. In the initial stages of Hitler's invasion, the Russians surrendered by whole divisions and hailed the Germans as liberators. Communism would have been finished then, had it not been for the incredible stupidity of the Nazis. They shot their Soviet officer prisoners, devastated the countryside as they advanced, slaughtered half the population, and destroyed the towns. Naturally, once the Russians realized what they were up against they began to fight back."

"Do you think the Soviet troops would betray the Kremlin now?"

"Yes; given the chance. The trouble is that since Tito's secession the whole situation has been changed by the Soviet's success in developing the atomic bomb. Atomic warfare could be launched by a handful of picked men whose interests are bound up with the survival of the Party. That is why it would be dangerous to challenge the Kremlin direct. But their censorship is so complete, and their internal propaganda so all-pervading, that they would find no more difficulty in saving face if they were forced, bit by bit, out of central Europe than they did when they were forced out of Yugoslavia."

"Such withdrawals would have very serious economic effects on Russia."

"Yes, they would undoubtedly aggravate the pernicious anæmia to which Communism is inevitably subject. But the process would naturally have to be a gradual one, as the Kremlin might be maddened into throwing down the gauntlet if too much were asked from it at any one time. It may well be twenty-five years before all the subject territories have been liberated and Russia herself is freed from the tyranny under which her people now groan. The only thing we can say with certainty is that Communism is a dying faith, and that everyone of us has it in our power to contribute something towards hastening its death."

Fedora and Nicholas had finished their meal, and their host now got up to bring them coffee. As he set the tray down on the table the telephone rang. Going into the next room, he answered it, and they heard him say: "Yes" three times at intervals; then, setting it down, he returned to them and said:

"That was Lutonský. He has seen Jirka and he thinks that to-morrow he will be able to get you both on the one o'clock 'plane for Frankfurt. Lutonský agrees that it would be all to the good if you could be got out of Prague while darkness lasts, and if I can take you to him he will put you up for the rest of the night. That depends on whether I can borrow a car; and I know of only one place where I might do so at this hour. If I fail we must get you to him not later than midday; but that should not be difficult. I will go out now, and if the car is available I will be back in it to collect you in about half an hour."

When they had thanked him he left them, and they drank their coffee. As Nicholas finished his, he said: "Owing to that long sleep I had this afternoon I don't feel at all tired; but you must be. Why don't you snatch a nap, while I wash up?"

"I don't feel particularly tired either," she replied. "I'm still too wrought up. I'll just stay quietly in the sitting-room."

He carried the things they had used for supper into the well-equipped little kitchen, and washed and dried them carefully. As he put the last plate in the rack he glanced at the clock. It was ten past one, and Mr. Smutný had been gone about a quarter of an hour.

It was at that moment that the alarm bell shrilled.

CHAPTER XVI

TRAPPED

FOR a moment Nicholas stood rigid, the blood slowly draining from his face. Then he ran towards the sitting-room. Fedora had already thrown open the door and was standing in the doorway. The bell continued to ring with a shrill, high note. They stared at one another in dismay.

"It . . . it may be only burglars," he faltered.

"Or a rat. One may have jumped against a trip wire."

On a simultaneous impulse they ran along the hall-way. Mr. Smutný had left the trap-door open and the ladder was hanging from it. They peered down into the darkness below. Beyond the circle of faint light that lit the ladder from above, the stacks of cases made a well of blackness. Both of them strained their ears; but the shrilling of the alarm made it almost impossible to catch any sounds that might have been coming up from the warehouse, and Fedora exlaimed:

"For God's sake find that bell and stop it!"

Nicholas had already noticed it, up near the low ceiling, just outside the kitchen door. Running back there, he pushed the door open, snatched up a table mat and stuffed it between the gong and its clapper. When he rejoined Fedora she was kneeling down, still listening; but now the clangour of the bell was stilled, the flat and the depths below it were as silent as the grave.

"I had better go down and investigate." Instinctively Nicholas spoke in a whisper.

She gave him a doubtful look, and whispered back, "You would never be able to find your way in the darkness. And if it is the Coms you might run right into them. It would be wiser to pull up the ladder and lie doggo here. Pan Smutný said that only a few of his most trusted workmen know about this penthouse, so the police might search the building all night without finding the trap-door that leads to it."

"It was of Mr. Smutný I was thinking. If it were a false alarm, well and good; but if the place is being raided we ought to try to warn him, otherwise on his return he may walk straight into the arms of the Coms."

"You are right about that. But I don't see how you can manage to warn him before he enters the building, and by then it will be too late."

"I can fire some shots through a window. The neighbourhood appears to be deserted, but it's extraordinary how a crowd collects from nowhere at the first sign of any excitement. He will see it as he comes back along the street, realize what is happening, and sheer off."

"All right, then. But will you be able to find your way back here?"

"There is a spare torch in the kitchen, I'll take that."

She got to her feet and laid a hand on his arm. "Nicky, do be careful. If it is the Coms, and they see a light approaching before you spot them, they will shoot first."

"I'll be as careful as I can." He gave her a reassuring smile, and pulled from his pocket the small automatic he had taken from Kmoch.

As her glance fell on it she said, "That's all right for close work, but you would be better off with something bigger for a job like this. Beside, Kmoch fired it three times and you did once, so it can have only half a load left in it. Pan Smutný must have some weapons up here. While you get the torch I'll see if I can find a man-sized gun."

He collected the torch and rejoined her in the sitting-room. She was rummaging in Mr. Smutný's bureau, and when she got to its bottom drawer they saw there three pistols and a store of ammunition. Selecting a big Luger, she loaded it and two spare clips with bullets for him. As she handed them over she said:

"Give me the little gun. I may need one before we're through, and it will easily go into my bag."

Having exchanged weapons, they hurried out into the hall and knelt down to listen by the trap again. There was still no sound from below, so he said, "Here goes," and slid his legs over the edge.

"Good luck, Nicky!" she whispered. "I pray to God it was a false alarm. Good luck, my dear."

"Thanks," he murmured, and slid down the ladder. After a final wave from the floor, he tiptoed round the end of the stack of boxes. Beyond them it was pitch dark, so he had to switch on the torch; but he held it so that its beam shone downwards about a yard in front of his feet, and used his pistol hand to screen the bulb from direct sight.

With his ears cocked to catch any sound he advanced on tiptoe down the narrow alley formed by two walls of crates, until he reached the first staircase. There he paused to listen, but he could hear nothing except the steady gnawing of a mouse. Gingerly he made his way down the flight, then through a maze of turnings, trying to memorize the merchandise stacked on each corner, so that he would be able to find his way back.

At the second staircase he halted again. There was still no sound from below. Somewhat reassured, he crept down it, and on the next floor went forward a little more quickly, urged on by the thought that Mr. Smutný would soon be due back, and that if anything was wrong no time must now be lost in creating a situation which would warn him of what was afoot.

Including its ground level the warehouse had five floors, and he was now half way down them. At the head of the staircase leading from the second to the first floor he again stopped to listen. His heart began to beat more rapidly. For a moment he was not certain; then a raised voice came distinctly to him. There were people moving about and calling to one another somewhere below him in the darkness.

There was still a possibility that they were burglars. If so, to fire off his gun through a window would be to invite real trouble. It would bring the police on the scene, and that was the very last thing that he wanted. With a sharp intake of his breath he realized that there was only one thing for it. He must go down and find out for certain who the intruders were.

Very cautiously now he tiptoed down to the first floor, then put out his torch. Flashing it only at intervals, when he bumped into bales and boxes, he felt his way along the alleys, until he reached the lowest staircase. The voices were clearly audible now, and a glow of subdued light was coming up from the ground floor.

At the stairhead he knelt down and peered over the edge. He could hear the intruders moving about but could not see anyone. Craning forward, he leaned over further. The light from torches held beyond his view made weird shadows move across the floor. One bright beam cut a circle of light upon a stack of large cardboard cartons near the foot of the stairway. The circle swiftly increased in size. Nicholas could hear the footsteps of the man who held the torch approaching just beneath him. He drew back a little, and held his gun ready in case he had to use it.

Suddenly there was a movement on the far side of the stairway. A man had stepped out from the shadows. He must have caught sight of Nicholas as he moved, or heard the slight noise he made as he drew back. He was staring straight up into Nicholas' face, and he was wearing the uniform of a State policeman. As his hand jumped to the pistol at his belt, Nicholas fired.

The man clawed at his chest. His eyes opened very wide, then his head fell forward and he went down with a crash across the lowest steps of the stairs. As Nicholas sprang to his feet the man with the torch ran out from beneath where he was standing. Again Nicholas fired. His bullet caught the policeman in the left shoulder. He was knocked sideways and stumbled over the body of his dead comrade. His torch was dashed from his left hand and went out; but in his right he still clutched his pistol. Swivelling round, he fired wildly up into the darkness that shrouded the top of the stairway. One bullet smacked into a beam just above Nicholas' head; three more thudded into the ceiling further off to his right at intervals of a few feet.

By now pandemonium had broken loose on the ground floor. Evidently a dozen or more men had been systematically searching it, to make certain that no one was hidden there, before proceeding to the upper floors. At the sound of the shots they had all come running back down the several alleys that converged on the open space at the foot of the stairway. Above the noisy trampling of their heavy boots came shouted orders and counter orders:

"Guard the door against a break out! Get up those stairs! Show a light! Don't shine a torch where they can see you! Shoot at sight! No, no! Comrade Frček said take them alive if possible. See if there's another staircase, some of you! Get on, damn you; rush those stairs!"

As a burst of bullets spattered past Nicholas, he leapt back, sent one last shot blindly down the well of the stairs, then turned and ran. Enough light was coming from below for him to see his way round the first turning, but he had to switch on his torch to find the next. He was hardly round it when he heard feet pounding up the wooden stairs. A third alley led him past an end wall of the building. In it two windows were very faintly outlined by starlight just percolating through glass encrusted with the dirt of half a century. On passing one of them he sent a shot through it. The crack of his pistol and the tinkle of falling glass brought another chorus of cries.

"They are down that end! Who are they firing at? Quick; after them; they're going to jump out of the window!"

Nicholas had found the second staircase and was up it. His pursuers reached the window. Someone shouted. "There's only one pane smashed. They're still in the building." Then they too found the stairs and charged up them.

His heart hammering wildly, Nicholas raced down a long corridor formed of bales on the second floor. In his haste he missed the turning he should have taken. To his horror, at the end of the alley he found himself in a *cul-de-sac*. Facing about, he ran back. To find the turning he should have taken he had to flash his torch. Its beam had just fallen on the opening when the darkness ahead was stabbed with a spurt of flame. A bullet whistled past his ear. There was no time to aim, but he pressed the trigger of his gun. As he flung himself round the corner, a cry told him that he had had a lucky shot. His pursuers had been bunched together at the far end of the narrow canyon formed by the bales, so he could hardly have missed; but it did not halt them. As he ran up the third staircase he could hear the relentless pursuit coming after him in full cry.

On the third floor he lost his way completely. In an agony of apprehension, expecting every moment to get a bullet in the back, he stumbled from turning to turning, no longer daring to flash his torch, even for a second. Suddenly, he heard Fedora's voice call softly from somewhere up in the darkness above him:

"This way, Nicky! This way."

With a gasp of relief he ran towards it; then tripped and fell on the lowest step of the fourth stairway. As he picked himself up there was a shout behind him. He had dropped his torch but still had his gun. Swinging round, he fired twice in the direction from which the shout had come. A scream rang out; a heavy body thudded on the floor, and near it an automatic exploded. Fedora was standing at the top of the stairs. As the flashes from the guns momentarily lit the darkness she saw Nicholas clearly. He bounded up the stairs and her outstretched hand met his left arm. Sliding her fingers down it till they found his fingers, she clasped them firmly and drew him along behind her.

"Thank God you came to find me!" he panted. "In another minute I should have run right into them. I dared not show a light, and I was hopelessly lost."

"I was afraid that might happen," she replied quickly. "That is what decided me to come down directly the firing started."

Fedora had had the forethought to count the paces from turning to turning on the top floor; so, without a moment's delay, they were able to hurry through the darkness to the final enclave. In it, the ladder hung bathed in the gentle pool of light from above. Three rungs at a time, they sped up it. As soon as Nicholas had tumbled after Fedora through the trap door, they drew the ladder up, laid it along the hall, and closed the trap. Still kneeling there, struggling to get their breath back, they stared at one another with consternation on their faces.

"How . . . how many of them are there?" she asked with a catch in her voice.

He shook his head. "I don't know. Eight, ten, twenty maybe."

"Then it's not just one of the arbitrary searches that the patrols often carry out in the hope of finding arms or an illicit printing press?"

"No. They are after us. I heard one of them say 'Comrade Frček wants them alive'."

Fedora swore. "How the hell can they possibly have traced us here?"

"God knows; I don't!"

"I suppose there is no chance of breaking out? I mean by going down again, and trying to sneak past them in the darkness?"

"I'm afraid not. There are too many of them. They were searching the ground floor systematically. It is certain that they would have left someone to guard the door."

"Did you get any of them—besides the one I saw you shoot just now?"

"Yes!" He was still flushed with excitement, and his voice held a jubilant note. "My opening shot was a bull's-eye, right on the fellow's heart; and I wounded two others."

"Well done!" she smiled, and her green eyes showed a glint of amusement, as she went on, "You've soon got over your squeamishness about killing Coms, haven't you? But it's like getting kisses, or olives out of a bottle—the first one's difficult, the rest come easy."

Her mockery caused him an acute twinge of distress. His mind flashed back to his righteous disgust at such killings by the character he had thought of to date as 'that imperialist-capitalist-bandit', and the idea that his recent doings had a quite definite similarity to those of Mr. Gregory Sallust momentarily horrified him. Then that hangover from his old beliefs was swept away by his now positive conviction that these police were not the decent representatives of law and order, but licensed gunmen richly rewarded for maintaining a barbarous tyranny.

His reactions to Fedora's grimly humorous comparison occupied only a few seconds; yet, before he had time to reply, the telephone buzzed and, jumping up from her knees, she ran into the sitting-room to answer it.

He dragged an old oak chest, that stood in the hall, over the trap-door, so that it could not be forced up from below, then followed her. She was holding the instrument to her ear. After listening for a minute or so she said:

"Thank you very much indeed. But I'm sorry to say they are already here."

As she hung up, Nicholas asked, "Was that Mr. Smutný?"

She shook her head. "No; a woman who works in the office at the Moulin Rouge. I don't know who she is. She rang up to warn us to expect a raid, but she couldn't get away from the club till nearly one, and then had a job to get through. Anyhow, it has solved the riddle of how Frček's boys managed to trace us. That brute of a waiter was found when the staff began to clear up, soon after midnight. You remember he followed me back into the box after I had been out to telephone. He saw me in the booth. When they got him round he gave the police the time I had made my call, and they got the number I had rung from the record kept by the girl on the switchboard. From that it was easy for them to get the address of the warehouse."

Mentally, Nicholas groaned. Fedora had certainly not foreseen this, or they would not have been there, but when she had urged him to kill the old waiter her instinct to take no chances had been right. By refraining from doing so he had again brought her life, as well as his own, into imminent peril. In addition he had been the means of giving away the secret quarters in which Mr. Smutný had lived comfortably and securely for so long. Nicholas expected her to reproach him, but she generously refrained, and said:

"It's no good crying over spilt milk, and we have no time to lose. As soon as they've satisfied themselves that we are not hiding somewhere on the fourth floor they will try to find a way up to the roof. I expect all the old ones are blocked, but they'll break through somehow; so we had better get away across the neighbouring roofs as quickly as possible."

8*

Switching out the lights as they went, they made for a door at the end of the hall-way and unbolted it. As they had supposed, it led on to the open part of the roof, which was much larger than that occupied by the penthouse. It was surrounded by a low parapet, inside which there was a walk-way; its centre consisted of a series of pointed ridges that embodied skylights, but all of these had been covered and sealed down with tarred felt.

As they glanced about them they were filled with dismay. The warehouse formed an isolated oblong block. All the roofs of the other buildings adjacent to it were several feet lower and some distance off. It seemed that there was no means of escape and that they were trapped there.

"Pan Smutný must have some emergency get-away!" exclaimed Fedora. "But I've got a rotten head for heights. Try to find it, then come back for me."

Leaving her by the doorway of the penthouse, Nicholas hurried round the three open sides of the roof, taking cautious peeps over the parapet as he went. The two longer sides faced on to narrow streets, but the roofs of the buildings opposite were well over thirty feet away. The shorter side, at the extremity of the roof, looked on to the canal that they had twice crossed when trying to find the warehouse. There was no wharf; the wall of the building dropped sheer to the water, so that barges could come alongside and be loaded or unloaded by hoists which projected from each floor level.

For a moment Nicholas peered down at the hoists, wondering if it would be possible to drop from one to another; but the distance between them was much too great, and he decided that even a monkey would not have risked it.

From a steel stanchion near him a thick telegraph cable, encased in some tarred material and having a smaller cable running in long loops below it, stretched in a graceful curve across the canal to a slightly lower building some sixty feet distant. The cable was thick enough to provide a good hand grip, and Nicholas thought that a trained trapeze artist could have crossed by it; but he felt sure that his own muscles were not up to such a strain, and as Fedora suffered from vertigo, that put out of the

question even the wild idea of making an attempt. Hurrying back
to her, he said glumly:

"I've had no luck out there. The streets on both sides are full
of police and cars. Even if we could lower ourselves to the top
of one of the fire escapes that come up to the fourth floor, we
should be spotted coming down. There's no one covering the
far end; but they don't have to. The canal is there, and there's
no way down at all."

"That's bad, Nicky!" Fedora did not attempt to disguise
how worried she felt. "If we had been able to lie doggo they
might never have found the flat. Once they had searched the
warehouse they would probably have decided that we must have
been warned and got away before they arrived, or had never
come here at all; but now they know we are here for certain
they'll take the building to pieces rather than give up."

Her words were symbolically prophetic. It was at that
moment they both smelt smoke. At first unnoticed by them in
the dim light, a wisp of it was curling up from a crack in the
covering of a skylight only some ten feet from where they were
standing.

"Good God!" Nicholas exclaimed. "Surely they don't mean
to burn the place down."

"They may," Fedora replied grimly. "You say there were a
dozen or more of them chasing you. That's more than enough to
have searched the fourth floor thoroughly in the ten minutes
since we got back here. Having failed to find us they probably
think we have gone to earth in some crates previously emptied
to form a hiding place; so they have set about smoking us out."

Nicholas nodded. "I see. Then by now they are down on
the third floor with their torches on the stairway and their guns
in their hands, waiting for us to be driven into their arms. Of
course, they can call up the fire engines to stop the blaze spreading downwards, or to other buildings, but in half an hour's time
the whole of the top here may be a raging furnace."

"You've said it! But I can't believe Pan Smutný would allow
himself to be caught in such a trap. There must be an escape
route from the dead end of the penthouse, where it's flush with

the fourth side of the building. The gap to the next roof may be narrower there."

Turning, Fedora ran back through the hall-way, switching on the lights as she went. At its far end were two bedrooms. She dived into one and Nicholas dived into the other. The windows of both had been screwed down and painted over. Knowing that it was now futile to maintain the secret of the flat, they both smashed panes of the windows, regardless of lights being seen up there from below. From both rooms the outlook was the same; a sheer drop to an alley, no sign of a ladder, and a yawning gulf of from thirty to forty feet to the much lower roof of the next building.

In the hall they met, their drawn faces reporting without words their failure to find an escape route. Parting again, they ran into the other rooms, seeing frantically for some indication of a way to get out of the flat, other than by the trap-door or on to the open roof. They could not find even a clue to work upon.

Back in the hall, Nicholas dragged aside the chest and was about to open the trap-door, when Fedora came upon him.

"What are you doing?" she asked sharply.

"I thought that if the fire is only at the far end, we might go down again," he muttered. "Then we could anyhow get to one of the fire escapes. It would be better to go down that and be shot than to be burnt alive."

"You can if you like," came the quick reply. "But they wouldn't shoot you. They would wait until you had emptied your gun, then take you alive. I'd rather throw myself off the roof."

As she finished speaking he got the trap open. If he had had any doubts about the soundness of her view, that settled it for him. A great puff of black smoke billowed up into the hall. Choking and spluttering, he slammed the trap to again. No one could now have got more than a dozen paces along the floor below without suffocating.

Half blinded by the smoke, they staggered back, covering their smarting eyes. Then, in desperation, they again ran along the hall to the door that gave on to the open roof. Even in the few minutes since they had left it the evidence of the fire had multiplied tenfold. At intervals along each pointed ridge there was now a glowing patch indicating the position of the skylights. Their wooden frames and tarred felt made them more vulnerable than the slate-covered sections between them. Spirals of smoke were issuing from their tops, bottoms and sides, and in some places little fountains of sparks spurted up into the darkness.

Their hearts numb with fear, they stood staring at the scene, so fraught with awful prospects of an agonizing death from which there was no escape. It was then that the telephone rang again.

As though galvanized by an electric shock, Fedora gave a violent start, swung about, and dashed down the hall to answer it. Nicholas was hard on her heels. He saw her pick the receiver up and say into it eagerly, "Yes . . . yes . . . yes." Then he saw her jaw drop, and her eyes become distended with fright, before she muttered a final "Yes" almost below her breath, and hung up.

"Who was it? Why are you looking so scared?" he asked impatiently.

"It . . . it was Pan Smutný," she stammered.

"Then this riot we've created saved him from running his head into a noose. That's something. But what did he say? What did he say?"

"He . . . he rang up to let us know his escape route. He tried before, but the line was blocked. That other call. It . . . it's along a telegraph cable that crosses the canal."

Nicholas no longer wondered that Fedora's thin cheeks had gone a greenish tinge. He shook his head. "Even if you were good at heights, we couldn't make it. To carry one's whole weight on one's arms across sixty feet of space would need the muscles of a Tarzan."

"It's not as bad as that," Fedora gulped. "Pan Smutný said there is some special apparatus to take the weight, under the bed in his bedroom."

"Praises be!" cried Nicholas, pivoting on toe and heel and

rushing from the room. A moment later he was dragging the escape gear from under Mr. Smutný's bed. There was enough for four people. Each set consisted of a six-inch broad leather belt, into which was sewn the end of a two-foot length of wire hawser, having at its other end a strong iron hook. The way in which it was intended that the gear should be used was obvious. One had only to buckle the belt round one's waist, put the hook over the telegraph cable, and jump off the parapet. The apparatus took the whole weight of the body, but, by using one's own strength when hanging on to the cable, one could lift oneself enough to enable the hook to slide a few inches at a time, and, as the cable sloped downwards, little impetus would be needed to carry one across to the building on the far side of the canal.

Grabbing up two of the belts, Nicholas hastened back to Fedora and held one of them out to her. "Here!" he cried. "Buckle that round you, and we'll soon be out of this."

She waved it away. "I can't, Nicky! I can't! The very thought of hanging from a telegraph cable absolutely petrifies me!"

"You've got to," he said angrily; and as soon as he had done up his own belt he strapped the other round her waist. Then, seizing her by the wrist, he dragged her after him out of the room and along to the door that gave on to the roof.

Now smoke lit by a reddish glare was billowing up from outside the parapet, tongues of flame had broken out from several of the skylights and showers of sparks were being blown about by every breath of wind. From below there came a fierce crackling and it was clear that before long the whole roof would be ablaze.

Pulling the terrified Fedora after him, Nicholas made his way along inside the parapet to the canal end of the building, where the telegraph cable swung from the tall steel stanchion. Halting by it, he said to her:

"For God's sake pull yourself together. You have only to do as I tell you, and you'll be perfectly all right."

"I can't!" she moaned. "Please, *please* don't make me!"

"You've got to," he insisted.

"No! No!" she tried to twist away from him. "You go. Leave me behind."

"Is it likely? Fedora, you've been so splendid up to now. Come on! Make an effort. Shut your eyes."

Jittering with fear, she obeyed him, and let him help her up on to the parapet. Feeling for the long strap of her pouch bag, she slipped it over her head, so that it should not slide from her shoulder; then she opened her eyes and looked down. At the sight of the water glinting faintly sixty feet below her, she let out a low wail and swayed outward.

Nicholas caught her only just in time. His grab at her arm drew the upper part of her body inward, but her legs folded under her and she toppled right on to him. As he staggered back under the impact he realized that she had fainted.

Behind him there was now an angry roaring. One of the skylights fell in with a faint crash. From the aperture it left, a great tongue of flame shot up fifteen feet above the roof level. It was no longer possible to see across to the penthouse through the dense smoke and clouds of drifting sparks. The air had become hot and searing. It was difficult to breathe and the fumes made every breath painful. Nicholas knew that if he did not get away in the next few minutes, he would never get away at all.

There were no means and no time to attempt to revive Fedora. She was right out, and as limp as if she were dead. For a moment Nicholas stared down at her as she lay, face up, sprawled half across the parapet; then, seizing the hook attached to the belt round her waist, he tried to get it over the cable. Almost at once he saw that it could not be done. With only one hand he could not lift her high enough. He wondered how he could possibly save her. To pick her up and carry her across in his arms was out of the question, as he would need both his hands to propel himself along. Taking out his silk handkerchief, he mopped away the sweat that was streaming from his face.

The feel of the handkerchief gave him an idea. It was the same one which he had used to bandage his eyes in the X-cell that afternoon. Laying it on Fedora's chest, he quickly made a corner to corner bandage of it again, folding it now as many times as he could. Crossing her wrists one over the other on the centre of it he bound them together, tying the ends of the handkerchief in a reef knot, so that the greater the strain upon it the tighter it would become. Then he stooped his head and slid it between Fedora's arms so that her bound hands were at the back of his neck.

There came a moment when he feared he would never manage to accomplish the next stage. He had to lift her, climb up on the parapet and get the hook attached to his own belt over the cable. He was within an ace of overbalancing; but, with a frantic effort, he got the hook over just in time. It took their combined weight, and he breathed again.

Half-blinded by the smoke and choking from fumes, he pushed off. Instantly Fedora became a dead weight round his neck. The hook jerked the leather belt up so that its edge cut into his ribs, and he let out a gasp of pain. Tightening his grasp on the cable, he endeavoured to take his own weight and hers on his arm muscles. For a moment he managed to support it; but the hook did not slide along the cable because the angle was not steep enough, owing to the slight dip it made at the point from which he hung.

Spurred to a fresh effort by the scorching blast now rising from the roof beside him, he did a second pull up; then knocked the hook with his left hand while supporting himself with his right. It moved a few inches.

After resting for a moment, he repeated the movement with the same satisfactory result. Hope now battling with fear he continued the jerky motion, edging his way out from the burning building across the yawning gulf. But every few inches of progress was bought at the cost of a greater agony. When he rested his arms it seemed as if the leather belt was going to cut him in half, and each time he took the strain on his arms it seemed as if they were being torn from their sockets.

He was fifteen feet out when he heard something snap. He could not see anything by looking down, as the unconscious Fedora's head, hanging backwards so that her chin jutted up towards him, blocked his view below chest level. But he felt sure that some part of his belt had given.

Next moment, as he let their full weight be taken by the hook again, there came a tearing sound. Hastily, he tightened his grasp upon the cable, then gradually relaxed. Swiftly the full horror of his situation was borne in upon him. The gear had been made to take only one person, and the combined weight of two had proved too much for it. The two-foot length of wire hawser, to which the hook was attached, was tearing itself from its setting in the belt.

Once more he moved a few inches; but as he let himself down the belt refused to take the strain. He now had to hang on without respite. Sweat was streaming down his face. Every muscle in his body was as taut as a bow-string. The pull of Fedora upon him had the same effect as if his limbs were being slowly wrenched apart by the pulleys of a medieval rack. He was barely a quarter of the way across the chasm. He could not go forward and he could not go back. The cable hurt his palms intolerably. His grip began to slip. His left hand opened and only its finger tips still kept a precarious hold on the cable. Suddenly they slid from it. He was hanging now only by his right hand. For another moment he remained suspended by it. Then that opened too. With a groan he let go, and together they plunged into the dark abyss.

CHAPTER XVII

ORDEAL BY WATER

NICHOLAS' left arm had fallen to his side. His right remained stretched to its utmost reach above his head, as though in some parody of a Fascist salute. At the final sharp rending noise, as the last stitches that held the short length of wire hawser to the belt had given way, the two bodies fell like a plummet.

Fedora was still completely out, hanging by her arms from Nicholas' neck, her head at his chest-level lolling limply back. His head too was thrown back. Despite the pull he had forced it back as, his eyes bulging from the strain, he had kept them riveted on his hands, the cable and the hook. Now, as he shot downwards, he had the illusion that he was not moving. Instead, it seemed as if some unseen power had suddenly snatched the cable and the hook upward from him. At one moment the cable had been as thick as the double barrel of a sporting gun; at the next it was no more than a black thread against the starry sky. In that same moment the sky itself seemed about to be swallowed up in darkness. As he had hung from the cable staring upwards, the buildings on either side of him had been outside his cone of vision; as he fell their tops came into it, then their black bulks, rushing together with the speed of express trains, as though about to collide, disintegrate, and crush him under a mountain of rubble.

Yet, had he and Fedora practised that inverted dive scores of times to make a living by it in a circus, they could not have performed it better. It was their absolute rigidity which saved them from any serious harm. Fedora's toes, hanging a foot or more below Nicholas' feet, formed the arrow point of their combination as effectively as would have a diver's out-thrust hands; the faces of both were upturned, and the back of her head broke the force with which the water would otherwise have hit him under the chin. With scarcely a splash they pierced the surface and disappeared beneath it.

The canal was only about eight feet deep. Although the water checked the speed of their fall, they plunged to its bottom almost instantly. Had it been man-made, and concreted, the legs of both of them must have been broken; but it was an old river-bed thick with the silt of ages. Yet this very fact which saved them from crippling injuries now threatened to bring about their deaths. Fedora was plunged in the mud up to her knees, and Nicholas well past his ankles.

Only one factor gave them any chance of surviving. As they had struck the water feet first and face to face, the breath had not been driven from their bodies. That saved them from instant suffocation and left Nicholas with enough strength to struggle.

For a moment the nightmare of an agonizing death down there in the chill, pitch darkness was strong upon him. It seemed as if his feet were gripped in a rubber vice and that he would never be able to get them free. Panic seized him. He found his hands grasping Fedora's shoulders. Thrusting down upon them with all his strength, he arched his back and tore his feet out of the mud. But her arms were still locked round his neck so he could not push himself up to the surface.

It was then he felt her move. The shock of the cold water had brought her round, and she too had begun to struggle. Seizing her round the waist he strove to draw her upward, but she was too deeply imbedded for his efforts to raise her, even a few inches.

His lungs now seemed on the point of bursting. Stars and circles danced wildly in front of his closed eyes. Desperately he tried to think clearly and co-ordinate his movements so as not to waste his failing strength. But he could not. He gulped in a mouthful of evil-tasting water and it caused him excruciating pain as it gushed down his throat. Wildly now, he struck out in all directions. Then something hard but supple hit him on the head and slid down over his face.

Groping at it with both hands he found it was a rope. In his straining chest his heart leapt with new hope as he pulled a length of it towards him. By frantic fumbling he managed to thrust a bight of it under Fedora's right arm and round her back, so that he could clutch it firmly with his right hand; then with his left, he began to jerk violently on the vertical length that ran upwards to the surface, praying that whoever had thrown it would take his jerks for signals that he had secured himself to it.

An age seemed to pass before anything further happened. Despite himself his mouth opened again and gulped in more water. Renewed panic and terror made him kick out afresh; but Fedora was still fast in the mud and formed as effective an anchor for him as if she had been a ton of lead. At last the rope tightened. Then a new agony began. Fearing that he might not prove strong enough to keep hold of the bight of rope round Fedora, he had slipped his forearm through it. Now his arm was caught and crushed against her ribs and, although protecting them, felt as though it was being cut through.

As the strain increased, he could have screamed with agony; but Fedora too was conscious that an attempt was being made to rescue them, and was exerting every ounce of her remaining strength in an endeavour to kick herself free. As she got one leg out, its sudden release caused them to lurch sideways. The rope slipped higher, giving him momentary relief; then as the strain was taken up again it caused him fresh torture by cutting into his bicep. Another moment of excruciating pain, and the ordeal was over. The mud released its last hold and, though the rope slackened, they were drawn to the surface.

During the next few minutes neither of them had a very clear impression of what was happening. As they gulped air into their bursting lungs they smelt the stench of the foul water, and felt rough hands dragging them from it. For a brief interval they lay sprawled on the hard boards of a deck, vaguely conscious of the lurid fire still raging far above their heads, drifting clouds of smoke, and the mutter of low, urgent voices nearby. Then all these were blotted out by a big tarpaulin being hastily dragged over them.

When, after a few more minutes, Nicholas' thoughts became coherent again, he could hear Fedora breathing fast but regularly as she laboured to restore her respiration to normal; so he knew that she could have suffered no great harm. His next thought was that while they were exceedingly lucky to be alive at all, they were still luckier in having fallen into friendly hands; for it seemed evident that they had. He had registered just enough of his surroundings to know that they had been hauled aboard a motor river barge, and he felt sure that the tarpaulin could have been thrown over them only to hide them from any police who might be watching the canal, as the barge chugged past the streets adjacent to the warehouse. Temporarily relieved of any immediate fears, he gave his mind to the minor physical ills he had sustained, spitting out the filthy water he had swallowed, gently massaging his arm where the rope had chafed it, and generally pulling himself together.

Five minutes later his surmise, that they were among friends, was confirmed. The tarpaulin was lifted off them and a gruff voice said, "We are just about to turn into the river; but I take it you two have no wish to be landed yet awhile?"

The man who had spoken to them was a big, bearded fellow, wearing a square pilot jacket and a peaked seaman's cap. Swiftly and simultaneously the two fugitives answered him, saying they would prefer to remain on board. At their eagerness he laughed, and said while helping Fedora to her feet:

"When I saw you hanging from that cable, and all those Coms down in the street, I guessed it must be you that they were after. No one who was not on the run would have taken such a suicidal risk to escape the fire alone—not when they could have signalled for a fire ladder to be run up to them. But come down to the cabin and get your wet things off."

Still holding Fedora by the arm, he led the way across the deck and down a short steep ladder to a low cabin which was dimly lit by a single oil lamp. As he turned up its wick he went on: "My name is Sova—Karel Sova. Don't tell me yours if you'd prefer not to. I'm the master of this barge, and we're taking a cargo of army boots down the Moldau as far at Litoměřice."

"We owe our lives to you, Pan Sova," said Nicholas with deep feeling; and Fedora chimed in, "Indeed we do, and there are no words with which we can thank you."

"It is God you should thank," came the quick reply. "For this night, He clearly had His hand over you. Since you did not break your necks in your fall, you should certainly still be stuck in the mud at the bottom of the canal. At that hour, the chances against a barge passing the place at which you dropped, close enough to mark the spot and throw you a rope, must be at least a thousand to one. And I was due to sail at midnight. Had not my wife been suddenly taken ill I should by this time have been an hour and a half's distance away down the river."

"Surely more even than that," Nicholas murmured, "as it must be getting on towards morning."

The bearded Sova pulled out an old-fashioned turnip watch, and glanced at it. "Not much," he said. "It is now twenty minutes to two, and it can hardly be more than ten minutes ago that we picked you up."

It had been ten minutes to one when the alarm bell had gone in Mr. Smutný's penthouse. Nicholas found it almost impossible to believe that all the frightful experiences he had undergone, from that moment till he had been pulled out of the water, had occurred inside forty minutes. Yet there was no contesting it; and it was even more remarkable that only owing to the sudden illness of a woman they had never seen, he and Fedora should be alive.

As Fedora said she hoped Mrs. Sova's illness was nothing serious, the barge-master produced from a locker the inevitable bottle of Slivowitz and glasses. Setting them on the square table that occupied most of the floor-space of the cabin, he said:

"Thank you, *Slečna*, it might be worse. Five years ago, before we knew better about such things, several hundred women marched in a procession to protest about the price of bread. The Coms dispersed them with rifle fire and my wife was among the wounded. She recovered, praise be to God; but twice since, when she has over-excited herself, the wound has reopened, and it did so again tonight. So I had to make her as comfortable as I could, and leave her behind."

"She usually comes with you on your trips, then?" said Nicholas.

Sova nodded. "Yes: and that is fortunate as matters have turned out. It will enable me to provide some woman's clothes for the *Slečna* while her own are drying. It is lucky, too, that the night is so fine and warm, otherwise you might already have caught a severe chill. But you both look very white and shaken by your terrible experience. Drink this, and it will put new life into you."

As he spoke he pushed two tumblers that he had half-filled

with Slivowitz across the table, and motioned them to sit down to it. The plum brandy was raw stuff and burnt their throats as it went down, but it was just what they needed to prevent them from collapsing after the shock they had sustained.

While they were drinking it the barge-master opened two low doors; one on either side of the cabin. The first was that to the galley, in which a small stove was glowing brightly; above it he pointed out some racks which were specially constructed for drying clothes. The second led to a double sleeping cabin, and as he showed it to them, he said:

"My crew of two sleep forward. These are my married quarters, and I fear you must share them whether you are married or not, as I have no others to offer you. But you will be safe and comfortable here; and you will find plenty of dry clothes belonging to my wife and myself. Please help yourselves to such night things as you want. If you put your own things on the racks in the galley they will be dry long before morning. And you have no need to worry about me. In any case I should take several hours at the wheel, and I often stay on deck all through these short summer nights."

When they had thanked him, he was about to leave them, but Fedora said, "One moment please, Pan Sova. As you are going down river you will pass quite near the Ruzyně airport, won't you?"

"Fairly near," he agreed. "It lies about four to five kilometres from the right bank of the river."

"Then could you possibly land us somewhere near there? We have friends who live near the airport and are willing to hide us. In fact we were waiting for a car to take us out to them when the warehouse in which we had taken refuge was raided."

He nodded. "I could land you; but it will still be dark when we pass that bend in the river; and as I am late already I dare not wait about until it is light before putting you ashore. Do you know the district well?"

Fedora shook her head. "No; hardly at all."

"Then, unless you have very urgent reasons for trying to get to your friends before morning, I certainly would not advise you to attempt it. All the chances are that you would become hopelessly lost while striving to find your way across country in the darkness."

"But it is urgent!" Nicholas put in, suddenly alarmed by the thought that unless they got off the barge fairly soon they might be carried many miles down river. "It is terribly urgent. Whatever happens we have got to be at an inn near the airport by midday to-morrow."

Sova smiled. "Ah! that is rather different. And in that case I think I can help you. A kilometre or so past the bend there is a hamlet, and a cousin of mine owns a farm there. I could land you practically at his door, and I am sure he would put you up for the rest of the night. Then in the morning he, or one of his people, could drive you over to Ruzyně."

Again in Nicholas' mind the necessity for stopping Bilto leaving England had assumed priority over all else; so it was with great relief that he exclaimed, "If you could do that, we'd be most terribly grateful."

Fedora added her thanks, then asked, "About what time should we reach this hamlet where your cousin has his farm?"

"About four o'clock," replied Sova, after a moment's thought. "That means you have a little over two hours in which to rest and dry your clothes, so I should lose no time in getting them off. In case you drop asleep, I will come down at about ten to four and give you a call."

Once more they thanked him, then he went up the short ladder to the deck and closed the hatch behind him.

Nicholas looked across at Fedora. She was in a shocking state. Her satchel-bag was still slung round her neck, but she had lost her beret in the water, and her coronet of plaits had come undone so that they now hung about her head in a ring of sodden rat's-tails. Her face was begrimed, blood was seeping from a cut on her neck and her hands were filthy. To drag herself free from the grip of the ooze she had had to abandon both her shoes, and she was smothered in mud nearly up to her waist. Raising a smile, he asked:

"How are you feeling?"

"I'm alive," she replied. "But that's just about all. And even that I owe to you. I'm thoroughly ashamed of the exhibition I made of myself up on the roof."

"You needn't be," he assured her sincerely. "You are the bravest woman I've ever met, Fedora. And if you hadn't come down to the fourth floor to guide me back, we'd neither of us be here now. So that makes us quits. Come on, now, let me play lady's-maid again and help you get your wet clothes off."

She shook her head. "No, Nicky. I can't face it. That rope with which they pulled us out gave my back hell. I'd rather let my clothes dry on me."

"You'll catch your death of cold."

"What's it matter? We are clear of the Coms now. They must believe that we were burnt to cinders in the pent-house. Anyway, there is no possible means by which they can trace us; so, unless we get a shockingly bad break, by this time to-morrow we'll be in bed and asleep in London. Having caught a cold won't spoil that for me."

"Nor me!" he agreed feelingly. "All the same, I'm going to get my things off; and you might as well let me take off your frock, anyway. Then if you sit by the stove your underclothes won't feel so cold and clammy."

To his last suggestion he persuaded her to agree, and having settled her in the galley he retired into the little sleeping cabin. On one of its bulkheads hung a mirror. When he glanced in it he hardly knew himself. His hair was a matted tangle, his eyes were bloodshot and his face, which seemed much thinner, was streaked with soot marks.

One end of the cabin was occupied by a dressing chest and the other by a broad shelf that formed a wash-stand. Having got his clothes off, he gave himself a good rub down, slipped on Sova's dressing gown, and carried his own things through to dry. Then he had a good wash and brush up and, now feeling considerably refreshed, decided that he must do something about Fedora. Refilling the wash basin, and collecting some towels and toilet things, he carried them through to her.

While talking with Sova she had given the impression that she had recovered remarkably quickly from her ordeal; but Nicholas realized that must have been a flash in the pan, as she now appeared thoroughly exhausted. Seeing that she was incapable of making any effort, he washed her face and hands for her, then undid the plaits, dried her silvery-gold hair, and gave it a good brushing.

When he had finished she took his hand, pressed it, and smiled up into his face. "Thank you, Nicky. You are being awfully good to me; and I don't deserve it, as I got you into all this."

He returned her smile. "No, I got myself into it; and you, too, in a way. If I hadn't impersonated Bilto in the first place you would never had been sent to Prague. Anyhow, the object of both of us was to stop him, and if our luck holds we'll succeed in that yet. That's the only thing that matters."

As they were both only partially clad they remained in the warm galley, sitting on two boxes of stores, with their backs against the bulkhead and their feet thrust out towards the stove. After Nicholas' ministrations Fedora felt much more comfortable and fell into a doze; but his brain remained too active for him to get a nap.

In considering their prospects, he decided that if they could reach the inn owned by Mr. Lutonský there seemed no reason why they should not get away as arranged. Even if the two telephone conversations between Smutný and Lutonský had been taken down by some spy in the exchange, nothing could have been made of them, as they had been couched in such cryptic language. That Smutný had escaped capture was evident from his telephone call about the apparatus for crossing the canal by the telegraph cable; therefore the police had nothing at all to go on which could connect Fedora and himself with Lutonský or Jirka.

But he was by no means so optimistic about Fedora's idea that they might sleep the following night in London. Apparently the 'funnel' was a well-established escape route in frequent use; so, barring unforeseen accidents, it should get them to Frankfurt. About their onward journey from there, though, although there would be no dangers, there would certainly be difficulties. They had no money for fares and their passports had been taken from them; so they might be held for several days before they could fully establish their identities and get themselves repatriated.

It occurred to him that as Fedora had been working against the Communists in London she must have contacts in the British Secret Service, and that through them she might be able to short-circuit many official bottle-necks; but, even so, it would take her several hours, at least, before she could secure a clearance through them, and the means to fly on to England.

However, all that was really immaterial. Once they had got to Frankfurt, or even to the nearest town on the other side of the Iron Curtain, there would be nothing more to worry about. The Americans would certainly not deny them facilities for telephoning to London, and he had no doubt at all that once he had spoken to Scotland Yard, Bilto would be arrested within the hour.

His thoughts then drifted back for a while to the terrifying experiences he had been through during the day; but cleaning himself and Fedora up had taken longer than he supposed, so he was quite surprised when the barge-master came down to tell them that it was getting on for four o'clock, and they were nearing their destination.

Sova put a pot of coffee on the stove, then left them to dress. Nicholas' suit and shoes were still a little damp but the lighter garments had dried out well. Among them was the big silk handkerchief that he had used to tie Fedora's wrists, as Sova had brought it down after untying them. Since she now had nothing to put on her head, and her long fair locks were loose again, Nicholas suggested that she should make them less conspicuous by using it as a head scarf. As she tied its ends under her chin she looked down ruefully at her ruined stockings and shoeless feet, and said:

"I hope Mr. Sova can find me something to walk in, even if it's only an old pair of gym-shoes."

When he rejoined them, she asked him what he could do, and he found for her from among his wife's things a pair of open-topped leather boots, typical of those worn by Czech country-women. As they proved too large, he gave her a pair of socks, and with these over her stockings the boots fitted fairly comfortably.

The coffee was the usual ersatz stuff, but with a shot of Slivo-witz added it did not taste too bad. They had only just finished it when there came a hail from above and the barge began to slow down. Sova ran up the ladder and they followed him. Crossing the short after-deck, he took the wheel from an elderly man, who wished them 'good morning', although the first light of dawn had not yet come. The placid river was faintly lit by starlight; there were no other boats in the vicinity, but about a hundred yards ahead they could make out a deserted jetty.

As they came nearer to it they saw that it was little more than a ramshackle landing stage with a solitary lean-to on its land-ward side. Sova stopped the motor; the barge drifted on, gradually losing way. A man holding a rope in the bows jumped on to the wooden staging; a moment later the elderly man near them followed suit, and the barge was made fast. Fedora, Nicholas and Sova stepped ashore. The two former shook hands with the crew and thanked them for the part they had played in the rescue. Both men wished them good luck, and cursed the Communists. Then Sova told his men that he did not expect to be gone for more than twenty minutes, and led the way to a cart-track on the far side of the lean-to.

The track ran inland for some two hundred yards, then en-tered a tree-fringed road. As they turned north along it the sharp roof lines of buildings among the trees ahead stood out against the night sky. They passed two cottages standing a little way back from the road, then a long, high barn that ran alongside it. At the end of the barn there was a gate to a farmyard. Halting at it, Sova said:

"It would be best if you wait here until I have made certain that my cousin Otokar is still in possession of his farm. He was a fortnight ago; but one can hardly be certain of owning the clothes one stands up in from day to day under our Communist rulers."

As the barge-master set off across the yard to the house, Nicholas asked Fedora, "Are things really as bad as he suggests?"

She nodded. "The Coms can take anything they want on the excuse of Sovietizing the country. You must know the first principle of Socialism, 'From each according to his means and to each according to his needs'. That can be made to cover any outrage. I have seen a Com tart take the fur coat off an old lady's back while the tart's policeman pals stood by and laughed. But, of course, the State is the all-time high-robber; and Mr. Sova was referring to the enforcement of the Collective Farm system that has been going on for some time. His cousin's farm may have been taken over without warning or compensation."

"What will have come of him if it has?"

"Oh, he will still be here. That is, unless he resisted and endeavoured to prevent the seizure of his property. In that case he would be shot. Otherwise he would be kept on as a labourer, under some slave-driving brute who has failed at farming himself but knows just enough about it to have got a Government job by joining the Party. They are the boys who collect all the pigs in a district at one farm, where there are no pig-sties, and all the chickens at another, where there are no hen-coops. Most of them get bumped off for incompetence in due course, but that doesn't do the wretched farmer who has been dispossessed any good; and there are always young thugs being educated up in the Party 'Youth' organizations to carry on the slave-driving."

Twelve hours before, Nicholas would not have believed her; but he did now, and said with a sigh, "It all sounds quite frightful. Still, as far as we are concerned, if he is still here, even if he has had the bad luck to be taken over, he will be able to give us a shake-down until morning."

"I doubt it. All the odds are that his house would have been given to someone who bears him a grudge, so that they can keep an eye on him—some lazy swine whom he has sacked, or one of his workmen with known Com sympathies—and that he will be sleeping in the attic or the cellar. Anyhow, if a Com is in possession it would be much too dangerous for us to stay here."

Fedora had hardly finished speaking when they were relieved of their fears that the pessimistic picture she painted as yet applied to the Sova farm. Two figures emerged from the darkness; the stalwart barge-master, and with him a tall, thin man whom he introduced as his cousin Otokar Sova.

Otokar proved to be a not unkindly but gloomy man. He said that he would willingly have taken the fugitives in but was unable to do so, because the authorities now compelled him to house all his work people who could not find other accommodation. In consequence, owing to the general housing shortage there was not a room at the farm that had not someone sleeping in it. However, if they cared to doss down in the barn, there was plenty of hay there and he could let them have a couple of blankets.

They were glad enough to accept his offer, and while he went off to get the blankets they said good-bye to Karel Sova; repeating more than once, in spite of his protests, that they would never forget what a good friend he had been to them.

The barge-master had not long disappeared in the darkness when Otokar Sova reappeared carrying a lantern as well as the blankets. As he led them into the big barn the oasis of light made by the lantern was just enough for them to realize that it was a fine old building with great oak cross-beams and a vaulted roof. The greater part of it was empty, except for a few piles of sacks; but at its far end, about one third of its length was divided horizontally by an open loft some ten feet from the ground, and it was upon this that the hay was stored.

Having set up a ladder against the open end of this upper floor, the lugubrious Otokar told them that his wife would bring them something to eat in the morning, then held up his lantern for them to mount to their resting place. As soon as they had reached it he wished them 'good sleep' and, evidently in no mind to risk a fire, went off, taking the lantern with him.

By groping about in the darkness they soon had enough loose

hay to make a soft couch and, having spread the blankets out on it, lay down side by side.

After a moment's silence, Fedora said: "I love the smell of hay."

"Were you brought up in the country, then?" Nicholas asked.

"No; in Prague. My father was a Czech businessman, and we weren't well-off enough to have even a cottage in the country. I love the smell of hay because it reminds me of New England, where my husband's home was. His parents had a farm there, and we used to go and stay with them sometimes on our leave. I liked it so much better than living in Washington."

"I hadn't realized that you married an American."

"Yes. He was an Intelligence Officer, and came here with the American mission in 1945, before the Iron Curtain closed down. I was only nineteen then; but we fell in love, and he married me and took me back to the United States."

During nearly the whole of the time that Fedora and Nicholas had been together they had spoken to one another in Czech, but he now recalled the slight American accent that he had noticed when they had first met and she was talking in English, as he asked:

"For how long were you in America?"

"Three years. It was during that time I taught my husband to speak Czech. How I wish to God now that I hadn't."

"Why?"

"It was that which led to our being sent back here. In those years between the defeat of Japan and the opening of the Korean War the prospects for a young regular Army Officer weren't up to much, and we had very little money. When they found out that he spoke Czech fluently, as well as having a Czech wife, they asked him if he would agree to be transferred for a tour of duty with a civilian outfit. They promised that it should make no difference to his seniority; and, of course, the pay for under-cover work was about four times what he had been getting. We fell for it and came back as stooges on the staff of a trade delegation. Our idea was that living being so cheap in Europe to dollar earners, we'd be able to put by a fine fat wad, then buy ourselves a nice little home for keeps when we got back to the States. But it just didn't work out that way."

All that Nicholas could think of to say was "That was rotten luck. You've had a hard deal, Fedora." But he stretched out a hand in the darkness, found one of hers, and pressed it.

"Thanks, Nicky," she murmured. "But I'm not complaining. I've had a lot of fun, and I've been lucky enough to help save a few people from a very gruesome finish. I've a feeling now, though, that I'm pretty well finished myself. I can't explain it; because if I were going to die I ought to have died tonight at the bottom of that canal. Perhaps it is that I have nothing left that I want to live for."

"Oh, come!" he protested. "You mustn't talk like that. You're a very lovely woman, and still quite young. From what you've just said you can't be much more than twenty-seven. It's certain that you'll fall in love again. Next time that may mean a home, security, jolly children, and all the sorts of steady-going happiness that you seem to have missed so far."

The hay rustled, as she shook her head. "No, Nicky. I'm not that sort of a girl. For a little time I thought I was; but I'm not. I've lived too hard and too dangerously these past few years. And somehow this last business of Bilto's having let me down makes me feel all burnt out. I wouldn't mind if I died to-morrow."

"I wish to God I'd never told you about that woman that Bilto was going to meet in Prague."

"You didn't know that I cared about him, then. But as he has been separated from her for years, it's quite understandable that he should have consoled himself with me in England. That's life. Men and women may carry an ideal love for another person in their hearts all their lives long, but that doesn't alter the fact that they can love another person with their senses from time to time; and I'm sure that Bilto loved me that way."

Again she was silent for a moment, then she gave a little laugh. "I wonder what would have happened if it had been you I had met in the first place, instead of him. You are awfully like him physically, but nearer my age, and at rock bottom a much finer person."

"No, I'm not. He's kind and generous, and a much stronger character than I am."

"That's not altogether true. He can be very weak at times, and he is not open, like you are. He has plenty of good points; but, loving him as I do, I know him well enough to recognize his bad ones."

"Ah, that's just it. You may know his, but you don't know me well enough to know mine."

She sighed. "And I don't suppose I ever shall. As things are that makes you all the more attractive. At this moment, for me, you are all the best of Bilto without the worst. Did you mean it just now when you said you thought me a very lovely woman, or were you just being nice?"

"No. I meant it. When I saw you first I thought you striking, yet hardly even pretty. But you grow on one; and the extraordinary thing is that you don't need any trappings. That pale face of yours was still lovely when you were covered with muck, after they pulled us out of the canal."

Once more there fell a short silence, then she asked, "Tell me, Nicky. What would you do if this was your last night on earth?"

The pressure of events in the past thirty-six hours had forced the circumstances in which he had left Birmingham so far out of his mind that it now ignored them; but as he consciously drew in the sweet smell of the hay it brought him a vivid memory of the unforgettable afternoon that he had spent years before with a girl in a haystack. Spontaneously he replied: "I should make love to you."

She slid an arm round his neck. "Then let's pretend it is. I want you to. Please, Nicky; love me to sleep."

For a good two hours they slept soundly; but as the full light of day percolated into the big barn Fedora became restless. She began to talk in her sleep and turn about uneasily. Nicholas roused up, and when he touched her cheek he found that it was hot and dry. He knew then that sleeping in her damp under-

9

clothes had given her a chill and that she had a touch of fever. He did not waken her, but dozed beside her for another hour or more, until she woke herself, to complain that her head was aching and her throat parched.

He was wondering if he dare go out to the farm to get her something to drink when a plump middle-aged woman appeared, carrying a basket over her arm. Climbing up the ladder, she introduced herself as Božena Sova, Otokar's wife, and took from the basket the bread, cold bacon, cheese and milk she had brought for their breakfast.

She said that she had not come earlier as she had wanted to give them as long as possible to sleep, and would have given them still longer, but for the fact that Sunday service was to be held in the barn in three-quarters of an hour's time.

On Nicholas looking rather mystified, Fedora told him in a quick aside that the Coms had closed nearly all the churches as places liable to be used for reactionary gatherings, and forbidden the holding of religious ceremonies in private as anti-social activities; so they now had to be held in secret.

Mrs. Sova said she understood that they would be leaving that day, and asked if they would like a parcel of food to take with them, or if there was any other way in which she could be of help.

Nicholas thanked her and declined the food, but said that they wanted to be at the Ruzyně Airport by midday at the latest, and they were not certain either how far off it was or how to get there.

"That is simple," she smiled. "The airport is only about six kilometres away, and the left-hand fork of the road south leads right past it. As for getting there, my good man can easily drive you over in the gig, after service."

"We must not put him to that trouble," said Fedora quickly, "and it is just possible that if he is seen with us he might be questioned afterwards. We can walk that distance in a little over an hour."

The apple-cheeked farm-wife had already been regarding Fedora's flushed face and feverish eyes with concern. "No," she said firmly. "Perhaps it would be wise for him to drop you half a kilometre this side of the airport, but he shall certainly drive you that far. You are in no state to walk, my dear, or travel at all for that matter. I wish I could put you to bed in the house. As that can't be managed, why not let me make you as comfortable as I can here for a day or two?"

Fedora shook her head. "It's terribly kind of you, Paní Sova, but we have a date with friends who hope to get us away, and it is very important indeed that we should stick to our arrangements. I would be grateful, though, if you could let me have some aspirin."

"I'll bring you some when I come back for the breakfast things," Mrs. Sova agreed, "and some lavender water to cool your poor forehead."

When she had left them Nicholas made a good breakfast, but he could persuade Fedora only to swallow a few mouthfuls of bread and bacon with the milk. It was clear that she was running a high temperature, which was not to be wondered at in view of all she had been through the previous day; but, worried as he was about her, there was nothing he could do, except hope that the aspirin would bring it down before they had to make a move.

Soon after they had finished eating, Mrs. Sova returned with it and, having given Fedora a couple of tablets, insisted that she should take the rest of the bottle with her. Then she sponged the girl's forehead, cheeks, neck and wrists with home-made lavender water, and told her to lie quiet until it was time for her to go.

But to that Fedora said, "If I may, Paní Sova, I would very much like to come down and attend the service. I'm sure that wouldn't make me worse."

The good woman smiled. "God forbid that I should restrain anyone from worshipping their Maker, child. You will be welcomed by both Him and us. But it would be better if you don't join in the singing or exert yourself more than need be. It will be starting in about ten minutes' time."

As she descended the ladder to the floor two men carried in a small harmonium and set it down at the far end of the barn. Soon other people began to collect, until a small congregation had assembled consisting of eight men and about a score of women. Nearly all of them were middle-aged or elderly and all were of the peasant class.

Fedora got up to go down and join them, but after a moment's hesitation she turned to Nicholas and asked, "Wouldn't you like to attend the service too?"

He smiled up at her a shade apologetically. "I'd rather not; if you'll excuse me. I gave up all that sort of thing when I was a boy, so I'd only feel embarrassed. But perhaps I'll say a private prayer up here."

He watched her join the group of women round Mrs. Sova, then saw the pastor come in. At his entrance a hush fell on the congregation and they quietly took their places: the men all together at one side and the women at the other, in the old Lutheran manner. Seeing that the service was about to begin Nicholas felt that it was not proper for him to remain there sitting up aloft like a spectator at a barn-play; so he got up and clambered over some bales of hay to the back of the staging.

Behind the bales it was almost dark; so, noticing a wooden door in the side wall of the barn, he pulled it open a few inches and sat down beside it. The door looked out on to the road and was about nine feet above it, so that wagons could draw up immediately below and load or unload crops direct from or to the loft.

It was a lovely May morning with the peace of Sunday on the countryside. Soon, as he sat there, the murmur of prayers, the clear voice of the pastor, and the chanting of age-old litanies came to him. He rather wished now that he had accepted Fedora's invitation to join in, for he had suddenly become strongly conscious that there was something fearless and fine and indestructible about these people's simple faith.

Their voices were raised in a hymn when he saw a big furniture removal van come round the bend of the road. To his surprise it slowed down and pulled up immediately beneath the door behind which he sat half concealed. From the seat next to the driver, a young boy of about eleven jumped down. Waving his hand excitedly, he shouted something and pointed to the barn.

Next moment a single-decker bus came into view and jolted to a standstill behind the lorry. Out of it poured a score of State police. Following the boy, they ran towards the gate of the stable yard. Springing to his feet, Nicholas pushed the door to from which he was looking. Out of the blue an evil fate had struck at him, Fedora and their friends. The barn was about to be raided: and from it there was no escape.

CHAPTER XVIII

DECREE OF FATE

FOR a moment Nicholas stood stockstill. To have rushed out from behind the bales of hay and shouted a warning to the congregation would have been futile. By the time he made himself heard above the singing, the leading men in the running squad of police would be at the main doors of the barn. It was already too late for anyone to get out that way without being caught. There remained the small door to the loft, near which he was standing. For the congregation to escape that way was equally impossible. The police would follow, call on them to halt, and open fire if any of them attempted to jump down into the road. For him alone it offered a means of escape, providing he did not involve himself with the congregation, and providing that no police had been left on watch with the vehicles below.

Realizing that, as far as he was concerned, everything hung on this last point, he opened the door a crack and peered through it. The roof of the big removal van blocked a large sector of his view. Beyond it the road was empty, but he could hear voices.

He felt certain that someone was standing on the far side of it, talking to its driver.

Suddenly the singing ceased. The harmonium played on for a moment, then died in a wail. For a matter of seconds there was a tense silence. It was broken by the bark of a harsh order. Hard upon it came a babble of mingled shouts of anger and cries of fear.

Nicholas pulled the Luger, which he had used in the warehouse, from his pocket. He knew nothing about weapons and wondered if its immersion in the canal had rendered it temporarily useless. The pistol had been well greased and, to his relief, he found that its recoil chamber still slid back easily. Pressing the magazine button, he quickly removed the clip, and saw that it had only three bullets remaining in it. Ramming it into his pocket, he reloaded with one of the full clips that Fedora had given him. Then, holding the weapon at the ready, he clambered back across the bales of hay until he could see down into the middle and far end of the barn.

Crouching there, still under cover, he took swift stock of the situation. The police already had the little group of men covered with sten-guns. They were crowded into a corner with their hands above their heads. Their faces were sullen but resigned. It was clear they realized the uselessness of putting up a fight. The women were proving more difficult. They were screaming abuse and, in several cases, attempting to break through the police in the hope of getting away. Fedora was among them. She was struggling wildly with a tall, dark man. Stooping her head, she bit him on the wrist. With a curse, he let her go, but hit her. She fell to the floor. He dragged her up and hit her again.

Nicholas was desperately tempted to intervene; but he was not a practised shot with an automatic. He knew that at that distance he was just as likely to hit Fedora as the thug who was maltreating her. Another thought also restrained him. There was more at stake than Fedora, or himself, or any individual life. Unless one of them could stop Bilto he would leave England that night. To-morrow it would be too late to prevent him making a present of the secrets he held to the men who ruled behind the Iron Curtain, and were endeavouring to force their hideous tyranny on the whole world. That Fedora should have been captured was tragic, but that made it all the more imperative that he should do his utmost to retain his freedom, so that he might yet get back across the frontier and telephone a warning to London in time.

In any case, no one man could have rescued Fedora now, in the face of a score of armed police. Had Nicholas attempted it he would have been shot down long before he could reach her, and thrown away his life to no purpose. That thought allayed a little his feeling that it was cowardly to play the role of an on-looker; but he could have cursed aloud with fury at his impotence to help, as his gaze continued fixed upon her.

At the second blow she had fallen again. Now she was lying on her back at the side of the barn, sprawling half across a pile of cattle-cake. Her right arm was flung out at an awkward angle above her head, and she lay quite still.

As Nicholas stared at her, he recalled the gloomy thoughts that had obsessed her when they had first settled down in the loft some six hours earlier—her feeling that she was finished, that she was burnt out and had nothing left to live for, her wish to pretend that it was their last night on earth. Had that been some strange foreboding that her death was imminent? He was no believer in fortune-telling and the 'mumbo-jumbo of the occult', preferring to explain away the inexplicable by attributing it to the as yet little understood affects of cosmic rays, or by other meaningless pseudo-scientific jargon. Yet he knew that there were cases of incontestable authenticity in which people had received previous warning of their own deaths. Had Fedora had such a warning? Had the policeman's last blow broken her neck? Had her gallant heart at last failed, after she had been through so much, at learning fate's decree that she was not to escape after all? As she lay slumped and twisted there, was she already dead?

The police now had the whole congregation under control. The officer in charge of the raid took a paper from his breast pocket and in a careless gabble read it out. It was a decree by the People's Government of Czechoslovakia prohibiting all religious assemblies held without an official permit, and making anyone caught attending such an assembly liable to a minimum penalty of one year's labour in the uranium mines.

Stuffing the paper back into his pocket, the officer gave an order, and his men began to hustle the cowed peasants towards the doors of the barn. He was standing near the pastor and, turning, gave him a vicious kick on the behind with his jack-boot, as a send-off in the right direction.

Not long since, Nicholas had inveighed against priests of all denominations as parasites, and propagators of outworn super-stitions the continued observance of which was not consonant with the 'Dignity of Man'. Yet his gorge rose, not on account of the physical brutality of the act but from an instinctive feeling that the indignity had been inflicted upon something in essence higher than any individual man, of which this humble Lutheran pastor was only the representative.

As he continued to stare down at the heart-rending spectacle of the Sovas and their fellow-worshippers being hurried from the barn, he saw Fedora move her arm, and the policeman who had hit her pulled her stumbling to her feet. His heart leapt with relief at the knowledge that she was not dead, but had only fainted.

Next moment he was given swift cause to think of himself. The boy of eleven who had led the raid was standing near the officer. He had caught him by the arm and was pointing to the loft. Owing to the hubbub which was going on below, Nicholas could not catch his words; but it was clear that he was suggesting that before they had entered the barn some of the congregation might have hidden themselves up among the hay, so the loft ought to be searched.

Without waiting for further indications of his peril Nicholas scrambled back. Next moment he was again standing in the semi-darkness beside the door of the loft. It was, as he had left it open a few inches. He peered through. There was no one in sight, but he could still hear voices on the far side of the removal van, and at any second now the police would be bringing their prisoners out from the yard into the road. If he jumped down, capture was as good as certain.

The reason why the police had brought the removal van was now obvious. It was the perfect type of vehicle in which to lock up and cart away a score or more of men and women. Apparently it was in normal use during the week and commandeered only for such raids on Sundays; as on its top, which was heightened by the usual two-foot board along its sides and ends to keep light goods stacked there from slipping off, there lay a pile of hessian wrappers and a tarpaulin.

In a flash of inspiration Nicholas saw the chance it offered. He had only to step out on to the roof of the van and pull the furniture wrappers over him to escape detection. As he opened the door he heard footsteps running up the ladder on the far side of the hay. Without the loss of a second, he pocketed his gun and stepped across the yard-wide gap which was all that separated him from the roof of the van. Throwing out his hands, so as to fall upon it with as little noise as possible, he dived below the level of the side-board, which then screened him from anyone approaching along the road. Grabbing the coverings with both hands, he pulled the whole bundle on top of himself and lay still, so that if the searchers who had come up the loft chanced to look out of its door they would see nothing to arouse their suspicions.

He had been lying there no more than a minute when he heard sounds beneath him. Someone was pulling open the doors at the back of the van. There came a trampling of many feet approaching along the road, with which mingled cries and curses. The noise increased to a din as the twenty to thirty people who had made up the congregation were herded into the van. Gradually the commotion subsided. The engine started up, the van moved slowly at first until it had backed round to face the direction from which it had come, then drove off.

For several minutes Nicholas did not dare to put his head out from under the coverings, as it was possible that some of the police might still be at the door of the loft, or, if they had gone

9*

into the farm, be looking out of one of its windows; but as soon as he felt confident that the van was out of sight of the hamlet he raised himself on one elbow and took a quick look round.

Behind the van the road was clear. In front the single-decker bus that had brought the raiding party was churning up the dust two hundred yards ahead. As he watched, it perceptibly increased its lead. In the distance, to the right, he could see the river; but they were veering away from it; so it was clear that outside the hamlet the van must have taken the left-hand fork and was on the road that led both to the airport and to Prague.

Now, for the first time since the raid, Nicholas had the chance to assess the new situation. That he and Fedora should have been caught up in the Communists' campaign to suppress religion was the most appalling luck. By what practically amounted to a miracle they had escaped from their pursuers, leaving no trace, and were by now almost certainly assumed to be dead; yet the arrangements for their flight from the country were in hand, and within another hour or so they should have been making their final preparations with Mr. Lutonský for a clean get-away. It was indeed a bitter pill to swallow that, through having chanced to spend a few hours in the Sova's barn, rather than in any one of the scores of others in the district, they should now again be prisoners.

That Nicholas had managed to escape actual arrest was true, but he was as much a prisoner as Fedora, because he could not get off the top of the fast-moving van without the risk of breaking his neck; and when it did pull up all the odds were that it would do so in the yard of some police headquarters, so to climb down then would mean immediate arrest.

Prague was only some twelve kilometres away, the van was going in that direction, and there was no town of any size nearer; so it seemed certain that it was going to the capital and would not stop before it got there. The fact that it would actually pass the airport added to Nicholas' bitter fury; but it seemed that his only possible chance of escaping capture lay in remaining hidden under the coverings until night, then endeavouring to get away unseen from the garage or yard in which the van was parked after it had unloaded its human cargo. But, even if he succeeded in that, he would then have missed the plane, and all chance of stopping Bilto would be gone.

It was not until the van had covered a couple of kilometres that it suddenly occurred to him that he might manage to stop it while it was still out in the country. The bus containing the raiding party had gone on ahead and was now out of sight. It seemed certain that they would have left guards with the van, but he still had his pistol; so if there were not too many of them, and he could take them by surprise, there was at least a chance that he might get away.

Crawling to the back of the roof, he peeped cautiously over the ridge board. Six feet below, on the tail board, two guards were sitting. He could easily have shot both of them from above; but that was not necessarily going to stop the van. If the shots were not heard by the driver, the two guards would simply roll off the tail-board and the van go on. If, on the other hand, the driver did hear the shots and pull up, that would be far from the end of the matter. The driver was probably armed, and the odds were that he had one or two more guards sitting on the box with him. If so, they would jump out into the road with their guns ready in their hands, and before Nicholas could possibly get away he would be shot himself.

The only alternative was to do the job the other way about and, if possible, shoot the driver first. That would result in the van careering on till it ran off the road and crashed into a tree or overturned. The risk entailed was considerable, as Nicholas knew that he would be flung from its top, and perhaps be seriously injured. On the other hand the men on the box would almost certainly be trapped in the smash, and the two guards on the tail-board flung off. There was also a fair chance that if the doors of the van had not been fully secured the prisoners might break out. That offered a prospect of rescuing Fedora, and if they escaped injury, they might be able to get away in the confusion.

Having weighed the chances, Nicholas decided that the risk was worth it. He alone would know when the crash was coming, so would have a much better prospect than the guards on the tail, of landing safely. The question now was, could he get into a position from which it would be possible to shoot the driver?

On hands and knees he crawled forward to the front of the van. Beyond the ridge-board projected the lower roof of the cab. It appeared to be made only of match-boarding, and he considered shooting blind down through it, but decided that the possibility of missing the man altogether was too great. Turning to the side of the van, he peered over. He could now see the cab a few feet below him, but not the man in it. To lean over meant that he would have to fire into it from a very awkward angle, but that seemed to offer a much better chance of wounding the driver than firing through the roof.

The road in front was clear. A glance over his shoulder showed that nothing was coming up behind. They were passing through a wood, so there was no chance of his being seen from a distance, and it would provide good cover for flight if he survived the initial stages of his coup. Taking out his gun, he clicked a bullet up into its chamber. The van was approaching a bend in the road. With difficulty now he fought down the urge to get the desperate business over, and waited until they were within fifty yards of it. Then, leaning over as far as he dared, and with his elbow crooked, he fired three shots down into the driver's cab.

He heard a faint shout, but nothing else happened. He thought he must have missed. If he had it was to be expected that the van would pull up, and that frightened, angry men would soon be shooting back at him; yet it ran on steadily. It had almost reached the corner, and there was still no indication whether his shots had taken effect. He seemed to have been crouching on the angle of the roof for an age, waiting for the van to swerve and run off the road. Round the bend he glimpsed open country. If he could not halt the van before it came out of the wood his chances of getting away would be enormously reduced. Seized by panic, he leaned over to fire again.

It was not necessary. Even as he gripped the front-board with his free hand, to prevent himself being sent over the side by an unexpected jolt, he saw that the van could not now get round the bend. It was still running straight. As he pulled himself back, its front wheels went over the grass verge. The grass was fairly level but sloped down sharply. Without changing speed, or even a perceptible bump, the van left the road. Another moment, and it was charging down the bank towards the trees.

The instant Nicholas realized that his plan was, after all, succeeding, he turned and endeavoured to scramble to the rear of the roof. He hoped that if he could get there before the van crashed he would be able to shoot one, if not both, of the guards on the tail-board. He might have done it, had he known even half a minute earlier that he had accounted for the driver; but now it was too late. The sharp tilt the van took as it charged down the bank sent him slithering back. Scared now that he might be caught unawares if the van turned over, he got his feet against the front-board, wriggled round and sat up.

The wood was not dense; its trees were, on average, forty feet apart with low scrub between them. The van, now bumping wildly, was about to career through a gap between a big oak and a beech, but their boughs almost met, and the lowest were a little less than the height of the van. With dilated eyes Nicholas saw that he was about to be swept from its top: yet he managed to keep his wits. As the nearest bough of the oak scraped the roof of the cab, lifted and rushed upon him, he thrust the gun into his trouser top and grasped at the bough with both hands.

For a moment he fumbled wildly, as the twigs and leaves were dashed into his face, then his clutching fingers found a firm hold. The van careered on beneath him; he was dragged to the rear end of its roof, bumped painfully on the back edge-board, and over it. Now that there was nothing to support his weight the bough bent under him. Still hanging on to it, his toes were no more than five feet from the ground. Letting go, he dropped, made an effort to keep upright but fell, and rolled into some bushes.

As Nicholas staggered to his feet the van hit another oak, fifty feet away, head on. He was just in time to see the two guards flung off the tail-board. He could have run for it then and there, and got away, but he was checked by the thought of Fedora. Given a little luck now he might save her, and the unfortunate peasant congregation, as well as himself. If he could catch the guards before they had a chance to recover from their shaking, he could hold them up and force them to undo the doors of the van. Automatically now, his hand went to the pocket in which he carried the pistol.

Before his hand was half way there he remembered that he had not had time to thrust it back before the bough hit him, so had stuffed its muzzle into his trousers' top; but it was not there either. It had been knocked or jerked away during his fall from the van. Hastily he began to search about for it among the bushes.

Barely half a minute had elapsed since the van crashed, but already muted sounds of commotion were coming from it. There was a banging on its doors, a dull thump and a loud creak as a concerted effort was made against them. The lock was not strong enough to withstand the weight of a dozen bodies. With a rending noise the doors burst open and out tumbled the mixed crowd of men and women.

At the sound, Nicholas looked up. He saw that one of the guards had been thrown head-first against a tree-stump, and was lying there either dead or unconscious. The other was on his feet and had drawn his gun. He was shouting at the crowd tumbling from the van to stand back and put their hands up.

From the front of the van a small figure scrambled down, and limped painfully away into the undergrowth. It was the boy who had acted as guide to the police when they had raided the barn. But no guards came running from the driver's cab, so Nicholas felt confident that, if any of them had been riding there, the crash had put them *hors de combat*. It looked now as if only the survivor from the tail-board stood between the whole crowd of prisoners and their freedom; and his back was turned to Nicholas.

Frantically Nicholas resumed his search for his lost gun. If only he could find it, he could take the remaining guard in the rear; without it he was as helpless as the others, for, had he approached, the rustle of the undergrowth would have given warning in ample time for the man to turn and shoot him. On hands and knees he groped around beneath the bough from which he had dropped, turning his glance swiftly from side to side, but his desperately searching eyes were not rewarded by the glint of sunlight on metal.

Suddenly a single shot rang out. Jumping up, Nicholas looked anxiously across the bushes. The peasants were all bunched together just outside the doors of the van. In the second rank he caught sight of Fedora's pale face beneath his silk handkerchief. In front of it a wisp of blue smoke was curling up. Covered by the people in front of her she had got Kmoch's little automatic out of her satchel-bag and fired between them.

Her bullet had hit the guard in the thigh. As he staggered the peasants launched themselves at him in a body. It was only as they surged forward that Fedora was fully revealed to Nicholas with the wisp of smoke curling up in front of her. The guard's gun went off once. A woman screamed and fell. Before he could fire again the rest of them were upon him. He was seized, struck, scratched, kicked, borne to the ground and trampled upon. One moment he had been a fine powerful young fellow; the next he was a torn and broken body with not a flicker of life in it.

As Nicholas ran forward several of the crowd ran at the other guard, who had been knocked unconscious against the tree-stump. Sova was the first to reach him, and pulled his pistol from its holster. The rest seized the helpless man and treated him in the same way as they had his comrade. Like a pack of ferocious wolves they worried and milled round him, until his body was grotesquely twisted and his face an unrecognizable mass of pulp.

When Nicholas reached Fedora she was pushing the pistol back into her bag. Her green eyes were brilliant with fever and her voice a trifle hoarse as she cried:

"Nicky, by all that's wonderful! Wherever did you spring from?"

In a few brief sentences he told her; and waving aside her praise for his having brought about the release of the captives, he added quickly:

"We've got to get away from here, and the sooner the better. When the van fails to arrive the police will send a motor-cyclist to find out what has happened to it; then the whole bus-load of them will return, and probably more. They'll be searching every inch of these woods in an endeavour to round up their escaped prisoners."

She nodded. "You're right! But they must have been taking us into Prague. That is a quarter of an hour's run from here. They'll give the van ten minutes' grace, then they've got to send someone out and he'll have to find the nearest telephone before he can report. We should have three-quarters of an hour clear, at least, and the airfield can't be much more than a mile away. We should easily be able to reach that pub, the Soviet Worker-Hero Air Mechanic, and go to earth there before the hunt gets going."

"All the same it would be asking for trouble to remain with this crowd a moment longer than we have to."

"I quite agree; but you must allow me long enough to have a word with the Sovas. All these poor people have now forfeited everything; yet some of them may be foolish enough to go home in the hope of being able to collect their most precious possessions before the Coms arrive. If they do that they will be caught for a certainty, and now that police have been killed in this affair, sent to the uranium mines to work there till they die. Their only hope is for them to abandon any thought of returning to the hamlet, and disperse as quickly as possible. I must warn them of that."

"Of course," Nicholas agreed. "To see tragedy overwhelm little community like this is positively heartbreaking. Do your utmost to advise them how best to act. A few minutes either way are not really likely to make any difference to us. While you are talking to them I'll have another look for my gun."

He was still hunting about unsuccessfully among the under-growth when he heard a shot. Looking up, he saw Sova stagger and fall. Fearful that by some awful trick of fate another police-man had unexpectedly arrived upon the scene, he dived for cover; but he was soon aware that no one else had done so, and no more shots followed.

Coming out from behind the oak tree, he approached the crowd which was now gathered about Sova's body. Fedora emerged from the crush and came to meet him.

"What happened?" he asked. "Did that gun go off by acci-dent."

"No," she said sadly. "He shot himself. When we were cooped up in the van I heard him say that he couldn't bear it, and meant to commit suicide at the first opportunity."

Nicholas frowned. "But why? He was only in for a year in the mines then, and he looked a strong, healthy chap. He ought easily to have survived it."

"It wasn't that. It was shame. Did you see that boy who brought the Coms on us? That was the Sova's son. For Pan Sova the thought that he, and his wife, and his pastor and all these other people had been betrayed by his own flesh and blood was too much. He couldn't face life any longer."

"What a frightful thing!" Nicholas said in a low voice. "The boy must be either mental, or a positive little fiend, to do a thing like that."

Fedora passed a hand over her eyes and sighed. "No; he is not abnormal. That sort of thing is happening in some house-hold every day now. The Coms get the children young and poison their poor little minds. You remember what Pan Smutný was saying last night about so many teachers for a long time past having ridiculed the Commandment which says 'Honour thy Father and thy Mother . . .' Well, this is the logical extension of their atheism. The children are taught that loyalty should be

given only to the State. They are encouraged to distrust and
spy on their parents, and to report any of their secrets that they
can ferret out. That boy will get a medal for this; a nice bow of
bright red ribbon with a portrait of Comrade Gottwald, or
Stalin, attached."

"By God, he'll get us too, unless we're quick!" Nicholas
exclaimed. "He was on the box with the driver, and he wasn't
badly hurt in the crash. I saw him run off into the wood. By
this time he may have found a patrolman on the road. Unless
we get away from here in double-quick time we'll find ourselves
back in the bag."

As he spoke he took Fedora by the arm and began to hurry
her further into the depths of the wood. Turning her head, she
shouted a warning to the crowd round Sova's body that his son
had got away and might bring the police on them again at any
moment, then she let Nicholas draw her with him towards the
denser thickets.

When they had gone some distance Nicholas queried the
direction they were taking, but Fedora said she felt sure they
could not be far off the mark. Shortly afterwards she was proved
right, for they came to the edge of the wood and from there
could see a large aircraft, about a mile away, slowly sinking towards the airfield.

Beyond the wood were some fields, then another screen of
trees. They could not see the road, which lay some way to their
left, but its position was marked for them by a line of telegraph
poles, and they could have seen the top of any vehicle that was
coming along it. The road was empty and, now that the aircraft
had gone down behind the tops of the trees ahead, nothing in
the whole landscape stirred.

Again there came upon Nicholas that sense of peace, so bound
up with the countryside on a still, sunny Sunday morning. It
seemed difficult to believe that less than half a mile behind them
they had left still warm bodies that had been terribly mutilated,
a suicide, and a dozen or more families who, without a moment's
warning, had been rendered homeless and, now destitute, were
about to be hunted as criminals. Had he been alone he might

almost have thought it an evil dream, but Fedora's presence and her pitiful state were concrete evidence of the brutalities enacted during the past half hour.

Had there been no raid, and had Sova driven them as arranged in his country cart to a spot near the airfield, her fever might have abated, or at least have been kept in check by the aspirin she had taken. As it was, the savage handling she had received from the policeman, whom she had attacked in desperation, the ride in the dark van with a herd of frightened pushing people, and its crash, had all contributed to worsen her condition. A glance was enough to show that she was running a dangerously high temperature. Her eyes held an unnatural light, and as she walked she was gasping for breath.

They crossed two fields and reached the trees, which proved to be on the edge of a smaller wood. As she jumped a small ditch that ran just in front of them she stumbled up the opposite bank and fell. Nicholas helped her to her feet and, much concerned about her, said:

"I think we had better rest here for a while. It can't yet be eleven o'clock and we haven't got to be at Lutonský's till twelve, so we have lots of time."

"All right," she agreed, half collapsing on the grassy bank. "Just for a few minutes; but we mustn't stay long. Once the police learn about the wrecking of that van hordes of them will be sent out here to scour the countryside; so we shan't be safe until we have gone to earth at Lutonský's inn.

Sitting down beside her, he drew a deep breath. "Yes; this morning's business was a frightful bolt from the blue, and in getting away we've had all we can expect of fortune. If we are caught again we'll never get that 'plane. Have you any idea what time it arrives at Frankfurt?"

"It is roughly an hour and a half's flight, so we should be there about half-past two."

"Good. Then allowing an hour for arguing our way past minor officials, we should be able to get through to London between half past three and four."

"Oh, no. London is about another two and a half hours on,

and we may have to go via Paris or Amsterdam; so I don't think we can expect to get in before six, anyhow."

"As far as we are concerned I should think we'll be lucky if we get back to-morrow. I meant get through by telephone."

She turned to stare at him. "Telephone? Who to?"

"Why, Scotland Yard, of course. To have Bilto arrested."

For a moment Fedora said nothing. Her feverish eyes dilated, then she exclaimed, "You'll do nothing of the kind! I won't let you."

He frowned. "What on earth are you talking about? That is the only possible way of stopping Bilto for certain."

"It is not. Once I get face to face with him I can stop him. I'm sure I can. Anyhow I shall move heaven and earth to do so; and I'll not agree to have Scotland Yard called in unless I fail."

Her rasping voice and feverish face made Nicholas think that she was slightly delirious, so he attempted to reason with her calmly.

"That is all very well. I know you are greatly attached to Bilto. For that matter, I'm very fond of him myself. Neither of us wants to see him get ten years. But there is too much at stake for us to allow our personal feelings to weigh with us in this. Neither of us has passports, so when we get to Frankfurt we are bound to be held up. It might even be days before we can establish our identities and get permission to fly on to London. That is unless you have a contact with some of the American Military Intelligence people there, and can get us specially passed through."

"I haven't. I am not connected with either the American or the British Secret Service. I've been working only for the Czech Underground; but they have a headquarters in Frankfurt, and they will fix things for us somehow."

He gave her a dubious look. "That is going to take time; perhaps several hours. Then what about money for fares; we have only a few pounds between us?"

"They will fix that too."

"There is much more to it than that, though. How about the

air services? They don't run every few minutes, like tube trains. By the time you have seen your Czech friends the odds are all against our being able to catch a plane that will get us into London this evening."

"Then I shall charter one privately."

"That will cost a packet. Do you really think the Czech Legion people would be willing to fork out for it? That is, unless you are prepared to explain how urgent it is for us to get to London by blowing the gaff about Bilto to them?"

"No, I don't think they would; but, if the worst comes to the worst, I can pay for it myself." As Fedora spoke she pulled her satchel-bag round in front of her, pressed a hidden spring in its bottom and produced from a secret pocket a fine solitaire diamond ring. Showing it to him, she said:

"Bilto gave me that. If necessary I'll cash it in to get the money to charter a private plane."

He shook his head. "I'm sorry, Fedora. It's all too sketchy and full of uncertainties."

"It is not," she insisted. "The Paris plane does not leave London Airport till ten o'clock. That gives us nine hours, and the actual flying time between Prague and London is only about four. If we do get held up in Frankfurt for longer than I expect, and we find our margin is a bit narrow, we can wait at London Airport till Bilto turns up, and head him off there."

"Good God, no! Now you really are going haywire. That chap Konečný will probably be acting as his courier, and would go to any lengths to prevent your speaking to him. Anyhow, you couldn't possibly have a show-down with him out there. Having got that far I doubt if he would even listen to you."

"In the last event we could call in the police to prevent his boarding the plane."

"There is always the chance that we might miss him. I have an idea that there are two night services to Paris, and that one of them goes from Northolt. He might take that."

"When we arrive we can find out if the Czech Embassy has booked two seats on the Paris plane. If they haven't and there is not enough time left for us to catch Bilto before he leaves the Russell, we can motor over to Northolt."

"Fedora, the sort of things you are suggesting would make the whole business the wildest gamble!"

"I don't agree!" she said hotly. "In the event of a definite hold up, making it impossible for us to land at London Airport before half-past nine, I'll consent to your telephoning Scotland Yard. But not otherwise. With any luck we should get in between six and seven, and easily be able to catch Bilto at dinner."

"I don't believe there is the least hope of our doing that, and I'll not risk it."

"Yes, you will. I insist on my right to endeavour to make Bilto change his mind."

"If we had twenty-four hours to work in, I'd give it you. As it is, I can't."

She was trembling all over as she cried, "I won't have you rush in and ruin his life, when it still may be possible to make him see sense and go back to Harwell!"

"Even if we caught him, all the probabilities are against his doing as you wish."

"Why?"

Nicholas felt that he had made every reasonable allowance for what he regarded as wild ideas produced only owing to the feverish state of Fedora's mind, and he said sharply, "Because he doesn't love you. He is in love with another woman, and he is expecting to marry her when he gets to Prague."

She winced. "That may be true. But he did love me. And I still love him."

"Perhaps you do," he shrugged. "All the same . . ."

"It is not a question of 'perhaps'; it is a fact," she cut in angrily. "And don't let any idea about the way I behaved towards you in the barn lead you to think otherwise. What you told me about Bilto yesterday had made me miserable; I was not myself either physically or mentally, and I most desperately needed comforting. That is all there was to it. When I said I thought you were a finer person than Bilto, I meant it. But women don't love men for their rectitude; they love them for just something that no other man has got. You may be like Bilto to look at, but you are not Bilto and never can be. You are a nice fellow, Nicky, but I'd throw you to the wolves without a second thought if I could save Bilto that way; because it's him that I love."

He nodded. "I quite understand that, Fedora; and I've never kidded myself for a moment that you have fallen for me, any more than I have fallen for you. We were just two people who had been through a whole series of acute emotion crises and dangers together, so it was a natural impulse for us to seek security for a while in each other's arms. Love had nothing to do with it, and it has nothing to do with this other matter either."

"It has. I love Bilto, and I mean to protect him from himself as long as there is the least possible chance of my doing so."

Nicholas stood up. "It's no good our arguing further, Fedora; and if you are rested I think we had better be getting along."

"Do you mean that you still intend to telephone from Frankfurt?" she asked, slowly getting to her feet.

"Yes. Immediately we arrive I shall ask to see the American Military Intelligence people, tell them the truth about this whole business and ask them to get me put through to London."

"I won't let you."

"I'm sorry, but I must. And if you were in a normal state I'm sure you'd agree that I've no choice. Your plans for getting us to London by this evening are completely wild and unreliable. We can't possibly allow any personal interests to count against the imperative necessity of stopping Bilto. To telephone Scotland Yard is the only way to stop him for certain, and that's what I am going to do."

"I won't let you!" she repeated hoarsely.

"You can't stop me," his voice was firm as he turned away. "Come on, now. Let's go."

"Oh, yes, I can," she cried. "Remain where you are! Don't move a step."

Swinging round, he was aghast to see that she had whipped Kmoch's little automatic out of her open bag and was pointing it at him.

"Fedora!" he exclaimed. "For God's sake be careful! Put that thing away!"

"Thanks for the warning, but I've had plenty of practice in handling a gun." Her green eyes blazed at him, and for the first time in several hours he noticed the cast in the left one.

"I . . . I know you have," he stammered. "But . . . it might go off. You're overwrought. If you weren't half crazy with fever and anxiety you would never behave like this."

"Oh, yes, I would."

"Listen!" He tried desperately to coax her. "It can't be more than a quarter of an hour's walk to Lutonský's place. When we get there you can lie down and we will talk over all this quietly."

"We are not going to Lutonský's place. At least you are not."

Fear suddenly gripped at his heart. His mouth went dry as he stared into her wild eyes, but he managed to gasp:

"Fedora! What do you mean? For God's sake . . ."

She cut him short. "I'm sorry, Nicky. If you believed in God I'd ask you to give me your oath to do as I wish, and I'd take it. But you don't. There is no way in which I can be certain that you won't double-cross me. You've got to die."

Perspiration had broken out on his forehead. His hands felt clammy. His heart was thudding like a steam hammer. She was a little above him on the bank and a good five feet away from him. He knew that he had no chance of rushing her. He could see from her face that she was not bluffing. In the hope of yet being able to save Bilto from prison, she meant to kill him.

Suddenly a forlorn hope by which he might perhaps save himself came to him. He shrugged, turned on his heel and began to walk away, praying desperately that she would not shoot him in the back.

It worked. Instead of firing, she cried, "Stop! Halt or I shoot!" but still she did not fire. Then he heard her running after him. A few paces brought her to within a yard of his back. Side-stepping, he swung round upon her, shot out a hand and grasped her wrist above the gun. She staggered and he was already off balance. They fell in a heap together with her underneath. The pistol exploded.

Wrenching the gun from her hand, he stumbled to his feet. She gave a groan and remained lying there. For a moment he stood staring down at her, then he cried:

"You're hit! Where? Oh, God, how awful!"

She moaned and put a hand to her side. Her voice had suddenly lost all its grimness and anger, as she murmured, "Here. The bullet . . . went in . . . under my ribs, I think."

Desperately he gazed round. "We . . . I must get a doctor."

"You . . . you must not risk yourself."

"I can't let you . . ."

"Die here," she finished for him. "Yes, you can. And I'm going to. I really am a . . . a dead duck this time . . . Nicky."

"There must be a farm nearby somewhere. I'll run for help."

"No!" Her voice was suddenly firm. "I haven't got long. Please stay with me."

He knelt down beside her. "Oh, Fedora! What can I say! It was an accident. I swear it was."

"Of course." She smiled faintly. "I know that."

With a shudder of pain she wriggled over a little, and he caught sight of the place where the bullet had entered her side. It was seeping blood only very slightly. Obviously the bleeding was internal, so there were no means of checking it. All the same, he asked:

"Is there nothing I can do?"

She shook her head. "Only see Bilto for me . . . whatever happens. Give him back my ring. Tell him . . . tell him that I've always loved him. Ever since we met. Even . . . even when I was still married to my first husband."

At her whispered words something clicked in Nicholas' brain. His conversation with Bilto over dinner at the Russell flashed back into his mind. Bilto had said 'My girl—or woman,

I suppose I should say, as she has already been married twice.'
He had gone on about her being a Czech who had been forced
into doing secret work, but who he believed had since become
a willing agent of her employers. Then he had said that he had
first known her several years before when she had been married
to her first husband. And several years before both Bilto and
Fedora had been living in the United States.

"I hadn't realized that you had been married twice," he said,
staring down at her.

"Yes," she murmured. "Terrance and I parted after . . .
after we'd been back in Prague a year. It was fifty-fifty. But
Bilto was out of reach. And . . . and I'd fallen for Honza . . .
by then. It was him the Coms took apart. Terrance went back to
. . . to the U.S."

She stopped speaking for a moment. Perspiration had broken
out on her forehead, and flecks of blood stained her pale lips.
With an effort she went on:

"It was after Honza was caught the Coms found out that . . .
that I'd known Bilto in the States. That's why . . . why they
sent me to England to act as his contact." Wearily she closed
her eyes.

Nicholas bent lower. His voice was urgent and miserable
with remorse. "Fedora! Fedora! I've made a terrible mistake.
Bilto's woman! It was you he was talking about. You are the
widow who had been married twice. It was you he wanted to
free from having to work for Vaněk. He had no idea you were
on the other side. It was you they promised to have in Prague
to meet him; but of course they never meant to keep their word.
Oh, Fedora, my dear, I see it all now. It was you with whom
Bilto has been in love for all these years."

She opened her eyes. They were misted over, but he could
see that she understood. Her lips drew back in a tremulous
smile, and she gasped.

"Thank you . . . Nicky! Give him . . . my love."

Suddenly a spasm shook her. She half sat up, her face con-
torted, and she vomited blood. Swiftly she seemed to recover.
Her voice came strong and clear.

"The spirit of John Huss lives on! God bless Czecho-slovakia!"

Fedora's eyes started from her head. Her mouth fell open, and she dropped back dead.

For a few moments Nicholas continued to kneel beside her, trying to take in the fact that she was really gone. Then he straightened her limbs and closed her eyes. All the fever, the tiredness and the pain had vanished from her face. It was serene and once more beautiful.

He had no option but to leave her there. Lutonský, he felt sure, would arrange with a pastor that she should receive proper burial. From her satchel-bag he took the diamond ring. Then he untied his silk handkerchief from over her silver-blonde hair. He had intended to use it to cover her face, but suddenly it seemed to him a pointless thing to do; because without it she retained the appearance of having just fallen asleep.

Instead, he put the handkerchief up to his eyes, and walked away weeping.

CHAPTER XIX

THE MORNING AFTER

On the Monday morning Professor Nicholas Novák took his class in Political Economics at Birmingham University as usual. He had given the same lecture on several occasions to other classes; so, without having to think very much about what he was saying, he delivered it with his usual ease and fluency. He had gone to bed in his lodgings at his usual hour the night before, slept soundly, and eaten a good breakfast. In consequence, he looked quite well, and none of his students—even Wendy Stevenson—noticed the least thing unusual about him.

When he finished his discourse he did not look at Wendy, but made a pretence of jotting down some notes, in order to give the rest of the class time to pack up their books and leave the room.

As he doodled with his pencil he was thinking, 'If it were not for the bruises on my arm the whole thing might have been an appalling dream.'

Except for his fare to London, the weekend had cost him nothing. His suit-case would still be in the cloakroom at the Russell, and he had only to write a line for it to be sent back to him. He still had his wallet and all his clothes—even to the silk handkerchief that Wendy had given him, with which he had covered his eyes in the X-cell, tied Fedora's wrists, and had lastly removed from her silvery-gold hair.

Again he went over in his mind all that had happened after he had left her. He had found Lutonský's without difficulty, and the Legionnaires there had been expecting him. They had asked for his solemn promise that in no circumstances would he ever reveal how the secret method of smuggling people out by air, known as the 'funnel', was operated. Naturally, he meant to keep that promise, and the journey had not even proved particularly uncomfortable.

At Frankfurt, as it was a Sunday afternoon, he had had some difficulty in getting himself taken to a senior officer of the American Military Intelligence; but the Colonel before whom he was eventually brought had proved to be a very live-wire indeed. By four o'clock they had been on the telephone to the Special Branch at Scotland Yard, and they had agreed to take Bilto into custody pending Nicholas' arrival in England to furnish full details.

By five o'clock the Americans had put him on one of their military aircraft that was leaving for Mildenhall, in Suffolk. There he had been met by officers of the Special Branch. They had informed him that, at a little before five, when on the point of being arrested, his cousin had pulled a gun from his pocket and committed suicide. Afterwards they had taken a full statement from Nicholas; then the ever-hospitable Americans had given him dinner in their mess and placed a car at his disposal o take him back to Birmingham. By a quarter-past eleven he had been in his bed-sitting-room with his own familiar things about him.

It had not dawned upon him until he woke up in the morning that fate had decreed that he should receive very handsome compensation for the trials he had sustained during the week-end. But he was Bilto's only living relative in England and next of kin, so automatically his heir. From what Bilto had said when giving him the Power of Attorney, he knew more or less what he might expect. Even after death duties were paid and everything settled up, there should be about two thousand pounds to come to him. That was a comfortable thought for a needy young Professor who had never been able to put by more than forty pounds in a Post Office savings account. It was enough to furnish a small house with nice things and leave a nest-egg of a few hundreds over. In addition to that there was Fedora's ring, to which, as Bilto's heir, he was also fully entitled.

The students had gone, except for Wendy. Her face was grave as she left her desk, and came towards him. With her usual directness she said:

"Well, Nicky. Have you made up your mind? I haven't changed mine, and I want to know how I stand. Must this be good-bye or . . . or can we go on together?"

He smiled, and produced Fedora's ring.

"Oh, Nicky!" she exclaimed, her face transformed with delight. "Does this mean . . ."

"Yes." He nodded. "I'll come with you to your aunt's next weekend, and anywhere else you wish. I was terribly near to losing you; but I've done a lot of thinking during Saturday and Sunday, and I know now that I can live the sort of life that will make you happy."

"Oh, Nicky, my own!" Tears started to her eyes, and she flung her arms round his neck.

It was several minutes later before he could put the ring on her finger. As she held it up and the splendid stone caught the light she said in an astonished whisper:

"Darling, it's marvellous! But how could you possibly afford to buy such a lovely ring as this?"

"I didn't," he confessed. "I inherited it. And I've come into a little money too. About a couple of thousand. The ring belonged to a very brave woman. That's why I'd like you to have it, rather than sell it and buy another with what it fetches; unless you'd rather we did that."

"No; of course I'll keep it. We couldn't find anything lovelier. You must tell me all about her."

"I will, some quiet evening when we've got lots of time."

"Nicky. About politics. I want to say this now and we won't refer to it again. I know how you feel, and I promise I won't be difficult. We both want the same thing really; to make life happier for people who get a poor deal. Somehow, I'm sure we'll manage to get nearer in our points of view."

He smiled. "Thank you, my sweet; I'm sure we shall. As I told you, I've done a lot of thinking this weekend, and I'm quite certain now that politics won't come between us."

She squeezed his hand. "Oh, I'm so glad! I've suffered agonies these last two days at the thought that I might lose you! Our being really engaged now makes me terribly, terribly happy. Did everything go well for you during the weekend?"

"I . . . I suppose so," he hesitated. "As a matter of fact it turned out very differently from anything I had expected. During it I went through some . . . some rather shattering experiences."

"You poor darling!" she exclaimed with concern.

"It's all over now, so you've no need to worry about me," he reassured her quickly. "I'll tell you the whole story later on; but I don't feel up to talking about it yet. On Saturday afternoon, though, I . . . I got stuck for about two hours in a place where there was nothing to do but think. I recalled that conversation we had one evening about our beliefs. It struck me that mine had been based on a rather lop-sided view of things, and I wanted to ask you again about yours."

With a little shrug, she said, "Perhaps it sounds a bit pompous and theatrical, but I think there are three things that embrace everything that is brave and fine and decent. I believe in God, the Queen and England."

"You must tell me about them some time."

Wendy smiled. "Come right up to the top of the class, darling."

Nicky smiled back. "What about a little kiss from my teacher?"

THE END